A CALAMITY OF NOBLE HOUSES

Amira Ghenim

A CALAMITY OF NOBLE HOUSES

Translated from the Arabic
by Miled Faiza and Karen McNeil

Europa
editions

Europa Editions
27 Union Square West, Suite 302
New York NY 10003
www.europaeditions.com
info@europaeditions.com

This book is a work of fiction. Any references to historical events, real people, or real locales are used fictitiously.

First publication 2025 by Europa Editions

Translation by Miled Faiza and Karen McNeil
Original title: نازلة دار الأكابر
(*Nāzila dār al-akābir*)

Library of Congress Cataloging in Publication Data is available
ISBN 979-8-88966-050-7

Ghenim, Amira
A Calamity of Noble Houses

Cover design and illustration by Ginevra Rapisardi

Prepress by Grafica Punto Print – Rome

Printed in Canada

CONTENTS

A CALAMITY OF NOBLE HOUSES

The beldi *families of Tunis are not to blame if their venerable sons look down on other people, if they strut, if they swagger, if they show off. Their egotism is no deliberate vice; nor is it a sin to tip the scales on Judgement Day. Arrogance is in their nature, like a cleft in someone's lip or webbing between their fingers: a congenital defect they're born with and can't be held responsible for.*

I am Hind, daughter of Mostafa Ennaifer, and, like most of the Tunis notables, I, too, was born with this defect. My uncle and father were born with it, as well. So, too, was my grandfather Mohsen—son of the great judge Othman Ennaifer—who remained imperious to his dying day, despite his buried secret.

During its long history of haughtiness and vanity, our sad family learned to hide its wounds from others' eyes. We wore radiant, proud smiles on our scar-covered faces. We covered our shame-crowned heads with hats of great deeds and wore gloves of glory and honor on hands deeply stained with vice and sin.

Our history is one woven with threads of secrecy, suspicion, and illusions. Clad in doubts, lies, and hypocrisy. Abounding in small treacheries, mutual accusations, and false allegations. Filled with plots, resentments, and insolence. Teeming, too, with aborted love stories, slaughtered fetuses, and secret beds.

This is the history I'm sharing with you today, my darling daughter. It's my origin and yours—or, if you prefer, my shackles and yours.

There's something my grandmother, Zbaida Ali Rassaa, used to say to me when I was young, her eyes filled with a laughter I now recognize as that of a trickster: "You, Hind, are the granddaughter of Tahar Haddad!" How could I have known she meant more than what she said?

Today, my daughter, a jinn of truth is emerging naked and barefoot from an abandoned folder in the basement. I will furnish it with shoes of ink and paper to help it reach you, to tell you of our secrets and our shame.

Today, this jinn of truth will recount the confessions of those who saw the pain of my grandmother Zbaida in her husband's (and father's) house, and will put in your hands the lost letter of Tahar Haddad.

Today, my daughter, you will read what the members of the Ennaifer family, their in-laws, and their servants said about that fateful night, the one they hid from everyone for so long. Don't let the numerous characters, diverse voices, and many names confuse you; all of them (except for Khala Luiza, who you know) are like a single sick body that conspired and united against their disabled victim. And even those who didn't raise a whip or throw a stone were false witnesses in the silent crowd that tormented her.

Examine our family tree closely, my daughter, and you will see how evil spreads from limb to limb like fire through dry wood. Check its knots and branches, and you'll see with your mind's eye what offenses sinful hands, rigid brains, and sick hearts have committed against life, love, and justice.

Now, with trepidation and concern, I'm offering you these painful stories, contemplating with new eyes my face and yours in the mirror. We both have more scars and defects, but less narcissism. And after the sharp blade of honesty has done its work, won't we be cleansed forever of these inherited defects? Is there any better remedy for false grandeur than dispelling old illusions? Is there any better remedy for egotism than exposing hidden shame?

Family Tree

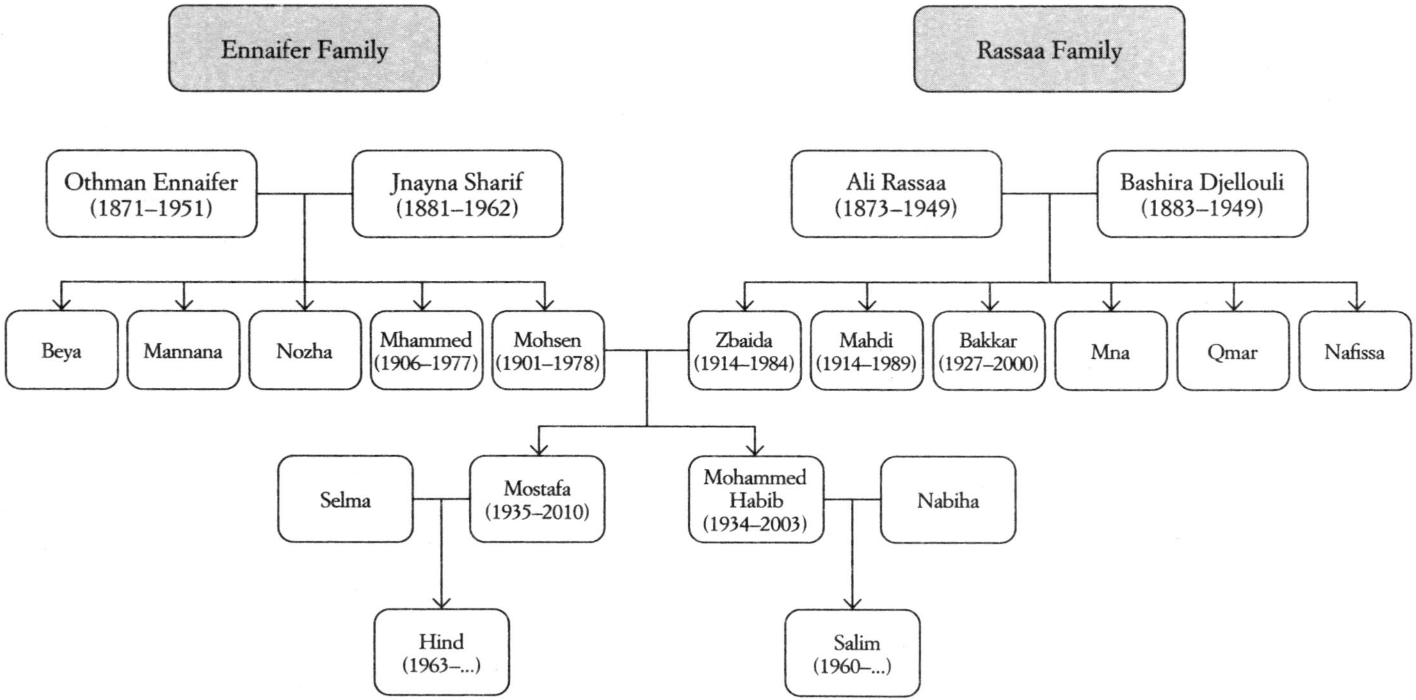
Ennaifer Family
Rassaa Family
Othman Ennaifer (1871–1951)
Jnayna Sharif (1881–1962)
Ali Rassaa (1873–1949)
Bashira Djellouli (1883–1949)
Beya
Mannana
Nozha
Mhammed (1906–1977)
Mohsen (1901–1978)
Zbaida (1914–1984)
Mahdi (1914–1989)
Bakkar (1927–2000)
Mna
Qmar
Nafissa
Selma
Mostafa (1935–2010)
Mohammed Habib (1934–2003)
Nabiha
Hind (1963–...)
Salim (1960–...)

1
The Tale of Khala Luiza
(*El Menzah VI, Fall 2013*)

I

My instincts didn't fail me, Hind. At dawn on that cold winter day, they'd already warned me of the ill omen lying in wait for us at Sidi Othman Ennaifer's house.

The harbingers of calamity came in the dead of night, when the hand of Boutelis, the jinn of sleep paralysis, snatched me by the neck out of a deep slumber. The damned creature knelt on my chest, pulling my tongue with his claws and pressing his heavy weight down into my ribs until my bones almost sliced my flesh open. If not for the barrage of prayers I assaulted him with in my head—as my Lella Bashira had taught me—he wouldn't have let me go alive.

In my long life, that jinn of sleep has only visited me twice, Hind. In both cases, the next morning brought an appointment with disaster.

On the morning following his first visit, when I was still a child, I received news of my father's death. Word came down from the mountain while I was in the capital, at Lella Bashira's house on Rue El Azzafine. Based on what my maternal uncle, Dhawi, told the gendarme, Baba was killed by a kick from his gray mule next to the door of our house. When questioned, Khal Dhawi told the gendarmes that Baba's mule surprised him with a kick to the stomach as he unloaded her, laying him out flat, near-dead. Then, as if the mule still wasn't satisfied, she trampled him, kicking him repeatedly with her hooves in a sudden fit of rage. My mother was the last person to see Baba alive. After the funeral, and to her dying day, she never spoke to my uncle again. She kept his secret, but she never forgave him. My God have mercy on her and forgive her.

Boutelis's second visit augured what was to happen in Sidi Othman's house, which I'll describe to you now, and which must remain a secret. Promise me that you won't share it with anyone, Hind, not even your husband—this is a family secret not for the ears of in-laws.

That night I said a short prayer of protection as soon as I managed to move my tongue, then with trepidation fell back into a fitful sleep plagued by nightmares. When I heard the dawn call to prayer coming from the Sidi Makhlouf Mosque, I dragged my exhausted body out of bed. I needed to start my daily chores for Sidi Othman's household, starting with heating up the water for the family members to perform their pre-prayer ablutions.

But just as I began to slip my feet into my clogs, a scream shook the walls and ceiling of the dark house. It was coming from Lella Zbaida's room.

My heart leapt out of my chest with fear and worry. Lella Zbaida was still lying in, having just given birth to your father, Sidi Mostafa. It had only been two or three weeks since the birth, and it had been a hard labor. I was afraid something bad had happened to the baby, like what happened to his older brother, Sidi Mohammed Habib's twin, a year and a half before. On that night, he nursed until he was full, fell asleep with rosy cheeks and regular breath, then never woke up. Although he was barely forty days old, many people attended his funeral. The status of the dead in the capital is measured by their lineage, rather than their good deeds.

That dawn, I hurried down the hall with my head uncovered, holding my clog in one hand and a lantern in the other, not caring if one of the men of the house saw me in immodest clothing. They all knew that Lella Zbaida wasn't just my lady; she was like my sister. Otherwise, she wouldn't have insisted on bringing me with her to her husband's house. Her mother, Lella Bashira, hadn't wanted to let me go, and her new mother-in-law, Lella Jnayna, had given the superfluous maid a cold welcome.

The maid's room was located between the kitchen and the storage room in the western section of the house; Lella Zbaida's room was in the southern section, on the upper floor designated for her and her family. The owners of the house—Lella Zbaida's mother-in-law, Lella Jnayna Sharif, and her father-in-law, Sidi Othman Ennaifer—had rooms surrounding the central courtyard, along with Sidi Mhammed, their youngest son (who would be a source of tribulation to them but at that time was a student at the university of the great Zaytuna Mosque). The girls' rooms—your father's paternal aunts, Mannana, Nozha, and Beya—had been closed up, one after the other, as they married and took their places in their husbands' homes.

I flew across the courtyard like an untamed filly toward Lella Zbaida's room, but a light rain had fallen in the night and left the smooth floor wet and slick, so I had to slow down to avoid slipping. As I neared the covered stairs leading to the upper floor, Sidi Mohsen came out onto the balcony overlooking the courtyard, wearing his burgundy burnous. When he saw me, he gave me a sign with his hand, reassuring me that your grandmother and her newborn were fine, then sent me down to the storage room to bring him the skeleton key. I realized that Lella Zbaida's seizures must be back. We'd almost forgotten this old affliction of hers. We all thought it had been cured, thanks to Lella Bashira's offerings at the shrine of Lella Aisha Al-Manoubya and the animals she sacrificed at the shrine of Sidi Mehrez.

I remember the first attack as if it were yesterday. (Yes, Hind, the memory of this old woman—the one your father, God rest him, left you the responsibility to bury—is still sharp! The years may have taken her eyesight and sapped the strength from her legs, but she can still remember every detail of past events. How strange, though, that she can recall ancient history but not, in the morning, what she ate the night before!) That day, your great-grandmother, Lella Bashira, was busy distilling sweet geranium water, *atarchya*, with Hedda. Hedda was a skilled woman, always in demand among upper-class Tunisian ladies for her expertise in making and preserving all kinds of provisions. Remember that back then, you couldn't just buy unflavored couscous and *mhamsa* in plastic packages at the store, like you can nowadays; you couldn't buy spices that were already prepared and ground for you. Instead, every season had its own provisions to be prepared and added to the pantry in rich people's homes. Spring was the season of distilling orange blossoms, sweet geranium, native roses, sweet briar, and other fragrant plants.

The task for someone my age then was to take the glass *fechka* from Hedda's hand when it was full and plug it up with a special piece of cloth, to make sure it was airtight and that none of the fragrant scent was wasted. This was toward the beginning of my time living in Lella Bashira's house, and I hadn't yet acquired the knowledge and skills of the city dwellers, so I sat gaping like an idiot at the drops streaming from the spout into the neck of the *fechka*. I had no understanding of how the cold water that Hedda was pouring into the upper part of the alembic was transformed into that warm liquid with its greasy top layer that looks like oil but isn't, and which filled the house with its sweet scent.

Lella Zbaida was a few years older than me and was busy chasing bees away from the piles of geraniums that had been brought from the souk by Sidi Hajj Ali's porter. They were heaped high next to Hedda, waiting their turn to be boiled in the bottom part of the alembic, which was sitting atop a crackling fire. I got bored waiting for "the head"—what people in the city call the first distillation—so I decided to help Lella Zbaida. I alerted her to any bees hiding between the green leaves and inside the small purple flowers of the sweet geranium. We would laugh whenever we found one.

Suddenly, Lella Zbaida shrieked, just like on that fateful dawn, then fell to the ground, staring without seeing, her body shaking. Lella Bashira jumped up in shock, knocking the alembic and its contents to the ground without noticing. I can still hear the alembic's terrifying blast as it echoed through the kitchen, and smell the sweet scent emanating from the water that streamed from its many holes.

Lella Bashira searched the uncovered parts of the young woman's body for the bee sting she thought at first had caused the attack. She thought it must have been a poisonous sting by a queen bee, but when she didn't find a mark and realized that Lella Zbaida was still shaking, she looked at me with sudden understanding. She asked me, sharply, "What on earth did you do to her, you damn girl?"

I burst into bitter, oppressed sobs that would become familiar to me in Lella Bashira's house. But I want you to know, Hind, that I don't hold any resentment toward your great-grandmother. I forgave her from my heart the day she asked for forgiveness, lying on her deathbed, and that day I shed more tears for her than I had over the death of my own mother. She was a second mother to me, despite everything.

Did she, after that question, slap me on the face once or twice for a sin I hadn't committed? I don't remember. But I do remember that Lella Zbaida stopped shaking and came to her senses as soon as Hedda placed a heavy iron key in her hand (I don't remember where she got it from). A smile and rosy glow returned to my beautiful little Lella's face, and she went right back to chasing bees before I had even stopped sobbing, both from my personal distress and my concern for her. That incident was the beginning of a series of seizures that began to slowly space out until they had almost disappeared. This was thanks to the blessings of the holy saints that Lella Bashira visited and gave offerings to behind her husband Sidi Hajj Ali's back. Meanwhile, Lella Bashira learned how to heal her daughter with that metal tool. After her marriage, I brought the tool hidden in her trousseau; I showed her husband Sidi Mohsen where it was and taught him how to use it. So he knew to ask me for it on the dawn of that ill-fated day.

The big iron skeleton key, which was hanging from a bent nail in the pantry, had to be spun in the soft, tender part of the palm for a few seconds, making seven circles, no more and no less, until the trembling body calmed down, the stiff muscles of the face relaxed, and the flipped eyeballs found their way back to the middle of the socket. Then the green almond-shaped eyes would regain their familiar twinkle, and the incident would disappear as if nothing had happened.

The movement in the house died down after we used the key, and the men left to pray the dawn prayer at the nearby mosque. Lella Zbaida's mother-in-law didn't ask about her daughter-in-law but rather made a gesture from behind the window of her room that opened onto the courtyard. She made a circle resembling the shape of a *kanoun,* as a sign for me to fill the house with incense.

She had taught me from my first day in her home how to mix the incense with precision and walk through the house with the small clay *kanoun* in my hand, the incense burning on top of the charcoal. As the smoke wafted through each room, the household would reap all the benefits of the incense, both the pleasing scent and the banishment of evil spirits. Every Thursday evening, I would circle through the house seven times with the incense burner. I would also dangle it inside the high-necked well. Wells have been the abode of jinn from time immemorial, even in the countryside where I came from. So are those bathrooms you have in the city, as well as the drains. If your grandmother Lella Zbaida had listened to her mother and aunts before she was hit by the jinn's evil—if she'd stopped pouring hot cooking oil on the heads of our otherworldly neighbors down the drain—she wouldn't have angered them so much that they sent her these seizures as punishment, their means of torture.

Remind your daughters of this advice, Hind! They've been spoiled by their schools and won't listen to a senile old woman anymore. Those daughters of a dog—no offense to the noble line of Sidi Mohsen Ennaifer—they laugh in my face when I warn them not to provoke the jinn.

Lella Zbaida was also spoiled by the nuns' schools, or that's what Lella Jnayna would say when she caught her making fun of our customs and traditions. She liked the smell of incense but didn't believe it could bring about any good or prevent any evil. She looked down on visiting the shrines of holy saints and waved her French books in people's faces when they told her she should. "These are my saints," she would say. "The good ones leave useful knowledge for the people, not fairy tales and superstitious nonsense." Then she would name some French saints Lella Jnayna didn't know. Saint Jacques Rasseau and Saint Victor Hugo and Saint Charles Beaudelele. May God forgive me if I mispronounced their names; I don't want to mess with saints, even if they are French.

Why are you laughing, Hind? Are you wondering whether the old woman has gone senile and gotten confused? Listen to this, then. Your grandmother Lella Zbaida used to make fun of the black cloth women put on their faces when they left the house, out of modesty and virtue. Imagine, she compared it to the muzzle people put on dogs' snouts (excuse the mention) to prevent them from biting people. Sometimes she even compared it to the mask a thief uses to cover their face and avoid the police. I have no idea where she came up with these strange images, but they used to drive Sidi Mhammed crazy. He was a student at Zaytuna University in those days. He would lose his temper and start accusing her of things I didn't understand, but I think they revolved around loyalty to the French and acting like an unbelieving European woman.

Sidi Mohsen also got his share of scorn over Lella Zubaida from his spoiled younger brother. Sidi Mhammed, the political activist and member of the Destour Party, used to openly condemn your grandfather for marrying the "Frenchified" daughter of the Rassaa family. He thought her brain had been poisoned by a European education and her behavior ruined by the Rassaa family's failure to zealously guard its women. It's possible that he was also hinting at Sidi Mohsen's loyalty to the French colonial authority. That was clear enough from the promotions he got, one after the other, over his Tunisian colleagues at the Tax Office where he worked. But your grandfather was a forbearing man who responded to anger with contentment and to a scowl with a smile. He probably interpreted his younger brother's temper as simple youthful exuberance, and justified his enthusiasm for anti-protectorate views by his lack of experience and wisdom. Things between them didn't explode until that fateful day. But after that, they didn't speak to each other for many years. They reconciled only when Sidi Othman was on his deathbed and threatened not to forgive them if they didn't make peace.

When the men came back home from the dawn prayer that day, I was still walking the courtyard with the *kanoun* in my hand, seeking to protect Lella Zbaida and her two boys from the clutches of jinn. My prayers were not answered, though, and the crackle of incense couldn't trick the fate that was barreling toward us.

As the men raised their voices in prayer, asking God for forgiveness, Sidi Othman stumbled on Sidi Mhammed's burnous, his silver cane falling to the ground. It broke in two with a deafening crack that reverberated in the echo chamber of the entrance hall. Lella Jnayna told me a few hours later that the Hajj himself almost fell flat on his face, but your grandfather Mohsen, may he rest in peace, helped steady him. He twisted his left foot, though, and his ankle had started to swell by the morning.

The series of accidents on that fateful day didn't stop there. These ill omens were nothing but a small prelude to the catastrophe that was to befall us, Lella Zbaida and I, a few hours later.

II

That morning, I was helping Lella Jnayna prepare lunch in the kitchen. Which is to say, she was giving the orders, and I was carrying them out. I washed and peeled the vegetables, separated the good beans from the bad and cleaned them, and handed her the spices—all without touching the pot. My lady used to say that she didn't like maids' cooking, because you could taste their inferiority in the food, no matter how long you'd spent trying to teach them. My lady felt the food they cooked had an inescapable Bedouin taste that she despised. This is what she used to proudly explain to those distinguished *beldi* wives who visited her over the holidays. Your grandmother Lella Zbaida wouldn't eat from my hand until the day your father, Sidi Mostafa, took us to his house outside the old city walls after marrying your mother.

One day Khaddouj, the black maid, burst in as we worked in the kitchen. She was a middle-aged woman, tall and nimble with broad shoulders and cheeks marked with old smallpox scars. She'd been serving the household for a long time and was as mean as a snake to me as long as she lived. She called over to me in a raised, sing-songy voice, making sure Lella Jnayna heard her: "The baker's boy from the shop on Sidi Mansour's at the door for you. He says it's urgent."

Lella Jnayna dropped the wooden spoon she was holding and gave me a look fit to kill. "My God . . . You good-for-nothing wench! Is this what we've come to? How could you let a baker's boy knock on Si Othman Ennaifer's door and ask to see one of the family women? What were you doing on Rue Sidi Mansour to begin with, that you know baker's boys?"

I gaped, not sure how to answer, since I was as surprised as she was. What could possibly have made the Rue Sidi Mansour baker remember us, so many years after our story with his friend?

I said, trying to hide my distress, "Lella Bashira must've sent something with him for our young Lella. Sidi Ali goes there sometimes because Lella Bashira loves his bread."

She clapped her hands, perturbed, and pursed her lips in disapproval. "The Rassaa family buys its bread from the baker like commoners? How people have changed!"

I gave her a smile to convey understanding and total agreement, thinking, let her curse Sidi Ali Rassaa and his family all she wants, just don't let her pry any further. I excused myself and ran toward the entrance hall, covering my face with the black veil women wore back then. In your grandmother's time, going out unveiled in a big city would've been a scandal, even though country women like me were unveiled by nature. Of course, when Bourguiba became president after independence, he made it possible for Bedouin and city women alike to go without.

The baker's boy was at the door, holding a white bundle. I assumed from its heft that it was several round loaves of bread set atop each other, wrapped in a clean white cloth and gently tied in a bundle. As I stuck my head out from behind the wicket gate, he whispered to me that his master wanted the letter delivered directly into Lella Zbaida's hand. He didn't give me a chance to ask him about the letter's contents, but took off running through the zigzagging alleys until he disappeared.

I closed the door and stood for a moment behind it, unsure of what to do with the bundle. Should I take it upstairs directly to Lella Zbaida's room, or should I pass by the kitchen first so Lella Jnayna saw it, to banish her doubts in me?

The footsteps of Sidi Mhammed coming from the corridor toward the main door increased my trepidation. I could tell his slow footsteps from everyone else's; his light limp gave them a unique rhythm. He was born with one leg a little longer than the other, which gave him an inferiority complex as a child; this was probably the source of his ferocity and introversion. But his small disability had secured him a special status at home: he was Lella Jnayna's favorite. He had a special place in her heart, and she loved him more than her older son Sidi Mohsen, to say nothing of her daughters.

I hurried toward him to avoid arousing suspicions about why I was loitering behind the door. We met in the middle of the corridor, which was unlit, save for a small glass skylight. One of us had to move aside so the other could pass, so I pressed myself against the wall waiting for him to go by, my eyes cast down. To be honest with you, before the incident, I used to find him handsome, despite his extra weight and plump cheeks. Perhaps I had a crush on him and, like any maid with a rich, single master, I secretly wished he'd throw open the doors of paradise and make me the lady of the house overnight.

In summer, I was captivated by his hay-colored linen *jebba* and used to steal glances at the silk-embroidered tunic beneath it. When I hand-washed his *sirwal*, I would imagine how he pulled the drawstring tight around his generous waist. I also liked how solid and broad-shouldered he looked in his summer clothes as he swaggered past in the evenings, his white *balgha* slippers releasing the fresh scent of new leather into the air. But when he wore his Hanafi finery on religious holidays—his *chokha*, *qaftan*, and *farraja*, with a red felt chechia on his head and a jasmine *machmoum* behind his ear—with Lella Jnayna trailing after him, slipping black cumin seeds into his pockets and reciting prayers to protect him from envy and evil in the name of God, His prophet, and the virtues of His name, the most beneficent, the most merciful . . . Well, at those times I avoided looking at him at all, out of fear that my eyes might reveal my hidden feelings to the lady of the house.

In those days, I was still unaware of his aberrant inclinations, so my heart raced when his hand moved toward my chest. I clung to the wall like a lizard, waiting for him to continue on his way toward the door so I could run with my bundle to Lella Zbaida's room. But the extra caution with which I was holding it had attracted his attention, and he grabbed at it. He'd probably heard Khaddouj's disapproving insinuations all the way in his room—the damn woman had trumpeted the story like she was the king's herald. I shrank with fear, still stubbornly holding on to the bundle, and said without looking at him, "It's bread, Sidi Mhammed. Lella Zbaida was craving it."

"Good, give me a loaf for the road, then."

"Ask Lella Zbaida for some, Sidi, I have to give her the bundle as is, without anything missing."

"Is the Rassaa family servant refusing me a loaf of dry bread!?"

As he spoke, he tried to snatch the bundle away from me. He pulled, and I pulled back, and the tie came loose, and what was to happen happened. The bundle's contents fell to the ground between his feet, and he beat me in the race to pick up what was destined to be picked up . . . and there it was, the calamity.

III

Had I died at that moment, Hind, it would've been easier on me than what happened next. For many days afterward, I kept wishing that Khal Dhawi had thrown me from the top of the mountain or drowned me in the river or buried me alive—anything other than selling me to a well-off family in the city before I'd even grown new incisors to replace my baby teeth.

As I stood in front of Sidi Mhammed trembling, terrorized and crowned with shame, hugging what remained of the open bundle, I remembered myself standing in the entrance hall of Lella Bashira's house the day I arrived from the mountains, a skinny girl with dusty hair, a patched dress, and bare feet. Then, too, I was embracing a small bundle, that one containing the summer and winter clothes my mother had gathered for me, all the while crying and saying, over and over, "May God curse you, Dhawi!"

On the third day of Eid al-Fitr, Khal Dhawi put us, my three sisters and me, on my father's two-wheeled cart, which he had taken possession of (along with some other things) after he had framed him at the beginning of Ramadan and got him thrown in jail. When I was a little older, during the few visits I made to our house in the country, my mother told me about the root of the problem between them. My father had a feud with his brother-in-law because of my mother's share of the land and livestock that her late father had left behind. My uncle had decided to take possession of the entire inheritance and deprive his sisters of their rights, even if those rights didn't amount to much. The truth is that the habit of disinheriting women and giving all the inheritance to men is common among us in the countryside. But my father was a fair man who cared about justice. He was also a poor man providing for four girls and their mother, and the pennies he made on the French settler's farm were barely enough to put bread on the table. His physical strength tempted him to take by force what my uncle refused to willingly give his sister. So one morning, he grabbed a cudgel and went to seize some sheep—the number he estimated to be legitimately hers—from the flock grazing in the foothills. Then he herded those sheep to the souq and sold them, using the proceeds to buy material to fence off a section of my grandfather's land and plant it with beans.

My father didn't enjoy the success of his raid for long; he was taken from the settler's farm in handcuffs after some good people had told the farm owner that Sassi Weld Aarem was transferring bags from the storage room to his land on the mountain under cover of darkness. The next day, the police found those bags beside the fenced land.

A few days later, my sisters and I found ourselves on a cart heading to the capital, followed by my mother's wailing and her curses on Dhawi, may God give him his due on Judgement Day.

I don't remember how I arrived in the Rassaa family's entrance hall or how my sisters and I got scattered. I probably fainted during the trip from all the tears I shed, and that's why I don't remember anything about our farewells. All I remember is a massive wooden door with two panels reaching up toward the sky shutting behind me, making an ominous creaking that would haunt my nightmares for years. I also remember with strange clarity that feeling of disconnect when my bare feet first met the marble of the entrance hall. No one can understand that feeling, Hind, except people used to walking on stones and thorns and feeling the warmth of the sun in the dirt.

We were at the end of fall or perhaps the beginning of winter, and the bumpy trip on the cart had made me lose one of my shoes, or both, I'm not sure. When the door closed behind me, the door that would permanently, harshly cut me off forever from my old world, and my bare little feet touched the marble of this new one, my senses received two conflicting messages: with the smoothness, an impression of gentleness and luxury, and with the coldness, harbingers of cruelty and terrible indifference. So the young girl with the long braids didn't know: should she look for calm and good fortune after her life of poverty and hardship, or should she fear the cruelty the future would bring, a cruelty colder than marble?

Hind, the days to come would teach me never to trust sleek, polished things. The maid expecting luxury from the marble of her master's house is like a cow expecting pleasure from the sharp knife. The truth is that your great-grandmother Lella Bashira was never absolutely unfair and was never absolutely fair. If she got angry with you, it always felt like she would never get over it. And once she got over it, it felt like she would always be happy. Sidi Ali used to avoid getting into fights with her, however high his self-esteem and determination, because when she was angry with her husband, my lady didn't care if she got cursed by angels all night until morning. She would take her pillow to one of her daughters' rooms and keep away from him until she felt better. I often heard one of her half-sisters warning her, in a tone both compassionate and preachy, "Keep being stubborn, you foolish woman, and he'll bring home a second wife. Then you'll say my sister Najiba was right."

Based on what I gleaned from her rare visits, Najiba had drunk repeatedly from that cup of bitterness and knew its discontents. Her husband was among the city's wealthy, as well as a respected religious scholar who believed that limiting oneself to a single wife was a sign of ungratefulness and scorn for the permissions God had bestowed on His pious servants. So he didn't deprive himself from taking a second, third, and fourth wife—in addition to being, according to his wife, angry at the bey who had abolished slavery in Tunisia in his father's time. Perhaps it was this abolishment of the slave market and the end of concubinage that forced him to make the most detestable (albeit permissible) choice of all: none of his four wives was safe from being divorced whenever he wanted to marry a new one. I memorized all the proverbs about men I learned from this Najiba, who would raise a warning finger in her sister's face whenever something unusual happened, saying, "Men and time are untrustworthy" or "Foolish is the woman who says her husband loves her, for he will eventually betray her" or "Don't put your trust in men any more than you trust water in a sieve."

However, the warnings of the experienced sister were not able to sway even a strand of hair on Lella Bashira's head. She would let her say what she had to say and answer her with a single proverb and a cryptic smile, "One's fingers are not all the same length, Najiba." By which, of course, she meant that her situation and her sister's were not comparable.

I believe that Lella Bashira was right and that the faith she had in her husband was genuine. She was sure of Sidi Ali's love for her, and no other woman could make her feel insecure. She would test his patience, keeping her distance until he proved that he was anxious and longing for her. She sashayed in front of him with her voluptuous body and glorious backside until she melted away the last drop of his resistance. No one knew when he made peace with her or how, but suddenly, after days—sometimes long, sometimes short—of not sleeping next to him, she would take her pillow out of the girls' room and put it next to Sidi Ali's on their platform bed before evening came. Early on the same day, a messenger would hurry from the Rassaa house to bring Fatima the henna woman to wax and beautify the lady as if she were a new bride, filling the house with the scent of incense and melting sugar mixed with lemon and honey. When Lella Bashira was ready, a fancy carriage would be waiting at the door with Sidi Ali in it. Lella Zbaida and I would watch from behind the *mashrabiya*, stifling our laughter at the sight of the dignified old man waiting outside the main door, smoothing his mustache and fussing with the red chechia on his head, waiting to help his beautiful Princess Bashira bint Djellouli into the carriage.

Where they went during these excursions, which lasted from afternoon until evening, remained a secret we often speculated about but never solved. Then Lella Zbaida learned from her friends in the French school that Monsieur Rassaa and his wife Madame Bashira would reserve Hammam Saheb Ettabaâ, a Turkish bath in El Halfaouine, for their exclusive use for the evening in exchange for thirty francs. Can you imagine, my dear Hind, that the owner would close the public bath in his customers' faces and open it only for this couple, so they could bathe by themselves in that intimate atmosphere where the steam would mix with sweat in the hot room—and you know the rest of the story. What man would spoil his wife this way?

During that time of my life, I didn't realize how unique the Rassaa lifestyle was, what with Sidi Ali's openness and modesty with his children, his full confidence in his wife and daughters, and the large margin of freedom he gave them. I used to think that this was normal for the *beldi* city dwellers. I didn't realize that I had ended up, by mere coincidence, in the house of a singular man (by the criteria of that era) until I moved with Lella Zbaida to Si Ennaifer's house. There, I discovered a completely different style of upbringing and another kind of philosophy of how to treat women. Unlike your grandfather Mohsen—who received his degree from a German university and was influenced by German culture—Sidi Othman was jealous and controlling with his wife, overbearing with his sons, and strict with his daughters, who he didn't allow to attend school. Sidi Mhammed had inherited all these faults, but with none of his father's good qualities. So I was certain on that fateful day that falling into his hands would end badly. I immediately gave up the idea of begging him to keep the matter between us, and not reveal to the family what was exposed to him by chance. I already knew that relying on his gentlemanly discretion was a lost cause.

Despite his lame leg, he bent down quick as an arrow to pick up the folded paper that had slipped from between the loaves of bread and finished its journey between his feet. So here's the letter, you stupid baker's boy! Wouldn't it have been safer to put it directly in my hand, instead of this convoluted stage play that caused all these problems? As he picked up the piece of paper, I saw a savagery in Sidi Mhammed's face that reminded me of a hawk, swooping down on a rat in our mountain countryside. But the rat hadn't given up yet. It said to itself: I'll try my luck. I offered him a loaf of bread with one hand and tried to retrieve the piece of paper with the other before he could open and read the note. He extended his arm in front of my face, giving me back the loaf of bread with a derisive smile. I said to myself, I'll snatch the letter from his hand before he reads it; I'll crumple it up and put it in my mouth and swallow it so there's nothing left.

But it was impossible. He opened the piece of paper with a flick and started reading it.

IV

I have more regrets in my long life than I have hairs on my head, my dear Hind.

I regret, for instance, that I didn't report Khal Dhawi to the police when my mother told me, when she sensed her time was near, how my father had really died after he got out of jail. Not under the hooves of the gray mule, but beaten to death by a cudgel.

I also regret that I didn't say yes to Husain the engraver's apprentice when he asked me to run away with him to his hometown on the East coast. I also regret marrying Amer the fried dough maker. It was a horrible marriage. Barely two months passed before I returned to where I came from—Lella Jnayna's house—with a broken heart and broken other things. (Though with something else that was meant to have been broken still intact.)

I have regretted many things, but time has a way of feeding on your regrets, diminishing them night after night until they fade away completely and are forgotten. My regret for not learning how to read, though, never faded, Hind. Time hasn't softened it; it's alive and painful to this day.

If I had learned how to read when I had the chance at Sidi Ali's house, I would've found a solution that day. I could've read the letter over Sidi Mhammed's shoulder, then found the perfect lie to get Lella Zbaida out of trouble no matter what, even if it meant getting into trouble myself. What did a young maid, not yet in her twenties, have to lose if her master questioned her behavior? She would be beaten and would, worst-case scenario, end up with a broken arm or leg and be sent back to her family or discarded at the foot of the old city wall. As for beatings, I had learned how to bear them, and my skin had grown thicker from Lella Bashira's pinching and biting until it was like a donkey's skin, almost impervious to the blows. As for losing my job and going back to my family's home, I would've been overjoyed to go back to the mountain and avenge my father. I would be the mule that would kick Dhawi with her hooves until his flesh and bones were mashed into a paste. My father would rest peacefully in his grave, proud to have a daughter better than a thousand men. And the street—what would the street mean for me? It would be nothing but an interlude that would end when another rich family picked me up and I began a new episode of the never-ending series of slavery. Whatever might have happened to me that day, had I succeeded in protecting Lella Zbaida's secret, would have doubtlessly been easier than what did happen.

Sidi Mhammed's eyes bulged out as he read the letter, so I knew for certain that disaster was looming. The paper was thin enough for me to see that there were at most two lines of writing in black ink, in a delicate hand. Could two little lines make a reader so angry that his chin would shake, his eyelids would flutter, and his eyes would bulge out of their sockets?

He cursed me with a curse too vulgar to repeat and then started beating me like a drum on Eid. He hit me and slapped me, punched me and shoved me, but I didn't get my share of kicking because of the leg problem I told you about. When he realized that I wasn't reacting to his violent behavior or screaming, to avoid causing a scandal, he shouted to the family to come over so he could tell them what he'd just witnessed.

He kept repeating a single refrain between blows and slaps and jabs and uppercuts. He was using it, or so it seemed to me, to provide a kind of rhythm to change up his beating style and the spots he aimed for. He was beating me and saying, "Who is Tahar, you whore?"

I remained silent, further enraging him. I was afraid of saying anything that might contradict what he'd read in the letter. So I decided to wait for another question, hoping to figure out a way to trick him. But when the rest of the family ran towards us, including Lella Zbaida herself and Sidi Othman (dragging the bandaged ankle he'd twisted that morning), I had no choice but to take a risk and do something. So I said, "I don't know him."

He didn't believe me, of course. But his parents' presence prevented him from resuming his cutting insults, so he started repeating my answer to himself with a mixture of sarcasm and indignation: "You don't know him, you tramp, you don't know him?" I suddenly realized, as his fists were raining down on my back, that complete denial was a bad plan, because even if it helped me clear my own reputation, I might unconsciously incriminate Lella Zbaida. I changed tack and said through gritted teeth, "Tahar is my cousin, Khal Dhawi's son."

I was lying, of course: Dhawi had neither a wife nor children. My father, peace be upon his soul, used to rile him up when they fought by never calling him by his name but rather by an insult he came up with, a word that rhymed with his name and implied effeminacy and impotence. But I had made another mistake with that answer. It was unfortunately not believable, based on the content of the letter as I came to understand it from his next questions. I saw Lella Zbaida's face turn as pale as death. The poor woman understood the whole story when she heard the name Tahar and saw her brother-in-law raising his hand, pointing at her in condemnation. We silently looked at each other, powerless as two doves fallen together into the same trap. I can still recall the details of those moments with such clarity, as if this didn't happen more decades ago than I can keep track of. All I wanted at that moment was to open an exit in the trap for my lady, even if that cost me my own life.

You couldn't understand, Hind, your grandmother's place in my heart. The Ennaifer family didn't understand it, either, when they discovered the truth. They were astounded that I was risking myself to prove her innocence, that I was doing everything I could to frame myself. Sidi Mhammed threatened me with utter ruin when I insisted on my first version of the story. He said, "I'm going to call the bey's police and have you thrown in a dungeon so deep and dark you'll never see the sun again."

Deep down, I didn't believe him. I'm not so naïve as to believe that the bey's police would take orders from this lame boy. But his talk about dungeons made me more determined than ever to protect her from his rage. They had reminded me of Lella Bashira's cellar and the horrors that haunted me during my youth, horrors that were only eased with Lella Zbaida's support.

There was a cellar in your great-grandfather Sidi Ali's house, where Lella Bashira kept big earthenware jars filled with olive oil and pickled olives. At the end of fall, she would receive sacks of olives from her father's farm in the countryside of Bou Achour, in addition to jars of new olive oil. The arrival of the sharecropper Aammi Sadok with his load was a holiday for the children of the house. We would race to the courtyard with blankets and old sheets and spread them carefully on the tiles before gently pouring the olives out onto them. We spread the olives one by one on the sheets and blankets until there wasn't space for even a single olive more. Sidi Mahdi, Lella Zbaida's twin, was our leader in that game that we simply called "the olive market." He would put on a chechia and a *kadroun* that he had borrowed from Khmayis, Aammi Sadok's son who would also play the game with us. He would sneak the necessary tools for the game out of the kitchen behind his mother's back: a small chair that we would put behind the sheets and sit on, a few dried beans that he would put in a tin and shake from time to time to sound like coins. And we girls would wrap ourselves with whatever old sheets were left. We would spread them over our heads and tie them around our waists like women do with their wraps. We would carry large baskets and fill some little bundles with fava beans and chickpeas, pretending they were our money bags; then we would hide behind the cracked doors of the rooms, waiting for the leader's signal. Sidi Mahdi would then raise his voice, trying to lower its pitch as much as the throat of a ten-year-old boy allowed, "Olives! Olives from Bou Achour! Come and get 'em, one cent a cup!"

Then Lella Zbaida and I would go out with her two sisters Lella Qmar and Lella Mna, along with Khmayis. We would strut by the display, pretending to examine the goods, then we would open our money bags and take out a bean or two for the olives. For the cup, we used Sidi Mahdi's chechia, which he would take off his head with a quick movement and then use both hands to fill it with green or black olives, depending on the wish of the buyer. The fava beans we paid with might be more than the price he asked for, so the honest seller would give us change in chickpeas or fava beans based on his calculations. We sometimes bargained with the seller over the price, or criticized his product, or asked him to fill up the measuring cup properly so he wouldn't end up in the place in hell reserved for crooked salesmen. Sidi Mahdi would get angry for real and flip the display over, saying (in imitation of Sidi Ali), "I won't sell you anything, get out of my sight!"

I still remember how Lella Zbaida would insist on me playing the game with her and her siblings, as if I were one of them. Her older sisters Qmar and Mna would force me to play the role of the maid in the game, just like my role in real life. They would put the baskets on my back and keep the money bag and ask me to walk behind them without talking to anyone. But Lella Zbaida would get angry and threaten to spoil the game, saying, "In the game Luiza's the same as us, or else nobody plays."

Lella Bashira would see and listen to the skirmishes between her daughters because of me and would not interfere. She would let me play with them if there was no urgent work that needed to be done. She would even take the green soap from my hands when she saw my tears mixing with the bubbles and water because the girls were playing without me. She would push me towards the game, saying, "Laundry can wait, Luiza. Go and play with them."

I often heard her rebuking Lella Mna, who was hostile to me for no reason. She would hold her by the ear and say, "I will let her sleep in your bed and make you sleep in hers to teach you not to be such a smartass." I believe that, despite her strictness with us maids, she hated arrogance and arrogant people. Quite the opposite of Lella Jnayna, Lella Bashira never prevented her maids from doing anything she allowed her daughters to do.

What was forbidden to one was forbidden to all, and what was available to one was there for all, as well.

But descending into the cellar was forbidden, summer or winter; it was out of the question. We would peer into it with children's curiosity through a squat, wide opening built into the lower side of the courtyard wall. It had short, thick steel bars to which Sidi Ali used to tie the rams that were waiting to be sacrificed for Eid al-Adha. To be honest, we didn't need any warnings from Lella Bashira to keep us away from the cellar. During the windy days of early winter, terrifying sounds came from it, sounds made even scarier by Lella Bashira's stories. She would tell us that a female jinn was tied to a stake at the bottom, by special order of the King of the Jinn. She was bound, said Lella Bashira, because she had intentionally trampled "God's gift"—that is, a loaf of bread—underfoot. So we would try as hard as we could to pick up God's gift quickly if it fell; we would kiss it and place it on our heads as an act of blessing before putting it somewhere high up, away from the feet of people walking. We also kept our distance from the squat cellar door, not letting ourselves be tempted to explore its secrets, not even by its zigzagging, dark stairs. These were revealed to us whenever Lella Bashira opened the door to get some olive oil from one of the earthenware jars or to store extra old furniture until she could donate it.

One day when we were playing the game, Lella Bashira needed to go down to the cellar. She disappeared for a moment, then came back carrying something in both hands, I don't remember what. Whatever it was kept her from closing the cellar door, so she left it ajar, most likely expecting to come right back. But she got busy and didn't come back. The game had at that point begun to lose its luster, and it suddenly occurred to Lella Zbaida to give it some new rules. She snatched the chechia off Sidi Mahdi's head as he sat behind his display and ran with it to the cellar. In one graceful movement, she threw it towards the open door, and we all watched it disappear into the darkness inside. We went silent, and she dissolved into laughter. Sidi Mahdi was furious; he saw her actions as disrespectful to him, the older brother, and an attack on a merchant's dignity besides. He ran for his mother, his eyes already filled with tears, planning to complain about it. At that moment, Lella Zbaida realized the enormity of what she'd done, so she started trying to smooth it over and apologize. But he insisted she go down into the cellar by herself to bring back the chechia, since she was the one who'd thrown it. In those days, bravery wasn't one of my lady Zbaida's distinguishing characteristics, and she turned pale and looked at me, as if asking my advice.

I walked up to Sidi Mahdi and spoke firmly, struggling to hide my fear, "I'll go down there for her and bring you back your chechia, if you promise not to tell on her."

I went down the twisting stairs with my knees trembling. I closed my eyes to avoid seeing the female jinn tied to her stake. I followed the stairs to the right and felt my way along the wall as I descended. At the bottom of the stairs, I stumbled over something heavy. I screamed in spite of myself, and then I heard something like the glug of water pouring out of a waterskin. A sticky liquid soaked my feet, and a familiar scent filled the place, covering over the cellar's smell of rot. Have you ever heard of the "leaning earthenware jar," Hind? Well, this leaning earthenware jar was now leaning in pieces across the ground after a blind Luiza stumbled into it—and Lella Bashira's supply of olive oil was all over the cellar floor.

My punishment for going down to the cellar without permission was to spend the night there, and my punishment for spilling olive oil and breaking the earthenware jar was to clean it all up. I was to spend the entire night sopping up the oil on the cellar floor with a piece of sackcloth, so it was completely clean by sunrise. I didn't try to clear myself by blaming Lella Zbaida, and she didn't admit anything to her mother anyway. Come sunset, Lella Bashira was pulling me down to the cellar like a lamb to the slaughter, and I was screaming for help and kissing her hands and feet and whatever part of her clothing my lips could reach. Lella Zbaida came out of her room holding her pillow and blanket and told her mother, in a tone of fear mixed with defiance, "If you make Luiza go down to the cellar, I'm going with her."

She probably thought saying that would make her mother change her mind about punishing me, that she would forgive me rather than see her daughter spend a night in the damp-walled cellar, haunted by spirits and God knows how many creepy crawlies. Zbaida's plan failed, however: her iron-willed mother snatched the pillow and blanket from her and pushed her with me into the cellar. Then she threw us an old straw mat and a matted sheepskin, saying, "I am afraid the pillow would get stained with olive oil and the jinn will steal the blanket. Good night, and don't forget to clean the olive oil off the floor before sunrise; otherwise, you'll be guests of the jinn for a second night."

As Sidi Mhammed threatened me with the dungeon and the bey's police, I remembered that night. No dungeon could be worse than Lella Bashira's cellar was for a young girl of not even ten. And I was not going to betray my lady, even if this hot-tempered man killed me. It's like I can see him now, Hind, dragging me by my hair from the entrance hall into the courtyard, the crowd marching behind me: Lella Zbaida stumbling on her *fouta,* your Aammi Mohammed Habib (who had just learned to walk) in her arms, Lella Jnayna holding a wooden spoon in her hand, coming from the kitchen in a state of shock when she heard her perfect, beloved younger son start ranting, Sidi Othman holding the newspaper that he'd been reading in the sitting room, black Khaddouj with a smile of satisfaction. Everyone except Sidi Mohsen, who hadn't yet gotten back from work at the Tax Office.

Sidi Mhammed put his hand on my neck and shook me violently, "Does Khal Dhawi's son write books and compose poetry, you rube? Does he leave copies of his books for you at

Sidi Mansour's bakery, so you can read them with all your vast knowledge?"

The story, then, included books and poems. The noose had started to tighten around Lella Zbaida's neck. Most likely, this sly fox understood that the letter was addressed to his brother's wife, rather than her maid, but he wanted me to confess on my own so he couldn't be accused of slandering a chaste woman. I kept silent and was ready to do whatever it took not to say anything that might be used against my lady. I saw from between my tears Lella Zbaida moving your uncle from her arms to the floor, her legs no longer able to support her, let alone carry a child. I was afraid that she might have another epileptic fit, as her body started to shake and her face started to take on a bluish tone. Pushing his hands away from my neck and struggling to catch my breath, I said, "My cousin Tahar works at Madrasa Al Khaldounia as a security guard. I asked him to send me a book."

No need to suppress your laugh, my dear Hind. This old blind woman hasn't lost her ears yet, and I can hear you laughing. You're right. It was clearly a bold-faced lie: an illiterate maid requesting a book! How I wish I'd learned how to read at Sidi Ali Rassaa's house!

Your great-grandmother Lella Bashira never objected to me attending Arabic courses with her daughters in the sitting room every Tuesday and Friday evening. While the Ennaifer daughters received sewing, embroidery, and lace-making lessons at the house of a female teacher—under strict supervision on the way there and back—Sidi Ali had chosen a private French school for his daughters, with a mixed student body of Jewish, French, Italian, and upper-class Maltese girls. The only flaw of this school, based on what I heard from Sidi Ali, was that it used French only. He rectified this flaw in his daughters' education by hiring a student from Zaytuna University to teach them the Quran and Arabic grammar at home, in return for a weekly salary. This was how Si Tahar entered the house of Sidi Ali.

I hadn't in fact witnessed his first visits; they were before my arrival to the Rassaa house. But Lella Zbaida told me that when the Hajj, her father, had brought him the first time to teach her older sister Nafissa, he was preparing for a prestigious theology degree that I think was called the *Tatwi.* He visited the house frequently for two years, then stopped coming for a long period. But Sidi Ali, after having seen how knowledgeable and polite he was, sent after him, asking him to teach the rest of the girls when they reached Lella Nafissa's age. Lella Zbaida told me that he demurred at first, saying that his charity work, and other things I don't remember, took up all his time. He was probably also too proud to take payment from Hajj Rassaa after obtaining his university degree. But Sidi Ali, being both tolerant and charismatic, insisted until he couldn't refuse the request. I still remember the first lesson I attended with the girls, and many more of his lessons after (before I gave up on them, seeing as how I was apparently too simpleminded).

He entered the house with a smile on his face, as confident as if he were a family member. When he saw me standing shyly at the door, he motioned me over to the table my ladies sat around, their notebooks and inkwells in front of them. He asked me about my name, my age, and where I was from. There was a look of pity in his eyes. He also asked me if I wanted to learn reading and writing, and I nodded. Lella Mna, my age-old enemy, was watching with displeasure and annoyance. She was most likely annoyed that the teacher was giving the young maid such attention even before talking to the elegant, upper-class mademoiselles. When she spoke with him in French, which I didn't understand, his natural sweet brown color turned dark red. Nodding at me, he signaled for me to sit down and said, "First, you're not allowed to speak French during your Arabic lesson. Second, the maid is a girl exactly like you, and she should have the same rights you do, but she'll never be able to take advantage of them without an education. Join us, Luiza."

Lella Mna pursed her lips in irritation, and Lella Qmar didn't seem to have heard the conversation at all. As for Lella Zbaida, thirteen years old then, her eyes shone with the light of victory.

Who would have thought that Si Tahar would reappear after all these years? What would I say to the people surrounding us, ready to aim their spears at my lady's chest the second my tongue slipped in this violent interrogation?

His father's intervention saved me from the clutches of my executioner. He hit Mhammed on his shoulder with the folded newspaper, ordering him to get away from me. Mhammed reluctantly let me go. Sidi Othman took the letter from him and looked closely at it. Then, out of the corner of my eye as I ran to hide behind Lella Zbaida, I saw his expression change and his mustache begin to tremble. He paid no mind to his wife Lella Jnayna, who was about to die of curiosity, asking everyone around her what was wrong and not receiving an answer. He folded the piece of paper back up and came towards me, dragging his injured leg. I huddled closer to Lella Zbaida's back, like I did as a child when my mother chased after me to punish me. The way I positioned my body was wrong, though, like most of what I did and said on that joyless day. I should have shielded her, instead of exposing her to the cane the old man used to hit her shoulder. Lella Jnayna ran to her, repeating "Bismillah" and cursing Luiza, the face of this evil omen, thinking for a moment that her husband had mistaken her daughter-in-law, who had recently given birth, for the guilty maid. But her mouth soon fell open in shock and disapproval when the respected sheikh threw the folded piece of paper in Zbaida's face and followed it with the newspaper in his hand, saying, "The letter has reached you too late, Miss Zbaida Ali Rassaa. I'm sorry for your loss: Tahar is dead; his obituary's in today's newspaper. Is this what the noble families' daughters do? This is what you get for teaching girls. Damn you and damn the people who raised you."

V

I'll never know what was in that letter or who wrote it. Was it Si Tahar himself or another person on his behalf? Did he know about it, or it was written after his passing and without his permission? Lella Zbaida will never know, either. Neither of us saw the piece of paper after that incident, and we don't know whether another family member kept it or whether it was swept away with the dust-covered bread under Sidi Mhammed's feet. All I know is that that day became the dividing line in our life at the Ennaifer house. Nothing was the same after that. Just as its bad events had started at dawn, the awful incidents continued through a large portion of the night.

When Sidi Mohsen returned from his work at noon, he was bewildered by the silence that reigned over the house. The stove was cold, and the meal in the pot atop it was half cooked. His father, his mother, and his brother were gathered in the sitting room, their heads in their hands. They were silent as statues, an empty look in their eyes. Even Khaddouj, the black maid, seemed grouchy and sullen when she greeted Si Mohsen lukewarmly from her seat on the threshold of the maids' room, not even raising her eyes to look at him. A weak, intermittent crying, coming from the crib of your father, Sidi Mostafa, in Lella Zbaida's room on the upper floor, was the only sign of life in the house. When he looked up, he saw me pacing the upper balcony with a swollen face and wild hair, carrying your Aammi Mohammed Habib on my shoulder, trying to put him to sleep. His mind flew to only one question, "What happened to Zbaida? Where's Zbaida?"

I couldn't answer him; I burst into tears. I knew he loved her, despite her coldness and the way she turned away from him to focus on her books and imaginary worlds. Sidi Ali forced her to marry him when she was seventeen years old, and I think it was the first time I saw him be harsh and domineering with his daughters. The day Lella Bashira told her that Mohsen, the son of Othman Ennaifer, had asked her father for her hand, she laughed dismissively. She was reading an Arabic book, one of those books that Si Tahar would lend her when he came to give lessons. No one persevered in their studies but her. Lella Mna got bored quickly, after only two or three lessons, when she found out he wasn't fluent in French. She, with her *beldi* complex, felt even more contempt for him because of his stories, during the breaks, about his Southern roots and his pride in his family and tribe, which hailed from El Hamma and had mostly settled in Sidi Mansour in Tunis. She started making up reasons to miss either the Tuesday or Friday lessons; then she started missing them both. Before long, she was engaged to her cousin, and she stopped attending completely when she moved in with her new husband. Lella Qmar, who married another Tunis notable that same year, followed her. By then, none of the Rassaa family daughters were left in the house except the youngest, Lella Zbaida, who was joined by her twin, Sidi Mahdi, in the lessons.

I was with her in her room when she received the news of her engagement. She was reclining on the bed reading her book, sometimes translating bits of it into Tunisian Arabic for me as I sat on the carpet next to the bed. I was heating the swaddle blankets for Sidi Bakkar, Lella Bashira's youngest and the pampered baby of the family. My lady came in with an expression of joy on her face and said, "You have the devil's own luck, my useless Zbaida!"

The word "useless" is what we used to describe women like you and your daughters, Hind. I mean, women who are bad at housework and don't know how to embroider or sew or clean the offal of the Eid lamb to make *osban*. And who don't know how to prepare difficult meals like *madfouna*, or *akod* or *molokhiya*. Your great-grandmother wasn't maligning her; your grandmother Zbaida, who spent most of her time immersed in books and magazines, truly was useless.

Lella Zbaida answered her with a smile on her face, making

room for her mother next to her on the platform bed. "Well, don't you look happy, for the mother of a useless girl?"

"Your father says that Mohsen, son of Othman Ennaifer, who has a college degree from Germany and is a senior employee at the Tax Office, his father asked for your hand today in the barber's shop."

Lella Zbaida let out a mischievous laugh, then looked at me and said, "Did you hear that, Luiza? And, Lord, did you understand it? 'The son of Othman, his father asked for your hand.' Which one is my prospective groom, Boshra? The son or his father?"

Lella Bashira answered back with one of her creative curses whose origin no one could pinpoint, then started listing the groom's many good characteristics: "Mohsen the pampered," "the son of nobility," "descendant of the Turks," "he beautifies the door at which he stands," "he has the posture of a bey," "well-bred," "fair skin and rosy cheeks," "tall and broad-shouldered," "smooth hair" . . .

Lella Zbaida couldn't stop laughing during this recitation, teasing her mother. "Wait a minute!" she said, putting on a false French accent. "Where did you see all zis? Fair-skinned *and* rosy cheeks and smooz 'air? Do you meet ze men behind Monsieur Hajj Ali's back, Madame Basheeeera?"

Lella Bashira fumbled for words before finally saying, "Bite your tongue! I've never seen him. Hajj Ali saw him and described him for me. But I'll see him soon, and he'll become one of my children, you lucky girl."

"Let him marry Luiza, then, if you're so eager to see him and enjoy the view. But this lucky girl's not marrying anyone. Also, who told you that I like fair-skinned men with rosy cheeks and smooth hair? I want a black man with blue cheeks and curly hair. Nobody gets to decide my taste."

Lella Bashira spit into her shirt pocket several times, the way city women do to seek God's protection from an evil mentioned in their presence. Then she said, as an end to the conversation,

"God forbid. Mohsen the pampered is a perfect fit for Zbaida the pampered. As for Luiza, we'll find her a husband that fits her, someone cut from the same cloth. Land birds and sea birds don't mix."

Then she added, raising her hand to her mouth, "Trill with me, Luiza!"

Lella Zbaida didn't take the matter seriously, and she probably never considered the idea that her father might force her to accept a husband she didn't want. Especially seeing as how he'd raised his daughters on the principles of freedom of choice and responsibility. She asked her mother to tell her father she wasn't in favor of this marriage, and she thought her refusal was enough to settle the matter. Lella Bashira was flummoxed by the young lady's stubbornness. She told her, "Do you think a son of the Ennaifer family isn't good enough for you? Are you waiting for the son of the bey to ask for your hand?"

Zbaida didn't answer her. As it happened, she was waiting for the bey himself to ask, in only a few days, as he'd promised. "The bey of my heart," she would say, staring at the ceiling with dreamy eyes. I had already noticed a change in her behavior before she decided to say anything to me. She'd started to take more care of appearance. She would drown her hair in olive oil on Monday night, and when she woke up in the morning, she would wash it with argil mixed with rose water. After it dried, she would pull it into a ponytail, then wrap it with a long stocking, one end gently tied to the top, and she would ask me to knot it at the bottom so it wouldn't get loose. Then she would keep her hair this way until just before Si Tahar's lesson on Tuesday evening. Only then would the young girl liberate her hair so it flowed over her shoulders, smooth and soft as if she'd just come from a Jewish hair salon. She would sit for a long time in front of the mirror touching the fine hair growing above her upper lip or at the edges of her temples, wishing she could remove it with a single quick stroke of sugar wax. But that was out of the question. Tradition was strict: the eyebrows could not be plucked and excess hair could not be removed from the face or body until the virgin became a bride, getting ready for her wedding night. It would be scandalous—and insolent—to do otherwise, because then what would be the difference between virgin girls and married women?

However, I had witnessed how Lella Zbaida excelled in finding tricks to display her beauty despite the obstacles. She would put a special kind of white stone in the mortar and crush it (quietly, to avoid attracting Lella Bashira's attention). When the stone became as smooth as flour, she would mix it with rose water to make a thick white face mask. When she washed it off with water a few minutes later, her skin was brighter, clear of any blemishes. I had also noticed that she'd started to wear jasmine perfume and spent more time than usual choosing her clothes and coordinating their colors. Time and again, she would distract me from my work, asking me to prepare some embers for the iron to smooth out her new pistachio dress or the shirt embellished with ricamo that the Italian tailor Madame Regina had made. When I asked her what was behind this transformation, she didn't deny it but instead told me everything.

When I learned about the proposal, I feared that her romantic dreams would fade away, but she stayed calm and confident. She explained to me that women had the right to accept or reject the men who wanted to marry them; this was what Si Tahar had told her. She also said that, in a few days, he would publish a unique book that would bring him great glory. She didn't elaborate, but she said, "A book about women, Luiza—a book about how their rights have been violated because of the stubbornness of religious scholars and their misunderstanding of Islam."

She added, seeing my blank look, "Weren't you telling me about your Khal Dhawi and how he stole your mother's share of the inheritance? Don't you remember the story my sister Qmar told about her sister-in-law, who was divorced by her husband in a tantrum? Then, when he regretted it, he started looking for a *muhallil* to marry and divorce her, so he would be allowed to remarry her. And have you forgotten what my aunt, Khala Najiba, told us about her husband, who divorced one of his wives because she peeked her head around the door without wearing a hijab?"

She stopped for a moment as if she were remembering other events, then put her hands on my shoulders and said, "When Tahar's book comes out, Luiza, and people read it and understand, you'll never hear about atrocities like these again. Do you understand?"

I didn't understand then, of course, though I pretended I did. It took me a quarter of a century to understand. I heard people in the markets talking, shortly after the departure of the French troops, about the new laws the leader Bourguiba had issued for women, and I ran to Lella Zbaida and told her what I'd heard. She didn't comment. She closed her eyes for a long moment, and then I saw a tear slipping from under her eyelashes. She quickly wiped it away and said, "Rest in peace, Tahar!"

VI

When Sidi Mohsen got engaged to Lella Zbaida, Si Tahar hadn't shown up for class for the past three weeks. The strange thing is that my lady, who usually got upset with him when he cancelled class, appeared happy beyond description during that time. She said that his book about women had been finally published, after a long wait, and that he was busy preparing for a launch celebration in his honor at the Casino du Belvédère, the municipal pavilion in the Parc du Belvédère. Some well-known people in Tunis were supposed to attend it. He brought an invitation for her father, Sidi Ali, and insisted on him attending. He promised Lella Zbaida that he would talk to him and ask for her hand immediately after the party, taking advantage of the celebratory moment to bridge the class differences between them.

Lella Zbaida waited anxiously for Sidi Ali's return from the party, loitering behind the *mashrabiya*. When she finally saw him come through the door, she expected that he would send someone to come get her, or that he would send her mother with the good news. But she waited in vain. When she could bear it no longer, she said, "Go to him, Luiza, and see if he needs anything. He might ask for me if he sees you."

However, many days passed, and the Hajj didn't say anything. Si Tahar himself didn't come for the next scheduled class, the week after the party. Lella Zbaida felt the week passing as if it were an eternity. She suspected that Si Tahar had renounced her when he saw how people celebrated him. "Do you think he lied to me, Luiza?" "Did he change his mind about asking for my hand?" "Why didn't he come this week?" I saw her anxiety but could do nothing but share in her torment. Then, that weekend, we thought relief had arrived. Sidi Ali sent someone to ask Lella Zbaida to join him in the sitting room. He didn't return her greeting, but took off his fez and put it on the small table in front of him. He put his palms on his knees, preparing himself, then leaned forward and said, "Mohsen ben Ennaifer has asked for your hand, and I have accepted. The women of both families will meet in two days to plan the wedding. We won't wait until summer. You will get married this month."

Lella Zbaida stammered, trying to say something. He stood up, straight as a spear, his eyes fixed on her. A month later, Lella Zbaida arrived a teary-eyed bride at the home of the Ennaifer family, and I, Luiza, her loyal maid, followed her.

2
The Tale of Lella Jnayna
(*Rue Tourbet El Bey, Summer of 1956*)

I

My dear Mustafa, your late grandfather came to me last night in my dream. He was surrounded by a halo of light. In all his finery and his judge's turban, he looked like a groom on his wedding night. He held my hand and took me into a spacious room filled with people, its floor covered with a handmade carpet. He gently pushed people aside to open a path for us. There was reverence and respect on their faces. When we made it to the front of the room where some people were seated, he waved his hand, and a lamp on the ceiling lit up as if it were a twinkling star. In the seating area stood a man in his fifties, of average stature, wearing European clothes and a Tunisian fez. The light dazzled me, so I couldn't see his face, but I heard him say, with a voice so deep it seemed to come from another era, "Seat her on her rightful throne, Othman."

I don't know the meaning of this dream, my boy, but it filled me with joy and fear. I told your Aammi Mhammed about it this morning as he sat reading the newspaper, but he didn't seem to care. He started sighing, wiping sweat from his brow, and shaking his head indignantly. I don't know what's bothering him now; after all, didn't what he was waiting for come true? Didn't Bourguiba kick France out of the country and declare this so-called independence last spring? So why is your Aammi Mhammed, who spent the prime of his youth as an activist for the Destour Party, still irritated, even though it's already summer? Also, could somebody explain to me the gist of this new "Personal Status Code" that your aunts are applauding, but that angered your Aammi Mhammed so much? Is it true that your aunts' husbands can no longer divorce my daughters with a word or a piece of paper, or threaten to bring other wives into the house? Your Aammi Mhammed doesn't answer when I ask him. This morning, he clenched his fist and started beating it against his palm as he looked at a picture of some important men in the paper. One of them I recognized as Bourguiba. He started to boil over and say to himself, "*Et tu*, Ben Ashour? You, Sheikh of Islam!?"

I asked him about the news, but he didn't answer me. He took the newspaper with both his hands, balled it up, and threw it away. Then he said, walking quickly to the entrance hall, "They've made Zbaida have the last laugh, Mama. The enemies of Tahar Haddad, who accused him of heresy just yesterday, are applauding Bourguiba today. Your husband, the great judge of Islam, Othman Ennaifer, is rolling in his grave. Did we kick France out of the country for this?"

I've been worried about your Aammi Mhammed, Mustafa, ever since he divorced that snake Fawzia. He says strange things and talks a lot about the dead. What on Earth could have reminded him of that man called Tahar and his story with your mother? And why would he open up a wound that's as old as you are, twenty-one years now? I know that snake Luiza has seeded anger in your chest against your uncle; God only knows what kind of lies she's made up to convince you that he's the reason for all the misery that has befallen us since that awful night. Now, though, you're a man with the ability to distinguish right from wrong, and it's important that you know the whole truth.

You were very young when the incident happened. We concealed the story and hid the scandal, but that damn Luiza had to open her mouth and speak. Two days later, our neighbor Manoubia, the wife of Aroussi Fayash, came over, pretending she wanted to visit your mother and congratulate her on her newborn. I served her coffee and sweets, and asked her to taste the *bsissa* we served after a new baby. I told her, "Zbaida is sick and can't see guests."

She laughed a fake laugh and said, in the tone of someone calling you a liar to your face, "Sick? I hope she's okay. It's God's will, Jnayna. As our ancestors used to say, everything in life is fate and luck, but some of it is breeding."

May God cut off her tongue, my boy, and the tongues of anyone who badmouths my darling Mustafa, son of my oldest male child, my darling Mohsen. Your birth has never been the cause of misfortune in the family. It is Luiza the ill-fated who has spread her bad luck everywhere she went.

We haven't seen any good in the Ennaifer house since we saw Luiza. She came to us with your mother's trousseau from the Rassaa family and inhabited our house like a persistent cold. It's been a quarter of century now or more, and Luiza is still sitting on the chests of everyone in this house, growing ever more insolent and vulgar. I believe she'll outlive us all, just as she outlived our maid Khaddouj and your grandfather Si Othman and your Aamma Beya after that.

This was your mother's condition for your father before their marriage, that that cursed maid of hers would go with her wherever she went. And your father, as you know, is weak with Zbaida and never refuses her anything. He told me about it, and I grudgingly agreed because I didn't think she would last very long. She was fourteen years old then, and no one expected her to stay single like Khaddouj; I figured that she would eventually get married. But I didn't realize how difficult an endeavor it would be, finding a husband for the blurry-eyed Luiza. Don't be fooled by her looks nowadays, especially after her skin color got lighter and her backside rounded out, her body becoming plump when she reached her forties. That's all owing to the bounty of the Ennaifer family, which made her soft and tender after she came to us from the Rassaa house like a solid dry stick.

After eight or nine years, when the great war broke out between Luiza and Khaddouj, I thought the crisis had finally ended. A fried dough maker from the region of Ghomrassen, an acquaintance of Si Othman, agreed to marry her. He had lost his wife, and all his daughters were married, so he needed someone to take care of him. Si Othman told him, "She is an obedient and warm orphan girl. She'll prepare your food and wash your clothes and will help clean the shop if needed."

I gave her the trousseau I had prepared for Khaddouj and sent her off with honors to the house by his shop in Bab Mnara with everything she needed. I compensated my poor fallow maid with a five-hundred franc note, telling her, "God will reward you, Khaddouj. The wool would've been eaten by moths if we'd kept it in storage much longer, and cotton eventually turns yellow from the humidity. When your Prince Charming comes, I'll make it up to you with something better."

Nor did Lella Bashira fail to add to the trousseau. She didn't break her promise to never set foot in our house again—after that fateful night, she swore she would never again enter our house or share in any of our celebrations. But she sent her maids with some woolen bedspreads and ceramic dishes, the bride's clothes, and a golden bracelet, earrings, anklet, and moon-shaped necklace studded with diamonds. She said, may she rest in peace, "Luiza is like one of my daughters. I had hoped she would marry when she was living in my house."

We made her a wedding just like the weddings of the city girls. Every day for a week, Lella Bashira sent the same henna lady who had prepared her daughters, asking her to consider Luiza the fifth daughter of the Rassaa family. Seven days and seven nights of non-stop *darbuka* music in our house, accompanied by the trilling of Khala Rebh, Luiza's mother, after we sent someone to bring her from the countryside of Zaghwan to attend her daughter's wedding. She was a thin woman with a hunched back; anyone who saw her would think that she was very old, but in reality she wasn't even sixty. There were still traces of beauty on her wrinkled face, despite the harsh effects of the sun and of poverty, though she hadn't passed any of it down to her daughter. But there is always a light shining from the face of a virgin bride, regardless of whether she is beautiful;

it's a divine light by the grace of God and His generosity. With her traditional costume embroidered with silver, her embellished hat perched on her hair, which had been softened by henna and was hanging over her shoulders, she looked so much like a bride from an upper-class family that her mother could hardly recognize her.

But a dog's curly tail can't be straightened. Two months or less after the wedding—the color of henna on her hands and feet not yet faded—her husband, the fried dough maker, threw her in our entrance hall with her trousseau and the divorce papers. He told Si Othman with a tone of pain and resentment, "She denies me my marital rights, hits me with whatever her hand can reach, and leaves the house without permission."

And she said, in tears, "He's an impotent deviant! He deflowered me with things I'm embarrassed to tell you about, so I hit him and ran away."

She was less modest when she told your Aammi Mhammed the details of her first night with him and claimed the fried dough maker had assaulted her. Then she dissolved into laughter when she told him about how she got her revenge the next day with a fiendish plan that couldn't have occurred to anyone but Satan himself: "I snuck into the shop, which is connected to the house, in the middle of the night when everyone was sleeping. I had the oil lantern in my hand. His young servant who stays in the shop was sound asleep on some empty sacks of flour. There was no way to enter without stepping over the shrouded body. I became frightened and hesitated, imagining what might happen if he opened his eyes and saw me there. But his continued snoring encouraged me to go on. I held the hem of my dress with my teeth and raised one foot and then the other. Half of the mission was successful so far; all that was left was to find the container where he mixes the flour and other ingredients to rise. It wasn't easy to empty out all the small tin dishes that were piled in it, waiting for the dawn customers. But finally, there it was in my hand. I carefully poured in a spoonful of oil from the lantern and started coating the inside, bottom and sides, of the container with it, then threw in some flour to make sure it stuck. I thought for a moment of adding a few drops to the used frying oil in the big pan the fried dough maker uses, but I was afraid it might cause a fire. So I just sprinkled it on the bags of sugar and flour."

Poor man, he nearly went crazy the next morning when his riff-raff customers started to pelt him and his employees with beignets and dishes, demanding their money back. With that evil act, Luiza had lost him most of his customers. In the two months she spent at his house, she ruined the reputation of thirty years of hard work. His marriage to her was jinxed, just like her arrival at our house.

She hated us, my dear Mustafa, from the moment we met at Lella Bashira's house. Your maternal grandfather, Si Ali, had sent word to your grandfather Si Othman in the fall to inform him of his acceptance and asked him to start preparing for the official engagement and the wedding. Your father was overjoyed, so I didn't want to spoil it for him by asking why the rush, especially after such a long silence from the Rassaa family. We'd thought it was a polite rejection of the alliance. I was honest to God wishing for your father to find a bride other than Zbaida. I was wary of how the Rassaa daughters had been spoiled, and of their Western lifestyle and their disregard for tradition. But Mohsen, who had dated the daughters of unbelievers in Germany, rejected all the girls from upper-class families that the old matchmaker showed him, stubbornly repeating, "I won't marry someone I know nothing about!"

Until one day, by chance, Zbaida, the daughter of Ali Rassaa, was mentioned, and how she went to school with European girls at the nuns' school and went with her father to the theater and concerts. Your father's face lit up, and he said, "This is the one, Mama."

I tried to change his mind but couldn't. I told him about the strong personality of his future mother-in-law, Bashira

Djellouli, sister of the grand vizier, Taieb Djellouli, and what the people said about her overbearing nature. I told him, "Like mother, like daughter."

I told him I was worried Zbaida might make him her plaything if she followed her mother's style in controlling and oppressing her husband. But he acted as if enchanted; he didn't listen to me, or maybe didn't care. I think he must have watched her during some of her promenades, seen her riding in their carriage or coming out of it, and that made him insist on marrying her. The day your grandfather Ali Rassaa sent his messenger asking us to begin the engagement period, Mohsen raised his voice in the courtyard singing one of Cheikh El Afrit's songs. Even now, I can almost hear him singing with Khaddouj, may she rest in peace, repeating after him with her beautiful Bedouin voice: "We sent a messenger and told him to see how beautiful she is . . . I can't wait, go and tell her . . . And talk to her with a genteel voice . . . I will surely ask for her hand . . . Zbaida, my neighbor . . . Lella Zbaida . . . "

II

On the day of the engagement, Luiza sneered in our faces as soon as she saw us entering the Rassaa house behind the silk-wrapped baskets and the bundles of white candles tied into gold-embroidered napkins. She met us with an angry grimace on her face and saw us off with a frown. And when Zbaida came out from her room swaying in her costume, her face covered with a light veil made of silver mesh, Luiza raised her hand with the women as if she was about to trill but instead let out a long wail that sounded like she was howling. The guests around her expressed their disapproval, and many women from the bride's side raised their voices reprimanding her for what they saw as an evil omen on a happy occasion. The women whispered that she was jealous of her lady's good fortune in marrying the elder son of the Ennaifer family. But Zbaida didn't notice anything. It was as if she was lost in her happiness, her eyes misted over with joyful tears.

Luiza started her second week at our house with a fight with Khaddouj that left her with damaged hair and bruised skin. Khaddouj, whose real name is Anbra, wanted to boss around the new arrival. She started giving her orders: "Bring the large copper bowl from the maids' storage room . . . Wash the sack-cloth and put it on the line . . . Boil the water to wash the clothes . . . Get the bucket out of the well . . . Don't poke the broom into the drainage holes . . . Don't forget to fill the clay stove with wood."

She had likely, in addition to that, prodded or pushed her or talked to her harshly. I saw what was happening between them, and I had to remind myself to stay neutral—though I had a natural bias towards Khaddouj, of course, based on what I had observed of Luiza's negligence and rudeness.

During that time, we were still taking meals up to the newly-weds' room, to pamper the bride and extend the periods of intimacy between her and her husband. When it was lunch time, the dishes and glasses were prepared, and Khaddouj called on Luiza to take the tray upstairs. When she was about to lift it up, some dishes shifted and collided with each other, spilling some stew and soiling the white tablecloth with its crocheted border. Luiza didn't seem to be concerned about what had happened, or maybe she didn't notice. Khaddouj, however, started to scream and curse, not knowing that I could see and hear her from my window. "You idiot—are you blind? Do you have two left hands?"

She added, taking the tray from Luiza's hands almost violently, "At the Rassaa house, you might eat like Bedouins on dirty tablecloths, but here at the Ennaifer house, we change them."

Luiza froze for a moment, not knowing what to do. Then she took the dishes from the tray and calmly put them on the kitchen table. Then she said, coldly, putting on a new cloth without raising her head, "The Ennaifer family must have learned civilization and finesse from your great-grandfather and his great-grandfather at the grand palace of the Negro dynasty. Unfortunately, the Rassaa family's freed slaves were coarse and unrefined, unlike you. Isn't that true, 'Anbra' or 'Dung' or whatever your name is?"

That day the newlyweds' lunch was delayed until after 4 P.M., and no one was able to save Luiza from Khaddouj's nails except your grandfather Si Othman and his cane.

I don't know what that damn Luiza told you about your grandfather and his cane on the memorable day of the scandal. I think she exaggerated the story and blamed your grandfather for what happened. Mohsen wasn't there the day of the incident, either, and he heard her version of the story instead of listening to ours. She opened the door for him, crying and screaming with your brother, Mohammed Habib, who hadn't yet turned two, in her arms. You, however, were with Zbaida in her room. She locked you inside with her, bolting the door so we couldn't get inside, despite your bitter tears over your empty stomach and the dirty diaper irritating your skin. We don't know what she told him. He was trying like a crazy person to break down the door to get to your mother, who wasn't answering him. He couldn't see anything from the window because the curtains were closed. The window was covered with the wrought-iron spirals and circles of its bell-shaped bars, which made it impossible for him to reach the wooden shutters to open them. He came down when he failed to force entry through either the door or the window. He was as angry as if he'd been possessed by demons. I had never seen him like that in my entire life. He pulled Mhammed from his chair with both his hands and started shaking him violently, in a blind anger, "Where's this paper you want to ruin my family with?"

"I gave it to the Hajj."

He repeated the question to his father, his tone polite but

his teeth clenched as he tried to control himself. Si Othman answered him almost scornfully, "We gave it to the person it belonged to. The messenger's duty is but to convey the message."

"What was written on it?"

"Ask your respectable wife, the educated woman, to tell you what was in it."

Mohsen looked at me, entreating. Before his arrival, Si Othman had summarized the content of the letter for me, asking God for forgiveness and protection from Satan. He said, "Your daughter-in-law, Zbaida, is seeing a man from Rue Sidi Mansour."

He added, clapping his hands together in frustration and despair, "The man is known, Lella Jnayna, to be an infidel and a heretic."

I didn't understand most of what he said that day. He repeated the letter, which was written in Standard Arabic, from memory. It was difficult for me to decipher the code, but I gathered that the man was called Tahar Haddad. Or maybe it was some man named Tahar who worked as a *haddad*—you know, a blacksmith—next to the bakery, and that's why the letter was camouflaged inside a bundle of bread. He also said that the man had died before his letter reached Zbaida, and told me that he knew about his passing only by chance from the newspaper. Otherwise, he would never have been able to make the connection between the Tahar mentioned in the letter and Tahar Haddad, and he might have believed that the message was meant for the maid and not his daughter-in-law. Honestly, Mustafa, I was astonished that the newspapers published obituaries for blacksmiths, but I didn't dare refute the Hajj's words.

I couldn't repeat all of this to Mohsen that day when he looked at me, his eyes pleading for someone to put end to his pain and confusion. I was flummoxed and didn't know what to say, so I said something stupid that only an idiot would say. "Anyway, the man is dead, thank God!"

After a few months, when everyone had calmed down and

the animosity had faded, that comment (I don't know where on earth I got it from), became an inside joke in our house. We would repeat it whenever one of us regretted a clumsy answer that was useless for whoever had been asking a question. Luiza was the only person who didn't think it funny, her face scrunching up with suppressed anger.

III

Luiza never forgave your Aammi Mhammed for what he did to her the day of the incident. Her stupid dreams of having him crumbled in the courtyard under his violent fists. She thought I hadn't noticed the ardent glances she cast at him, both coming and going. I didn't care about the matter in the beginning. I was naive and thought that that ugly, skinny teenager couldn't attract the attention of an old monkey, let alone my dear, handsome son Mhammed. However, I started to worry one day when I saw her secretly smelling his clothes before washing them. She put his shirt on her eyes and buried her head in his trousers and was frozen there for an hour, doing nothing but breathing in and out. When I confronted her, she gave me a laughable lie as an excuse. She said that her master Mhammed's clothes reminded her of those of her late father, who was recruited by the French army and killed in an air raid during the Great War. Can you imagine? The clothes of your Aammi Mhammed ben Othman ben Hmida Ennaifer reminded her of clothes belonging to dirty mountain dwellers in the countryside? I would find out later on from your grandmother Lella Bashira that Luiza's father was a day laborer who had stolen from his French employer and been sent to jail; after he got out, his brother-in-law killed him because of some old feud. It's a family of gangsters. God help us!

After that, I forbade her from washing Mhammed's clothes and assigned that task to Khaddouj. But she didn't give up. I saw her once from my window sneaking into his room and opening his dresser. I rushed to her, tripping on my long *fouta*, heedless of everything around me. She was, after all, brought up by the late Bashira Djellouli. Stories don't come out of nowhere, and as wise people said a long time ago, "The egg doesn't make a cracking sound unless there's a crack in it." I don't want to speak ill of the dead; your grandmother is now in the abode of truth, and I am in the abode of falsehood, but . . . women would talk when they were alone together, in the bathhouse and the *zawiya*, about your grandmother Bashira and her amazing abilities. Some of them said: "Bint Djellouli has a magic power: she's made the head treasurer at the prime ministry like henna in her hand, and on her foot as well! She's in charge of everything. He's never said no to anything she's asked him for."

How else do you explain your grandmother's control of your grandfather, Mustafa? What do you think women do to control men? Luiza acted confused when I surprised her at your uncle's dresser, her hand in his folded clothes. She laughed at me, the hussy, when she saw me throwing all his clothes on the floor and searching the shelves and his pockets for an amulet or a talisman or one of those things like that that women use to put a spell on men. She said, raising her eyebrows and pursing her lips, "I'm looking for Sidi Mohsen's cream-colored shirt. Lella Zbaida couldn't find it, so I thought Khaddouj might have put it by mistake in Sidi Mhammed's dresser."

I looked at her helplessly and said, "Your plots won't work, Luiza bint Bashira."

I don't know what Luiza did to your uncle, Mustafa, what kind of concoctions she slipped into his meals or sprayed on his clothes or scattered in the corners of his room during the time she lived in our house. However, seeing the hate and disgust in his eyes when he looked at her assured me that our countermeasures would, God willing, frustrate her efforts to bring him to her. Khaddouj used to pour sea water on the threshold of his room and under his bed, and I would hold salt in my hand and rub his back when he put his head in my lap, and recite *ruqyah* to protect him every morning and evening. My fears, however, returned when I saw your uncle reach his thirty-fifth birthday and still refuse to get engaged or married. I invited him to join us whenever Fatima the matchmaker came over, but he would come in a bad mood and rush to leave, as if he were sitting on an ember. I started urging her to exaggerate the beauty of the girls she described, hoping that one of them would fall into his heart, the way Zbaida fell into Mohsen's. So Fatima would let her tongue go and start weaving some amazing images. "Her name is Aziza, and she lives up to her name. Her beauty is perfect, and she has the best mind, sweetest soul, and most beautiful eyes. She hails from an affluent family. She is the lady of ladies. She is Jazia El Hilalia strutting in her long hair. Her skin is so translucent you can see the water in her throat when she drinks, and her smile can light a dark room. She is the one and only. Her lips are the color of coral. She is tall like a moringa branch. She has the eyes of a gazelle, and her hair is dark as the deepest well."

As much as I admired her powers of description and rhyme, your Aammi Mhammed's objection and disgust only got stronger. I was very confused and not sure what to do, my dear Mustafa, so your Aamma Nozha, your father's sister, advised me to consult a soothsayer: it was possible that the boy was suffering from a spell or had been harmed by envy. I sent for an old Moroccan lady; I forget her name. She lived on Rue du Morkadh, and I learned about her from a woman who works as the keeper of the Sidi Brahim Riahi Mausoleum. She asked me for a piece of his clothing that had his sweat on it, along with two eggs from a red hen with no yellow on them and a complex mixture of incense called *fasoukh*. On Thursday evening, at the end of visiting hours, we met in the mausoleum. I gave her the undershirt Mhammed had worn that day, and she spread it out and began to chant incantations over it; they were unintelligible, but I didn't think it was from the Quran. After the mausoleum keeper arrived with a *kanoun*, she took one of the two eggs and put it in the ash under the embers in the *kanoun*. She wasn't satisfied with just the incense I had brought at her request, but also pulled another kind from under her shirt: it was dark-colored and had a putrid smell that made you short of breath, and it made black smoke instead of white when you put it in the fire. As for the other egg I still held in my hand, she wrapped it in a white cloth that smelled like saffron and had writing on it in yellow ink. She had me hold the cloth and said in Moroccan Arabic, in a tone that sounded like singing, her body swaying with her words, "Your son is tied up, Lella Jnayna. He's tied with chains, not ropes. The chains are heavy, and the woman bewitching him is dangerous. The key is hidden in your house, but have faith and show the egg and remember what I tell you . . . "

I put the money she asked for in her lap and gave the mausoleum keeper the same amount. They put me in a circle of candles with the piece of cloth and its egg in my hand. The keeper sat far away on a low wicker chair, watching what was happening, and the old Moroccan woman bent so far over the lit *kanoun* that I was afraid the fire would burn her scarf. She started moving the embers with a wooden stick, and her lips made shapes like words without producing any sound. The egg suddenly exploded in the clay stove, making a crackling and gurgling sound. In the middle of the two halves of the broken shell, I saw a small swath of wool covered with dark red. I was surprised it hadn't been burned. That was half of the spell that had been prepared for your uncle Mhammed. The old Moroccan woman was able to recognize and neutralize it. It was a swath of wool plucked by hand from a live horned ram and soaked in impure blood on a Thursday night in the month of Muharram. This is what the soothsayer said. As for the remaining half, she said, it was still hidden in a high place in our house, and we should use the remaining egg (the one wrapped in the cloth with saffron writing on it) to find it. Before I left, she made me memorize what was expected from me in the next steps. She said something in her Moroccan dialect that the mausoleum keeper helped me decipher: "Hard boil the egg in salted water and add seven cloves to it, no more and no less. Once you're sure that the yellow and the white of the egg are stuck together, put it, still in its shell, in a clay vessel and place that against a bench in the entrance hall or the courtyard or wherever there are benches in the house. Cover it with the cloth for an entire night, making sure to leave a little opening for air. If you follow this prescription faithfully, the spell shall reveal itself after three cycles."

After the three days passed without any development, I was devoured by fear and regret. I remembered what Si Othman said about women who consult sorcerers or soothsayers: God will make them look ugly in this life and will not look at them in the next. Though I've never seen anything like that happen. Look at Lella Bashira, who only became more beautiful and obtained more prestige and power over her husband year after year, until she died of grief after his passing.

However, at the beginning of the third week, an old nest started to fall down from the southern porch roof. It had been used every migration season for a long time by a pair of swifts; we always considered the presence of the nesting couple and their chicks a blessing, so we didn't dare get rid of the empty nest, even when it had been abandoned for years. When it fell, I was shocked to see the dry body of a small bird fall down among the mud and fine straws. No one could mistake this bird for a swift, given its color and the distinguished crest on its head. I had never in my life seen a hoopoe before that day, but Zbaida was able to recognize it and was surprised to find it in the nest. She said that it's one of the most popular birds used in black magic—though she added that those practices are nothing but cock-and-bull stories told by swindlers, and that they can't hurt anyone but those who are weak-willed and gullible.

With the exposure of this dirty plan, Luiza went pale, but

she denied any wrongdoing or knowledge about who did it. I refrained from blatantly accusing her, out of respect for Zbaida and because of the lack of evidence. But I asked Khaddouj to keep an eye on her so she wouldn't get the chance to do something else. Two days later, after the incident, I hurried to summon the matchmaker again because I was certain that the problem was solved. However, your Aammi Mhammed became even more stubborn and started to say loudly, if he was certain that Mohsen couldn't hear him, "I won't give up my freedom, and I don't want to be made a cuckold by any woman."

I spent a lot of money on soothsayers, enough to buy the palace of Lamine Bey. But I got nothing in return but the resentment of Hajj Othman, who found out about my frequent visits to shrines and *zawiyas* carrying gifts and sacrifices. So he decided to forbid me from leaving the house, and that ban didn't end until his death, may God rest his soul, a year after Mhammed's marriage to that piece of bad luck that he ended up divorcing.

IV

Mhammed only obeyed me after ten years of daily begging that rose to the level of insistence, ending with crying and cursing. I believe that what Luiza accused him of, and the rumors that she spread, my dear Mustafa, made him rush to get married to prove her wrong and stop people from spreading lies.

You probably heard the story of the shed from her. She probably made it sound vulgar in a way that's not appropriate for a young man your age to hear from a woman. You know, of course, that your Aammi Mhammed made the shed on the roof into a sitting area for him and his friends. They could go up from a private entrance in the courtyard and would sit there for hours playing cards and backgammon and smoking hookah, and just chatting without bothering anybody. One night in the middle of Ramadan, you and your brother were guests at Lella Bashira's. That year, she had insisted on bringing all her family members together (except Zbaida, of course) for iftar every night of Ramadan, as if she knew, may she rest in peace, that she and her husband would not live to see the next Ramadan.

That night, after the *Tarawih* prayers, your Aammi Mhammed went up to the shed with one of his friends and asked Khaddouj—who in that period had begun to be riddled by illness, though we were not yet aware of it—to prepare Turkish coffee for them and to serve it with *zlabia* and Béjean *mkharek*. He instructed her to leave the tray at the bottom of the stairs, as usual, so as to not tire herself, and also to allow the young men to speak as freely and dress as lightly as they wanted on those hot summer nights.

Your grandfather Si Othman had taken your Aamma Beya's children to watch the Ramadan puppet show in the nearby square, while Zbaida, Beya, and I sat in the roofed part of the courtyard, eating hazelnut *bouza* and drinking cold lemonade. We were enjoying a lovely chat that got even more fun when the Om Kalthoum song "May My Beloved Be Happy" started playing on the radio in the living room where Mohsen was sitting. When your grandfather brought the kids back around 10 P.M., they made a lot of noise in the courtyard: they had brought sticks from the street and covered them with rags and napkins to make puppets out of them, and they started acting out the characters they saw in the puppet show. It seems that the noise they were making bothered your Aammi Mhammed because he shouted down at them from the edge of the roof. A few minutes later, Beya noticed the absence of her youngest child, Sulaiman. We looked for him all over the house but couldn't find him, so Zbaida suggested a possibility we hadn't thought of: "He probably climbed the stairs up to the roof to join his uncle Mhammed."

We started calling to Mhammed to see if the boy was there or not, but he didn't answer. So Luiza (who'd been looking for an excuse to visit the shed for a while) ran towards the stairs, as the rest of us returned to the courtyard where we'd been sitting, waiting to get it straight from the horse's mouth.

A few minutes later, that cursed Luiza's screaming tore the veil off the moonlit night. Your Aamma Beya and I were faint with worry, thinking something bad must have happened to the three-year-old boy. We ran towards the entrance hall, along with Mohsen, who was faster than us. As soon as we reached the stairs, Luiza appeared holding Sulaiman and looking frightened, unable to talk or breathe. We couldn't get anything out of her intermittent gasping to solve the mystery of what had paralyzed her with fear.

The evil that had broken out between your uncle and your father the night of Zbaida's letter scandal was still present, despite the long time that had passed, so Mohsen decided not to go upstairs to check on his brother. He made do with interrogating Luiza, who started shaking her head and lifting her hands in the air as if she was suffering from something unbearable and serious. She started repeating one sentence over and over, as if she had lost her mind, "Good heavens . . . Good heavens . . . Good heavens!"

We were still in a state of chaos, between fear and relief, when we saw Mhammed's companion shoot down the stairs like an arrow and rush through the entrance hall, running towards the door. Suddenly that damn Luiza started spitting at his back in an insolence that I've never seen in my life saying, "May God curse you, you dog . . . Impurity in this holy month?"

After that, she left us standing there like idiots as she ran to her room, locking the door behind her. Our gathering ended, each of us certain that the young man had harassed her behind Mhammed's back when she went up there looking for Sulaiman. We settled on blaming Mhammed for hosting the trash of society who violate people's honor.

However, during the pre-dawn suhur meal, Luiza came back with another story that nobody could have made up but a wicked person. She fabricated from her own imagination some disgusting details that she claimed she witnessed when she looked at Mhammed and his friend through the window of the shed, searching for Sulaiman. She told Zbaida that fabrication, who passed it on to Mohsen before it reached me. Mohsen told me, trying not to look me in the eyes, "I am passing the news on to you so that you can be on your guard. I don't have time to follow him in the streets and alleys to know who he hangs out with. But keep an eye on the shed and its visitors."

Hajj Othman was the only person who didn't hear anything. I was afraid if he found out what the maid had accused his son of, he would have killed her with his cane before even realizing what he'd done.

V

The next day, I told Mhammed about Luiza's false rumors, wanting to encourage him to end that cursed celibacy that allowed low-class people to slander his reputation. What really surprised me was his tolerance and control of his anger, especially since I was expecting that he would be satisfied with nothing less than firing the maid and sending her home to her original masters. But he went silent for a long time as he listened to me, holding his head between his hands, then said in the tone of someone surrendering to their fate, "You want me to get married? Fine . . . choose a spinster based on your criteria, and I will marry her."

"Spinster? Don't be silly. I'll choose the best girl for you, one who will be suitable for my darling son, the master of all men."

However, the best girl—chosen for your uncle from an upper-class family—wasn't any less disastrous than the queen of disasters, that cursed Luiza. I strongly believe that when the curses of those two women gathered together by some miracle at our house, under the same roof, they passed the limit of what

God's mighty providence could do to save us. The tragedies started the moment the new bride entered our house and never stopped.

There were bad omens that appeared a few days before the wedding, which we'd had to postpone many times. As soon as we began preparing for the marriage contract ceremony, we received the news from the Rassaa family about your grandfather Si Ali, who had lost consciousness two days before. Suddenly and without any warning, his head had fallen onto his chest as he ate dinner with his family, chatting and telling jokes. He told them while biting into a fig, "These figs are delicious. I'll bring you another bag tomorrow from the market." Then his eyes got bigger and his face muscles cramped up, and he fell forward onto the table. Lella Bashira screamed, thinking that his time had come. She asked the neighbors for help, and they took him by car to the Hôpital Sadiki. But the doctor who saw him didn't see any point in keeping him at the hospital, so he asked them to take him home. He told Lella Bashira that he had only a few days left to live and that he would most likely never regain consciousness.

After a thirteen-year rift—from which you and brother escaped only because of the two adversaries' agreement—Mohsen, Zbaida, and I knocked on the door of the Rassaa house on Rue El Azzafine. Zbaida was despondent on the way there, overwhelmed with missing her mother and fearing for her father's health. Mohsen and I, while showing her sympathy and support, were in fact delighted for this precious opportunity that destiny had provided. There would be no better occasion to close this disagreeable chapter with our in-laws than by visiting the dying man. It wouldn't have been fitting to postpone the reconciliation visit until the funeral day.

In the end, a miracle happened, and Si Ali belied the French doctor's opinion. Zbaida and her mother couldn't stop hugging all the way from the entrance hall to the courtyard, their words of reproach mixing with tears, and their feelings of concern over the sick man getting mixed with the joy of seeing each other again after so many years. Then a weak voice came out from the main room. We listened carefully. "Zbaida . . . Zbaida . . . Zbaida."

We rushed to him, following his wife. He was sitting in his bed, adjusting the woolen pillow behind his back with one hand and, with the other hand, patting the head of his youngest son, your Khal Bakkar. Bakkar was so shocked he couldn't speak, so he just cried, kissing his father's knees before he gave up his place to Zbaida after a long hug. The maids' trilling in the house spread the good news, and Lella Bashira started welcoming the neighbors who came over, bearing sweets and drinks. Whenever anyone asked how it had happened, she would tell them, in the honest, sincere way of someone who is cleansed of old grudges, "May God bless and keep the Ennaifer family. They are the visitors who brought Si Ali's healing with them."

I seized the opportunity of the happy moment to invite them to join us in celebrating your Aammi Mhammed's marriage contract ceremony three days later. I convinced Si Othman to visit them that very evening and invite them himself, in a show of respect to them. He told me, while talking about his visit to the Rassaa house, "Si Ali, God bless him, welcomed me standing up on his own two feet, his cheeks rosy and his clothes perfumed with musk. As if he had never missed a moment from this life."

The women gathered on Thursday afternoon, the day of the ceremony, in the house of the bride, while the men gathered at the mosque of Sidi Yahya with the marriage officiants, to sign the contract after the *Asr* prayers. During that time, I entered the room of the viper who was to become my daughter-in-law. I wanted to make sure that she had taken off her belt, as required by our traditions, and that she had put the piece of sugar under her tongue and contemplated her face in the hand mirror, following the rituals of the marriage contract ceremony. Brides should be as sweet with their grooms as the taste of sugar in the mouth (may God make her mouth bitter now, wherever she is). And the groom should never see anything but the image reflected in the mirror in her hand, the image of her face and no other (may God make her face ugly, and bring her shame among women).

As soon as I finished putting the silk bridal veil on her head, I heard a noise from the courtyard, where the women attending the party had gathered; I could distinguish Luiza's voice, wailing and screaming something I didn't catch. I was sure it was a disaster, and it came into my head that the cursed woman was trying to spoil Mhammed's wedding by fabricating some calamity. But then the voices got louder, rising from every direction: "God is great . . . *Allahu akbar* . . . Life is transient . . . May God have mercy on him and give you comfort, Zbaida . . . Only God is immortal . . . "

Mohsen told me that Si Ali had collapsed in the mosque courtyard. The jasmine *machmoum* had fallen from his hand as he was walking between his two sons and his son-in-law, walking strong with his tall stature and charisma that were well known among both his loved ones and his enemies. When your Khal Mahdi bent over to pick up the *machmoum*, he saw his father lose balance and fall on the ground on his face, his turbaned fez rolling on the ground before him. After a short moment of trembling, he made a gurgling sound, and his movements ceased as his soul left his body to meet its creator. People couldn't believe that he had died: they waited for him to open his eyes and talk to them. But a miracle doesn't strike twice. The wedding contract ceremonies were canceled and instead of reading the Fatiha over the marriage contract, the men read the Fatiha over the old man's body, shrouded on the mosque mat in his red *jebba*. Then they worked together to carry his body on their shoulders to his house.

And the strangest thing was Mhammed's joy in postponing the marriage contract ceremony. As if his heart was telling him, my dear Mustafa, that the bride was a you-know-what and that his marriage to her was destined to fail, if not today, then tomorrow. I saw him that day, when I scurried home from the bride's house to take off my formal clothes, kohl, powder, and other finery. I saw him taking off his formal clothes and putting on the clothes of mourning while whistling a dancing tune. He refused outright after that to conclude the marriage contract ceremonies within a small family circle, even after the forty days of mourning had passed. He told his father in a strange tone, "It's not right, father, please. What would people say about us? The dirt in our father-in-law's grave is not even dry yet, and we are throwing a party? It is absolutely not right. We should wait until next spring, out of respect for Zbaida, or even next summer, if you wish."

God fulfilled his wish without any effort from our side or his. Bashira joined her lifelong companion after a malignant tumor grew in her chest and rushed her off to the cemetery. Then Khaddouj died of the same illness after a short stay at the hospital. The bride's family threatened to cancel the engagement if we continued to postpone the ceremony, so we held the wedding in the early summer, and neither your father nor your mother attended. Your mother didn't attend because she was still mourning your grandparents, may God bless their souls. Your father's absence was purportedly to support his wife, but in reality he did it to spite Aammi Mhammed, as he hadn't yet forgiven him for what he did on the night of the big scandal, when you, Mustafa, were still an infant in your cradle.

VI

I knew that Mohsen loved Zbaida, but it never occurred to me that his love for her would reach the level that I saw with my own eyes and heard with my own ears that night. After I said that ridiculous thing I told you about ("Anyway, the man is dead"), I briefly explained the crux of the matter to him. I said, choosing my words carefully, "Your wife received a letter, sent to her by a man from the Sidi Mansour quartier, and it was hidden in a bundle of bread. Mhammed found it by chance in Luiza's hands after she received it from a messenger. The man's name was Tahar Haddad, and he died today or yesterday based on what the Hajj told me. Your father lost his temper and hit Zbaida with his cane."

I said all that together in one breath, like someone who is trying to get rid of a heavy weight. I waited to be bombarded with questions asking for clarification about the letter's contents and the name of the sender, but he only said, "The Hajj hit Zbaida?"

Si Othman answered him in a mocking tone, "No, I kissed her on the lips then expressed my condolences about the passing of the great scholar Sidi Tahar Haddad, God rest him."

Mhammed smiled as if he found his father's answer funny. Mohsen looked at him angrily and said, "Oh, you're laughing are you, Big Man?"

"Do you want me to cry? Mama is telling you we intercepted a letter on its way to your chaste wife from a strange man and you're asking whether the Hajj hit her?"

"Shut up and stay out of it. This is a private matter for me to solve as I see fit."

Mhammed was about to answer him back, but he caught my eye, which at that moment was visibly scolding him, so he was forced to keep quiet. But the sarcastic smile didn't leave his lips.

Mohsen turned back to me, asking, "Why did Zbaida lock herself in the room? Why doesn't she answer me or calm Mustafa down? I can hear him crying in his crib. Is she okay?"

I pursed my lips and raised my eyebrows to show that I had no idea why, but Mhammed decided to continue where he'd left off. "Why don't you tell him the truth, Mama? Tell him that Zbaida locked herself up so she could cry undisturbed and mourn her sweetheart, that unique man who will be sorely missed by the Ennaifer family and the entire province of Tunisia."

Mohsen bit his lower lip so hard I was afraid he was going to make it bleed. He was staring at your Aammi Mhammed and seething. Anyone who saw him wouldn't need to be that clever to understand that he was forcibly holding himself back from answering with his fists rather than his tongue, out of respect for his father's presence.

My dear Mustafa, I don't recall your father ever losing control of his tongue. Even when the situation got very bad, with the interference of Lella Bashira and Si Ali on the night of the incident, your father kept as calm and composed as if his nerves were made of stone. I see that you take after him in your forbearance and patience when making decisions—the opposite of your brother, Mohammed Habib, who takes after Zbaida in his irascibility, impatience, and recklessness. While your Aammi Mhammed's upbringing was exhausting and difficult for me, your father was like a full-grown man from the beginning. He was never frivolous or thoughtless. However, he has one bad trait that has remained with him since childhood, and I don't think he'll ever be cured of it: a legendary stubbornness that could blunt metal.

When Mohsen decided to move to Germany after finishing lycée—a decision that surprised all of us—nobody could change his mind about it. The common path was that the best students would go to France and then come back from its universities as doctors or lawyers, and your grandfather Si Othman had prepared him for this path. This is why he chose not to register him at Zaytuna University after he graduated from the Quranic school, to save him from becoming a judge, and instead provided him with a modern education at the Collège Sadiki and then at Lycée Carnot de Tunis. Your grandfather was hoping that his firstborn would become a doctor. He was planning to open a private clinic for him at a location he had inherited from his grandfather, Mhay Eddine Ennaifer. His grandfather, along with his partner, the Jewish merchant Isserine, had several silk shops in Souk El Grana. Even before Mohsen could walk, he would look at him and say, "Inshallah the nobility of Tunis will pass by the clinic of my son Dr. Mohsen ben Othman Ennaifer!"

I would tease him, saying with a laugh, "What kind of prophecy is this, Si Othman? Are you foreseeing a new epidemic for Tunis that will bring down all its nobility?"

Then your grandfather would stand up and pat your father's head and say laughingly, "Who cares, my dear Jnayna, as long as we have the protection of this hero."

But Mohsen disappointed him when he refused to take the second part of the secondary school diploma exam after receiving a high grade on the first part. We didn't take his refusal seriously at first, since none of us believed it was possible for someone to arrive at the finish line and not cross it—but that's just what Mohsen did. When anyone asked him why, he would answer with one unchanging sentence, "Because I don't want to."

In his anger, Si Othman tied him to that column you can see in the middle of the courtyard for two days, wearing nothing but shorts. He almost broke Khaddouj's back with his cane when he caught her trying to loosen the rope pressing on Mohsen's chest and legs, out of love and sympathy. But that didn't stop her from supporting him with whatever she could manage. When that late summer heat we call *aoussou* became brutal around noon, she would hang big blankets on the clothesline to shade him and prevent the sunlight from reaching him, and she would even soak those blankets in water so the Hajj wouldn't suspect why she'd spread them on the line that way. She would go to him every now and then with cold water, and when he quenched his thirst, she would pour the rest on his body to cool him off. I suffered a lot during those two days. I fed him secretly and spent all day running between him and his father: pleading for the Hajj to forgive and untie him, and pleading with him to apologize to the Hajj and promise him to make up for what he'd missed in the most recent examination period. The Hajj agreed by the end of the second day to forgive him, but Mohsen didn't agree to apologize or make any promises. He told me, rubbing the spiral blue lines that the rope had left on his body, "I will never change my mind, not even if you keep me tied up till I die. No one will decide my future for me unless I'm six feet under."

That incident changed his relationship with his father. I believe his decision, after he came back from Germany, to marry the daughter of the Rassaa family, despite their European lifestyle, was a matter of him choosing the opposite of the strict lifestyle that had been imposed on the family by your grandfather. I remember that the Hajj asked for him in the dining room on the morning after his wedding. He told him, smoothing his mustache, "Tell your wife, Zbaida Rassaa, to forget everything she's used to in her father's house. The laws of the land here are the laws of the Ennaifer family. Leaving the house should be only for a good reason. This is a conservative house."

Mohsen smiled, nodding. That same night, we heard Zbaida's high heels clicking across the courtyard tiles in rhythmic steps. She was wearing a long black cloak and had covered her head with an embroidered cotton scarf. On top of everything, she had wound a white silk *safseri* that didn't cover much of what was under it. Your father was walking behind her, wearing a gray European suit, his coat over his arm. I went out to them, very concerned, thinking that they had had a fight after Mohsen informed his wife of his father's instructions. I was afraid that he was returning her to her family house in the darkness of the night, divorced and heartbroken. But I was met with two bright faces greeting me with a smile. That calmed me down, and I heaved a deep sigh of relief. I followed them with my eyes, a thousand questions in my mind. When I was looking at the entrance hall, hesitating between asking them about their destination on this dark night or staying quiet and returning to my room, damn Luiza suddenly appeared out of the blue, covered with her white cotton *safseri*, as well. She said from behind her black face veil when she realized that I was trembling with fear, "God protect you, Lella—I didn't mean to scare you. I would sprinkle some water on you to calm your nerves if I weren't in a rush. But the concert will start soon: Sidi Mohsen is taking us to the 'thearter' to see Fadhila Khetmi."

Si Othman was busy reviewing some notebooks just then, and I'm not sure if he really didn't notice what was happening or was just pretending. I imagine that, with time, he came to understand that Mohsen ben Othman Ennaifer was going to deal with his wife based on his own rules. And they eventually became the rules of the Ennaifer family, as well, after they were altered by the stubborn boy.

The next day, I started rebuking your father, deliberately lowering my voice, warning him that the matter wouldn't have gone so smoothly if Hajj Othman had noticed them going out at night. Mohsen kissed my head, smiling, and answered me in a whisper, in a tone that was either serious or humorous, I couldn't tell, "If my father finds out about us going out at night, then give him the thick rope from the maids' storage room, and advise him to fashion some handcuffs from it."

VII

If not for my fear of Hajj Othman, my dear Mustafa, I would have asked Mohsen to take me with him and Zbaida, even just once, to a restaurant, to the theaters, or to the concerts he took her to on the weekends. I would become filled with envy when I saw that cursed Luiza hopping along behind my son and his wife towards the main door and getting into the carriage, as I watched from behind the *mashrabiya*. Then the next day, I would hear her singing the songs that were stuck in her head from the concert the night before while mopping the floor, as if she were trying to aggravate me. My ears would prick up when she started telling Khaddouj about the details of the concerts. Khaddouj feigned indifference, but I knew she was dying of jealousy, same as I was.

She told her once about an old Italian man who threw ten thousand francs to Chafia Rochdi in only one night. She told her on another occasion about how a drunk Maltese man started tearing his clothes in appreciation of Cheikh El Afrit's singing, until he was almost naked and was kicked out of the theater. Khaddouj would get caught up listening to her, her mouth open, then would quickly right herself when she saw the look of victory in the malicious girl's eyes; she would go back to pretending to be busy and stop listening to her.

Once Khaddouj called to me to listen to what Luiza was telling her. The wicked girl was relating secrets that she had learned in Khemaïs Tarnane's concert about the hideous murder of the singer Habiba Msika, who had been set on fire. Her neck was swelling with pride as she confidently told her, "Habiba Msika wasn't killed by her lover, like people say. The poor guy died with her, trying to save her. A hit man with Italian roots was hired by her aunt, Leïla Sfez, and set her on fire. She paid him two hundred thousand francs to do her dirty work."

To this day, Mustafa, I still don't know whether Luiza really discovered these secrets while eavesdropping on a conversation between two men in the audience, as she claimed, and whether one of them actually did confess to killing Habiba Msika. Or if she just made up the story to impress us and make herself out to be someone who knows secrets.

The truth is I dismissed the story pretty quickly, as I had learned over time that spinning tales and fabricating stories was something that cursed Luiza was very good at and had made her craft. Didn't she fabricate from her sick imagination that dirty story about your Aammi Mhammed and his companion in the shed? I don't know why I was surprised that she was the one who fabricated the painful details she relayed to the Rassaa family the night of the incident with Zbaida. The story that sent Lella Bashira out of her house in the darkness of the night, stumbling on her clothes, to knock on our door at the Ennaifer house.

3
The Tale of Si Ali Rassaa
(*Rue El Azzafine, Summer of 1949*)

I

God has brought me back to life, Bakkar, to make peace with your sister Zbaida, and he will take me again whenever my time is up. I believe, now that she and I have reconciled, that I will be bidding you a final farewell soon, and I'm ready and happy to leave this world.

Ahh, my dear Bakkar, have you started crying again? Did you think I didn't notice when I was unconscious? No, my boy, I could see you squatting there on the edge of the bed, playing with the fuzz around your mouth and fancying that you finally had a mustache. I could see you all—or maybe I was just imagining it. I'm not sure.

You were crying like a woman, Bakkar. You started sobbing with your nose buried in my chest until my clothes were wet with your snot, and I almost woke up from disgust. Your brother, Mahdi, is stronger than you, or maybe he's just better at hiding his tears. He would pretend to wipe his face from forehead to chin, spreading the tears on his face so whoever saw him would think it was sweat, not tears. As for your sisters Qmar, Nafissa, and Mna, let me tell you! They started crying and counting my virtues and lamenting me before I was even dead. I was able to see you all, Bakkar, and hear you, too. I could also see Bashira and hear her weeping. I could have laughed when she put her hand on my chest in the same place where your nose had run like a tap. I can almost see her now, lifting her hand as if she'd been stung, losing her place in the *ruqyah* she'd been reciting. So she closed her eyes, waiting to organize her thoughts, then returned her hand to my shoulder, pretending to massage it when, in reality, she was wiping the mucus from her hand onto my shirt.

The only person I didn't see among you when I was unconscious was Zbaida. When I looked beyond that vast whiteness around me, I could see that face I hadn't seen for thirteen years, ever since that hellish night at the Ennaifer house. I hear her crying out in pain like all of you, and I remember her voice saying: "I swear to God I'm innocent, Baba." Whenever I wanted to answer her, my voice would get stuck and my throat would tighten up. But then I heard her talking to your mother in the courtyard, and my tongue suddenly broke free.

Would it have been possible for me to wake up if Zbaida hadn't disobeyed me and entered my house while I was still alive? Did she consider my state a postponed death, so she hurried to visit me and saved my life? Would I have felt at peace if I'd left this world while Zbaida and I were still angry at each other? I still ask myself, Bakkar: who was to blame for the tribulation that befell us the day Tahar Haddad died? Was it that idiot baker in Sidi Mansour? Or Luiza, who brought us news that should have stayed buried at the Ennaifer house?

You were young, my dear son Bakkar. You were three years old when Zbaida got married, and you were eight when the incident happened. You were the one who opened the door for Luiza that rainy night in December 1935. We had just finished our dinner in the dining room, and your brother, Mahdi, jumped up on his chair as usual, rehearsing for us the fiery speech he would give the next day at the meeting of the Destour Youth, the splinter group from the old party. Suddenly, we heard an alarming banging on the main door. Bashira jumped up from her seat and started pushing Mahdi with both hands, trying to hide him who knows where. Your mother still hadn't forgotten how your brother was chased by the police a year and half before when he was carrying pamphlets inviting the people to resist. They were calling for the return of the Neo Destour Party's leaders, the ones who were taken from the capital and had been imprisoned in the south of Tunisia since September 1934. The police officers saw him run into our house that morning and bar the door behind him. They started knocking violently until Bashira opened it for them, angry and roaring like a lioness. She denied that she had a son and that anyone had entered her house. She also threatened to report them to the grand vizier for trespassing at the home of one of the nobility. The poor officers apologized and retreated, assuming that they had mistaken the address, since most of the defectors from the old Destour Party were riff-raff from the countryside.

Mahdi didn't enjoy his escape from the police investigation for long, however: no sooner had the police officers departed than he found himself in the clutches of the military court detective Bashira Djellouli. She rebuked him with a long, improvised list of curses and insults, "May God blacken your future, Mahdi . . . May God burn you to a crisp . . . May you fall into a deep well that no one can get you out of . . . "

She also threatened to cut off his head with a cleaver and then barbecue it on the stove if he didn't stop doing this "politics," which was going to ruin his future career and afflict his mother with diabetes, high blood pressure, and heart disease and make her die young. She softened, however, when he started patiently explaining to her what the demands of the Tunisian national movement were. He also described how Habib Bourguiba, Tahar Sfar, and the rest of the exiled activists were suffering in Bordj le Bœuf, without having committed any crime except demanding justice, human rights, and the establishment of a Tunisian parliament. He was telling her, in the tones of an orator, "Freedom doesn't come as a gift, Mama; you have to fight for it."

And she answered him, surrendering, "May God unleash your tongue, my son."

So when we heard the violent knocking on the door that night, Bashira was sure the police officers were at the door to arrest her stubborn son. He had been hosting some of his fellow activists in the entrance hall, where they'd been working for quite a while to prepare banners and come up with slogans for a big upcoming protest. They were planning to march from Place El Halfaouine until they reached the government palace in La Kasbah, to show the people's support for the exiled leaders. But Luiza's arrival instead of the police didn't make Bashira any less frightened; she could see the traces of violence around Luiza's eyes and the tears that had mixed with the rain and soaked the black veil on her face. At first, I thought the Ennaifer family had kicked her out; when I saw her trembling with fear and cold, I wondered what kind of terrible thing she could have done that would justify expelling her before morning. I felt angry, to be honest with you, before she could say a word; I thought that, whatever crime Luiza may have committed, she couldn't have done anything that atrocious. The Ennaifer family had to remember that that girl was one of us, and that any assault on her was a violation of the ethics of kinship and pleasant manners. You can imagine after that my feelings when Luiza pulled your two-year old nephew Mohammed Habib, wrapped in a blanket, out from under her wet cloak, and dropped her bomb while unwrapping him, "Sidi Othman beat Lella Zbaida."

Bashira didn't believe her ears, so she asked Luiza to take a deep breath and repeat what she'd said, so that we could understand her better. She repeated what she'd just said and added, still gasping for air, "Sidi Mohsen and Sidi Mhammed are fighting."

We listened in shock, waiting for an explanation for these riddles, but when she opened her mouth, it was only to add one more: "The newborn, Sidi Mustafa, is very hungry and thirsty." She stopped talking for a moment to wipe away the water dripping from her hair and pooling on her eyebrows and the edge of her nose. Then she resumed, rocking your nephew Mohammed Habib on her knees, "Lella Zbaida hasn't said a word since this morning."

At that point, Bashira lost it. She grabbed the baby from Luiza's lap and put him in mine, where he burst into tears, but she didn't care. She grabbed the poor girl's arms and started shaking her, screaming, "Why are you being so cryptic? Tell me what happened to Zbaida!"

Luiza answered in a hoarse voice, avoiding our eyes, "She received a letter today from Sidi Tahar."

Bashira didn't seem to understand anything and at first didn't even remember who Tahar was. She kept shaking her head, her eyes fixed on Luiza's lips waiting for a clarification. But for me, these words had made everything clear. I had the feeling of someone who'd suddenly been stabbed in the stomach by a hot metal spear.

That evening, I had met with my cousin Sheikh Hmida Bairam at Younes's barber shop. Hmida, God rest his soul, was an interesting man. He combined piety with a strange ambition that he called the "trinity desire." He used to say, "A table is stronger with three legs."

Most of our friends thought that what he meant by this was marrying three women. But once he laughingly explained to his close friends that what he meant was combining the three positions: sheikh of Islam, grand vizier, and the minister of justice. Hmida kept his position as the sheikh of Islam for more than twenty years, but his attempt to complete the other sides of the triangle made him a serious threat to the vested interests of the state, including your uncle the grand vizier, Taieb Djellouli, may God rest his soul. The latter had such a serious personal feud with Hmida that, after he left the ministry, he worked to remove him from his post as the sheikh of Islam. Hmida not only lost his triple dream but was greeted with the reality of being back at square one. The fired sheikh found himself unemployed and his arrogance from his days in power faded away. He started frequenting his childhood friends again, until his death two years after this meeting.

As soon as I entered Younes's barbershop, he rushed to tell me about the passing of Tahar Haddad. He said, setting up chess pieces on the board, "Today he will be punished for his disbelief, and he will wish that there was an eternity between him and his work."

I answered him, taking my seat. "Say 'may God rest his soul,' Hmida. Or are you more knowledgeable than God about how He will call His creations to account?"

He moved one of the pawns, nodding for me to do the same, and said, "The man rebelled against the consensus of all the imams of Islam and denied universally accepted wisdom. And as if corrupting morals and leaving behind Islamic traditions wasn't enough, he even mocked the prophet, peace be upon him, and disparaged the Prophet's wives—the Mothers of the Believers, may God be pleased with them. He insulted his teachers and cursed them. How do you wish God to have mercy on him? It's true that God is the pardoner and all merciful, but He's also the giver of severe punishment, and as it is said in his holy book: "Allah loveth not those who reject Faith."

At this point, Younes broke in, taking a towel off the neck of his last customer. "You're talking about that infidel who wanted to forbid what God has permitted for us, and to permit what He has forbidden?"

"Amazing! You've already given a legal opinion about his unbelief and made a judgment? You should rush to get there before his coffin and stop them from burying him in an Islamic cemetery."

Hmida got agitated and hit the table with his hand, scattering the pieces on the chessboard. He put them back in their places again and said, "I swear to God, if the matter was up to me, I would have enforced the sharia punishment for apostates on him as soon as his book was published. But what could you do with the feeble Bouhajeb government? He barred Haddad from serving as a legal witness, but he didn't authorize banning the book and stopping its distribution, even though we alerted him that it was published without the permission of the Great Mosque."

"Good God, Hmida! You all made such a fuss because one

man among you took a different approach to interpreting the Quran. You ruined his career and life because he called for an end to oral divorce and a ban on polygamy. Where was this zeal for religion during the Eucharistic Congress, when the Catholic Church marched through the streets of Tunis with crosses, just a few months before Haddad's book was published? Where were all you warriors of Islam when the Christian monks set up shop in Place Ali Azzouz and handed out green pamphlets to Muslim residents, urging them to convert to Christianity? Did you say a word when the students—including your Aamma Nafissa's son Salah Eddine—were thrown in jail because they stood up against the education ministry's plan to host the nuns from that Crusaders' display at Collège Sadiki? Didn't some of you actually work together to ensure that shameful congress would be a success?"

Hmida's chin trembled involuntarily, as it always did when he got angry, and then he said, raising his voice, "Are you condemning me, Ali, because I was in the honorary committee that planned the congress? Am I better than Ahmed Pasha Bey, who was its president? Or am I better than the senior statesmen who participated and applauded it, including your in-law Taieb Djellouli? Were any of us expecting what happened there?"

"You said it yourself, Hmida: Many bad things happened at the congress, but you, the Maliki mufti Tahar Ben Ashour, and the other imams of Zaytuna Mosque didn't seem to care. We didn't hear any of you raising your voices to condemn what happened, and we didn't see any of you defending Islam. You did nothing at all until Tahar Haddad published his book. Can you explain away that hypocrisy, Hmida?"

A new customer entered the shop, and Hmida lowered his voice. He moved the rook, saying with malice as he avoided the question, "Are you trying to defend that unbeliever, Ali? Have you forgotten what he did to you when you opened your house to him and entrusted him with your daughters?"

"I haven't forgotten. I haven't forgotten. Checkmate, Hmida."

II

Of course I still hadn't forgotten, my dear Bakkar, my last meeting with Tahar Haddad. So Luiza's words about his letter to Zbaida ripped through me like a thunderbolt. I had believed, until that moment, that I had taken care of the matter at the Belvedere, with the conversation we had following the launch celebration of his controversial book. I hadn't told anyone the details of his offense against me, except for some very close friends like Hmida. As for Bashira, I was afraid of her reaction if she found out what Zbaida had been doing behind her back, so I didn't dare tell her what had happened.

Tahar had visited me in my office at the ministry at the beginning of the week, looking very cheerful. He told me that his small book *Our Women in Sharia and Society* had come out just two weeks before. It was made up of a collection of essays he had written and published in the *Assawab* newspaper over the last two years. It also included other chapters that had taken a great deal of effort. He said that these reflected the religious knowledge he'd gained during his time at Zaytuna University, where he studied *ijtihad*, the role of thought and reasoning in Islamic law. He gave me a copy of the book, in addition to an elegant invitation to attend a celebration in his honor on Friday, October 17, 1930, at 4 P.M., at the Casino du Belvédère in the park. I still remember the precise date because many newspapers mentioned it later when they smeared the ceremony and its guests. Even I was not immune from their systematic smear campaign, and I got my share of it in the hallways of the ministry.

I arrived that day about fifteen minutes early. At the door of the pavilion, I found a young man waiting for me: Tahar's best friend, Ahmed Deraai. He kissed my forehead and escorted me through the crowd that had gathered in the exterior courtyard of the majestic Moorish building, leading me into a lounge designated for the guests of honor. He introduced me to the others there, embarrassing me with his effusive praise. The boy still hadn't forgotten my support when Tahar brought him to my office seven years before. I still remember the details of that meeting, Bakkar. Tahar said, after introducing him to me, "My friend Ahmed received his diploma from the Grand Mosque, and now he's continuing his education at the Lycée Alaoui to become fluent in French. After he gets his diploma, he's planning to focus on law."

I was about to commend his ambitions and his interest in modern education, but Tahar continued, saying, "He is currently accused of committing an offense against his majesty the Bey, and might have to go to jail. I'm hoping you can intercede with your acquaintances at the Ministry of the Pen and spare him any time in jail."

The reckless young man had sent a telegram to Muhammed Habib Bey, protesting the decree issued by the French Protectorate authorities that allowed Tunisians to become French citizens. He included in his telegram a sarcastic old expression that he directed at the Bey himself. He told him in plain language that accepting naturalization orders would make his authority "a title without power, like a cat puffing itself up to look like a lion." I couldn't stop laughing as I listened to him defend himself, whispering so people in the offices next to mine wouldn't hear us. "Tell me Sidi Ali, was what I said a lie? How could he be a prince of the Tunisian state and still accept the decrees of naturalization? Should we act like the bey and keep silent about such a diabolical plan? It's targeting our Tunisian identity, ultimately hoping to integrate the kingdom of Tunisia into French soil!"

I liked his enthusiasm and respected his bravery. I also didn't want to disappoint Tahar, my daughters' teacher, in the only favor he'd ever asked of me, so I bailed them out—Deraai and one of his friends who had also signed the telegram—so they wouldn't be subject to the six-month jail verdict. Deraai had been grateful ever since and never forgot to send me a card for any holiday occasion. When he became famous in Francophone journalist circles, he took your brother, Mahdi, under his wing. As their relationship developed, Deraai was the first person to train him how to write his fiery articles. You can bear witness, Bakkar, that he still cares about maintaining our good relationship, even after the alienation between me and his friend.

Hardly had I taken my place in the Casino du Belvédère's lounge than I heard a tumult in the courtyard and, through the window, saw Deraai running towards the exterior door. People craned their necks to see, and most of them thought the guest of honor had arrived. But formulas of prayer and safety rose up when the crowds saw a dignified old man entering, leaning on a cane and supported by the arms of some young men. His face wore an expression of acute pain. I would find out from the conversation that took place between him and Deraai and some of the attendees with us in the lounge that he was the man who'd been chosen by the organizing committee to preside over the celebration. He was a Tunis notable, and his name was Rasheed Ben Mostafa. It seemed that while he was on his way to the pavilion, he got into an accident on the tram tracks connecting the municipal slaughterhouse and the Parc du Belvédère. His features drawn, holding Haddad's book in one hand and massaging his left leg with the other, he said, "No man can escape his fate. I was hit by the tram while crossing the tracks. I'm truly sorry to inform you that I will not be able to preside over the ceremony because I have to leave soon. The pain in my leg is getting worse, and I'm afraid it may be broken."

He went quiet for a moment, as if overcome by pain; then he looked at a strong man in his fifties sitting to my right, dressed in a brown *jebba*. On his knee was a sweet girl of seven or eight, wearing a brightly colored, striped dress in the European style.

She was looking around at the attendees with mischievous eyes. Ben Mostafa said to him, smiling and opening his arms, calling the girl. "I expect this little girl is keeping you company, Sheikh Salem."

He added, giving the child a kiss after her father gave her to him, "I will be with you to welcome Si Tahar when he arrives shortly. Your daughter, this beautiful girl from Akouda, will present him with a bouquet of flowers as we planned. Then I will read my short speech at the start of the ceremony, before I give you responsibility to preside over it, Sheikh Salem. I hope that you accept. A great orator like you won't be afraid to deal with an emergency."

Sheikh Salem caressed his beard, answering him seriously in the distinguished accent of the East coast Sahel region. "I'm sorry about the accident, Si Rasheed. I wish you a speedy recovery. I'm happy to take over your duties, but I haven't read our friend Tahar's book yet, and I don't think it's a good idea to talk about something I don't know."

Rasheed Ben Mostafa laughed and said in a low voice, inclining his head towards Si Sheikh Salem, "God bless you, Sheikh Salem Ben Hmida. Whoever named you 'The Philosopher of the Sahel' was right. Are you apologizing because you haven't read the book? Have any of us finished reading it? It just came out in print—the ink's not even dry!"

Then he looked at me inquiringly, with a crafty smile on his face. "Unless our friend here, who I haven't had the chance to meet yet, has finished reading the book before us, and we should let him preside?"

Sheikh Salem introduced me to him as I shook my head with a smile, not saying a word. Then he said, thumbing through the pages of the book, "The book title reveals its content." He seemed a bit taken aback, trying to remember the title before going on, with feigned enthusiasm, to cover up his confusion, "Our son Tahar Haddad, God bless him, is known for his bright ideas, his strong spirit, and his clear vision. His book can be nothing less than another brick added to the edifice of enlightenment that was initiated by Ibn Khaldoun and continued by Hayreddin."

He kept talking in general terms about things such as the great men of Tunisia and the value of empowering women to reform the society until Deraai interrupted him by announcing that Tahar's car had arrived. I saw from the window of the lounge the invitees spread out in the exterior courtyard, standing in two receiving lines to greet the guest of honor. He looked elegant, slowly walking between them, wearing a white silk *jebba* and a fez on his head. The brightness of its wool hinted that it was being worn for the first time. He answered the applause and cheers with genuine smiles and started serenely shaking the hands of the attendees who surrounded him on all sides and then followed him into the building. When he got to the lounge and saw me, he beamed with joy and gave me a big hug, thanking me repeatedly for accepting the invitation.

I saw him that day with a new eye, Bakkar. He showed great taste in the choice of his traditional clothes, which imitated the prestige of the nobility. It was amazing how much respect and veneration the audience showed him. I honestly felt pride and fervor when Tahar held my arm and started walking with me towards the big hall, where elegant round white tables were arranged in rows and encircled by young men, adults, and seniors.

The table at the front was reserved for me, and there was an elegant sign on it with my name written in Kufic font: "The Honorable Sidi Ali Rassaa and Family." Did Tahar hope I would bring Zbaida to see his success and the high status he enjoyed among the intelligentsia? I asked before leaving whether she would like to accompany me, but the sly girl refused. She undoubtedly knew about the plan Tahar had prepared. I sat there alone for a little while, surrounded by six empty chairs, until some men—commoners—joined me. I understood from the notebooks and pens in their hands that they were journalists, or possibly informants. I noticed that they were looking at me with curiosity, as if they were trying to get me to talk and reveal why the event organizers had seated me in such a special place. The truth is that I was more surprised than they were at first, though by the end of the night, I understood the reason all too well.

As soon as Rasheed Ben Mostafa gave the reins of the ceremony to Salem Ben Hmida, excusing himself to the audience because of the pain in his leg, the tongues of the people sitting at my table took off. One man was skinny, with a head so narrow that his fez ate all his forehead and almost swallowed his eyebrows. He kept having to push it back, trying to fix it, but the fez would slide down again whenever our friend looked down to scribble some notes. I watched him paying attention to the successive speakers above glasses that also slid down, towards the tip of his nose. Then he nudged his colleague with his elbow saying, "Ben Mostafa's a smart politician, 'praying one night alongside Caliph Ali, then eating dinner the next night with the caliph's enemy Mu'awiya,' as they say. Now he's presiding over the ceremony to please the reformers, and then he'll abandon them to please their opponents. What a great lesson in social hypocrisy!"

I interrupted and shared what I'd learned in the lounge about the accident and the injury. But the little man with the fez answered me sarcastically, all but laughing out loud at my naivety, "Did you believe, sir, that an old man could be hit by a tram and still walk into this room? It's just a pretext for him to throw the noose around Salem Akoudi's neck and get himself out of the dilemma with minimum damage."

I became curious and asked him in a whisper about this dilemma—I wasn't yet aware of the plot that was being hatched against Tahar and his book before the celebration took place. He swelled with pride at my interest in the secrets his small head was hiding. He looked around, as if fearing a danger that no one knew about but him, and beckoned for me to bring my ear close to the foul air issuing from his mouth. In a rush, as

Sheikh Salem gave his fiery speech, he told me about the Friday sermon that day at the Great Mosque. He said, struggling again with his fez, that his majesty the Bey had reinstated the fired imam Sadiq Ennaifer under the recommendation of some political parties in the country. He was charged to give the sermon that afternoon, instead of the official imams, and many were invited to listen. In the sermon, the imam attacked Tahar and his book and described its content as dangerous heresy. Then he called for a boycott of what he called an anti-Islam ceremony at the Belvédère and the shunning of its participants.

Then our friend added, putting his hand to the side of his mouth to ensure that the others at the table couldn't read his lips, that some men from the Destour Party had started a rumor campaign against the book. They claimed that it was nothing but atheism, apostasy, and an attack on religion and declared their intention to organize a protest against the celebration and even stop it by force, if necessary. Our friend suggested that Si Ben Mostafa, when he heard about all this, feared the consequences and chose a middle solution that, he opined, no one but an unprincipled coward would choose.

After he used up all his ammunition, he went back to his notebook and pen, but not before winking at me, raising a skinny finger to his blue lips as a sign to keep quiet about the secret. I didn't think very much of what the man sitting next to me had said; I didn't even know his name. But I would come to read bits of his commentary in some newspapers in the weeks following the party, along with a lengthy article by Rasheed Ben Mostafa in the *Al Zahra* newspaper, distancing himself from the book and its author. In it, he apologized that he hadn't read the book before the ceremony, save for a few sections that weren't enough for him to fully understand the book and realize that it was against the principles of the religion and aimed to obstruct religious laws based on clear Quranic texts.

I turned to look at the young girl I had met in the lounge. She happily jumped up to the podium and started singing in a sweet voice a long five-part poem written by her father about girls' education and emancipation. She made pronunciation mistakes here and there, and sometimes her tongue would get twisted in the complex words, but that only made her cuter and added to the sweetness of the performance in the minds of the audience. The speakers took turns at the podium after her, most of them male journalists or writers; I heard nothing from them but praise of Tahar and his good work.

However, I didn't fail to notice signs of resentment on the faces of the men sitting at my table, even though most of them gave me hypocritical smiles whenever we made eye contact. The young man sitting at the right side caught my attention. He seemed around the age you are now, Bakkar; I don't think that he was more than twenty years old. He didn't speak with anyone, and no one spoke to him; rather, he was fully absorbed in writing and didn't miss a single word of what was said in the speeches. His decent clothes and shiny shoes suggested that he belonged to a respectable family, and his blond hair, green eyes, and big nose hinted at a family resemblance with a prominent noble family in Tunis. My friend with the fez whispered to me when he saw me observing him, "That's one of Sheikh Mohieddine Klibi's followers; he's writing a detailed report for him."

When he saw me continuing to stare at him with bafflement, he went back to winking and raising his finger, ordering me to keep quiet. But curiosity devoured me, so I tugged on his shirt sleeve (which was so long it almost covered his fingers) and whispered, "Could my respected friend please clarify? Do you mean Mohieddine Klibi, the director of the Destour Party?"

He answered in a grumble, spraying my face with his flying saliva, "Give me a break, sir. Why would you ask such a stupid question? Are you one of our foreign guests?"

"All right, all right, but why would Mohieddine Klibi ask for a report about a celebration in honor of Tahar Haddad?"

He brought his lips so close to my ear that his fez would

have fallen on my face if he hadn't caught it at the last minute, and said a dangerous tone, "Listen to me, sir. The executive committee members of the Destour Party are in a meeting at this very moment at the club on Rue d'Angleterre. They are planning a campaign that they will launch in the newspapers and the public opinion against Haddad and his book. Look at him now, how happy he is—this is the last time you'll ever see him like this."

It was as if he was reading the unseen, Bakkar. Indeed, I never again saw Tahar happy after that meeting. In fact, I didn't see him again at all, despite continuing to follow what he wrote in the newspapers and what the newspapers wrote about him, until his news faded away and people forgot about him. I watched him during the celebration that night with real affection. I involuntarily smiled whenever I saw him scratching one of his temples out of modesty and dismay when he felt a speaker was no longer being objective and had started to exaggerate. He laughed, embarrassed, when Deraai started comparing him to Descartes to determine which of them was superior in terms of accepting different ideas and weighing them on the scales of reason. I noticed, however, that he went silent for a short moment, his face grim, when Deraai read a letter from his friend, the poet Aboul-Qacem Echebbi, apologizing for not being able to attend the celebration and explaining that his illness had worsened and his doctor had ordered him to avoid any mental effort.

At this, the man sitting next to me, whose head was so stuffed with secrets, went back to raising his eyebrows and, this time, didn't even bother lowering his voice: "Aboul-Qacem Echebbi is smart and doesn't want to stain his name by supporting someone who everyone will agree is the enemy of religion in a few days."

I didn't care about what he said, but from my seat at the front of the room I started to notice some unusual movement in the back, coinciding with the journalist Hadi Abidi's turn to speak. There was a big man with a thick mustache in a dark blue dungaree jacket trying to wade through the tables to reach the podium, as three young men held him back and pushed him, politely but with determination, towards the door. However, angry mumblings were heard by the front rows, and some attendees heard things like "carnival of disbelief," "polytheistic orgy," and "war on the Prophet." But the speaker raised his voice, trying to cover the noise, and started shouting with excitement, "We must shut out backwards opinions, so they don't disturb us with their nasty voices, crying over their worn-out shrouds. We want to get rid of those shrouds while we're still alive and among the people, but they want to carry them with them, dead among the living."

The audience became ecstatic, and their hands burned with applause. The small man next to me pursed his lips and opened his palms, as if bearing witness to the truth of the secrets he'd revealed to me.

III

After about three hours of successive speeches and poems, Tahar took to the podium for the last speech. I almost didn't recognize him as the shy, soft-spoken young man that I had become acquainted with ten years before. There was another Tahar in front of me, eloquent in his strong arguments, quick-witted, and interesting.

I never told you, Bakkar, about how I met Tahar, or how I asked him to come to my house to teach your sisters. I used to stop by the shop of my friend Othman Belkhouja at Souk Chaouachine from time to time. I would see a young man whose mustache hadn't yet grown in, busy reading or dusting the chechias on display. My friend Si Othman was a teacher at the Zaytuna Mosque University and one of the best scholars there, yet he was modest and didn't boast about it. And despite his prestigious rank at the university, he never gave up the craft of making chechias, which he inherited from his ancestors. I learned from him that the young man was one of his students; though his family was originally from El Hamma in Gabes, he'd been born in a modest neighborhood in Tunis. His father had a chicken shop in the Marché Centrale. Othman spoke to me about his intelligence, his strong love for his country, and his belief in freedom of opinion in legislation, despite his young age. I started chatting with him from time to time, until one day the subject of education in general, and specifically the education of girls, came up, so I mentioned how I had sent my four girls, one after the other, to the nuns' schools. I noticed something in his eyes that resembled sorrow, even though he tried to hide it out of respect. When I asked him about it, and then insisted, he said in a calm voice, avoiding my eyes, "Si Ali, I admire your eagerness to provide your daughters with a modern education. I also agree with you that the Muslim girls' schools established by the French Protectorate are basically no different from the vocational factories that teach girls weaving, embroidery, and sewing. These schools, even though they're new, aren't really any different from the vocational girls' schools that were common here before the protectorate. Their basic French and Arabic lessons aren't enough to provide a real education; they're just tacked onto the vocational one. But . . . "

He stopped talking for a moment, looking hesitant and embarrassed, but Sheikh Si Othman Belkhouja encouraged him to continue, assuring him that his friend was open-minded. So he went on, "But being dissatisfied with the Islamic girls' schools and the quality of education they offer is no reason to educate Muslim girls at the nuns' schools. The Catholic Church's schools, with their French education—undoubtedly colored by the spirit of Christianity—cut Muslim girls off from the roots of their religion and history, and prevent them from learning the language of their people and the history of their country. This gradually weakens every national sentiment they have and prepares them to fully assimilate into the foreign culture, and then integrate their children into it, in a way that eventually threatens the whole nation."

I said, trying to embarrass him, "And what is the solution, Si Tahar?"

"The solution is that we shouldn't rely on the protectorate government to find suitable solutions for us. The ones they offer are designed to fit their interests, not ours. But the solution isn't to boycott public education, either, if boycotting means going backwards and keeping girls at home again. We have to rely on ourselves to establish schools for Muslim girls as we see fit, based on our needs. And we have to make an effort and spend money. As it stands, we are being spendthrift on the superfluous, and stingy on the essential."

His logic seemed practical enough to me, far from empty idealism. He was a young man with his eyes on the sky but with his feet firmly planted on the ground. But I wanted to tease him a little bit, and it never occurred to me that the conversation would end the way it did. I said jokingly, "Do you mean that I have to rely on myself and establish a private school for my daughters, since the available schools are useless?"

He said, smiling, "In my opinion, the problem in your daughters' education could be remedied by hiring a tutor to teach them the principles of Arabic and some Islamic studies and history."

I answered him immediately, putting my fez on my knees, "Would you accept, Si Tahar, to take on this mission in your spare time? I promise I will do whatever it takes to support you."

A heavy silence came over the group. The truth is that I was as surprised by my offer as Tahar was. I had never thought about the pitfalls of the nuns' education, and it never occurred to me how to fix it. Finally, Si Othman Belkhouja said, "He's the best candidate to teach your daughters, Si Ali! Tahar is like a son to me, and he will never embarrass me with my friends. Isn't that right, Tahar?"

Tahar found himself compelled to agree, having walked into the trap on his two feet and fallen into it by chance and fate. But he stipulated that the matter remain a secret between the three of us, so that no one would say poverty forced him to make a living by teaching the daughters of the upper class. He first taught your sister Nafissa and refused to accept payment for his lessons—but I insisted until he finally accepted.

When I listened to his speech that day at the Belvédère, I realized how lucky your sisters were to be his students. He started speaking without reading from a paper, slowly and calmly, as if he were dictating his text within earshot of history. With that pace, he gave those sitting around me the opportunity to write down every syllable of his speech. They suddenly became dictation machines. Tahar's voice fluttered freely in the room and touched down in their notebooks to be quickly captured in the shape of lines on the page. I heard Tahar saying: "It is time for us to voice what we believe is the truth without fearing punishment. The hypocrites among us will grow accustomed to our voices ringing out as loud as truth itself. Even if they're bothered by it today because it sounds strange to them, they will learn their lessons in time."

Then I read in the journalist's notebook, "He said that he defied Zaytuna University's scholars, who he described as ignorant, hypocritical, and fawning."

I heard Tahar say, "We have no weapon with which to fight for women's causes but religion itself! We have declared war on its essence and meaning. We have mocked it in our way of life and work, yet remained fanatic towards it on its surface—a fanaticism created by our own prejudice and traditions."

Then I read in the journalist's notebook, "He's calling for a war on religion and is mocking religious people, describing them as fanatics and prejudiced."

I wanted to alert him to his misunderstanding, but Haddad's

voice began again, "We want to honor women and relieve them of the terrible nightmare that has befallen them. Nothing is preventing us from doing so."

Then I read, "He is comparing Islam to a nightmare and challenging Muslims."

I heard him say, "Those who are opposing us are people just like us, who eat food and walk in the markets. They may talk about Islam, but they are not more worthy or closer to understanding it than us. They may criticize us, but they, like us, are subject to criticism. Nothing is sacred to everyone except evidence in speech and honesty in action, for they are the scale that determines justice."

Then I saw the writing in the journalist's notebook: "He looks down on the Muslim scholars and denies their contribution to interpreting the religion. He denies the sanctity of everything, including the hadith and Quran."

When Haddad paused for a moment, they lifted their pens, but they quickly pounced again on their blank pages when he said, in closing, "Islam is on our side in the subject of women's emancipation, and the time is now. There's nothing left to do but the good work—that is what will outlast us. From now on, let us shout: Muslim women have allies fighting for them!"

Applause and cheers erupted in the room. I noticed that the man sitting next to me put down his pen and started applauding with those who were applauding and cheering along with them. I looked at the last thing he wrote. I saw a drawing instead of letters, a small circle with two thick dots in the top half and, below them, a horizontal crescent. He put a chechia on the circle, so it looked like a smiley face. Under the drawing he had written a short sentence in sloppy handwriting. I made a huge effort to decipher it and finally made it out: "The closing joke is nothing but fairy tales and illusions."

My neighbor caught me peering at his papers. He saw my astonishment over what I had read and chuckled with derision.

IV

Deraai stopped me at the door as I was leaving. A large crowd had gathered around Tahar after his speech, so I decided not to wait to congratulate him. I told myself I would see him soon enough at Si Othman's shop or at home when he came to teach Mahdi and Zbaida, and then I would talk to him and congratulate him. But Deraai insisted that I go back to the lounge. He said that Tahar would soon extract himself from his well-wishers and admirers and those who wanted him to sign their copies of the book. Tahar had something very important he wanted to talk to me about, he said, and he couldn't do it elsewhere. It occurred to me that he was going to tell me he was stopping the lessons, so I started preparing a speech to make him change his mind. Who else could I trust to come to my house? Over the years, he'd become a brother to my daughters and sons. However, I quickly changed my mind and even offered justifications for him. Was it appropriate for someone who had come into all this glory and been elevated to this level to knock on the door of a nobleman to give private lessons to his daughters? It was undoubtedly more dignified and appropriate not to insist, but rather to keep the friendship of this intelligent young man who had generously offered us his attention and time and honored us with his kindness for all these years.

Tahar came about ten minutes later and asked me to accompany him to the outdoor courtyard, to join in a group picture at the entrance of the grand building where the celebration had been held. There were about a hundred people standing in long rows on the stairs. On the front row, people were seated, with the guest of honor in the middle. Tahar indicated that he wanted me to be seated next to him, but he was too embarrassed to express that clearly to Sheikh Salem Ben Hmida or his friend Mohammed Saidi, who sat to his right and left. I didn't want that embarrassment, either, of course, so I quickly sat down at the edge of the first row, to the right of Haddad, leaning on my cane, which, in those days, was only ornamental.

When the crowd broke up, Tahar pulled me aside. We sat at one of the empty tables in the big hall. It started to get dark outside, and the noise was replaced by calm. I asked him, "Is everything okay, Tahar?"

He smiled uncertainly, wiping sweat from his forehead with a silk handkerchief. His eloquence had faded away; he was trying to say words but found he couldn't weave them together in an intelligible way. I felt sorry for him and wanted to make it easier on him, so I said, patting his shoulder, "Don't worry Tahar, my son. I understand that your new circumstances require you to adjust your relationship with us. That's life."

He looked confused and was silent, not knowing what to say. I became certain that my intuition had been correct. How could I have known that he would ask what he did? I added, putting on my fez and getting ready to stand, "Have you spoken with Zbaida? I mean, have you informed her of your decision?"

His jaw dropped, and his tongue tied. And since I still thought all this was about his leaving us as a tutor, I added like an idiot, "Zbaida won't find better than you, but I'm counting on you to find a replacement for her and Mahdi."

His tongue finally broke loose as my words took him back to square one. He saw the misunderstanding and said, "That's not what this is about, Si Ali."

"Didn't you ask me to stay so you could tell me you wanted to stop giving my children lessons?"

"Stop giving them lessons? No! But I do want to transfer that teaching in your home into another sphere, if you'll allow it."

I said with amazement, "Have you established a school like the ones you've been dreaming about?"

He fell silent again, shaking his head, a forced smile on his lips. There was something in his eyes that I didn't understand. A mixture of fear and hope. Soon after, I heard the adhan sounding the *Maghrib* prayer from the nearby mosque and started to lose my patience, so I decided to push him a little harder. "Are we going to spend the night here, Tahar? Tell me, what's the matter?"

Then I heard Tahar take a deep breath before, in one go, he poured out everything he had to say.

V

For years after that, I kept asking myself the same question, Bakkar: was I wrong to bring a young man into my home to teach my daughters? Am I the one responsible for what happened that awful night at the Ennaifer house? And what would have happened if I'd given Tahar a different answer that day? Could I have saved Zbaida the pain that she carried and will carry for the rest of her life?

I didn't believe my ears when Tahar told me, in a shaking voice broken by modesty, "Si Ali, I would like to ask you for Zbaida."

I said carefully, completely confused and not knowing whether to believe him or not, "You're asking for her for what?"

"I ask for her as a man asks for a woman. I am asking for her hand in marriage."

I could have politely refused, Bakkar. I could have said, for example, "Zbaida's still young, and I won't let her marry before she gets her university degree" or "Zbaida is engaged to her cousin" or "Let me consult with her, and we'll do as God wills," or anything else that would have delivered a rejection without disrespect. But, for some reason, I was enraged. Did I feel at that moment that he'd betrayed me, entering my house as a teacher but leaving as a lover? Or was I angry at him because he tricked me, luring me into a situation where he thought we were equals: my social class on one side of the scale and his knowledge on the other? The admiration I had felt for him during the celebration changed suddenly into resentment and hatred. I felt that he'd forgotten who he was and had betrayed our confidence. I felt the violence of betrayal, and my answer to him matched violence for violence. I said with a cold smile, standing up forcefully from my seat, "Well, I suppose if you lie down with dogs, you shouldn't be surprised when you get up with fleas!"

He was staggered, and his color changed. I saw his Adam's apple tremble as he swallowed with difficulty. I lost control of my temper completely and said, "Who do you think you are, boy? I trusted you with my family, and you made eyes at my daughters? It's true what they say: befriend a blacksmith or a coalman, and their filth will rub off on you."

And as if that wasn't enough, I added, turning and heading towards the door, "If you think that little book you wrote—the book you filled with the names of Tunis nobles and Zaytuna University scholars who graciously agreed to answer your banal questions—raised you to their level and prepared you to be their peer, that's just proof of your stupidity and faulty judgement. Go see Othman Belkhouja, who opened his shop for you and answered your stupid questions in that book. Go find out whether he'll let you marry one of his daughters. Go so you can wake up from your illusions, remember your place, and stay there in the future."

The poor fellow didn't say a word. To be honest with you, Bakkar, I later regretted every word I said to him that night. The day he died, I shed tears on my way home from Younes's barber shop with the sad news, and I begged God to have mercy on him and forgive me for my mistakes with him. But my sadness that day turned into bitter resentment and hatred on that horrendous night the second I heard Luiza talking about Tahar's letter to Zbaida. My head boiled with questions. How had they stayed in touch for five years after the celebration at the Belvédère? How had they fooled me and tricked Mohsen Ennaifer all this time? Hadn't I uprooted the evil when I agreed to marry her to Ennaifer's son, even though I'd been dreaming that she would finish lycée and get a prestigious position? Didn't I force her to leave school, despite her brilliance, to move to her husband's house—all so I could make sure her relationship with Tahar Haddad was over for good?

When Othman Ennaifer asked for her hand for his son one day at the barber's, I had delayed my answer. I told him, "Let me consult the girl and her mother," concealing a postponed rejection. I didn't yet know what was going on between my daughter and her teacher, and I didn't want her to get married before finishing her college education. Your sister, Bakkar, was no less qualified than Tawhida Ben Sheikh, her older classmate at the Lycée Armand Fallières. Tawhida became the first Muslim woman in Tunisia to earn a baccalaureate in 1928 and the first Muslim woman to come back from France with a university degree—as well as the first Muslim woman to become a doctor, not only in Tunisia, but in the whole Arab world. I dreamed that Zbaida would follow in her footsteps; she excelled in all her courses, and all her teachers spoke of how smart she was, in contrast to her sisters.

But Tahar's request reminded me of the well-known religious edict that "avoiding harm is better than reaping benefits" and made me change my mind. I saw from Zbaida's behavior with me after coming back from the celebration that she'd been aware of his plans and was complicit in them. I had to act quickly so as not to let things get out of my control: if she remained single, she would keep her hope of marrying Tahar alive, in her mind and his. So I sent someone to Othman Ennaifer to inform him that I agreed to the marriage of his son Mohsen to my daughter. So how could Luiza say that a letter from Tahar was sent to Zbaida? How could she receive a letter from him on the day of death? And what did Othman Ennaifer read in that letter that made him raise his hand against his daughter-in-law? Why would the brothers Mohsen and Mhammed fight, as Luiza said, unless the river had breached the dam, as they say?

I don't think these questions or anything like them occurred to Bashira that night. Her main concern was to make sure that her daughter was okay and to save her grandson Mostafa. Even when Luiza revealed that it was Tahar who had sent the letter to Zbaida, she just threw the first cover she found over her shoulders and said, "And what of it? Tahar's her former teacher, and we've never seen anything but good behavior and strong character from him. Maybe he wrote because he needs her help, for example through her husband Mohsen in the Tax Office? Is this why Othman Ennaifer hit her? May God break his hand and foot before I break his head open myself!"

I realized from Luiza's reaction that the damned girl knew the whole story. She kept sneaking glances at me as Bashira talked, as if trying to gauge if I believed the rosy, innocent possibilities that your mother, in her ignorance of the situation, was weaving. When she saw the fiery look in my eyes, she quailed, realizing that what had been hidden was now out in the open.

I sat glued to my spot as if I'd suddenly been hit by lightning, and Bashira paced in circles like a spinning top. She would calm down for a moment, only to head east, then west, then both directions at once. It seemed like she was about to sprout wings from the emotional extremes. Meanwhile, your brother, Mahdi, watched us with confusion and became very anxious. Bashira asked me to accompany her to the Ennaifer house right away. If you'd known what I knew, Bashira, you wouldn't have made that request. Should I go to the Ennaifer house to hear them say that my virtuous daughter, my hidden pearl, my well-behaved princess had dragged her husband's nose in the dirt and disgraced her family's honor? Should I go to support my daughter or to drink her blood? Had I lived so long only to see my educated daughters make my enemies gloat over me and see thugs chew on my reputation? These questions remained swirling in my mind as I sat still, unable to move, until Bashira yelled at me to stand up, saying with a voice broken by anger,

"Are you still sitting down, Si Ali? May God grant me a heart a tenth as cold as yours! Othman Ennaifer raised his hand to your daughter, and you don't seem to care?"

I thought about telling her everything, but it occurred to me that her reckless reactions might just make the matter worse. So I chose to keep quiet that night, just as I had when I came back home from the Belvédère and didn't say anything about the conversation between me and Tahar. It was also impossible for me to keep her from going, because there's nothing in the world that can stop a mother from running to her daughter if she senses danger. Luiza had said that Zbaida hadn't made a sound since morning. Bashira was sick with worry about her daughter, and there was no way to convince her that my staying here was better than going with her. She ordered Luiza to take Mohammed Habib from my lap and stay with him in the front room until we came back. Then she instructed Mahdi to throw on his burnous and join us. I had no choice but to follow them, against my will, not knowing what the next few hours of that fateful night had in store for us.

VI

The rain had begun to clear a little when our carriage stopped in front of the Ennaifer house on Tourbet El Bey. Under the dim light of the streetlamp at the end of the street, I could see the studded wooden door and the brass door knocker in the shape of a curled-up hand. It was very quiet, except for the street cats' yowls here and there; nothing warned of the intricate web of tragedy that fate was slowly weaving around us. The black maid opened the door for us after a short wait. The gloom made her skin darker, to the point that all we could see of her in the darkness of the night were her big teeth and the whiteness of her protruding eyes. Bashira rudely pushed her out of the way, storming the entrance hall and calling for

Zbaida. Lella Jnayna welcomed us stiffly into the house. Her eyes roamed over the floor as she mumbled with an anger she couldn't hide, "That idiot just couldn't keep her mouth shut. She left the house without permission and bothered you on this dark night. But of course, you're always welcome here . . . "

But Bashira answered her angrily, "We didn't come here to talk about Luiza or Aziza or anybody else, Lella Jnayna. What happened? How could something awful like that, something that only happens among common people—thugs!—happen here?"

Despite her words, she greeted her with two perfunctory pecks on the cheek as her eyes tried to penetrate the darkness of the entrance hall and get a glimpse of light inside that might reassure her that Zbaida was okay. Your sister's mother-in-law didn't say a word, just silently led Bashira into the house. Your brother and I remained standing in the entrance, waiting for one of the men of the house to come for us. After a moment, a pale-faced Othman Ennaifer appeared, walking with a cane and dragging one of his feet with difficulty, his ankle bandaged in a white cloth. I was still trying to choose the right approach to deal with the situation, but as soon as I found one, I would discover its pitfalls and move on to the next one. Many ideas occurred to me as I returned his lukewarm greeting. Should I do like Bashira: go on the offense from the start, with the confidence of someone who thinks they're in the right, demanding redress from those who wronged them? But how could I be like Bashira, so honest and guileless, when—while she had no doubts about her daughter's conduct—I had many? Suppose I threatened him, raised my voice, and acted angry. Couldn't my opponent insult me and take me down with a single phrase? How would I answer him if he said, "Your daughter, sir, is cheating on her husband," and then showed me proof? What could I tell him if he asked me, "Is this what you educated your girls for?" Wouldn't it be safer, better for my reputation and for avoiding problems if I hid and avoided such a conversation?

But wait a minute. Had I even considered that Bashira could be right in assuming good intentions? It was entirely possible that the letter was innocent and there was no reason for us to clear Zbaida's name. Hadn't Tahar been upright, well-behaved, and conscientious all the time I had known him? He had never exposed himself to criticism and never given people reason to doubt his morals. Also, didn't I bring up my children, boys and girls, to be virtuous and loyal, and to protect their honor? Why have doubts in my daughter, with no proof but some words that were spoken years ago? What was Tahar's mistake when he asked me for the girl's hand, in accordance with God's law? What was Zbaida's mistake when she assented to my choice and married who I chose for her, giving up the person I'd deprived her of? Don't they say, "One thousand men can ask for a girl's hand, but she will spend the night with only one?" Here is one from the thousand who asked for her hand; I refused and saw no insistence on his part that would disgrace him. Nor did I ever hear any harsh words, defamation, or attack from him. He has already passed away as I sit here talking to myself, so why was I committing a sin by thinking ill of him?

Those thoughts brought back some of my composure, and when I sat down with Othman Ennaifer, I was already feeling confident and less doubtful. But when his son Mhammed entered the room where we were sitting, with his big flabby body and his face colored with the evidence of fresh slaps, evil emanated from his eyes and made me rethink everything. If repairing what had been broken was not possible and the rip could not be patched, then perhaps the solution was to complete the tear and make a clean break.

4
The Tale of Si Mhammed Ennaifer
(*Tourbet El Bey, Fall of 1971*)

I

They detained you, my nephew, for five whole years in the aftermath of that horrible night, when that boney-assed Luiza kidnapped you and took you in your blanket to the Rassaa house. You forgot your mother, and you rejected your father. Mostafa grew up without knowing you, his big brother Mohammed Habib, and you didn't know him. Until one day when they came back to their senses and relented. Khaddouj's shoes had gotten worn out from walking back and forth between us and them, and your grandmother Jnayna had all but gone blind from grief over you. They threw you on us one summer evening, like someone being pushed into a predator's cage or into a hole occupied by ghosts and vipers.

I still remember how you entered the room, wearing your blue shorts and your red checkered shirt. Khaddouj, soaked in sweat and carrying two leather bags on her head, was dragging you behind her. Your grandmother Bashira had filled the bags with the European clothes they're so fond of in the Rassaa family. Every time I look at your son, Salim, now, whenever you bring him inside the city walls to visit his father's uncle, the lonely sheikh, I see the spitting image of you when you were his age. And I remember what you looked like on that day, long ago, when you entered our house like someone being led to their execution.

You didn't recognize any of us, and no one could blame you for it because you'd left us before you even turned two. Nothing could calm you: not the boxes of imported candy, not the brown-sugar-coated almonds, and not even the shiny coins your grandfather Othman put in your palm to bribe you to stop crying.

When we took you to your mother for a hug after five years apart, you started punching her with your small fist, scratching her face and pulling her hair. We heard nothing from you but a single sentence you kept repeating, crying and complaining in various tones, "I want to go back to Mama Bashira."

I've loved you ever since, Mohammed Habib, and you're still my favorite, as if you were my own son. It's not because you became my close friend and confidant over time, but because you were the only one who hated Luiza more than I did. Was it your child's instincts that showed you the evil lurking inside her? Or did your subconscious mind store images of the night she kidnapped you under her wrap, taking you to the Rassaa house on that cold and rainy night and coming back the next day without you?

The damn woman started trying to make you love her the evening Khaddouj brought you back for good from your grandparents' house. You were terrified of Khaddouj and cried hard whenever you saw her. Perhaps your child's mind made you believe that she was a mythical ghoul because of her coal-black skin and her hair, which was thick and wild like fountain grass. Your grandmother Jnayna, bless her soul, felt sorry for you, so she ordered her to go away until you were no longer terrified. That broke Khaddouj's kind and honest heart and filled the heart of Luiza with spiteful glee, because she replaced Khaddouj and took over serving you. But you were a good man, my nephew, a real man ever since you were small. You didn't buy her fake kindness or her forced smile. You had good instincts and could sense the evil she was hiding under that fake sweetness. I praised you to the heavens the day you treated me to the sight of her screaming and running like a crazy person in the courtyard. When she'd bent down to take you to Zbaida against your will, you'd bitten her semi-exposed breast with your small teeth, so hard you almost took a chunk out of it.

No one that day could calm you down and comfort you but me. I offered to show you the pigeons' nests on the shed up on the roof, and you contentedly gave me your hand. From that day on, you would wait at the door for me to come home from work at the notary public's office so that I could take you by the hand to our spot upstairs, where we could see the baby pigeons and listen to their pleasant cooing. Your father nearly went crazy when he saw you run towards me instead of him, but he couldn't keep you away from me. For months, you would only smile when you were with me, and within a year, I managed, little by little, to make you forget your time with the Rassaa family and get you to accept your new life with us.

There was only one thing that caused you pain and spoiled most of your days, sometimes sending you to me in tears: your extreme jealousy of your brother, Mostafa, because of the different way you were treated. He was closer than you to his mother, and he was his father's favorite. He was nurtured by his grandparents, as well; Othman and Jnayna provided him with a love and indulgence that you never got. Because you were proud and haughty—much like me—and you had the painful feeling that you were an outsider in a family that didn't treat you the way they treated someone who'd never left. But that cursed Luiza, may she die soon, could always fan the flames of your jealousy and discriminated against you in every way possible. Mostafa always got to choose first. If you quarreled and one of you hit the other, Mostafa was always the victim in her version of the story, and you were always the villain. The day Mostafa threw sewing scissors at you and left that scar on your forehead, Luiza ran to Mohsen before you got there, your face covered in blood, and swore by God that you headbutted the scissors in your brother's hands when you tried to take them away from him—that you were the aggressor, not him.

Your weight started to go up year after year, and your body started to get bigger before you even turned ten, exactly like mine had. It wasn't because you were a glutton or a gourmand because—also like me—you weren't a big eater at all. Instead, it was because of the painful feeling that you'd been betrayed twice. Once when you were uprooted from your home and family the night of the calamity with Zbaida. And again when you were forced to come back after the residents of the house had gotten used to their life without you and you'd gotten used to your life away from them. I could read on your body the lines of your daily torture and could see in your extra weight the intricacies of your personality as they grew and became even more complex. You were anxious, my dear nephew. When you chose not to speak, your body spoke in flesh and fat. The tragedy you lived through as a child ruined your sense of security and destroyed your self-confidence. To others, you seemed aggressive, short-tempered, and careless about consequences. But I saw in you a naughty little boy just trying to get his parents' attention, even if that meant screaming and throwing tantrums.

II

No one was able to understand your pain but me. I, who'd lived all my life trying to hide what couldn't be hidden and to camouflage what was plainly visible. That damn Luiza found out about me one night in Ramadan. She saw something she wasn't supposed to see and revealed the truth whose revelation had been my worst nightmare. The damn woman wasn't satisfied just to find out; no, she had to go and tell everyone. Mama Jnayna didn't believe her, but she started begging me every day to get married. Your father, though, believed her, and started watching me constantly and following me when I went for walks. He did his best to keep you away from me, as if I had scabies and he was afraid I might infect you. I wonder whether he also thought that I might assault you. The look of accusation on his face every time he pushed open the shed door on the roof, calling you, was the most infuriating and painful thing in my life. Whenever I noticed him following me in the old city, I would lead him to Sidi Abdallah Guech and other streets in the red-light district of Tunis, trying to make him think I was getting my pleasure from whores so his doubts would fade away. He would turn around quickly, not wanting to be seen in those shady places, and I would retrace my steps, as well, before I could get caught by one of the Jewish women hunting for customers in the street. I had an Italian friend who used to frequent a brothel for male prostitutes in Sidi Ali Ouaki in El Hafsia; he told me once that a man stopped by to ask the brothel owner about me, wanting to know if I was a customer. But—despite his short skirt and red lips, his wig and false eyelashes—Luigi was a real man and didn't tell him anything. He instead started to proposition him, offering him all he had to offer, till the man ran away without looking back.

What would your father gain from uncovering my secret? Would it have been possible, for instance, for him to go back in time and save me from the clutches of Ayad, that dirty young man our Quranic teacher hired to carry rugs and clean the floor?

When I was sixteen years old and a fat student at the Zaytuna Mosque who was sarcastically and disdainfully called "Baba Mhammed" by his classmates, I heard by chance that Ayad had died under the wheels of a tram. I felt both glee and an indescribable sadness. The glee was because he died the way I would've wanted him to die: flattened, ground, and mashed. The sadness was because I didn't see him like that, his brain mixed with his testicles, his blood swirled in with his sperm, and the solid parts of his body made softer than butter on the tram tracks.

He was a skinny, brown young man with only one arm who worked at both the Quranic school and the mosque next to it. His missing arm that had never grown always filled the children at the Quranic school with panic. We believed it marked him as one of the keepers of Hell that God uses to torture those He throws into the inferno. He was, in our imagination, stronger than the teacher, more powerful and cruel, especially when he snatched an unlucky student's legs with his one arm and tied them securely to the *falaka* post, then gave them over to the schoolteacher's rod to beat their feet. He was a solid young man. His fingers were solid when he poked you in your back, urging you to sit down and get out your wooden tablet. His voice was also solid when he asked you to share your snack with him, or when he asked for some of the treats your parents sent the schoolteacher. His gaze was solid when he stared at you as if he wanted to prey on you. He also had something solid he would poke your bottom with if you bent down in front of him to take off your shoes before stepping onto the straw mat.

One morning, I suffered from an unbearable stomachache and asked the teacher if I could go to the bathroom in the mosque next to the school. Ayad was there cleaning the ablutions area to prepare it for the *Zuhr* prayer. He let me use the toilet after he helped me pull down my trousers and to secure my feet around the marble hole. He gently slapped the plump cheeks of my buttocks, laughing, and for the first time, he seemed like a kind person. The bathroom was simply a short wall that jutted out from the back of the ablution room and ran parallel to the wall on the left, bending to form a right angle that narrowed its entrance and hid its user from view without having a door. I squatted and tried as much as possible to stifle the sounds one makes when relieving oneself, out of embarrassment because Ayad could hear. But what sounded like moans were coming from behind the short wall, drowning out the sound of the water that came from the pitcher I used to quickly wash myself. I ran out, thinking that something bad had happened, but instead saw Ayad sitting on a bucket that he had put against the wall across from the toilet entrance. He had pulled his trousers down to his knees and was playing with something between his legs and groaning in pleasure. I was five years old then, and all I knew about my penis was that it was a piece of limp flesh the size of a date that I used to go pee. You can imagine my amazement when I saw Ayad's hand filled with something that size; I was astonished that someone needed all that flesh to pee.

He had leaned back against the wall and extended his legs in front of the toilet entrance, parallel to the place where its short wall angled in. He was shaking slightly, licking his lips, and emitting short groans. He didn't seem to see me, so I advanced with caution towards the exit, walking next to the toilet wall and gluing my back to it. When I was about to reach salvation, he suddenly lifted one of his legs and leaned it against the wall, blocking me from leaving, so I had no option but to go back to the toilet or remain where I was standing and wait for Ayad to move his leg and let me go. My curiosity was stronger than my fear, so I stood rooted to the spot, watching what he was doing, feeling a strange tickling in parts of in my body I hadn't known could experience that feeling. He began to stare at me with those two solid eyes as he continued what he was doing, his breathing becoming more rapid and his moans louder, the hand holding his thing going up and down in a rhythm that increased in violence and speed. His movement didn't subside until something viscous and sticky spurted out from him and landed on my shoes. Then the leg that was pressed against the wall slackened, and an exit opened, so I ran back towards the Quranic school.

That scene remained in my head during the rest of the day and all night. When I thought about it, my saliva would dry up, and something like fever would flow in my veins. The next day, I avoided looking at him as he passed out the wooden tablets to us like normal, but he pinched my cheek and said with his solid voice, "Good job cleaning your shoes, Mhammed, but they'll get dirty again soon."

I swallowed with difficulty, turning my face away. I spent the rest of the day distracted, not able to concentrate and thinking back to the scene from the day before. I wasn't sure what to write on the tablet or what to repeat after the teacher. Once I'd made two or three mistakes, the teacher called on Ayad and asked him to take me to the mosque column. The column was a kind and merciful punishment that the teacher reserved for kids from important families, sparing them the *falaka*, which was mainly for the kids of poor or sometimes middle-class families. I walked silently behind Ayad until we got to the torture column, which was under a small covered area in the mosque courtyard. I had to spend a full hour standing on one foot, my face to the column and my hands on my head with fingers interlaced. I patiently stood as instructed, but my energy quickly faded, and my leg fell asleep. The pain tore at my forearms, and I started to sob, faltering. Ayad, though, just pulled a small, dirty jar of snuff from his pocket and sat on the threshold of one of the rooms, sniffing it and watching me from afar.

Whenever I tried to cheat by lowering my arms or using both my feet, he would yell at me menacingly, as if there were an old feud between us. After a while, I'm not sure how long, I saw him come closer to me on the pretext of making me stand up straight, as my back had arched out of fatigue. He put his only hand on my chest and pressed on my bottom and back with his knee and the inside of his thigh, ordering me not to slouch. I straightened myself up, but he didn't leave me. He pushed me to the column until my body touched it. He put his only arm around me from the back and held me tightly to him. My hands were still on my head when he knelt down to my level and started moving rhythmically and slowly behind me, first like a pendulum from right to left, and then like a coil moving up and down. Then movement behind me started to get more intense, and his breathing on my back got faster, and there was something sharp and hard that hurt the bones of my pelvis as it collided with it over and over. When his arm slackened and I felt something warm on the small of my back, I understood that my shirt today had received the same thing my shoes had yesterday.

He didn't spare me the hour-long punishment after that. He made me go back to my first position on one trembling leg, but he let me lower my arms and lean my forehead against the column. If you only knew what a great relief that was. He finally let me go back to school after he ordered me to keep quiet about our new game and bribed me with a honey fritter that he must've stolen from the presents our teacher had received that day.

In reality, I didn't need to be ordered to keep the matter secret. Even though I didn't understand what was happening, I sensed instinctively that it was a bad thing, and that my passive participation in it was a source of embarrassment and shame. These two experiences, however, led me to explore my body and its abilities to enjoy pleasure early. I tried to mimic what he had done, using my hand, or crawling on the floor, and discovered that my small, date-like penis could become a little bit erect and a little bit solid, giving me a strange feeling somewhere between pain and pleasure. I started to allow Ayad, whenever we got the chance to be alone at the school or the mosque, to touch me. My visits to the mosque bathroom started to become more frequent. At this stage, I didn't do anything but watch the sinful spectacle. Ayad got more pleasure when someone watched him doing what he was doing. He forced me to witness these masturbation parties of one but didn't ask me to participate in any other way. Over time he became confident that I wouldn't tell anyone his secret—and probably saw in the way that I looked at him that I would agree to actively participate. So he started demanding different things, depending on what circumstances allowed and his desire dictated. He smelled awful; his scent clogged my nose when he thrust into my mouth something that disgusted me and made me nauseous. I remember one day, after returning from time alone in the mosque, I started repeating after the teacher, "The most merciful taught the Quran," and in my mouth there was a short, thick piece of hair that I kept chasing with my tongue but couldn't get rid of. I developed a temporary lisp and nearly threw up on my classmate.

The matter continued to be bearable and sometimes came

with sweet pleasure, a pleasure augmented by its secrecy and violations of the forbidden. Then came the dark day on which I began to hate Ayad the way fire hates water, and started praying to God, wishing him ill. We were sitting around the teacher, repeating Surah Yaseen after him, when one of our teacher's acquaintances came into the room running and said, "Close the classroom, Zine Alabedine, and let the kids go home. There is shooting on Rue Sidi Bachir, and there are people dead and wounded. The protesters are coming this way, and the police and army are chasing them."

I would find out when I got older and joined the Young Tunisians and the Destour Party with Sheikh Abdelaziz Thâalbi that that fateful day of my life coincided with the Jellaz Affair. It was an important day in the history of the national resistance movement and was, they say, the first violent confrontation in Tunis between the Tunisian people and the colonial power. Many died, except those who ran for safety like our teacher did when he heard his friend's warning.

Our teacher was a coward. He threw his *burnous* over his shoulders as soon as he heard the news, then called Ayad. He gave him the heavy key to the room and asked him to lock it after walking us, one by one, to our homes in the neighborhood. Being a smart man, he suggested to Ayad (as he put his left foot in his right slipper) to start with the students who lived farthest away and take those who lived nearest each other with him. Being also, God bless him, an honest man, he insisted (as he reached the door) that Ayad deliver us to our families in person. Then he left at a run, without looking back. About an hour later, Ayad barricaded the door from the inside, having taken all my classmates home and left me for last. The place was plunged into darkness because the school was only a single room and, like the old shops in the area, was poorly ventilated, with no other opening but the wide door.

When Ayad approached me, I sensed the imminent danger. The look in his eyes was harder than usual. The noise of people running, the sound of the soldiers' heavy boots behind them, got louder outside, but, for some reason, I felt that outside was safer than inside. It was cold inside the room, whose walls were covered with mats stained from the mold and damp. Ayad started to take off his clothes, slowly humming a dirty old pop song. He stood in front of me naked. There was a protruding bone from his shoulder in the place of his missing arm. It was scary and disgusting and made me shrink in the corner, seeking refuge and waiting to be rescued. He forced me to inhale his awful odor, as usual, and I endured the ordeal as he pulled and pushed my head back and forth as per our old, familiar game. But it didn't end there. He suddenly forced my face to the ground and yanked off my trousers before pinning me down with his skinny, solid body. Then I felt something hard and sharp trying to penetrate me and screamed out in pain, trying to move my body from beneath him. But the hard thing quickly withdrew, and Ayad knelt beside me, putting one knee on my back to keep me down. I wasn't able to lift my head from the ground to see what he was doing to me, but I felt him turning, reaching behind him with his only arm to pick up something on the corner of the bench: the plate of olive oil and olives that our teacher kept to snack on during morning break. Before I had a chance to wonder about the reason for this sudden hunger, I felt the dish spill over me and the olives roll down my buttocks along with a thick stream of olive oil that Ayad pushed deep inside me with his finger. I screamed again when he started splitting me open with the rod, now slippery with oil, but he violently pulled my hair, yanking my head back with a terrible force until my neck arched and my windpipe closed. I couldn't do anything but produce a kind of weak death rattle as I struggled to grasp a breath.

When he got up off me after that indescribable pain, I thought I was dying. He took the piece of cloth students used to clean their tablets and started wiping the traces of olive oil from my body and the straw mat under me. When I stood up, while he was pulling up my trousers, I felt a warm liquid coming from the epicenter of the pain and was certain that I was going to poop out all my internal organs here on this straw mat. The strange thing is that there was no blood, despite all the pain. He had butchered me with a knife coated in olive oil, but not a drop of blood came out of the wound.

It would take me years to put a name to what I was subjected to the day of the Jellaz Affair. In addition to the pain and despair, I felt a terrible guilt. I didn't consider myself a victim or my aggressor a rapist until much later, when I was finally able to understand what had happened. Somehow I'd always felt like an accomplice. Our house was nearby, couldn't I have run there when Ayad left to take the last group of my classmates home? Instead, for some reason, I waited for him, as if I was hoping for what happened to me to happen.

No one before you has heard this story, Mohammed Habib. I've lived with its pain in silence for decades. My body spoke by gaining flesh and fat, like yours did, but for different reasons. After that, Ayad would rape me twice more in the mosque bathroom, and each time he threatened me: if I refused, he would tell his honor the judge, Othman Ennaifer. I wouldn't be free of him until the day our teacher fired him, after the worshippers at the mosque found out he was masturbating in the mihrab after the *Zuhr* prayers. But the impact of what he did to me didn't go away when he did. I started enjoying some secret, forbidden habits, sometimes involving the neighborhood boys behind our families' backs. No female has ever had the least effect on me, despite all the efforts I made to change my orientation. I tried so hard to become normal, but all to no avail.

When she asked for her divorce, Fawzia bint Abdallah told me I'd treated her unjustly by marrying her when I didn't like women. Is that true? Could *anyone* disobey an order given by Mama Jnayna, bless her soul? She forced me to marry against my will to quash the rumor that cursed Luiza had spread. But Luiza hadn't lied; she simply recounted what she had seen.

III

Larbi, the man that Luiza caught me with in the roof shed, was a waiter at Ali Bouna Café in Place Sidi Msharraf. He was over twenty years younger than me. Poor man, he would be killed in mysterious circumstances six years after that incident that separated us. He died at the notorious Prison de Lambèse in Algeria, after a military trial in which he was accused of killing a French officer.

He was then, in the mid-1940s, a young man of twenty-two. He was skinny and short, his facial features delicate and handsome. He would get shy whenever I caressed the small of his back as he bent over next to me to refill the hookah. As he moved between tables and took orders, his eyes never left the spot I was sitting in. He sat with me once when his boss wasn't watching. He claimed that he was a student and wanted to ask a question about some religious issues. When he found out about my activism with the national resistance movement, he started to come back every day with a new question. Sometimes he would ask me for news about Moncef Bey after he was removed from the throne. He wanted to know whether the king was continuing the struggle from his exile in the French city of Pau or whether he had withdrawn from politics and preferred silence. Sometimes he would ask about the destiny of Mongi Slim, Salah Farhat, and all the other national figures who had been imprisoned in the aftermath of the Night of Destiny Congress in August 1946. He asked me to explain to him the difference between the internal autonomy that the National Front demanded and the full independence that Salah Ben Youssef and his comrades demanded. He asked many questions about the meaning of the reform plan that the Resident-General of France in Tunisia Charles Mast had declared, and he talked about the scope of its agreement with the nationalists' demands. He would always praise the leader Habib Bourguiba and what he had done to draw international attention to the cause, whether from the party offices in Cairo or through the strategic visits to the United States he made in late November 1946.

I think about Larbi a lot these days when I watch the news, Mohammed Habib. I remember with great sadness his special praise for Bourguiba and his absolute loyalty to the party political bureau. I remember him every day as I watch Bourguiba's feverish effort to destroy all elements of Arab identity. I helplessly witness the war he has declared on Islam, ever since he announced these shameful laws to benefit women (his so-called Personal Status Code). Not content with just closing Zaytuna Mosque University, prohibiting use of the *Hijri* calendar in the administration, and confiscating religious land in the name of the state, he also attacked religious duties by encouraging people not to fast for Ramadan—all on the pretext of the public interest! I often tell myself, seeing what Bourguiba did to the supporters of his opponent Salah Ben Youssef, that God must love Larbi very much. He chose him, out of all the prisoners of Lambèse, to be a martyr, and so spared him the misery that all us old activists live in, as we see Bourguiba waging a war on his former comrades and sending some of them to the gallows.

I was impressed, my nephew, by Larbi's precise political education and his knowledge of details that common people rarely know. But he confessed to me at one of our meetings at the cafe—after he'd asked his confidants about me and felt more comfortable—that he'd been a member of an underground movement ever since he'd left prison seven years before. He had spontaneously formed a resistance committee with some of his young friends, with the mission of inflicting damage on the colonizer, in coordination with Congregation Council and the Neo Destour Party Political Bureau. He told me about his adventures, which included not only distributing pamphlets calling for mobilization and civil disobedience, but also attacks on electricity poles and phone cables, as well as blowing up military establishments and interests in and around Bourjel, Gambetta, Sayda El Manoubia, Mellasine, and La Kasbah. In the beginning, I hid my membership in the old Destour Party from him, since it didn't support vandalism, but I later discovered that he already knew and didn't care. Larbi didn't understand—or didn't care about—the disagreements between the different national factions. He also didn't differentiate between the executive committee and the political bureau, and didn't recognize the distinction between old and new when talking about the Destour Party. He used to say, as he rekindled the hookah embers with a small woven fan, "The important thing is to not let the fire of resistance go out. Everything that goes into the stove is fuel, Si Mhammed."

Our relationship became stronger over time, and I started inviting him to come over to chat in the roof shed. That was where he told me about his tragic childhood at the Sidi El Hari *zawiya* in Tunis. His father was a Sufi sheikh, one of the Isawiyya mystics. He'd been stung in his sleep by a yellow scorpion, one of the ones they eat alive in their performances. No one knew how it got out of its box, nor how it reached his bed. It stung him on his upper lip, causing his face to turn as black as coal, and he died after a night of terrible pain. Larbi was told that the Isawiyya mystics who hailed, like him and his father, from the order of Sheikh Sidi Ben Aïssa could not be affected by the arachnids' poison; it must have been an evil jinn who appeared to his father in the shape of a scorpion and infused him with the devils' poison.

His mother ran away with his sisters to her family in Meknes, Morocco, a month after the death of her husband when her brother-in-law, who had already taken his brother's position at the *zawiya*, tried to indecently assault first her and then her eldest daughter. So Larbi, who was not yet nine years old, was left unprotected. He left the Quranic school he'd been attending when his father was alive and started living like an animal inside the *zawiya*. He lived off what the visitors gave him and participated in the shows of the Isawiyya men by warming up the *bendir* and *nagara* drums and other percussion instruments. He also moved the heavy boxes filled with scorpions and snakes, and every tool needed for the Sufi Nouba ceremony, like swords, daggers, and knives, as well as the clay stoves and the wooden beds with long nails. But his uncle, who was a reformer, wanted to diversify the Isawiyya shows and infuse new blood into them. He decided to include his nephew in the ceremonies the men performed for visitors at the *zawiya* or in public squares and private parties. He started training him to swallow sharp knives, lie down on beds of nails, walk on hot coals, and jump on ground-up pieces of glass. His throat and vocal chords got inflamed, his butt and the bottom of his feet were lacerated, and the skin of his feet was burned. And all he heard from his uncle during this time was, "You are like bread that hasn't risen enough, Larbi. You're the son of the Sufi order, just like your father and uncle, but it seems that, in your case, fire has left only ashes in its wake. What a shame. Why aren't you strong, like your father? Why aren't you ferocious when fighting scorpions and vipers like me? You have to leave your body behind when you dance to the rhythm. Focus with the *bendir*, Larbi, and take off—far, far away."

Larbi took his advice to heart and set off for far, far away. He put a bundle on his shoulder the next morning at dawn and, walking on his wounded feet, left the *zawiya*, left the entire city, in fact. He was thirteen years old then and was dreaming of working at sea, so he rode the tram towards the suburb of Sidi Ali Beji. After a week of hunger and fatigue, he sold himself to an old French man for the price of a seafood meal at a restaurant by the sea and a good night's sleep on a real bed without nails. He sighed a lot while telling me the sad story. He said, "A heavy foot prodding my shoulder woke me up when I was sleeping on a sandy beach. I don't know whether I was sleeping or unconscious. The sun had dried my skin, and the heat had burned it. I realized that my nose was stuffed with damp sand, which had irritated the sensitive skin inside my nose, causing severe pain. My lips were glued shut and stuck to my front teeth like a piece of plaster attached to a wall. The roar of the sea in the dark night covered the man's voice, and the flickering lamps at the nearby restaurant overlooking the beach made it so I couldn't make out his features. I was horribly dizzy, unable to tell the land from the sky, the sand from the water, or the short figure standing next to my head from my body, lying like a dirty rag on the wet sand. I sat up with difficulty, holding my head between my hands so it wouldn't fly away from the pain. My stomach felt nauseous, or maybe hungry. I thought to myself that it was probably hunger, remembering that I hadn't eaten anything since the caretaker of the Sidi Bou Said El Beji *zawiya* kicked me out, after she caught me kissing her spinster sister behind the tomb.

"Zohra, yes—that was her name, or maybe it was just the name she liked men to call her during sex. My first night there, she came to where I was sleeping on the stone bench just inside the *zawiya* entrance. I opened my eyes when I felt her lustful hand running over my body. She didn't give me a chance to object. By the light of the pale stars, I saw her bare her small breasts and rub them against my face. My body tensed like a taut bow, and I didn't know what to do; I'd never touched a woman before. Very quickly she realized how inexperienced I was, and she started expertly guiding me with short sentences: 'Do this. Keep going. Wait. Harder. No, not like that.' In the process, she put dirty words in my mouth that she wanted me to address her with, so I repeated after her, panting, saying her name over and over like she wanted: 'Zohra.'

"After that night, she visited me again and found me more skillful and less hesitant. But when she didn't show up the third night, I spent the night sleepless until dawn. As soon as the old caretaker opened the door of the shrine, I snuck into the courtyard looking for Zohra. I found her sitting next to a large tub, washing clothes with her dress pulled up to her thighs. She smiled flirtatiously when I scolded her for her absence, cautiously so the old lady wouldn't notice. She said something I didn't understand then: 'I'm on my period.' She gave me a naughty wink. Her wink and her bare thighs excited me, so I signaled to her to follow me to the mausoleum. She left me waiting for an hour, my blood boiling and my body jittery from desire. Then she came in slowly, cautiously looking around her. I pulled her behind the tomb, blinded by desire and not thinking about the consequences, but she pushed my hand away when I tried to touch her in the place that, during our first adventures, she had encouraged me to touch. Laughing, she repeated, as to a stupid person who doesn't understand anything, 'I told you I have my period. Are you an idiot?'

"I made do with a deep, hot kiss that was interrupted by the old lady's scream when she entered the room carrying boxes of candles. Zohra suddenly became a ferocious beast, pushing me with one hand and slapping me with the other. She started screaming loudly and cursing me, the bastard who had tried to assault her before the eyes of her saint El Beji, may God be pleased with him.

"I left the *zawiya* like a cowardly dog being pelted with stones by children running after it. I walked on the beach for days, trying in vain to convince the small fishing boats' owners to hire me to help them collect the nets or bait the fishhooks or untangle fishing lines. Then I grew feeble because of hunger and thirst and woke up being prodded by the foot of this old Frenchman. I didn't know that he was European at first, until he spoke to me in broken Arabic with a foreigner's accent. He helped me stand up and started cleaning my hair and clothes from the sand as he pointed to the restaurant behind me and asked me with signs whether I was hungry. He led me to a corner next to the restaurant that was made of bamboo and had a shower in it for vacationing customers in the summer. He gave me a round pink soap with a nice scent, the likes of which I'd never smelled before. I had left my bundle of clothes on the *zawiya* bench when I fled after the scandal, so I had no option but to put my dirty and smelly clothes back on after the shower. I had hung them on the bamboo wall near the entrance, but when I reached out to take them with one hand, rubbing my soap-stung eyes with the other, I couldn't find them. After a few seconds of hesitation, I went out naked, covered by the darkness, and felt along the ground with my hand, thinking that the clothes had slipped and fallen on the other side of the wall. Then I saw him standing a couple of steps away, holding a flashlight that he aimed directly at me. He swept it up and down my body, exhaling a strange-smelling smoke from his pipe.

"I bent down, trying to cover myself with my hands, but he nodded at me and held up his hand to stop. There was a sly smile on his lips. I froze in place like a scared puppy with its tail between its legs. I heard him calling, 'Alice . . . Alice!' and then a blonde woman in her thirties appeared at the restaurant door. She was slender and curvy, wearing a short blue dress with a jasmine *machmoum* placed in the neckline between her breasts. I noticed that she was holding some white fabric in her hand. She threw it to me, commanding in a flirtatious voice, '*Mets ça, beau gosse*!'

"The truth is that I didn't know any French, but I soon came to memorize that sentence—*put this on, handsome*. She would repeat it dozens of times, in the same tone, when I lived at the restaurant, each time throwing me some women's clothes from her own dresser.

"That night, I ate a fancy dinner, sitting cross-legged on a Persian rug in a lacy silk nightgown. By the time the morning came, I had learned some new games in the house of Monsieur François. These games had astonishing socialist rules and needed three players: an old Frenchman, his thirty-year-old wife, and between them an obedient Tunisian boy, discovering his body and needing food and a place to stay."

After a few games, Mohammed Habib, Larbi gave up the idea of working as a fisherman and became satisfied with his work at the old Frenchman's restaurant during the day and in the couple's bed at night. The French police arrested him after less than a year when they found the restaurant owner strangled in his bed with his shoelaces. Larbi didn't know of any enemies that the Frenchman and his young wife might have had, and he hadn't heard anything suspicious on the night of the incident because he'd drunk half a bottle of wine left behind by a customer and slept like a stone until morning in his usual place in the kitchen. Since Larbi didn't speak any French but *mets ça, beau gosse*, he didn't know how to answer the questions posed by the police and didn't manage to convince the detectives of his innocence. He spent two years in the civil prison without trial. He was exposed to a lot of harassment from other prisoners, even though he was still just a kid. Those two years were also decisive in shaping his political consciousness, thanks to the friendships he struck up with the political prisoners who were denied transfer to the Prison de la Rabta, as well as the right of political status, by the protectorate authorities. Those prisoners turned the civil prison into a political academy, instructing young Tunisians in the principles of resistance and guiding them to various roads of activism. Larbi was released suddenly at the end of the two-year period for lack of evidence, so he took the initiative to contact some men from the resistance movement in Rue Bab El Falla whose names and addresses he had gotten from fellow prisoners. They found him a job at the coffee shop where we met and facilitated his enlistment in the underground movement.

They conducted a series of successful operations targeting the transportation system, economic establishments, and the port equipment. But then Larbi and some of his fellows were arrested when the French police confiscated an announcement at the Belvedere post office addressed to Radio Berlin, with the stamp of the resistance on it. One evening in the roof shed, Larbi laughed as he showed me the scars from cigarette burns on his chest and knees and told me the story of how he toyed with Commissaire Philippi and Gendarmerie Capitaine Cotaire, the two officers who took turns interrogating and torturing him. He said, "One evening, they stuck hot needles under my toenails, attached electric wires to my penis, and crushed my fingertips with pliers. At dawn, just as I was about to die from the pain, Detective Philippi came back to ask me if I had finally come to my senses. I gave him the answer he wanted, telling him that the typewriter we'd used to type up the flyers was at the bottom of the Mellassine reservoir. They hired a diver who kept diving, over and over, until that afternoon, as I stood between the officers, watching and silently gloating. Later, I was taken back to the endless fun of the Lafayette police station. Philippi and Cotaire promised to torture me to death if I didn't tell them where the typewriter was. They didn't know, of course, that I was from the El Hari *zawiya*. When I asked for the help of Sidi Aïssa, the saint's blessings were quickly bestowed on me. Whenever the sting of the whips got stronger, the sound of *nagara* and *bendir* drums grew stronger in my ears. I would focus on the rhythm, as my uncle had taught me, and my bloodied body would break free of its shackles and float away from that pain, far, far away."

After the violent but fruitless interrogation, Larbi and his fellow comrades were referred to the military court and were given the death penalty. After Marshal Pétain issued a pardon, however, the sentence was commuted to life in prison at the fortress at Ghar El Melh, with its dark tunnels and deadly diseases. Then Larbi was among the prisoners given amnesty by Resident-General Jean-Pierre Esteva, so he was released after a year, carrying many dreadful memories.

What hurt him most, though, of all his sad memories was one that, whenever he brought it to mind, made him feel as if his soul might spill out with his tears. It was the memory of that morning when he found out, while still a young boy at the shrine of Sidi El Hari, that his mother and sisters had abandoned him and left for Meknes in Morocco without him. He could never find any justification for their betrayal. He'd never forgotten them, and yet he never seriously considered going to look for them or join them. He would say, wiping his eyes, "A mother who abandons her son to a man capable of tearing open the bellies of venomous creatures with his bare hands—that mother doesn't deserve to be looked for. God will find her and exact my vengeance."

IV

You probably said the same thing to yourself, Mohammed Habib, or something similar, when you realized that your mother had abandoned you and given you over to your destiny at the Rassaa house, as if you were an orphan. I believe that you lived the same pain twice, when your second mother, Bashira, abandoned you, as well, returning you again to the woman who'd left you behind and didn't bother for five years to bring you home. And as if what had happened to you wasn't enough, we inaugurated your return to us by rushing to hold your circumcision ceremony. I wonder who the sage behind that genius idea was, with the excuse that you were almost eight years old and hadn't yet been circumcised? I had started, slowly but successfully, to ease your fear of us and replace your dislike of your new home with acceptance and familiarity. Then I found out that the preparations had started to enter you into Islam before the end of summer. They were rushing, thinking it unacceptable that your younger brother would go before you. It seems your grandmother Bashira thought it improper to cut your flesh, as they say, while you were so far from your mother, so she postponed it until you returned to us.

Mama Jnayna took care of everything. She sent Mohsen to the souqs to buy you the circumcision clothes, including a fine crimson chechia from Souk Chaouachine. Hanging from the top of the chechia was a horn of pure coral, a small decorative fish the size of a thumb, and between them a golden *hamsa*. You also received a burgundy *jebba* from Souk Trok, with a short jacket, *sirwal*, and a pair of fine leather slippers embroidered with silver silk thread from Souk El Blaghgia. Khaddouj and Luiza were busy preparing the table for the feast, making sure it was well-presented and filled with a variety of sweets, drinks, and jams, and decorated with candles and various flowers and aromatic herbs. Your grandfather Othman hired a group of Sufi men from the Sidi Abdelkader *zawiya* on Rue du Divan for the evening of circumcision, to chant Sufi odes like Qasidat al-Burda, along with Sufi music. As for me, I was assigned to prepare the pottery jars that would be thrown to the ground after the circumcision. I filled them with sugared almonds, candy, almonds, pistachios, pine nuts, and walnuts. I was also to arrange for a groom to bring a horse to wait for you in the entrance hall. It would be festooned with a beautiful golden saddle and green and red silk cloth, and would take you to the Sidi Mehrez *zawiya*, then back to the house where the *khatin* waited to perform the circumcision.

We paid attention to all the details, Mohammed Habib, neglecting nothing . . . except Mohammed Habib himself. You watched the ceaseless activity with fearful eyes. You were wearing beautiful clothes, but you were suspicious. You wanted to ask what everyone was plotting against you, but you didn't know who to ask. Everyone was too busy for you, while believing themselves to be busy *for* you. As for your mother, she ignored the whole thing. She secluded herself in her room and didn't participate in any of the preparations. She wasn't even willing to welcome the crowd of women who came over to congratulate her. When Mama Jnayna entered her room with the basin of cold water to put her feet in the moment the *khatin* started circumcising you, as is our tradition with the mother of the child, she looked the other way and said, "I don't need a cold basin. I've been at the bottom of a well for years."

I was standing in front of you with my face behind the *khatin* when he started tricking you into thinking that he was a tailor who wanted to measure you. As soon as he stood you up on the couch with the scissors in his hand and wanted to pull down your trousers, you became suspicious and stubbornly refused. You felt shy about being naked in front of the crowd that had filled the room to witness your ordeal. But his assistant betrayed you from behind. He yanked your trousers down, wrapping one of his arms around your knees and the other around your chest and arms. Our eyes met, Mohammed Habib, while you were shackled and oppressed, as the *khatin* grasped the skin and pulled it to him. Tears of terror covered your face, and your eyes held a look of great disappointment and indescribable accusation. I couldn't bear that look, so I withdrew from the room, running away before the deed was done, chased by your thunderous scream, which were soon covered by the women's ululations when the *khatin*'s scissors cut through the soft flesh.

Mama Jnayna took you in her lap for the rest of the day until the evening. We told you nice things and filled your chechia with riyals and francs, but you kept frowning, refusing to talk to us and refusing to eat or drink. The wound on your penis healed after a few days, and we thought the matter was done with. But you were not like other children. They get circumcised, they cry a bit, then they go and pee on the fragments of the candy jars on the ground in the courtyard; they laugh out loud then, and they forget the pain. You were like someone with an internal wound that festered over time, and you salved your pain with a startling cruelty that crept in and took up residence in your soul. You didn't vent your cruelty towards anyone but Zbaida, to the point that I almost felt sorry for her, even though she was the one responsible for what happened.

V

I had known Tahar Haddad for many years. I met him through the meetings of the Destour Party club during the days of Abdelaziz Thâalbi, as well as later on, when Sheikh Thâalbi was forced into exile in the East and Mohieddine Klibi became the leader of the party. But when I intercepted the letter that Luiza was trying to deliver to Zbaida, it never occurred to me that the Tahar mentioned in the letter was that heretic I'd met at the political party meetings. How on earth could I have known that that vagrant—who spent his days wandering with Mohamed Ali El Hammi between souqs, ports, and mines—knew my sister-in-law and was sending letters to my house? If your grandfather Othman hadn't learned of his death by chance that morning, no one would've made the connection between him and the scandal.

My relationship with him consisted of nothing more than exchanging cold greetings, yet I still found him repulsive. His behavior took on a snobbish and arrogant tone around the upper-class members of the executive committee, revealing a complex stemming from his southern roots. We spent many years looking at each other from a distance, until there was a clash that transformed our mutual neglect into resentment and hatred. One morning we were at a meeting at the political party club on Rue d'Angleterre, and Mohieddine Klibi was with us. Suddenly Tahar Haddad entered the room, whirling and spitting like a tornado, a copy of *Al Nahda* in his hand. He waved the newspaper in our faces, screaming in rage, "You stab these workers in their backs and conspire against them with their enemies, and then you release statements without consulting the bases?"

We all realized that he was angry about the statement we'd published the day before in *Al Nahda*. We had met with Joachim Durel, the secretary general of the French Socialist CGT, along with some high-profile members of the Destour Party and the

Reform Party, and members of the governing council. We had decided to join the coalition front that included the reformers and socialists and asked the workers to join the French union as it was a general international union. That would mean leaving the General Confederation of Tunisian Workers that was founded by Mohamed Ali El Hammi with the help of Tahar Haddad. The party members exchanged awkward glances at his outburst, but Mohieddine Klibi appeared oblivious. Speaking calmly to Haddad, he said, "Take it easy, Tahar. Why attack us without checking in first? What are you saying to us?"

Haddad pounded the table so hard that he nearly broke it in two, then bent over face-to-face with Klibi, yelling, "The statement has your signature, Si Mohieddine Klibi, and the signatures of all the other weaklings: Ahmed Al Safi, Hassan Klalki, Salah Farhat . . . "

His hand shaking in anger, he shook the newspaper to open it to the page with the statement and started going over the list of signatures, but Klibi became angry and interrupted him. He stood up and said, "Watch your mouth, Tahar, and don't push me. Remember that I respect you because of Sheikh Abdelaziz Thâalbi. If not for him, I would've told everyone about your nonsense ages ago."

"Oh, I'm so frightened of you, Klibi—I'm trembling with fear. If you truly respected Sheikh Thâalbi, you would've sought inspiration from his book *Tunisia, the Martyr* and the principles of the party that you ruined after he left. But you either have a short memory, Klibi, or you're too ignorant to read. Or else you'd have realized that your betrayal of the General Confederation of Tunisian Workers is a shameful denial of workers' rights. The right of workers, teachers, and employees to unionize and gather is one of the demands in Sheikh Thâalbi's book."

I interfered with the intention of calming the disagreement, but the words didn't come out of my mouth the way I'd planned. Instead, I found myself snapping at him. "Stop preaching, Haddad, and stop being such a zealot for Mohamed Ali El Hammi. We all know why you support him. Isn't it strange that you act based on tribal loyalty just like the people of the Jahiliyyah, even though you're a graduate of Zaytuna University? Can't you see what establishing this confederation has caused? What have the workers who joined your confederation gained? It only caused divisions among them and exposed these hard-working people to more abuse by the capital. Ever since El Hammi set up the Tunisian Economic Cooperation Association, getting ready to announce the confederation of workers, it's been one disaster after another for the laborers. And what did it lead up to? Blood spilled in Bizerte. I wish that you and your friend El Hammi had learned something from that tragedy, but instead you're still inciting revolution. You provoked the protectorate government until it accused us of allying with communists and conspiring against state security. One month ago, the French police raided the house of the party secretary Ahmed Taoufik El Madani and terrorized his family. Mohammed Ali himself has been in jail for a month and a half now on charges of conspiracy. Don't see that you're defending a lost cause?"

Klibi smiled, silently gloating, as I whipped Haddad with facts—facts that his tribal fanaticism blinded him to. But he took me by surprise with an enraged retort that made me lose my temper. I stood up, and we would have come to blows if not for his friend Deraai, who came up next to him and pulled him out of the club, cursing. He said, his words drenched with class hatred, "I'd advise you to shut the hell up, ben Ennaifer. How could you and people like you, who were born with a silver spoon in their mouths, understand the need for a union organization? You're like all the other members of the party's esteemed executive committee: a stain on Thâalbi's activist history. You don't believe in revolutionary nationalism! You declare your obedience to the protectorate state, then hold out your hands waiting for it to bestow a few crumbs of reform upon you. You've divorced yourselves from the masses and shut your ears against the pain of the oppressed. You don't talk to the crowd unless you're at a podium. You claim that the people are fallen, hopeless, and morally decadent, but all you're describing is yourselves. You use your activities in the party clubs as a coverup for the rich among you to generate authority and prestige through the vast publicity around your big names. God damn you all and God damn you, ben Ennaifer, for talking about things you know nothing about."

After that, Haddad stopped coming to the main branch of the party club, and we learned that he incited the regional chapters of the party to protest and write statements of complaint. Some of these chapters, such the Rue du Morkadh chapter, which was under his absolute authority, split off from the party and started encouraging other chapters in Tunis, Mateur, and El Kef to proceed in the same manner. Some of our friends, the informants, told us that Haddad gathered a gang of his friends and started planning at the Rue de Riadh chapter to establish a new party to replace the old one. Some of the people we trusted were informing us of the rumors Haddad was spreading about us, especially about Mohieddine Klibi, in his meetings with riffraff and thugs, all to stain the image of the leaders and make people leave the party. People had often told us about his well-known heresy, but we had always defended him. We had denied the rumors and accused those who spread them of exaggeration, but when his book about women's emancipation came out, that doubt became a certainty.

The truth, Mohamed Habib, is that we received his book with great happiness. How could we not, when it was such an exceptional opportunity to get our revenge on him? Mohieddine Klibi was the most excited and happy of all of us. He prepared a failproof plan to destroy the book and its author before people even got the chance to read it. And it was because Haddad had dissented from the party and tried to dismantle it.

VI

I was returning from the sharia court on Rue du Divan when Abdelwahab Bramli, one of my old classmates at the infamous Quranic school I told you about, stopped me at Rue de l'Eglise. Abdelwahab was an idiot. He had gotten used to the teacher's *falaka*, and it had gotten used to him. But despite our teacher's efforts to open his mind by beating his feet, he learned nothing more during the entire first level than a short surah from the Quran. He ended up working at a printing press on Rue de l'Eglise, having tried his hand at many jobs without success. Abdelwahab was a chatterbox who would chase you with his stories; if necessary, he would abandon his plans and walk with you a street or two to finish telling you what he'd planned to. Most of the time, it would be the kind of trivial news that would give you a headache. But the news that afternoon was so interesting that I couldn't wait until the next day to share it with my friend Mohieddine Klibi.

Abdelwahab said, grumbling and sighing, "For nine months this man has been visiting us twice a day. One day I got so tired of him that I suggested he rent the storage room next to the press so he could keep an eye on his precious book. Even the press owner got tired of him; he returned his manuscript multiple times and told him to find another press that would agree to publish a book that size for the paltry sum he was offering. For months, he brought in subscriptions he'd managed to get from selling the book before printing it, but Si Mohammed, the press owner, didn't think it was enough to cover the expenses. And then this morning, he showed up with a fat envelope and gave it to the owner, saying that he'd sold a property owned by his father to print his book. Imagine, Mhammed! Now they're selling land for papers that will end up destroyed by fire, ruined in water, or gnawed up by rats."

I answered him with a bored tone, moving at a near-jog and

hoping that he would leave me alone, "No doubt he's a crazy poet or some bohemian short-story writer."

"I wish he were, Mhammed; that would at least be an excuse. But he's a graduate of Zaytuna University."

I stopped walking, curious. I wondered who this student from Zaytuna University could be, who would sell property to publish a book? I asked him if he remembered the name of the author and the title of the book. He told me that the author was Tahar Haddad, and the book was about women, but he'd forgotten the title.

After I told Mohieddine Klibi about the matter the next morning, he insisted I introduce him to my friend at the press. I'm not sure whether he paid him money or tempted him with some political concessions in the party, but we didn't leave until he'd promised to give him some proofs of the book before it was published so we could check it out—to prepare a reception appropriate for Haddad's behavior and his attack on the old Destour Party leadership. So Mohieddine Klibi and I prepared articles attacking the book under pen names, and when the book came out—and after the ceremony—we rushed to publish them in different newspapers, such as *Al Zahra, Al Nadim, Al Nahda* and *Ezzahou*. We also contacted our friends in the executive committee, such as Rajih Ibrahim and Moncef Mestiri and told them about the issues with the book and encouraged them to be harsh in their reviews. We didn't stop there, either: we rushed to contact Sidi Ahmed Bey and asked him to take strict measures against Haddad's project to destroy sharia law. We also sent clear threats to those participating in the book celebration at the Belvedere; some of them decided not to attend, and others tried to take a middle road by leaving the ceremony early.

We incited thugs against him to the point that we made his life a hell on earth, and there wasn't a single place in Tunis where he didn't get harassed and cursed. I thought that we'd eliminated him, only to find out that he'd sneaked into my house and forever ruined my relationship with my brother. He also destroyed your childhood, Mohammed Habib, and weighed your mother down with a heavy burden she would carry for the rest of her life.

VII

I was astounded by your father's reaction to what happened. His calm when hearing about the repugnant news provoked me, and his defense of his wife, after she tampered with his honor, the honor of the entire Ennaifer family, enraged me. He started knocking on her bedroom door, begging her to answer him. But she just ignored him. He thought, because of his stupidity, that her silence meant she was unconscious or dead, so he was close to losing his mind. Wicked Luiza was adding fuel to the fire with her carrying on: crying, slapping her face and unveiling her head—anyone who saw her would think that a tragedy was imminent, if it had not already happened. I knew that they were complicit in the charade, since there is no better way to banish anger at a guilty party than worrying about them. The farce continued for hours, Zbaida unmoving and quiet, Luiza screaming, and Mohsen, in front of the door, a wreck: he stood, sat, peered in from the window and then the keyhole, stood again and tried to force the door with his shoulder, and paced the hall, sometimes slowly, sometimes rushing. All the while, the screams of the newborn Mostafa rose and fell, stopped and started.

I am actually not sure whether I got offended that your mother and her maid had toyed with my deceived brother and made him their puppet. Yet, and despite what had happened, I left the sitting room where your grandfather and I were and called up to him on the balcony to come down and join us. It seems that he thought we had finally decided, after some deliberation, to address his confusion about the contents of the letter, so he came to me with questions. However, as soon as he realized the reason we'd called him down, he started fuming with rage, and the situation between us got tense, leading to the animosity you've witnessed for fifteen years.

He grabbed hold of my collar when I contemptuously explained to him that Zbaida was fine, just pretending to be dead to transform his anger into fear and sympathy, and that Luiza was supporting her by her screaming to make the play successful and catch him in their trap. He spoke through gritted teeth, pulling me to a far corner of the courtyard so Hajj Othman couldn't hear him, "You idiot, do you think I need lessons from you? Don't you see that you're about to destroy my family because of your stupidity and meddling? If anything happens to Zbaida today, I will stomp the life out of you."

I couldn't believe what I was hearing. Mohsen ben Othman Ennaifer was a cuckold and wasn't even trying to hide that from his family? He was *reproaching* me for opening his eyes to his wife's infidelity? Did he want the matter to stay hidden, like a covered dish with rotting food inside? Maybe I should've extracted my clothes from his hands that day and stopped talking to him until my anger had faded. My blood, however, was boiling in my veins, and as you know, I'm very protective of my family. So instead, I pushed him away in disgust and raised my voice so everyone in the family could hear me: "Are you worried that something bad might happen to your faithful wife? Don't you care about your stained honor? No doubt you're the laughingstock of the entire Sidi Mansour quartier by now, and the news of your virtuous wife has already spread among the thugs and scum that ignorant atheist used to sit with. I swear to God that everyone who bought a loaf of bread today from that baker is now chewing Mohsen Ennaifer's honor along with the bread on their tables. And what are you worried about? The well-being of the criminal who dragged our noses through the dirt! If I were you, I would've strangled her with my own hands, but here you are, practically in tears you're so scared for her."

I was trying to escape from his hands when he started beating and slapping me. He called me lame and many other insults besides. But as soon as I fell to the ground in surprise, I lifted my lame foot and kicked him between his legs with all my strength, and he fell to his knees, making a sound like death rattle or a bull bellowing. Mama Jnayna and Khaddouj ran towards us screaming and started trying to separate us, but the battle was getting fiercer. The mute giant inside me suddenly spoke, and my fists started quenching the thirst of a lifetime of resentment and jealousy, covered with a veneer of brotherhood and affection. I remembered, rolling around with him on the ground, that he represented all the beautiful things that I couldn't have. A slender figure, an athletic body, and an iron personality. He had rebelled since his boyhood against the father I also wanted to rebel against but couldn't. I remained all my life under Othman Ennaifer's robes, walking straight ahead on the line he had drawn for me, and despite it all, I could see disappointment and disdain in his eyes because I was still unable to fulfill the role he had for me in his imagination. Mohsen boarded a ship and traveled abroad, and I stayed here fixed in place like a rusty knocker, left behind, hanging on a ramshackle wall. Mohsen went to Germany and came back, got engaged to a woman and married her, and fathered two sons. And all the while I sat with my failure like a dog, with my slanted inclinations and no hope of a family or children.

Those black thoughts that were fighting in my head filled it with so much strength that it butted Mohsen in the face and made him bleed from his nose and mouth. As soon as Mama Jnayna saw the drops of blood on the marble, her screaming became howling, as if the blood were a black omen of what fate had in store for us.

Is it true that marble has the bloodlust of a shark, that it gets excited by the smell of just a little bit and seeks to spill more? If not, how do we explain the great quantities of blood that soon quenched its thirst? Your father and I broke apart as a gentle smattering of rain slowly transformed the scattered drops of blood in the courtyard into small pink pools, and Luiza splashed through them as she ran, with you in her arms, towards the door you wouldn't enter again for five years. Mohsen went towards the kitchen with his hand on his nose, trying to stop the bleeding, Khaddouj following behind him. I went towards the sitting room, my mother behind me, not knowing whether to reprimand me or to console me. And in a flash of lightning, Mohsen was chasing after me, holding a metal poker that Mama used to stir the wood in the oven. The women's screaming got louder, and this time, all the signs of certain death were present. Your grandfather Othman, who had stayed neutral all through the battle, scurried out, trying to stand between me and your father. But his bad leg obstructed his progress, so he started wailing like someone who had lost their child, asking Mohsen to put down the poker and curse the devil. But then a voice came from the balcony, and everything stopped. The beautiful lady had finally decided to leave her bedroom and break her silence. She stood on the balcony, waving to Mohsen and beckoning for him to come up.

Mohsen threw away his weapon and ran to Zbaida, and the marble was forced to bide its time until another bloody round started in the dead of night.

5
The Tale of the Maid Khaddouj
(*Hôpital Aziza Othmana, Winter of 1949*)

I

I'm the one who gave the letter to Sidi Mohsen, Lella Zbaida. A yellowish paper the size of your palm with a few words written on it in black ink. I found it after everybody had left in the hands of little Mohammed Habib, who was playing with it. I hid it in my shirt, then gave it secretly to Sidi Mohsen.

Now I'm confessing this to you from my bed at the hospital. I don't think I'll see you again after today. You won't be back to visit me, and when I leave here it will only be to the cemetery. My mother died because of a tumor in her chest, too. But no doctor saw my mother, and no visitor checked on her. She spent her final days groaning in pain on a straw mat at the elder Ennaifer's house, then calmly died, just like any old donkey.

I still don't know, to this day, what was written in that note, Lella Zbaida. I don't remember the letters that Sidi Mohsen taught me when he was a boy in school. All I could remember was the mountain with the sharp summit divided by a horizontal line halfway up and the pregnant lady with her small head and big stomach looking to the right. Trust me, neither of these two letters was in the note I saved from Mohammed Habib. I found it by chance in his small hands. He was lifting it up to his mouth, trying to tear it apart. No doubt he had found it in the courtyard after everyone went to their rooms in the aftermath of the cane incident with Sidi Othman. I immediately buried it in my blouse, but I swear my intention wasn't to tell on you. I was afraid that Sidi Mhammed might spread lies about you or lie to Sidi Mohsen because of his jealousy of him. I wanted to keep the original message so he could compare it to what he had heard from his brother. I didn't want Luiza to see me giving him the letter, fearing that she would tell you about it in an exaggerated way, to make you angry with me. So I hid, waiting for Sidi Mohsen on the covered staircase that led to the upper floor where he was stationed by your room, and I slipped it into his hand as he came downstairs to fight with Sidi Mhammed. He snatched it from me and didn't take more than a few seconds to read it. Then he put it in his trousers' pocket and continued down the stairs. I didn't see any hint of either anger or satisfaction on his face. It was neutral, as if he were wearing a mask. Everyone thought, Lella Zbaida, that the letter had stayed with you after Si Othman threw it at you while raising his cane to you, so no one asked about it. As for Sidi Mohsen, he kept the matter secret and never told anyone that he had it.

Forgive me, Lella Zbaida, if I've done anything during the years I lived with you that upset you. Seeing Sidi Mohsen's pain made me hate you despite myself. Would you forgive me if I told you that your handsome white husband was the son of this ugly black woman, even though she's only ten years older than him, or less? I witnessed his birth in the room where you now live at the Ennaifer house. My two sisters and I were also born at that house. As was my mother. My grandparents and their children were the freed slaves of the family. Some of them who were stubborn decided to find a job on their own after the Bey's order to free all slaves, and they became homeless and hungry and died of disease. Whereas the lucky ones, like my father and mother, decided to stay, and worked for the family generation after generation.

When Sidi Mohsen was born, Lella Jnayna was twenty years old, and she had already given birth to Lella Beya, as well as a boy who was premature and stillborn. Her labor with Sidi Mohsen was difficult; she didn't stop screaming from dawn until evening, and the Jewish midwife's face blanched as she said over and over to whoever asked (and those who didn't), "The baby is breech, God help us."

When I asked my mother, running behind her on that difficult day, about the meaning of the word "breech," she told me, irritated by my questions, that it meant the baby had done a somersault in his mother's womb and was coming out from the exit feet first instead of head first like other babies. I was afraid to ask her about the exit. She seemed angry and tense, about to explode, as she boiled water in a tin bucket on the clay stove and carried it on her head to the upper floor over and over without rest. Before long, the story of the tumbling, acrobatic baby made me forget to ask more questions. I spent hours smiling and dreaming, imagining what this naughty boy would look like, the one who'd started playing tricks even before coming into the world. I wished that Old Lella, Lella Jnayna's mother-in-law, would let me come into the room to look at the baby wherever he was, since he was refusing to come out. But the door was covered with a colorful woolen rug that my mother had hung with thick nails on the frame, hiding the secrets of the dark labor room from the eyes of the curious children of the three sisters-in-law living in the big house.

Shortly before evening, when the laboring woman was exhausted by the fits of screaming that had become more and more frequent, the mind of the Jewish midwife came up with a genius solution. She saw me spying by the door whenever the rug shifted, as people brought in water or left the room. I heard her saying to Old Lella in a happy tone, as if she'd just found the key to salvation, "No one can help but this little black girl, Zina's daughter."

Suddenly, a sturdy hand pulled me into the room, and I was confronted with the frightening scene. Lella Jnayna was sitting on a strange wooden chair with a hole in the middle. Her legs were open, and she was bent so far over that her head was almost touching the midwife's chest. The midwife was sitting in front of her on a normal chair, her hands exploring under the chair with the hole, dealing with something, I didn't know what. Under the midwife's chair, I noticed a pottery dish with some things that you wouldn't expect to find together: a nail, a red chili pepper, a candle, a match box, a small knife, a red thread, and a small container that seemed to have either cumin or caraway seeds in it. There was something burning in the *kanoun* next to the door; I recognized the scent of lavender. Lella Jnayna's head was wet with sweat, her eyes bulged from the pain, and her face was swollen. Her older sister-in-law sat behind her with her hands stretched out, holding Lella Jnayna's belly and gently pulling her backwards, praying continuously: "Help her, God; help her, Prophet Mohammed; help her, our saints."

The midwife explained her decision to Old Lella as I stood shyly between them. "Lella Jnayna is under the influence of the evil eye, and no one can help better than black children to get rid of the evil."

She added, forcing me to kneel down by the chair with the hole, "With God's help, their blackness attracts the evil eye, and it will be hurled into them and not into you, so the victim of envy will be safe."

The older sister-in-law looked sad. She was a kind woman, and she was hurt to be the target of this indirect accusation. But Old Lella ignored her and asked me to put my hands next to the midwife's under the hole in the chair to receive the newborn. I did as I was told, even though I was disgusted by the blood collecting in the container under the seat. Lella Jnayna's screaming was getting more frequent and stronger. Her face was contorted, she was sweating heavily, and her legs were trembling in a scary way. Before long, I saw a small bloody foot. When the midwife gently pulled it, the full body of a boy, who looked like a skinned rabbit, his little clenched fists flailing, slipped out. As soon as the midwife put her fingers in his throat to clean it from the birth fluids, the newborn's screams rang out through the house, along with the women's ululations of joy. I quickly discovered the secrets of the pottery container, though I didn't see the nail and the chili pepper used for anything—I thought they were probably both used to fight the evil eye. When they failed that day to help with the labor, a black head, my head, was invited in for reinforcement. As for the knife, the midwife cut the umbilical cord with it, then tied the remaining part of the cord with the red thread. The candle was lit with a match from the matchbox and put near the newborn's face for blessing. The women praised his white skin that resembled the candle wax and prayed for him to stay in the light as long as he lived. Then Lella Jnayna chewed the cumin seeds into a paste and spread it on his face so he would grow up to be handsome and loved. He wasn't swaddled until Sidi Othman read a prayer in his ear, exhorting him to make his bloodline proud.

As God is our witness, Sidi Mohsen was a good, hardworking boy and has been a source of happiness to his family ever since he was born. On the day of his birth, Old Sidi, his grandfather, put a banknote in my hand: I still remember the sound of its rustle and the sparkle in my mother's eyes when she grabbed it from me to hide it in her blouse, great joy on her face. Ever since that day, Sidi Mohsen has been the apple of my eye. When he was just a year old, I would carry him around on my back as I helped my mother clean the house. When he was old enough to distinguish tastes, I started hiding whatever morsels of tasty food I could find that I thought he might like. I walked in front of him the day he was circumcised to keep the evil eye away. Sidi Othman put a red chechia like his on my head to make sure the eye was deceived. I cried with him that day, for just as long as he did, until the pain faded away and the wound healed.

To be honest with you, most of my crying that day was over my mother, who had died two days before the circumcision. But the Ennaifer family didn't temper their celebration at all, as if it was just an animal that had died. No one had paid attention to her pain over the previous two months. Her tortured face hadn't gone yellow or green but remained a brilliant black, proud of its blackness, defying her illness. Her energy waned a bit, so I started helping her take care of the big house chores that, for the first time, seemed too much for her. My two older sisters, Yakouta and Selma, were still with us then, before destiny scattered them: one to the home of her husband, a porter at the harbor, and the other to the psychiatric department at the Hôpital Sadiki. We shared the work without complaining as Old Lella whipped us with her non-stop orders and met our great efforts with frowns and dissatisfaction. And then, one day, my mother woke up and found her legs could no longer carry her. Whenever she tried to stand, she would fall down. If she tried to sit up, she felt dizzy, so she lay back down on her small bed on the straw mat in our shared room. She complained about an unbearable pain in one of her breasts, where a tumor the size of a ripe apricot had appeared, and then the pain spread all over her body, just as it's spreading in mine now. May God keep you healthy, Lella Zbaida. She hid her pain during the day, but at night when we went to bed, the pain became unbearable, and she couldn't suppress the moaning; her groans became more frequent, and she would toss and turn as if she were lying on embers. We couldn't sleep at night, and we stayed like that until morning, feeling helpless and speechless. It's astounding that none of the family's senior members thought to call the doctor or take her to the hospital. The preparations for Sidi Mohsen's circumcision were in full swing, so I guess no one paid attention to the sick maid lying in her corner, so long as her daughters took care of the house. One night, after many painful nights, we thought that God had heard our prayers and had pity on us; we became certain that she was getting better and would be healed soon, and we rejoiced for God's mercy. That night, our mother's tossing and turning calmed down until it stopped, her moaning quieted until it faded away. She seemed to us to be enjoying a good night's sleep, and her pain had been transformed into rest and serenity. This was the rest of death, and we were so young that we didn't know the tragedy awaiting us in the morning. My two sisters left the room before me to prepare the dough and bake. I didn't want to wake my mother before bringing her some warm bread with olive oil, as usual. She'd been refusing to eat for days, but I assumed that morning that her calmness during the night was a sign of solace. I even added some dates, which I'd kept hidden for Sidi Mohsen under a bowl in the kitchen. She was lying on her side facing the wall, and when she didn't answer me, I gently shook one of her feet, and the coldness of the corpse seeped into my hand. I had never believed she was dying. Does anyone believe that their mother is dying? Especially if that mother is in the prime of her life and able to grab up a big ram in a single swoop to hang it and skin it? If I forget everything else in my life, Lella Zbaida, I will never forget the Old Lella's response when I ran to her that morning to tell her about the tragedy. She was in front of a mirror, lining her eyes with kohl from a jar Old Sidi had brought back with him from his last trip to Hejaz. I said, between my sobs, "Lella, my mother died."

She looked at my reflection in the mirror in horror and threw the kohl jar onto the marble tabletop in front of her, where it broke into pieces, scattering the black powder. Then she said, wringing her hands, "She died? This is just what I need. Couldn't you have lingered a day or two, Zina? Just two days, until after the circumcision of Othman's son?"

Sidi Mohsen cried with me that day, and I felt for him. The coffin left the Ennaifers' house without anyone walking behind it. My middle sister Yakouta, who had started showing the precursors of insanity at around this time, started chattering away unintelligibly, moving her head in all directions as if she were possessed. My older sister Selma wept patiently, putting her arms around me so I wouldn't run in the street behind the coffin. Sidi Mohsen didn't see the departure of the corpse at noon because he hadn't yet returned from Quranic school. When he found out what had happened after he got back and saw my grief, he started wiping away my tears with his small hand until he got tired, and then he started crying, and I didn't know how to comfort him.

With the passing of my mother, Yakouta's insanity, and Selma's marriage, Sidi Mohsen became my entire family. When he decided at the dawn of his youth to rebel against his father Sidi Othman and leave for Germany, all the family members shunned him like a mangy camel, so I became his entire family, as well. Lella Jnayna's heart hardened against him, so she didn't help prepare his luggage and didn't help him with provisions or money. I gave him everything I had, and I didn't have much, apart from what Lella Jnayna had given me herself, during the many years I spent working for her and her mother-in-law before her. No one understood the secret of his stubbornness and his insistence on going to Germany but me. He hadn't told anyone about his story with Katarina, which happened when he was a young man of not even twenty.

II

Sidi Mohsen met Katarina on the beach of Hammam Lif in the aftermath of the Great War. She was a beautiful fifteen-year-old girl. She'd been born in a city called Strazbourch or Strasboorgh or something similar, the daughter of a French father and a German mother. Sidi Mohsen told me her story a dozen times until I had memorized it. He said that she fled with her mother and younger brother to Tunis during the war to live temporarily with her uncle, one of the French settlers in the region of Béja.

It was in these circumstances that Sidi Mohsen met Katarina at Hammam Lif. We were in the summer house (which you're familiar with) for the holidays, and the house next to ours was owned by the Bernaz family. They didn't come down that summer, so they rented it to some settlers. Life's coincidences decided that the settler who rented the house that summer would be Katarina's uncle, and that the window of her room on the top floor would face Sidi Mohsen's. Because Sidi Othman didn't permit the female members of the family to walk on the beach during the day and didn't allow them to see the sea up close—or, that is, only once or twice and only at night—Sidi Mohsen and Sidi Mhammed had gotten used to going to the beach with the neighbors' boys early in the morning. The change of the residents that year didn't stop them from knocking insistently on the door, so Katarina came out to them in her pajamas. At her uncle's farm in Béja, she had gotten used to being around Tunisian workers who didn't know French (except for a few words like *bonjour* and *merci*), so she spoke to them harshly. She didn't expect Sidi Mohsen to understand and answer her angrily in correct French.

Sidi Mohsen said that she followed him to the beach and started apologizing to him. When he ignored her and snubbed her, she started crying tears of pain and regret, but he paid her no mind. That evening, a stone flew through his open window, landing a few inches away from his head. It was attached by a thread to a jasmine *machmoum*. When he looked up in anger mixed with amazement, he found her standing at her window, cheerfully waving at him. He said to her, hiding his smile, "You almost broke my head, you reckless girl."

She answered him in a serious tone, "The head that doesn't understand deserves to be broken."

That night, they continued their conversation on the corniche. Sidi Mohsen bought her a paper cone full of roasted chestnuts from one of the street vendors who crowded the corniche that time of the year. He walked with her on the beach, as she held his hand and told him the details of their trip to Tunisia and her temporary life in Béja. She was sad but hiding her sadness with loud laughter and forced joy. When Sidi Mohsen asked her about her father's fate at the end of the war and the victory of France, she hid her face in his chest and burst into tears. She told him that the French army found her father in one of the camps where the Germans put the war prisoners, but they didn't see traces of torture on him like the rest of them. Nor was he emaciated, like the prisoners of Germany everywhere. Before he was released with the other prisoners, some of them denounced him as a secret agent for the Germans who had translated the confessions of prisoners and some of the secret documents they'd found. So one of the French officers executed him by firing squad, in front of the prisoners in the camp and without a trial. When the news reached her, Katarina's mother decided she would never again set foot in the land where her husband had been executed. She started contacting her family in Germany, planning for her final return there with her daughter and son.

Sidi Mohsen didn't tell me how far his relationship with Katarina had progressed until he became depressed when the summer ended and she went back to Béja, then, a few months later, to Berlin. But I'd become aware, more than once that summer, of him opening the summer house door after silence had fallen, when the family was fast asleep. She would tiptoe up to his room on the top floor and not leave until dawn. I would stay awake all night, waiting for her to leave safely and fearing that Sidi Othman or someone else from the family would notice her presence and turn the whole thing into a catastrophe. They exchanged letters for a year or more after her departure for Berlin. Sidi Mohsen was a student in his last year at lycée. He would be consumed by longing if her letter was late, and he would stop eating and drinking. Then I would get mad at him and start cursing her, so he would put his hand over my mouth, pleading, and say, "If you'd ever been in love, Khaddouj, it wouldn't be so easy for you to curse my beloved in front of me."

I would swallow the lump in my throat and keep myself busy with errands so he couldn't see the tears in my eyes. Indeed I hadn't been in love yet, Lella Zbaida, but I would come to know love after your marriage to Sidi Mohsen, and I would be silently burned by its fire. I can forgive Sidi Mohsen, who defied his family and chose to study in Germany to see Katarina, and I can forgive you too, after seeing what the love of that man who wrote the letter, Si Tahar Haddad, did to you.

III

Sidi Mohsen told me about the man who wrote that letter, Lella Zbaida. When the storm had calmed down, a few months after that horrendous night, he told me, praying for his soul to rest in peace, that he was a respected writer who was ahead of his time. I was so surprised to hear him praising the man who had caused the schism in his family and the destruction of his marriage that at first I thought he was being sarcastic. But he was sincere in what he said, insisting on it despite my astonishment. I asked him whether he knew him personally, and he nodded ambiguously without saying a word, so I chose not to embarrass him with more questions.

Sidi Mohsen is a well whose depths are unknown, Lella Zbaida. You think you know everything about him, and then he surprises you in ways you never expected. You think you're hiding secrets from him, only to find out later that he's known about them all along and never let on. I thought I'd hidden my story with Rezgui until a night came when I was so depressed that I took a rope to the covered part of the courtyard and attached it to the beam where we tie animals for slaughter. I'd decided to hang myself, but then Sidi Mohsen showed up in the darkness and cut the rope with a knife, saying, "Every problem has a solution, Khaddouj, and that son of bitch Rezgui doesn't deserve a single tear from you."

Rezgui was a white man. Yes, and don't be surprised. It's possible for a black woman's heart to beat for a man cut from a different cloth. Love is like water: it doesn't have a color, and no one can escape it. When it flows, it makes its own path wherever it wants. But it usually has a taste and a scent. When it spreads unintentionally, scandalously, without warning, it smells like treachery. God knows its taste is sweet in the beginning but bitter in the end. There's nothing that can match that sweetness, but there's also nothing that can match that pain. Rezgui was treacherous, Lella Zbaida. The agony of his betrayal made me forget the sweetness of being with him. I met him a year after your marriage to Sidi Mohsen, during one of my visits to my sister Yakouta. She was living out her days, after years of homelessness and working in brothels, at the insane asylum in Manouba where Rezgui worked.

IV

By about a year after my mother's passing, Old Lella was losing patience with Yakouta. She had taken to climbing the stairs in the middle of the night and singing out the call to prayer at the top of her lungs as people slept. She would also scream like a slaughtered rooster during the hot afternoon naptime to banish the *qailulah* demons. She poured boiling water on the flowerpots in the courtyard, hoping to kill the seed of evil. She imitated animal noises, talking to you in bleats, growls, and moos. She refused to sleep without a big wooden spoon under her pillow, to protect herself from an attack by the bogeyman, Boushkara, who she said lived on the moon and had threatened to kidnap her and take her with him in his sack, along with the other naughty children and garbage. She did many other things, too. I remember some of them but have forgotten most.

The straw that broke the camel's back was the day she soaked Sidi Othman's burnous with oil and gas because she heard the burnous, and not Sidi Othman, complain that fleas were biting its wool. That day, Old Lella decided she wouldn't let Yakouta spend another night in the house. And since the insane asylum in Manouba didn't yet exist then, at the end of the first decade of the twentieth century, she gave her husband three choices: to take the crazy woman to the police station and have her thrown in jail where she wouldn't get hurt, to send her to the Takiya house that had recently opened its doors to shelter the needy, or else to let her face her fate on Place Halfaouine or Place Sidi Abdeslam or any other square in Tunis. In those places, she could make a living with snake charmers and others selling illusions, like the other fortune tellers. But Old Sidi was merciful and didn't want people to say that the Ennaifer family threw their maids in the streets when they got sick. He found out that the Hôpital Sadiki administration had designated a wing for the insane. He contacted some of his acquaintances working there to ask about the procedures for admittance. Just one day and one night later, they sent two male nurses to our home, men with big bodies like professional wrestlers. After two or three slaps, they bound poor Yakouta in a white gown, her arms pulled tight across her back. They got her out from her hiding place on the roof. She was grunting and screaming like an animal in a way that broke your heart.

Many years passed, and all the while, I believed that Yakouta was residing at the hospital and that—to help her get better—she wasn't allowed visitors. That's what the Old Sidi had said, and later when he died, Sidi Othman said the same thing when I insisted on knowing. Then one day, I saw her as I was passing by Souk El Asr on Rue du Morkadh. Sidi Mohsen's trip to Germany was looming, and the still-angry Lella Jnayna had refused to prepare his luggage. So I started going out to the souqs (with her tacit approval) to shop for him and get him all the important things someone who is traveling abroad and planning to stay for a long time needs. I saw her turning onto El Eklil Alley, which leads to the square. I didn't believe my eyes because she didn't look like the sister I'd known my whole life. Also, she was wearing her *safseri* in a way that was the opposite of decency and modesty. We were separated by the crowds, and decorum prevented me from raising my voice to call after her. I started following her with some difficulty, hoping to discover what was really going on with her. Each time I was about to call out to her, I was unsettled by the behavior I was witnessing, so I told myself to wait, so long as she was still within sight. It seemed to me that she was bumping into some male passersby on purpose before apologizing loudly and touching the men's jackets as if they were good friends. I started thinking the worst, but I asked God for forgiveness for her and for myself and kept following her. It occurred to me that hiding from her at that moment was better than letting her see me.

We reached the area of Bab Jedid and walked a little bit before she turned into one of the alleys and I followed her. I immediately noticed that it was all housing for black people. And it was the strangest thing: some of its female residents stood up by the doors of their homes, calling out to passersby in an obscene way. I was cautiously advancing behind Yakouta, leaving a good distance between us, when an old black woman's voice issued from one of the windows: "Hey black girl! You new here?"

Yakouta raised her head and shouted an obscenity in response. I immediately recognized her voice. She said, after the insult, "Have you lost your mind, old lady? Or maybe you've gone blind. Don't you recognize the black pearl Yakouta bint Zina?"

There, she'd given her name, leaving no room for doubt. She had spoken the name of my virtuous mother in this dirty place. The old woman let out a whore's laugh and answered her with an even more obscene insult, then added, "Shut your nasty mouth. No one's talking to you, skunk! I was talking to the gazelle strutting along behind you."

Yakouta looked back at the gazelle before I could run away. Our eyes met; she recognized me and looked horrified. In a moment, she spun on her heels and started running until I could no longer see her. I stood rooted to the spot, feeling sick to my stomach. How did Yakouta go from the Hôpital Sadiki to Boussadia Alley? What must she have gone through to live like this among prostitutes? I leaned against a wall, thinking about my next step. Should I ask these people about her, to find out where she was living? Or should I go back home and think about the matter in peace? The voice of the old woman forced my hand. She asked, "Who are you, lady? Why did the crazy girl run away when she saw you?"

There, standing under her window, I told her the truth. I said that she was my sister, and that I'd lost her for many years. The old woman motioned for me to come in. I hesitated at first, fearing the place might be dubious, and I might get myself in trouble. But my desperate need for answers encouraged me to be bold and enter.

The place was more than dubious: it was an honest-to-God brothel! You entered via a spiral staircase until you reached a door covered by a red curtain. On the right of the door was an old table covered with a faded cloth, a metal box that looked like a safe, and a pottery vase containing dust-covered fake flowers. Behind the table, the old woman sat wearing a low-cut dress that revealed the tops of her dry breasts. She was looking out the window at the street and exchanging jokes with two girls wearing immodest clothes and scandalous makeup. My heart beat violently against my chest when I heard mutterings, laughter and moans coming from behind the closed doors lining the large, foul-smelling parlor. The old woman introduced me to the two girls, saying, "This young, single woman is the sister of Yakouta the *darwisha*. All the family members are artists. Amazing, isn't it?"

The women started giggling, which made me more nervous. I tried to cut the meeting short by asking my questions all together at the same time. But as soon as I started to speak, a skinny white man with a pale face and yellowish eyes entered the room. He coughed twice, then spit on the floor in a dirty, disrespectful way next to the old woman's desk. I expected her to reprimand him, but instead she stretched out her foot and wiped away the spit with the heel of her shoe, putting on a welcoming, satisfied smile. The man examined the two girls in front of him. They stared back at him insolently, chewing gum and blowing bubbles, then shamelessly running their tongues over their lips. He ignored them and looked at me. I was still wearing my *safseri*. I turned away, pretending to be looking out the window. But I was able to see him out of the corner of my eye, pointing at me and addressing the old woman, saying, "I want that one."

The old woman laughed, winking at him, and said, "That one will be available next time, Si Abdelwahab. She's not ready today."

"Your girls are fakes, Madame. I've been seeing you and the Italian doctor for a month or more now. His medicine hasn't helped, and your girls haven't helped me, either."

"Believe me, Si Abdelwahab, if you listened to me, you'd stop going to the doctors and keep on coming to the ebony beauties of Massouda El Baya, the queen of Boussadia Alley. I swear, your cheeks will become ruddy, your blood will strengthen, and you'll get rid of your illness. This is a proven prescription, and it's well known. But you're impatient, Si Abdelwahab, impatient and quick on the draw. No offense meant, I'm telling you this only because patience is needed in this case, if you want to get better."

A client exiting one of the doors off the parlor interrupted their conversation. He was in his fifties, wearing clothes that gave him an air of solemnity; if you saw him on the street, you would never have guessed that he frequented brothels. He was tottering towards the door, wiping his sweat with a carefully folded handkerchief; he appeared tired. The old lady immediately addressed him, seeking his endorsement for what she had been saying, "Tell him, Si Bashir: aren't my girls a cure for all illnesses?"

The man nodded approvingly at her words before saying out loud, in a voice thickened with alcohol, "Prima. Massouda's girls are *luxe*. Especially that Elgiya, she's an animal."

A mature black woman in a pink nightie came out after him. She started shaking her hands like people do when they're complaining about something tiring. She said, in response to his words but addressing the old woman, "You all need to forget about Elgiya right now. She has sold all her merchandise and closed up shop. That criminal is equal to four clients, Mama Massouda. Make him pay double the price or have him go to someone else next time. What in God's name was that?"

The man's neck swelled in pride. He smiled in satisfaction, closing his eyes. He started swaying towards the exit. When he was close to me, he pinched my nose between his index and middle fingers, saying, "Look how beautiful you are, new girl . . . next time you'll taste Bashir's honey."

He stumbled at the door and would have fallen if he hadn't grabbed the musty red curtain so hard that he almost pulled it down. This was all too much for me, and I couldn't stop myself: I pushed past him and ran down the stairs without looking back.

I hid the story of seeing Yakouta from the family. I kept waiting for the opportunity to go back to the old woman Massouda's brothel. I was sure that she was the only way to get to the truth. Two days later, pretending to be going to the souqs to shop for Sidi Mohsen, I drew aside the red curtain for a second time.

V

I introduced myself to the old woman with a fake name. Or, rather, with my real name that Old Lella had used until she died: Anbra. It means "ambergris," and I've always liked it. My father chose it for me but died before he could use it. But Lella Jnayna never liked it: she had difficulties pronouncing the "r," so she could never say it right, and that made people laugh. After Old Lella passed and Sidi Othman inherited the house, making Lella Jnayna the leader of the family, she decided to rename me. She called me Khaddouj and forced everyone to forget Anbra, as if she never existed. I myself forgot about it until it spontaneously came out of my mouth when Massouda asked me my name. I had meant to lie to her, but the lie was pure truth. Massouda said, offering me a cup of coffee, "Listen, Anbra. Your sister Yakouta was lucky enough to find a new life here. Madame Radhia, the owner of the first-floor brothel, found her in Souk El Salah eating garbage with the rats during the day and sleeping on the threshold of Al Haliq Mosque at night. Your sister was lucky: Madame Radhia had lost most of the girls in her brothel in the 1911 pandemic. One of them got infected by a client and infected the rest of the girls, and they started dropping like flies. Radhia was looking for new girls when she found Yakouta in the shape I just described to you. She dragged her here to our alley like a beast of burden, cleaned her, put new clothes on her, and had her stand at the door. She became the clients' favorite, and they always came back to her. She used to do some funny things that pleased the clients and would say strange things; when the residents of the alley found out about them, they spread the word that she was a *darwisha*. Since white men believe that sleeping with a black woman purifies the blood, Yakouta became a favorite among those looking for both pleasure and healing, thanks to her skin and the crazy things she would say and do."

Zbaida, Yakouta denied that she knew me when I went looking for her at the address Massouda gave me. She pretended that she had never seen me before in front of her madame. She claimed that she was an only child and that she had no siblings. When her denial made me more stubborn and obstinate, the madame called for Zbiba. Suddenly a large glowering man appeared, wearing a short white *jebba* and walking like a debauched woman. He rudely pushed me towards the door, cursing me in the language of old women. When I resisted, he hit me. Suddenly Yakouta changed her mind about knowing me; she jumped at his chest, scratching and biting him, forcing him to withdraw defeated. Then she held my hand and led me down a long hallway with many doors lined up along one side. She talked to me, crying, her tears getting mixed with her snot on the dirty comforter on her bed, which already held the dried traces of other liquids. She said, "I ran away from the hospital after two months. I said to myself, 'Yakouta, dying at the foot of the city walls from hunger and exposure is better for you than dying here slowly of electric shocks.' Can you imagine they were treating us with electricity? I heard them say that as they attached thin wires to our arms and feet, which were strapped to the table with leather belts. Then they would send a burning fire into our bodies that would convulse us and leave behind an indescribable pain throughout our bodies. My share of the electric charge was always stronger than the other inmates'. The nurse always reminded his colleague to make the shock stronger. He said that because of their build, black people feel less pain than white people. They shocked us with the electricity at night. They would come into our rooms with a mobile table that had belts and wires attached. They moved the inmates to it one by one, then put masks over our mouths, tied tightly so our screams didn't reach patients in the other wards. The doctor in charge of our ward, Monsieur Jacques, would join them sometimes to witness our terrible pain and take some notes. But if the nurses were alone with us and feeling sleepy, one of them would hurry his colleague along, saying, 'Shock them and be done with it!'

"How can I explain to you the pain caused by that electric shock? Imagine every part of your body is penetrated by big thick needles that go through skin, flesh, bone, membrane and ligament, and then a demonic hand shakes each of these spikes at the same time for as long as your electrified body is shaking. I truly wanted to die, and I begged God to take me to join my mother. But one day I had an idea: I started hitting my head on the iron bedpost and kept doing it until I started bleeding and passed out. They took me out of the high-security ward for the insane to another ward to stitch up the wound you can see here on my forehead. I waited for the right moment when no one was paying attention, then hid inside a garbage can in a cart that was sitting by one of the back doors. I stayed there for hours, in the heat of the summer sun, surrounded by bandages stained with pus and rotten blood. The smell was so awful that my lungs nearly exploded. When I had lost all hope and was about to leave my hiding place and surrender, I felt the cart move. Shortly after, when I could hear the noise of the street, I jumped out of my hiding place and ran like a crazy person through the shouting pedestrians."

Yakouta said that she spent some time on the street but that she couldn't remember anything about it. She probably felt embarrassed to tell me what she'd done during that time to feed herself, so she chose to just erase it. She also claimed that she couldn't remember how she arrived at Boussadia Alley or how she came to live in this house. She said, avoiding my eyes, "Khala Radhia, the landlady, is a kind woman. She welcomed me into her house among her girls and didn't ask for money in return for my food or lodging. God bless the hands that raised her; the woman is a saint."

I nodded, pretending that I believed her. What was the point of digging into the past? What was done was done. Our ancestors were right when they said there was no sense beating a dead horse. Yakouta asked me, as I was bidding her farewell, to say nothing about our meeting to anyone from the Ennaifer family or to our older sister Selma. As if I needed to be told! Selma had her own problems with her husband and had no time to hear the news of her prostitute sister. As for the Ennaifer family, if they heard about the scandal—well, needless to say, they wouldn't keep a maid who frequented brothels to visit her sister.

My visits to her became more infrequent, until one day when I asked about her at the normal address, I was told that she'd been moved to the insane asylum in Manouba. The kind lady who owned the place told me what had happened on that unforgettable day. "God damn that crazy girl!" she said. "She and her crazy tricks ruined the reputation of this brothel and made me lose half my customers. She tied a Maltese client's wrists together with a scarf, took off all his clothes, and then tied him to the bed. At first, he was into it, thinking it was some new trick of hers—all her clients knew how creative she was. But then she jumped on the bed by his feet and started singing, dancing, and randomly whipping him with his belt. I heard his screams along with her singing and laughter but just figured he was one of those perverts we sometimes get. Some of them like a little pain with their pleasure, so I thought Yakouta must be doing a great job. It didn't occur to me that anything was wrong until the man started screaming louder, asking for help in all the languages he knew. I ran and banged on the door, but she refused to respond. When my girls and I finally got the door open, we saw the weirdest scene. That crazy woman was wearing an unbuttoned white lab coat over her naked body. It was like the ones nurses wear, but it was filthy. God knows where she got it. She had a leather belt in her right hand and a broken chair leg in her left. She waved it in our faces when we tried to untie the man. She was screaming angry nonsense, some French words mixed in there, but all out of order. The only thing we understood was that she wanted us to leave her alone with her patient so she could give him the full dose of medicine and cure him. We would've spent the night at the gendarmerie if the man hadn't been so afraid of the scandal and his reputation that he left without making a fuss. But the fit didn't stop there. As soon as the man left, Yakouta was possessed by a wild bull, or an entire herd of bulls being chased by wolves. She took off the lab coat and started hitting the doors, the walls, and the furniture with the broken chair leg. When the piece of wood broke in her hand, she picked up another chair and attacked anyone in her way. She was foaming at the mouth, with a demonic glow in her eyes. She wounded poor Zbiba in the head when he tried to stop her, then nearly gouged out his eyes. This house is usually so safe and calm, but by then people were screaming, clients coming out of their rooms barefoot and half-dressed, running for the door. Then suddenly everything got quiet. The goddamn woman collapsed all of a sudden, like froth on the surface of boiling milk when you take it off the heat. She stared at our terrified faces and the destruction around her and said, all innocence, 'What happened? Why are you staring at me?'"

The brothel owner said she called the police, and they took Yakouta away, carrying her out like a sack after she pretended to have lost the ability to stand or speak. Later, she learned that they'd transferred Yakouta to a new hospital in the suburb of Manouba, built to accommodate insane people. That's where my story with Rezgui started.

VI

I hesitated for a long time before visiting Yakouta in the hospital; her words about the electrotherapy remained in my memory like a mill, grinding my nerves whenever I thought about her. I was afraid that if I visited, she would talk about her pain again, and I would be unable to save her from it, and then guilt would kill me, the guilt of leaving her to her executioners and going back to where I came from. I told Sidi Mohsen about the hospital without telling him anything about her past in Boussadia Alley. He was a new groom, enjoying the pleasures of married life, but that news ruined everything for him, and he couldn't feel better until he got me into a tram car to Manouba to check on Yakouta.

Rezgui met me at the door. He was leaning against the outer wall, smoking a cigarette and talking to the guard. I didn't know who I should talk to or who I should ask for permission to enter. I said, stuttering, after greeting them, "I've come to visit my sister. Her name is—"

Rezgui interrupted with a sly smile on his face, "Yakouta, the girl from Boussadia Alley."

His words seemed to hold an unmistakable accusation,

directed at me, and I was startled. I must have flushed, because he continued, laughing, "Don't think me too clever: we only have one ebony beauty like you, and her name's Yakouta. Isn't that who you're asking about?"

I nodded, speechless, so he raised his fist as if celebrating a victory, still laughing. The guard, however, said in a cold tone, not looking me in the eye, "The Negro woman isn't permitted visitors. She's agitated and dangerous."

To be honest with you, Lella Zbaida, I was glad they didn't let me visit her. My fear of seeing her in a sad situation had been eating me up the whole way there as the tram passed farms and fields on its way to the faraway suburb. If not for Sidi Mohsen, I would have turned back before reaching the hospital. So I left as soon as the guard said that no visitors were allowed, as if he had taken a very heavy burden off of my shoulders. But I had barely gotten two steps away from the building when Rezgui started calling out to me, "Hey, lady!" I pretended not to hear him and walked quickly towards the other side of the street, but he caught up with me. He said, "Don't worry about the doorman. Rezgui will take you wherever you want to go. Come with me."

I returned unwillingly, feeling that I had no choice. Suddenly the doorman had disappeared, and Rezgui didn't need to negotiate with him. It took me years after this to realize that this was a ploy they'd come up with together to trick naive women like me. I walked behind him down a long, dark hallway and noticed that he was purposefully slowing down to keep pace with me. I snuck a look at him. There were traces of old vitiligo that stained his natural white color with whiter spots. His nose was curved like an eagle's beak. He wasn't ugly, though. His laughter revealed straight, clean teeth, and above them was a short, elegant mustache. He tried to chat with me, but I kept giving him short answers until he gave up and stopped talking to me. He said, "Do you work?" I said, "Yes." "With Yakouta?" "No." "In another place?" "No." "Is it a secret?" "No." "Am I bothering you with my questions?" " . . . " "Okay, well at least tell me your name."

When I told him my name, Lella Zbaida, he said in a singsongy tone, "Lella Khaddouj." It was the first time in my life I had heard my name preceded by the word "Lella." No one before Rezgui and no one after him ever called me that. My name at that moment seemed to be prestigious, as if it belonged to a queen. I liked the man who pronounced my name that way. I immediately relaxed and smiled back at him, mirroring his generous smiles. Human beings so naturally look up to those who treat them well. He offered me a wicker chair in a narrow storage space at the end of the hall. In one of the corners were buckets stacked on top of each other, cloths, brooms, and cleaning solutions. He explained that the official visiting hours hadn't started yet, so I'd have to wait for the doctors and nurses to leave the ward and finish their morning inspection before he could take me to Yakouta. As he explained the way the hospital worked, he stood behind a small wooden workbench with a kerosene stove on it, a few pots for cooking, and glass jars filled with various herbs and spices of different colors. He started working the stove until he had gotten it lit, then put a teapot on top of it. He filled it with water then added some loose-leaf black tea and sugar. He had some quick business to take care of, so he asked me to keep an eye on the tea until he came back. Was it the sweet smell that came from the teapot when the water started boiling, or the organized cleaning tools that made the place feel somehow familiar? Or was it Rezgui's smile, when he returned carrying hot *tabouna* bread and fresh cheese? Or maybe it was all of that put together that made me feel so comfortable, calm, and safe that I didn't feel the time passing. I spent two hours talking with Rezgui, eating bread and cheese, and drinking tea with mint, before he decided to take me to Yakouta's room.

Her situation wasn't as bad as I'd feared. She wasn't agitated or dangerous, as the doorman had said. I found her sitting cross-legged on a clean bed in a shared room. She was deep in contemplation of a dark spot on the blanket and rubbing it with her ring finger in a nonstop, compulsive movement. She raised her eyes, looking through me, when I called her. She didn't react and remained calm, as if seeing me for the first time. Rezgui explained to me that she was under the effects of a medicine that put insane people into a middle stage between sleep and waking. I checked her wrists and her ankles, searching for the marks of restraints, but I didn't see anything unusual. I hugged her and kissed her, but she didn't react. She just kept moving her finger around and around on the blanket. Tears spilled from my eyes as I observed her coldness and absence from the world. Before I knew it, I found myself back in the wicker chair and narrow storage room, crying silently while Rezgui patted my cheek, comforting "Lella Khaddouj, whose tears are spoiling the beauty of her eyes."

Two weeks later, I found myself getting ready to go to Manouba again. I purposefully arrived a long time before visiting hours, but Rezgui wasn't at the door. I regretted coming and couldn't approach the guard, who was sitting as usual on his three-legged throne, occupied with whittling a piece of cork with a knife. But he saw me hesitating there in my *safseri,* a veil covering my face, and the sly man knew who I was and asked me to come closer. He winked, pointing at the door, and said, "Come in, Lella Khaddouj. Si Rezgui is waiting for you."

You might think that I am stupid, Lella Zbaida, but hearing that filled me with great pride. I raised my head high, straightened up, and swaggered inside the building, searching for the hallway leading to the storage room with its warm, pleasant atmosphere. It was a cold winter day in February, and the shy rays of sun shone through heavy black clouds. I found Rezgui at the end of the hallway, carrying a bucket and a cloth, busy cleaning the floor. He became flustered when he saw me and started drying his hands by rubbing them on his long gray apron. Words of welcome spilled from his tongue. His vitiligo seemed less pronounced this time. I ran my fingers over the traces of smallpox on my face, praying that God would hide them from his eyes, which were scanning my body with admiration but also respect, or at least that's what I thought.

He opened the storage room and asked me to make myself at home while I waited; he would finish his work and join me shortly. I hung my *safseri* on a hook behind the door. There was a worn-out woolen *burnous* hanging from the hook; its wool was tattered, and it had the smell of old sweat. I cleared the workbench of the breadcrumbs and olive pits scattered here and there. There was a paper bag with homemade harissa in it and another bag with eight eggs. I lit the stove and took one of the tin pots arranged on the workbench. I put the pot on the stove and added some oil that, from its smell, I recognized as cheap vegetable oil. I couldn't find any garlic, so I put extra harissa in the oil and mixed it with a little bit of water. I started smelling the bottles of spices until I found the caraway. When the harissa on the heat became thick, I put in four eggs and a sprinkle of salt and black pepper. I mixed it with a long wooden spoon hanging from a nail on the wall next to the workbench. The smell of the shakshuka spread in the small storage room, even more appetizing than the smell of grilled lamb or couscous. I felt an indescribable joy, listening to it as it bubbled. This might sound strange, Lella Zbaida, but you probably don't know that Lella Jnayna forbade me, after the death of Old Lella, from entering her kitchen and cooking her food. She said she detested the taste of food cooked by maids. So that short time at the stove in Rezgui's kitchen was a source of indescribable pleasure that gave me the illusion that I truly was Lella Khaddouj, taking care of her own house as she wished.

Rezgui came back just as I was putting the shakshuka into a deep dish. He started sniffing the air with joy, closing his eyes, his face tilted towards the ceiling. It occurred to him that we needed bread, so he took his burnous from behind the door—carefully, so my *safseri* wouldn't fall—and left. He came back quickly, carrying fresh flatbread wrapped in newspaper. He told me, shaking the drops of rain from his chechia and his thick, smooth hair, that it had started raining very hard in the suburb. He brought two extra chairs from the room next door. He sat on one of them and put the shakshuka dish on the other, between us. This was the most delicious meal I ever ate, Lella Zbaida. As Rezgui soaked his bread in the shakshuka sauce and our fingers touched, I felt a tingle of pleasure everywhere. To this day, the taste of harissa with eggs reminds me of that feast in the cleaning supplies storage room nineteen years ago.

The day got very dark in Manouba, even though it wasn't yet noon. Black clouds gathered and spread like a thick cover over the ground, like a piece of darkness that had gotten lost on its way into the night. It rained so hard that it became hard to see, and the water rose up to knee-level. The hospital medical staff left early, deviating from their normal schedule, hurrying to get home before the roads were closed. I only got to spend fifteen minutes with Yakouta before Rezgui came in, rushing me to leave. He told me people were saying that an old man and his donkey had drowned when Wadi Chafro suddenly flooded and swept them away. Leaving the building in that storm was an unnecessary risk, so I listened to Rezgui's advice when he proposed that I wait until the weather got better.

I went back with him to the storage room. The atmosphere was charged with a sweet electricity that the water murmuring in the gutters and the thunder shaking the walls only intensified. The room itself was completely silent, apart from the water simmering in the teapot, a gargle that started weak and intermittent but then became violent and continuous. There were embers of burning desire in my chest, and another sensation that mimicked that water—a bubbling or gargling. I don't know how Rezgui came to be standing behind me nor how he put his hands on my breasts, rubbing them softly at first, and then with an almost violent force. I was sitting on the wicker chair, watching with dreamy eyes as the spark of the stove grew bigger. I felt its flame burning inside my belly as Rezgui kept on massaging and rubbing, moaning deeply and exciting me. I held his hands to move them away from my chest, but he moved around to face me without releasing my hands from his. He pulled me to him, and I embraced him with a violence my body had stored up for forty years without ever being touched by a man. He quickly pushed me away and pulled a long broom from the corner. He angled its handle under the doorknob, making it a barricade between us and prying eyes. The rain outside had become a torrent flowing with the force of my desire. But I refrained. I tried to extract myself from his arms, but he started whispering in my ears, his voice scratchy with lust, "I love you, Lella Khaddouj. I love you, and my intentions are honorable."

My resistance collapsed like the flame of a candle taken outside on a stormy day. Rezgui pushed me with his body from behind until I reached the bench. He pressed his elbow into the small of my back until I was bent over so far my cheek almost touched the leftover shakshuka and breadcrumbs in the empty dish. He didn't let me go until the tea had boiled over. Its boiling had the taste of resting after tension and healing after sickness. The storm had also calmed down, and the sky held back its water. I left him after a long, deep kiss, and we set a date to meet again soon.

This situation continued for two years, Lella Zbaida. I ran to him whenever I missed him and could get permission from Lella Jnayna to leave the house. The truth is that Luiza unwittingly helped me with all this. Her outings to accompany Sidi Mohsen and you to parties and concerts made Lella Jnayna too embarrassed to keep me from my sick sister. There was no comparison between the theater Luiza went to and the insane asylum I wanted permission to visit. The worst part, Lella Zbaida, is that Yakouta died and was buried, and I didn't even know it. I didn't find out for six months, even though I kept visiting the hospital. I had slowly given up on visiting her, since she would just ignore me and treat me coldly. And I can't deny that I begrudged her that bit of precious time that I preferred to spend in the storage room with Rezgui. I made do with asking him how she was doing, and he hid the news of her passing from me to make sure I kept visiting him. Then the ultimate, inescapable thing happened. My period stopped, and I became so sick to my stomach every morning that I thought I would vomit all my guts out. I spoke with Rezgui, who already seemed less excited to see me and had begun to treat me coldly. I told him I was pregnant and he had to keep his promise to marry me. Do you know what he told me, Zbaida? He guffawed and stared at me with contempt: "You want me to marry a deflowered black spinster from Boussadia Alley? A woman whose rotten smell is only matched by her bad breath—do you really wish me luck *that* bad?"

I thought he was joking. With time, I'd uncovered his more unpleasant characteristics, but love is blind and deaf. But no, he escorted me to the door, saying seriously, "Listen up, Whatever-Your-Name-Is. There's nothing left for you here. Your sister died a long time ago, so why are you still visiting the hospital? If you're hoping I'll claim your bastard, you're both deluded and stupid. Look for a father for your fetus among your customers at the brothel. Me, I'm a respectable man with a wife and kids."

He walked me to the outer door, and I trailed behind him feeling lost and not knowing where to put my feet. When we reached the doorman, Rezgui told him, "This Negro woman's sister is dead. Don't let her in anymore."

VII

Had the baby lived, Lella Zbaida, he would've been your son Sidi Mohammed Habib's age today. But Sidi Mohsen, when he saved me from the rope I'd tied in the entrance hall to hang myself, gave me two pills wrapped in newspaper and told me to take them both on an empty stomach. I suffered severe bleeding the next day. I didn't tell anyone about it and pretended to be suffering from a stomachache, and Sidi Mohsen took me to the hospital, where the midwife did what was necessary. He told me that he'd been in contact with the hospital administration in Manouba and had inquired about Yakouta from time to time, as he intended to bring her back as soon as her condition stabilized. The administration called him at work one day to inform him of the patient's death and consult him on the burial procedures. I happened to be with Rezgui that day and had come back buoyant and joyful. He asked me, dumbfounded, whether I had seen Yakouta, and I told him that she'd sent him her best regards. He thought there must be a mix-up in the names, so he called the administration, but they confirmed the news and sent him the forensic report. Then he suspected that I must be visiting somewhere other than the hospital. He followed me one day from afar until he became sure of my destination. When he asked the doorman about me, the man said, "How does a respectable gentleman like you know these prostitutes? That's the girlfriend of a cleaner who works here. His name is Rezgui. She visits him from time to time." Sidi Mohsen didn't want to confront me with what he'd learned. He said to himself, "Khaddouj is not a child. She's a mature woman in her forties, and she knows how to differentiate bad from good and evil from virtue. She's probably found the man who'll marry her and make her lady of the house." He waited for me to open up to him, until he found me hanging the rope in the entrance hall and understood everything.

I still remember Rezgui to this day, Lella Zbaida. I cry when I remember his cruelty, but then I think about you, so I dry my tears and put on makeup. I comfort myself when I remember what falling in love with that Tahar Haddad did to you. I scold myself. "You should be ashamed," I say. And, "What have you lost compared to what your Lella Zbaida lost? Your simple scratch is nothing compared to her mortal wound." I also get ashamed of myself when I see Sidi Mohsen's patience. I know that he loves you, Lella Zbaida, but he's stubborn. His wound is still bleeding to this day. The blood spilled on the courtyard marble that fateful night was his blood, too. Your mother, Lella Bashira, God bless her soul, understood everything. But you didn't. You never understood anything, Lella Zbaida.

6
The Tale of Lella Bashira
(*Rue El Azzafine, Fall 1949*)

I

Blaming someone for something that has already happened is a heresy, Mohsen son of Jnayna. Whatever God has planned for us will happen, and "what has been written on the forehead, the eye must see." I'm not blaming you: who are you to stop fate or bring about the future? What is written is chasing us, and it will catch us. There's no escape from it, even in the belly of a whale.

Who would have thought that your father-in-law, Si Ali, would wake up from his coma after the doctor gave up on him and sent him home to die? God proved him wrong! And who would've believed that then he would sit up, walk on his own two feet, groom himself and put on cologne, and dress in his best clothes—only to collapse at people's feet at the mosque the night of your brother's engagement, and get carried home on a stretcher? So little separates life and the afterlife! In the blink of an eye, your father-in-law was gone, Mohsen, as if he'd never existed. God does what He wants, even in the short time between the *Maghreb* and *Isha* prayers. And here I am, your mother-in-law, Bashira Djellouli, walking in his footsteps and getting ready to meet him. Our fates have been written in heaven, ben Ennaifer, and we're following them on Earth whether we like it or not.

There's no point in regretting anything now, Mohsen. You said what you said, and the word that leaves the mouth can never be put back, even if you pay a fortune. But I wish you'd never told me. I wish you'd just left me alone, living out my days happily, believing that whoever could cross the sea, could cross the lake. But still, I don't blame you. Our ancestors were right when they talked about the one "you think is Moses who's actually a pharaoh." I don't want anything from you, after what you told me, except for you to promise me, ben Jnayna, that you'll keep your despicable act a secret and never let Zbaida know about it. Let her enjoy her ignorance and feel protected from tragedy, despite what happened.

My poor, poor daughter. Some proverbs sound like they were made for her. "How good and beautiful I am, but luck is not for me." It's as if enmity and hatred have stood between her and good fortune ever since she was born. As a child, the unlucky girl caught every imaginable illness, and she was the one, out of all her friends, who fell down on every playground. Isn't it a sign of her bad luck, what happened to her in your house? Otherwise, why all the fuss about a letter from a dead man, whose relationship with her never went beyond books and writing? Does this matter deserve all that spilled blood, the broken body, the heinous acts?

Was it easy for you, Mohsen, to treat your wife like that? It seems the price of silk is so low now it's being used to clean pots, the day Ennaifer's son has come to tell me about his championship title in betrayal and backstabbing. Gone long and come back all wrong. May God protect those who care. Did you consider my daughter, the apple of my eye? Did you think it through before doing the unimaginable? You betrayed the woman who chose you over her family that fateful night, who closed her ears to the entreaties of her mother and father, who decided to disobey them, against God's teachings. Even though they threatened to disown her if she stayed with you, if she didn't immediately leave that disgraceful house where your father, Othman Ennaifer, raised his cane to her.

My daughter remained humiliated in your house all these years, after she allowed her family ties to be cut to please you. She accepted a life of misery with your family, but that wasn't enough for you. When I kept her son Mohammed Habib in my house, hoping to force her to visit us to take him back, it didn't occur to me that she would choose the husband over the son. She left the boy with us for five years. If I hadn't feared that he would reject her and she would reject him, the boy would've remained at the Rassaa family home forever, without having anything to do with the Ennaifers at all, except his name on his ID once he grew up.

II

After I returned Mohammed Habib to you, his grandfather Si Ali refused to talk to me for a month or more. I would speak sweetly to him, and he would turn his face away. I would put my hand on his shoulder affectionately, and he would jerk away as if stung by a scorpion. He was punishing me with this malevolent silent treatment for hiding the matter from him. I was sure that he would flatly refuse if consulted, so I didn't tell him. I seized the opportunity of his trip to El Kef, where he went with a delegation of statesmen on the orders of the prime minister, Hédi Lakhoua. There were violent protests in the Sahel and El Kef regions, protesting the arrest of some resistance fighters. There were riots, led by some young people like Bahi Ladgham and his comrades. Si Ali angrily informed me that France was threatening Ahmed Pasha Bey with retaliatory measures if he didn't cooperate with the French Resident-General to calm the people and put down the uprisings. So he delegated some trustworthy statesmen to negotiate with the protesters and placate them. Si Ali was a member of that delegation, even though he hated to be included. He was a supporter of the secret resistance, which I'm sure you're aware of, especially after his son Mahdi became a member.

Your father-in-law was absent for two days, during which time I sent some of my maids to inform you that I was returning the boy to his mother. The decision wasn't easy, as Mohammed Habib had become, over the years, a piece of me and the joy of the house. But I was afraid of the days that would come and snatch the joy away, leaving only endless heartache. People are candles in the wind. What if, God forbid, the boy got sick and died? What if his mother suddenly passed away before she could hug him? What if I myself, his grandmother, passed away and left the boy to an old widower and two motherless young men? Those dark ideas kept spoiling the happy moments with my baby, your son Mohammed Habib, who knew no other mother than Mama Bashira and no father but Baba Ali.

In just a few months after his arrival, when I had sent Luiza back and kept him, your son became the center of everything in this house, to the point that I expected my sons Mahdi and Bakkar to be jealous of him. But his uncles became more attached to him over time and competed for his attention. And God knows, an uncle is practically a father for his nephew. Mahdi was spending most of the year in Paris, studying at medical school, but when he came back home during his breaks, it was never without something in his hand for the pampered boy. He would bring him almond candy, sesame candy soaked in honey from the Ouled Mezab Algerian store, or date cake that was as good as homemade from Aammi Youssef's bakery, or a half-melted gelato cone from Franco's gelato cart on Rue de Paris. Or sometimes it would be a small bag of walnuts, pistachios, and almonds, or fried chickpeas with raisins and sun-dried figs from the shops of Souk El Fekka or Souk El Grana. As for Si Ali, during the days of Eid al-Adha or Eid al-Fitr, he would not come home without stopping by the souk in La Kasbah to get something for Mohammed Habib—even before his nine-year-old son Bakkar—gifts like copper swords, wooden guns, leather drums, reed flutes, rocking horses, spinning tops of various sizes, multicolored marbles, and other toys, both cheap and expensive. The truth is that the love and joy Mohammed Habib spread in the house were a fair compensation for the painful void that the rift with Zbaida left. No one is dearer than children except grandchildren.

But I was overcome by worry about the future when the whooping cough almost took the boy from us in the beginning of his fourth year. He suffered three nights in a row with diarrhea and two nights of fever that rose water compresses on his forehead failed to bring down. I tried a traditional concoction, sweetened with sugar, and flax seed poultices on his chest; nothing helped. I didn't think the medicine the Jewish doctor prescribed for him was working either; every time he started coughing, it would get so bad that he seemed about to vomit up his intestines along with his saliva. I gave him a drink made of soaked herbs that some knowledgeable people at Souk El Blat, where medicinal plants are sold, told Si Ali about. I also applied a poultice of carob leaves to his chest. But the lukewarm drinks I forced him to swallow didn't stay in his stomach for long; as soon as the coughing got bad again, he would be hit by sudden cramps and vomit them back up. I also put hot cups on his back to suck out the bad blood, and made him gargle whale oil before breakfast, to wash his lungs from phlegm—none of it worked.

By the end of the third day, an old woman gave us the solution. She knocked on our door while Si Ali was at the mosque for the afternoon prayer, so Ouisha, our deaf maid, opened the door for her. The old woman was carrying a dirty and tattered basket, and on her shoulder she had a thick black cloth bag similar to the ones carried by fortune tellers. Since Ouisha knew that Si Ali couldn't abide tricksters entering his house, she rushed to kick her out, making her usual short, shocked screams and gesturing with her head and hands towards the street. However, the old lady pretended to be stupid, as if she didn't understand, and raised her voice sweetly as she pushed Ouisha aside and walked into the entrance hall, calling to the people who lived in the house. I was sitting next to Mohammed Habib, checking the rose water compress on his forehead. I hadn't left his side since morning; he'd started the day making scary phlegmy sounds in his throat every time he exhaled, and the fever had left him exhausted. I called him and shook him, but he didn't open his eyes and didn't moan, as if he were slowly sinking into a deep, quiet pit with no exit. I ran to the entrance hall when I heard the old woman calling. I asked her to open her bag and read the sand. I needed some certainty, any certainty, even if it came from a swindler. A drowning man will cling to a straw, and a hungry man is allowed to eat carrion.

That day, the old woman knitted her brows, her wrinkled forehead covered completely with blue Amazighi tattoos. She put a pile of sand on a piece of dirty yellowish cloth and started moving a small, crooked olive wood stick on it. She said, moving her eyes between the wavy lines of sand and my eyes swollen from crying and staying up late taking care of the sick child, "The dear one is going down into a hole."

I hit my face with my hands as if I had just received news of the passing of a loved one. The old lady understood that the matter was serious, so her stick started moving faster on the sand right and left before she whispered solemnly, pointing with the stick to a small path between two parallel lines, "Unless he takes this path."

Revealing the path required only a big bowl of couscous, left over from our lunch and still warm, with lamb, fried peppers, chickpeas, and boiled local eggs. The old woman put it in her basket while praying for the sick child. Before sunset, I was riding in a carriage, holding your son wrapped in linen cloth, headed towards the shrine of Barrek Jmel outside of Bab El Khadra. The shrine keeper took him from me after I explained to her that he'd been suffering from whooping cough for three days. She put him on his back on a straw mat next to the tomb. She took a black band off the cloth belt around her waist and told me to put it on his eyes. I was disgusted by the sticky texture of the band but had no choice but to obey. Mohamed Habib surrendered to the hands that lifted and lowered him with no complaints, as if he'd put his fate in God's hands. The shrine keeper disappeared for a moment, then came back with a small clay stove attached to a long chain and placed a large knife inside it. She started turning the knife over on the embers until its color changed to purple. She pulled out the knife and slowly approached the shrouded child, reciting Surah Al-Falaq. She gently lifted his chin to reveal his neck. She had already explained the procedure to me in detail, but still a cold shiver went down my spine, and I felt like I was about to faint. My tears were dripping onto his palm, which I had brought close to my face as I spoke to him to comfort him, as much for my comfort as his. The shrine keeper approached his neck with the knife. She said "Bismillah," then pulled the knife twice back and forth. Then she took the band off the boy's face, proclaiming joyfully, "God protect you, my son, the whooping cough has been slaughtered."

Why are you giving me that blank look, Mohsen? The slaughtering wasn't real, of course. It was merely a show that cured your son from his cough. With the blessing of Sidi Barrek Jmel, the fever was gone, and the diarrhea stopped. But the incident left a bruise on me that time couldn't heal. Nightmares haunted me for months. I would see Zbaida in my dreams, kissing Mohammed Habib's forehead while he was, God forbid, wrapped in a shroud. I would hear her crying, beating herself, and addressing the people at the funeral, saying that her mother took her son away and refused to let her see him until he died, far away from her. Then I would see myself, carried by pallbearers towards the cemetery, Mohamed Habib running behind the coffin calling after it. I decided, after much hesitation, to return him to Zbaida. I said to myself, her second son has grown up a bit now, and she's gotten used to her new life. With Luiza's help, she'll be able to take care of two boys who've both outgrown the stage of complete helplessness. But the whisper of emotions is sometimes stronger than the shout of the mind, so I would shake off the idea whenever I took the boy in my arms to play with him or sing him lullabies until he fell asleep. I tried to speak with Si Ali about the matter first. I chose a happy moment on a summer night, as we sat on a thick cushion by the night-blooming jasmine on the eastern side of the house courtyard. I was feeding Mohamed Habib *masfouf* with dates and, testing the waters, asked, "What will we do when Mohsen Ennaifer asks for his son back, and takes him by a court order?"

By then, Mohammed Habib had started playing his favorite game, climbing onto his grandfather's shoulders to pick the sweet-smelling flowers from the tree and scatter them on the heads of the family members sitting below. This game amazed Mahdi and Bakkar, who would exchange winks with something that looked like jealousy. Si Ali had always been conservative in showing his affection to his children; he wouldn't kiss them or pat them on their shoulders, despite his modern style of parenting. But he became more relaxed and less strict as he got older, allowing his grandchildren what he'd forbidden his children. That day, Si Ali held his grandson and put him on his back. When he tickled him, the little boy laughed, and the grains of *masfouf* scattered out of his mouth, making me worry he would choke. Si Ali didn't immediately answer my question. He covered the boy with kisses, on his stomach, chest, and neck, then said, putting him back on his shoulders, "Rest assured, no one will take Mohammed Habib from us, Bashira. Not as long as I'm alive."

I didn't dare open the subject again. Two full years passed, and I spent them torn by the unending dilemma, until Si Ali decided to circumcise Mohammed Habib at the beginning of the fall. The nightmares started haunting me again, and the *khatin*'s scissors got mixed up in my dreams with the knife of the Sidi Barrek Jmel shrine keeper. In my mind, circumcision became a crime committed against the boy while he was away from his mother. I secretly packed his bags, waiting for an opportunity, until Si Ali went to El Kef at the end of the summer. Then I sent the boy to your house. I swear to God, I swear to God, if I had imagined for one moment the enormity of the pain his departure would cause me, I would have never done that of my own free will. The house became a tomb the night he left. Mahdi was enraged; he stormed and threatened, then finally went into his room and locked it, angry and defeated. As for Bakkar, he hid his tears, saying reproachfully, "You should at least have told us, so we could've said goodbye to him. I don't think the Ennaifer family will ever let him come back."

As for Si Ali, when he came home from his trip and passed through the entryway, calling Mohammed Habib with bags of sweets in hand, he was met with absolute silence. When I confessed what I had done, he spoke to me in a language I would have never imagined he would use after forty years of pure companionship. He said, on the verge of exploding with anger, "I never thought you would betray me, Bashira. I swear to God, if not for the scandal it would cause, I would divorce you today, despite my gray hair."

III

Mohsen, Zbaida chose you over her mother and father and her darling eldest son. And here you are now, telling me about the reward you offered her in return for all her years of patience and loyalty. It's an awful act that only a depraved adulterer would even think of.

No, I'm not blaming you, ben Ennaifer; our religion allows you this. But it's no longer acceptable among the upper-class denizens of Tunis; it's something only louts, Bedouins from the mountains or countryside, do. Didn't your mother tell you that the *beldi* people of Tunis don't do this? And if any of them do, it's because their morals are corrupt or due to extreme circumstances. I don't believe you hid the news you told me from your mother, as you say you did. You and her are like two heads in one chechia. I think you did what you did with her blessing. Jnayna never liked Zbaida anyway, and I know she asked you after the incident to divorce her. Luiza doesn't lie. She heard you talking about it, and she told me everything.

I don't understand why you people at the Ennaifer house don't like Luiza. She's a poor girl who has spent her whole life serving others, and she's been patient with the bad treatment masters subject their maids to, whether intentional or not. As if taking her from her family when she was a child wasn't bad enough luck, then your father gave her away at the first available opportunity to an impotent husband the age of her grandfather. When she got her divorce and left him, crestfallen, your black maid used all her tricks to annoy and torture her.

That Khaddouj is a plague in human form. I swear to God, whoever said "I'll take a thousand jinn over a black maid" was right. When someone's grandfather's an onion and his mother's garlic, he's sure to have a stench. But God does exist, and whoever sifts through people to judge them, will be sifted in turn. That maid of yours is like a rag; whenever you're done with it, you throw it in the garbage. Had Luiza not threatened to expose her serious secret to her Lella Jnayna, she would have persisted in provoking and oppressing her to this day.

Luiza is smart, Mohsen. She's kind and has a good sense of humor. She's also discreet. She keeps secrets and doesn't permit herself to badmouth other people. But your black maid abused Luiza's patience with her repeated misdeeds, so she told me her story.

Luiza said you were complicit with the maid in keeping the secret. She respected you for this and considered it a noble, chivalrous act. She didn't tell anyone except Zbaida what happened, of course. But my daughter asked her, because of her good family line and clean conscience, to keep the matter secret and rise above petty personal problems. Luiza had been able to gather, thanks to her cleverness, the threads of the dubious story until she was able to weave it all together in her mind. She got the first knot started when she saw a stranger leaving your house some evenings during your absence.

You and the family were at your farm in Mornag spending the weekend, and Luiza got permission, as usual, to spend her day and night with us at the Rassaa house. Jnayna didn't have any problems with Luiza staying in touch with us, as long as she provided her with news of Mohammed Habib. That time, your black maid didn't go with you to Mornag under the pretext that she was sick. Luiza headed as usual to our house on Rue El Azzafine, but two days prior, we'd gone to Sfax for the circumcision of my older brother's son. When Luiza found out from the neighbors that we weren't home, she turned around. She decided not to go straight back to your house on Tourbet El Bey, and instead wandered in the souks and then went to read Surah Al-Fatiha at Sidi Ibrahim's tomb. She found the shrine courtyard filled with ululations and incense. There were tables covered with couscous and lamb, brought by someone to pay their due for a promise they had made to the saint. She ate with the visitors and danced with the dancers to the rhythm of the Sufi music. Then she went back to the Ennaifer house around the time of the Zuhr prayer. She knocked on the door for your black maid, who she'd left sick with a headache that morning, and waited for a long time, but the door didn't open, to the point that she even got worried about her nemesis and fellow servant. After some deliberation, she left the alley leading to your house, deciding to go for a walk in the streets of Tunis until she could figure out what to do. She was about to turn onto the main street when she thought she heard the familiar creak of the heavy door opening, then the clatter of the two knockers as it closed. When she went back to check, she saw a man walking quickly towards her in the street, as if he'd descended from the sky on a rope. He was fat, his face disfigured. There were traces of ugly vitiligo on his forehead and cheeks, and he was walking in a nervous way. As soon as he passed by Luiza, he started looking back at her, so she rushed to the house, feeling a bit scared of him. She knocked only once, and the door opened immediately, treating her to the sight of the black maid's face, kohl running around her eyes and red lipstick smeared on her chin and above her lips. Her smile immediately disappeared when she saw Luiza at the door, and she started wiping her mouth hurriedly and awkwardly, as if trying to erase the traces of the scandal. She'd undoubtedly thought her disfigured lover had come back for one reason or another, so she didn't bother fixing herself up before she opened the door. As soon as she had swallowed the surprise, she started rubbing both sides of her head with her fingers and went back to complaining about her headache. Luiza just smiled and didn't say a word.

Many weeks after that incident, Luiza realized that her roommate in that filthy room at your house had taken to eating a lot in the evening and throwing up in the morning. Then she started having severe crying fits in the middle of the night. A few days later, Mohsen, you yourself took her to the hospital and claimed that she'd been treated for an alleged stomach cramp. That brought an end, by God's will, to the voracious appetite, the vomiting, and some other symptoms like those common among women who give birth or get an abortion. Luiza noticed all this.

How strange it all is, ben Jnayna! You forgave your whoring nanny for her mistake and covered up for her. Meanwhile, you punished your virtuous wife for a crime she didn't commit. It never occurred to you to protect her; you just listened to people condemn her without saying a word. Wasn't it your mother who said, that fateful night, in front of everyone, "Women get sent to Dar Joued for less than this"? Dar Joued! My elegant and educated daughter in the prison for disobedient women?

It's unthinkable, my well-bred boy, that someone would say something like that to the daughter of Ali Rassaa. But what's even more unthinkable is for her husband to react with silence, as if he were deaf, dumb, and blind.

IV

Your mother probably thought, may God cherish her and enlighten the universe with her cleverness, that your father, the

Maliki judge Othman Ennaifer, was more powerful than my brother the grand vizier, Taieb Djellouli. She probably deemed us weak after Taieb left the ministry and imagined that his influence had diminished. If he, may God release him from his burden, had heard then of what happened to his niece, your father would probably have ended up in jail, God forbid. But your father-in-law, Si Ali, forced me to keep the matter secret from Taieb and the rest of the family. "Family keeps each other's secrets," as they say, though I never imagined that these secrets would, one day, reveal so much. You'll eat your fingers out of regret, Mohsen. There was nothing between Zbaida and Tahar that could dishonor her or him. I will testify this in front of God Himself if asked about it on Judgment Day. She never sat with him alone. Even after the marriage of her sisters Qmar and Mna, Mahdi would attend the lessons with Zbaida. When he couldn't attend for whatever reason, I would make Luiza attend the session and then check on them to make sure she was still there. Tahar, may God bless his soul, was aware of my vigilance and would, in return, make jokes about it and smile. He would've probably called Luiza back himself if the damn girl left because she was bored. To be honest with you, the man was noble, shy, sweet, and kind. He never did or said anything that might offend people around him. But in any case, he wasn't the kind of man Zbaida would be interested in. His attire was traditional, and he didn't look like the young blond men in the French magazines my daughters were fond of reading. He wasn't great at French, either, and if he used one of those common Tunisian words in his conversation, his tongue would twist, making my daughters Mna and Qmar wink at each other and laugh under their breath. Do you think that Zbaida, as you know her, is someone who would consider that kind of man? And he paid no attention to her, either. I wasn't born yesterday, and there's no way I could miss any signs of admiration. Even now, in my old age, I'm perfectly capable of deciphering the codes and secret perfume of love.

Nothing ever aroused my suspicions back when they met for lessons. Tahar, in fact, started missing his tutoring sessions a lot during his last year working for us. He was always pretending to be busy, and then he stopped coming at all for a long period, during which time Zbaida didn't ask about him—no one did. And of course we didn't! We were all busy preparing for your wedding, which was planned for a few weeks later. I was very upset at Jnayna that night for saying, hitting her forehead as if she'd suddenly realized something important, "Is *this* why her father rushed the marriage ceremonies? God knows how many other problems Mohsen hid from us."

V

That night Jnayna revealed her true face; a vicious, rude personality appeared from under her mask of politeness and kindness. Suddenly the smooth tongue put down its silk spinning wheel and picked up the wool carder, and the nasty words started hitting right and left. Her fake welcoming of us, Si Ali, Mahdi, and I, lasted for no more than a few seconds. Afterwards, the traditional rituals of greetings became clear provocations to bang the drums of war. Si Ali and my son Mahdi stayed at the entrance, waiting for one of the men to come out. For my part, I followed your mother to the roofed area of the courtyard, stumbling on the hem of my *safseri*, which had gotten dirty from the mud in the alley leading to your house. In the roofed area of the courtyard and under the light of a pale lamp, I noticed that there were scattered blood spots on the marble, turned pale pink by the rain. And since I didn't yet realize the extent of the disagreement between you and your brother, Mhammed, I assumed it was the effect of your father's cane on Zbaida's head. I could no longer hold myself together and started screaming and hitting myself in grief. But Jnayna just looked at me and sliced the air with her hand several times as a sign of rebuke, a look of resentment on her face. She reacted to my fear and screams with cold sarcasm and stared at me mockingly, making circles in the air with her head as an expression of disdain and disapproval. She violently shook my hand from her shoulder when I clung to her and screamed, in a voice hoarse with fear and anger, "Where's my daughter, Jnayna?"

She didn't answer me, but your black maid pointed upstairs, embarrassed, and I understood that Zbaida was still in her room, as Luiza had told me. I scurried towards the stairs leading to the upper floor, ignoring your mother, who gestured in the direction of the sitting room. But I had barely made it two steps before I heard the door creaking from the balcony and saw you coming out of your room, Zbaida behind you, chasing you with a scarf in her hand whose color I couldn't discern in the night. You went down in a rush towards the entrance hall, putting your hand on your nose with your head tilted back, like people do when they've got a nosebleed. Zbaida was running behind you, trying to convince you to use the scarf. A few minutes later, she was seated between me and your mother on the green couch in the sitting room. She gave short answers when I asked her what had happened. "It's fine, Mama, fine." She mumbled this with a voice that was practically inaudible, rubbing her eyes, which were swollen like ripe tomatoes. Jnayna didn't give me a chance to ask questions; she immediately commented in a mocking tone, looking at Zbaida with a fiery look in her eyes. "Fine? Blood has been spilled between brothers in the Ennaifer family because of you. And my darling Mohsen's reputation is being chewed on by the thugs of the Sidi Mansour quartier. And you say 'It's fine'?"

Zbaida's face got so pale I was afraid she might pass out, but your mother had no mercy. Turning to me, she leaned back in her seat, taking off her slippers and stretching out her legs, her palms on her temples, "By God, I never would have thought that a woman hailing from a noble family could do what she did, Lella Bashira."

I didn't know what to say. Seeing the blood on your face, Mohsen, flustered me and made me realize that the matter might, in fact, be worse than I'd thought. But despite that, I pretended to be strong. I ignored your mother and what she was saying, and reached to touch Zbaida's face, checking it on both sides as if looking for some traces on its page, and then I said, my voice breaking despite my attempts to stay strong, "Luiza said that Hajj Othman hit you. Did he really dare, Zbaida?"

Tears spilled from her eyes, but she didn't say a word. Your mother, though, straightened herself up violently in her seat and started talking ferociously, her chin shaking, "What are you saying, Lella Bashira? It seems you don't understand a thing yet. Your respectable daughter, my virtuous daughter-in-law, is receiving letters from men wrapped in a bundle of bread, Lella. Mhammed discovered her this time, God bless him. If it hadn't been for him, God knows for how long she would've continued this farce, and only God knows when it started! And you want her father-in-law not to teach her a lesson? Isn't Si Othman like her father? Would Haj Ali Rassaa approve of this?"

I leapt up, almost blind with anger. Your maid was coming into the room with two cups of coffee and some sweet *debla* on a silver tray, but a strong movement from my hand sent her and her tray back to where she came from. I was so furious I was shaking, and Zbaida sat still, looking down, glassy-eyed, quiet, like a beaten child. I had never seen this kind of submissive behavior from Zbaida. The Zbaida I knew didn't stay quiet when she was right, and didn't swallow insults easily. What happened to her that day to cloak her in shame? Doubts invaded my mind, fear and anger mixing. Was her silence a confession? Was she not defending herself because there was serious evidence that proved her guilt? Could Si Ali know something I didn't—and was that why he'd been so uneager to accompany me? Impossible. It was impossible that my smart, sensible girl Zbaida would drag us into that abyss. I shook those black thoughts from my mind as I stood before Jnayna like an agitated lioness. I would never believe that my daughter, who I myself raised, would wrong her husband and family by conducting a sinful relationship. Zbaida, who we raised based on the values of freedom and honesty, wouldn't violate that trust or betray any of us. I decided not merely to defend her but to launch a counterattack. I screamed at your mother, holding Zbaida's arm to force her to stand up in hopes that it would pull her out of her silence. "Watch your words, Lella Jnayna, and don't make accusations lightly. Her father and I are aware of everything. All the Rassaa daughters are more honorable than honor and more transparent than crystal. If that stupid baker is hiding a letter between loaves of bread, Zbaida shouldn't be the one paying for his foolishness."

I took a risk saying that when I didn't know—and still don't know—what was in the message. But I said to myself that Tahar, based on what I knew of him, was a polite young man and wouldn't do anything wrong. But your mother's temper immediately flared up, and we ended up with the rift and coldness you're familiar with. She jumped out of her seat, pushing the small marble-top table with her foot, and one of its sharp corners almost hit my knee. There were some small knickknacks on the table, little pink ceramic monkeys of different sizes, and they smacked into each other, making a loud clacking sound that made the atmosphere even more tense. She raised an admonishing finger in my face and started hissing, drawing out each syllable and stressing her words, "Well, well, the game has been played then!"

I shouted at her in warning, but she paid me no mind and continued in a voice dripping with sarcasm, "And you're saying that you're aware of everything? Then you know that your daughter is exchanging letters with her boyfriend from her husband's house? And her father knows, as well? Isn't that just lovely? I couldn't wish for better in-laws!"

I felt that the chandelier hanging from the ceiling had suddenly begun a feverish, circular dance. I almost lost my balance watching the alternating lights and shadows on your mother's face, which at the time seemed uglier than Satan's. Your mother continued saying hurtful things, threatening to send Zbaida to Dar Joued and hinting that you might not have properly assured her virginity on your wedding night . . . and other things in that vein that I've mentioned to you before. I also said some awful things, but I don't think there's any benefit in repeating them to you. May God forgive us; we were like two ferocious tigers, each one protecting her cub with claws and teeth. Neither of us paid any attention to that poor woman who stood between us, looking at us in terror, maintaining an oppressed silence, like the silence of a corpse being washed.

VI

The skirmish between me and your mother might have continued for a long time, if not for your raised voices coming from the direction of the entrance hall. I was able to distinguish Si Ali's voice, which was thunderous as he called for Zbaida. Our daughter ran to him, and I ran along with her. I knew we had reached a danger zone, because Si Ali, as you know, is very patient most of the time; he's not quick to anger and almost never loses his temper. But his wrathful tone when he called Zbaida sounded like he'd lost his patience and was losing control. He would tell me on the way home, as the carriage jolted quickly through the rain-covered streets of Tunis, about the conversation that took place between him and your father, Si Othman. That conversation made him lose his mind, to the point that he asked for his daughter back from the Ennaifer house, but she refused to obey him. He was as angry at you as he was at your father, because he saw your silence and your failure to defend your wife as cowardice and abandonment. When he called Zbaida and ordered her to leave your house immediately, he spoke to her with the tone of someone confident of being obeyed. He thought he was supporting her, restoring her dignity, and—with his faith in her—cleansing her from the muck her father-in-law had dragged her through in the presence of both her husband and father. He said to himself, "She will eat my bread and live in my house." But she failed him. Zbaida supported you and failed her father. And here you are, Mohsen, rewarding her with all that your treacherous character could offer. He who takes a giant bite finds his whiskers in a plight. A foul prize from a foul guise.

7
The Tale of Lella Fawzia, the Divorced Wife of Si Mhammed Ennaifer
(*Zawiya of Sidi Mehrez, Winter 1951*)

I

Oh, Sidi Mehrez! Sultan of Tunis, keeper of the holy secret, master of masters!

I am your daughter, Baba Mehrez. I'm Fawzia, the daughter of Douja, daughter of Sheikh Omran. Do you remember me?

Fawzia, the naughty girl with golden braids, the seven-year-old girl whose fever the Kouloughli doctor couldn't bring down. Desperate and hopeless, Douja brought her to you, and she left your shrine jumping and playing in the puddles on a day the skies opened up over Tunis.

Fawzia, the fallow twenty-five-year-old girl whose mother made vows to you, perfumed your tomb with incense, and brought you gifts. All to get close to you, asking you to help her daughter find her soulmate, to end the bad luck, and to bring her a good husband soon.

Fawzia, the twenty-seven-year-old, the beautiful bride wearing a burgundy *fouta*, the virgin who visited your shrine the day before her wedding night with Mhammed, son of Othman Ennaifer, to thank you and ask you to bless her from your abundance.

Yes, indeed . . . It's me. The short, plump, fair-skinned girl with long golden hair. The happy bride who untied the belt above her Arab lace *sirwal* as part of our ritual, here in front of your honorable tomb, with ululations and drums under the shrine flag and a lantern.

Can you hear me, Sheikh Mehrez? I am the bride who came to you early in the summer like a blooming rose and is now returning to you at the beginning of winter as a dry cactus. I ran away today from my husband's house. Have pity on me and look at me. Look at my skinny body, my gloomy face, and the state of humiliation I am in. Make your judgment, my master, that fair judgment that prevails over both humans and jinn.

Sultan of Tunis, I know you can see hear me. Forgive my audacity! And forgive me if I've disturbed your virtuous seclusion tonight by imposing myself on you as a guest at your shrine.

I had to trick the nice shrine keeper and hide under the curtains of your tomb, Sidi, so no one would interrupt my talk with you. I know God's saints can see and hear even from under the ground. I've been thinking about this plan for a month or more, and today I finally made my decision.

I left the Ennaifer house before evening without permission. I didn't take anything with me except the candle box you see over there, in the opening facing the tomb. I tiptoed out, holding the hem of my *safseri* in my teeth until I arrived at the entrance hall and, from there, snuck into the alley. The Ennaifer house usually becomes still and quiet between noon and the early evening in both summer and winter. They sleep like the dead, and all the noise and life drain out of the house. Only their maid Luiza stays busy, and today I snuck out when she wasn't watching. I closed the big door behind me and ran. No one will notice I'm gone until late tonight; it might even take them until tomorrow morning. The people living in the house don't ask about me; they're used to me hiding in my room the entire day, or sometimes for two days. My husband, Si Mhammed, leaves for work in the morning and doesn't get back until late at night. He doesn't talk to me when he gets home and doesn't turn on the light. He changes his clothes in the dark, then collapses into bed next to me like a pig and starts snoring in a way that keeps me awake.

I don't understand how a person who makes all that noise could fall asleep or get any rest. The racket that comes from his nose and throat! Hissing, grunting, neighing, clucking . . . The creaking of moving carriages, the gargling of bottles being poured, the din of a common brawl, and the bellow of bull camels fighting. All that in one snore. I swear by you, Sidi Mehrez, someone lying next to Mhammed Ennaifer in the dead of night might as well be trying to sleep in the middle of a busy souk at 10 A.M.. I thought when I first lived with him that his coldness and snoring were the worst parts about him, until I found out, as time passed, that they were the least of my worries.

I'll tell you everything, Sidi Mehrez. Everyone's gone now, and the shrine is closed and quiet. The keeper has blown out the candles surrounding the tomb and closed the door that separates us, you and I, from the big courtyard. Now I can leave my hideout in the dark and finally lay down my heavy load.

II

Fate didn't make it easy for me to be the bride of Si Mhammed Ennaifer. As soon as we made it past the engagement, each new step towards the wedding night was beset with calamity or problems. Ali Rassaa, the father of my elder sister-in-law, Zbaida, could find no better time than the evening of my engagement to fall down dead amongst those who'd gathered to celebrate. Shortly after that, his wife Bashira joined him, then the Ennaifer family's black maid . . . so we kept postponing the wedding, time and again. I probably should've listened to my mother when she opened up to me. She scratched her scalp with the handle of the kitchen knife, as she always does when she's feeling perplexed, and said, "There's something off, Fawzia. I would bet you money, my girl—something's not right."

My mother decided, without consulting anyone, to counterattack. At the funeral of Lella Bashira, the mother of Lella Zbaida, she purposefully sat next to my mother-in-law, Lella Jnayna, and her daughters. She asked them about the groom and how he was doing, and after a short chat, she asked about the wedding date. Lella Jnayna mumbled, hiding her mouth behind her hand, "Is this really the best time, Lella Douja?"

My mother puffed up in anger. She threatened to cancel the engagement if the groom's family continued to postpone the wedding on flimsy pretexts. I think she felt, with her mother's heart, that the groom wasn't serious about the marriage and was enjoying the delays.

But, God forgive me, I was like a cat in heat. No advice could stop me from dreaming, and I never stopped rushing and pining. I was waiting with suppressed lust for the promised day, when I would finally be behind closed doors with a man, any man. Si Mhammed, with his solid body, his elegant mustache, and his sharp look, was in my eyes the master of men. It's true that he was a few years north of forty, and it's also true that I'd only seen him once, the day he accompanied his father after our engagement to wish my father a happy Eid. But that single time was enough to make him the desirable hero of my fantasies every night. He had a small limp, but that only made him more handsome and manly in my eyes. His apparition visited me daily, making me neglect my prayers—not just the optional ones but even the required ones. And then, finally, a date for the wedding was set at the beginning of last June.

On the wedding night, he seemed preoccupied as he walked me to the room that would become my torture chamber, on the upper floor of the Ennaifer house. On our way there, we passed by a door that was slightly ajar, with a dim light coming from the crack. I couldn't see anything when I stole a glance at it, but from behind the door, I heard choked sobs, like wailing. That was the first bad omen, though I didn't realize it yet. I would later find out that this door led to the room my sister-in-law Zbaida shared with her husband, Si Mohsen. It was a bigger room, more luxurious than the one occupied by the newly wedded bride and groom, and there was nothing but a thin wall separating the two. If you pressed your ear against it, you could hear with shocking clarity every secret thing that happened in the dark.

When Si Mhammed got us into our room, me walking proudly in my wedding dress, he left the door open behind us. I only noticed when his older sister came and gently closed it from outside, laughing. I heard her shout down to my mother-in-law, who was unable to climb the stairs on account of her feet and had watched our procession from the courtyard, trilling joyfully. "The groom was so happy he forgot to close the door!"

Si Mhammed seemed neither happy nor sad, just silent and cold like a thick wall. So cold, in fact, that once we were alone in the room, with its blue velvet curtains and magical perfume, he didn't even look at me. He untied his shoelaces slowly, almost absent-mindedly, as if unaware of the virgin bride standing three feet from his bed, which was covered with silk sheets and jasmine blossoms, and unaware that she was patiently waiting for him to offer her a seat and lift her gold-decorated veil. She remained standing like a statue, furtively glancing at him as he sat on the couch and took off his socks. He lifted them to his nose to smell them like a common mutt before rolling them into a ball and throwing them at the feet of his confused bride, who still hadn't left her place near the door.

I couldn't believe what I was seeing. But the disgust wasn't enough to restrain the horses of desire rearing up inside me. I didn't know what to do. My body was on fire, but my mother's words about a bride's behavior on her wedding night were still ringing in my ears: "Don't initiate anything, not with a word, an action, even a breath. Don't start with a sweet word or caress. Let your husband lead you how he wants, and hold back a bit. Be modest. Proper girls don't put themselves forward."

I kept my eyes lowered, attached to the spot like a tent peg planted in the ground in some deserted place. My chest rose and fell rapidly, and I was flooded by mixed feelings of fear, desire, and anger. I felt insulted beyond imagination. I was like a lavish banquet spread in front of a vile man who was already full. I tried to be patient, telling myself that the groom was probably afraid on his wedding night, or confused, or shy, but my emotions were overwhelming, and I started crying, my kohl running and mixing with my face powder and lipstick. All the while, Si Mhammed was oblivious. He turned away from me and started slowly taking off his wedding clothes and hanging them with care on a wooden rack behind the door.

Suddenly I felt, in addition to the feelings of helplessness, a wave of heat that made the golden veil feel like a piece of hell. I ripped it off, releasing a loud and angry sigh. Then I saw him, from behind a transparent mist of tears, walking towards me in his underclothes. He uprooted me from my spot without gentleness, pulling my arm to seat me next to him on the edge of the high bed at the far left of the room. At his touch, all my pores opened up, like plants promised rain. I focused my eyes on his parted lips, waiting for my desired kiss, but instead those lips twisted into hideous, distressing words that promptly deflated me again. "God, are we already starting with this misery?"

He said that, then turned away from me again to light a cigarette, taking a deep drag and blowing smoke rings into the air with a provoking calm. I don't know how, by the time morning arrived, my soul hadn't liquified from all the tears I shed. Maybe it was his loud snores, which could wake the dead, that prevented me from dying that night. He avoided me for the entire month after the wedding night, as if I were a mangy goat. I thought in the beginning that he was impotent, but then, over and over, I saw him use his hand to pleasure himself in front of me, and I didn't see anything wrong with his equipment. Maybe he did it to try and excite me, so it would eventually be easier for him to get the dirty thing he wanted from me.

God forgive me. God knows I don't want to tell you these things, Sidi Mehrez. But even though I wasn't in school for long, I still know what God and his prophet said. Didn't they say, "There is no embarrassment in religion"? And don't people say, when someone gets married, that they've completed half of their religion? A conversation about marriage is a conversation about religion, then, so we shouldn't be embarrassed. Of course, obviously, I'm not so stupid that I believe what Si Mhammed has told me, and I know these things. I also know that God, even if he ordered women to obey men, also ordered men to have marital relations with their wives from the good place that religion allows, and forbade them from approaching them from the impure side.

The night that Si Mhammed finally approached me, after a month of purposeful neglect and intentional excitement, he found a body ready for any concession in order to quell its hunger, which deprivation and longing had only intensified. When he mounted my back, looking for a sheath for his sword, he found a woman broken by the long wait, unable to resist or stop him. He violently grabbed the pillow my face was planted in, and shook it with his free arm to remove its case. Then he balled up the pillowcase and stuffed it into my mouth when I started screaming from the terrible pain. With his other elbow, he pressed his weight into my upper back to prevent me from moving. I moaned from the pain and humiliation until the morning. My sister-in-law Zbaida must've heard everything that night because I saw something like pity in er eyes the next day at lunch. When I later asked her, the day I told her my painful secret, whether she'd heard the pain of the first shock, she neither confirmed nor denied it, just gave me an ambiguous smile. That woman is solid, despite all her disappointments. When I sit next to her, I feel like a small bird's egg next to a pile of solid rocks. She's strong despite illness, weakness, and the rumors plaguing her. And I am fragile, destined to fade away at any moment.

What can I tell you, Sidi Mehrez? Do you understand what it means for a bride to look, after the belated intimacy of her wedding night, for the precious pink blood spot on her bed sheet, and instead—still a virgin—find a thread of black blood spilled beneath her?

In the following days, Si Mhammed tried to convince me that all the openings in my body were made to fit his equipment. He compared them to the reservoirs God created as natural containers, meant to hold the excess water the ground didn't need. He compared my body to the deep, narrow holes he dug in the wet beach sand in Hammam Lif as a teenager and then had sex with after dark when no one could see him; mine were only better in terms of heat and slickness. He also said that there was no difference between the holes except how much pleasure they gave, based on the mind's ability to imagine. I didn't understand anything. When I complained about the severity of the pain, which took away all other feeling, he just said, "You'll get used to it. Just do what I say, and you'll get used to it."

I did what he said, but I never got used to it. Pain and despair canceled out nine tenths of the lust that had been pushing me to agree whenever he wanted me. As for the wounds to my soul and body, they never healed the way he promised they would. Instead, they got worse with every brutal attack; the bleeding got so bad that it was as though I was menstruating from my backside. I told no one, not even my mother, about my suffering for two months, until the day came that the secret was exposed.

I was drawing water from the underground cistern in preparation for the daily laundry routine. I took the large tub to the eastern corner of the courtyard and placed a short wooden chair behind it. Suddenly, Luiza, Zbaida's maid, ran towards me. She sat on the chair and started separating out the clothes piled next to the tub. She said, smiling, "I'll help you today, Lella Fawzia. You're looking pale and tired."

I thanked her and politely refused her offer; up to that point, there hadn't been the kind of affection or friendship between us that would make me comfortable accepting it. On top of that, Lella Jnayna had warned me about her just after I arrived, without telling me why. But Luiza ignored my rejection. She insisted, so I stopped talking. She took the water bucket from my hand and poured it into the tub, then separated the clothes by color and started washing the whites. The pain in the wounded spot had by then become unbearable, to the point that I couldn't sit next to the tub without breaking out in a cold sweat because of the strain on the affected muscle. So I didn't insist on refusing, though I wasn't overly enthusiastic in my thanks, either. I only bent over to pick up my underwear, stained by the secret hemorrhage, but Luiza was quicker. She decisively pushed my arm away and said, "Don't trouble yourself! You're like my sister, like Lella Zbaida. If Lella Jnayna hadn't forced me to do Khaddouj's work, God rest her, on top of my own, I would never have allowed you to bear your burdens alone, unlike the other ladies in the family."

I sighed deeply and didn't speak. It would've been rude to leave her and go do something else, so I squatted next to her, biting my lips in pain. Her sharp eyes evidently caught my facial expressions, so she dried her hands on one of Si Mhammed's shirt that hadn't been washed yet and stood to help me up the stairs. She took me to my room, saying in a sympathetic tone. "I hope you feel better, Lella Fawzia!" Then she added, in a clearly angry tone, raising her eyes and palms to the ceiling, "May God punish whoever caused this."

She may have been aiming blindly, but she hit the target dead center. I knew that she wanted to tell me a secret. Since it was still morning and would be a long time before Si Mhammed came back from work, I decided to give her the chance to tell me all the secrets she knew. As soon as I closed the door and invited her to sit down on the couch at the front of the room, she happily accepted, as if she hadn't left a tub full of clothes waiting downstairs. I asked her directly, without preamble, "What do you have to tell me, Luiza?"

She answered me without hesitation, "I wanted to tell you something I memorized from my first Lella, Lella Bashira, may God rest her. She used to repeat the proverb, 'The flawed one's defect can't be hidden.'"

She remained silent for a while, looking for the impact of her ambiguous proverb on my face, but it was clear I didn't understand, so she continued. "Lella Bashira also used to say, 'It all ends in death or revelation.'"

She paused for effect, moving her head up and down in circles as if remembering something or expressing regret over something from the past. "And I say, 'Or marriage.'"

Lella Jnayna's shouted call prevented her from elaborating or explaining. She leapt up and ran towards the door when she heard the old woman's voice screaming "Luiza." Any delay in answering Lella Jnayna meant a scandal that everybody, near and far, would hear about. One of the old woman's idiosyncrasies was that if she started calling for someone, she would repeat their name dozens of times without so much as a breath, as if she were calling for help. So whoever she was calling from a distance wouldn't have a chance to tell her that they'd heard her and were coming. She wouldn't stop calling until she saw that person directly in front of her. But I stood between Luiza and the door. How could I let her go after she kindled my curiosity with those enigmatic words? I pushed her back towards her seat, to no avail, and said, "I don't understand anything from your riddles, woman. Tell me what you mean."

She answered, slipping past me and opening the door, "Go ask Lella Zbaida to explain it to you. She knows not only the well's cover, but also its depths."

III

Has Zbaida ever visited you, Sidi Mehrez? Has she ever stood next to your tomb to ask God for healing? I don't think she's the kind of person who visits saints. So you haven't seen the clear white skin, the beautiful face, the poise and tenderness. Isn't it unfair that she's disabled, despite all that?

I don't know how her bottom half got paralyzed or when the

accident that disabled her legs occurred. The Ennaifer family are keeping the story secret. Even when they do mention it, their versions are suspiciously contradictory. Lella Jnayna told my mother that her elder daughter-in-law had suffered from postpartum depression after giving birth to her second child, Mostafa. She got a sore on the lower part of her back, followed by a severe fever that caused chronic weakness in her leg muscles and eventually left her unable to move them. Lella Jnayna quickly forgot that version of the story, though, and claimed to some neighbors that Zbaida stumbled on the hem of her *qaftan* after giving birth and fell down the stairs. The fall broke several of her vertebrae, and that paralyzed her legs. When I asked Si Mhammed, during a good moment between us, to tell me the truth about what happened, he harshly cursed his sister-in-law. He rubbed the traces of an old wound under his chin and then kicked me in the waist, ending the conversation. "The crazy bitch. Getting paralyzed was her own damn fault. Let's see if those books she reads morning and night help her now; may God blind her."

You've probably heard another version from the mouths of visitors in front of your tomb, Sidi Mehrez. Visitors? Vultures, is more like it! My cousin Jweeda told me that she heard some women in the hammam telling a story about a rich Italian trader named Franco. He fell so madly in love with the young Rassaa girl that he started throwing money left and right. He even asked a baker in Sidi Mansour to make some special loaves of bread so he could slip presents into the dough: a ring, a bangle, a bracelet or a necklace . . . or sometimes a bottle of perfume: jasmine, musk, ambergris, or oud. When those loaves, loaded with their gifts, were ready, he would send them with the baker's boy to the house of her husband, Mohsen Ennaifer, on Tourbet El Bey. With the help of her maid, she would open the loaves far from prying eyes to take out the hidden treasures. The situation continued for months, until one day the maid forgot the bread on the kitchen counter and got busy with something else.

Then Judge Hajj Othman Ennaifer, the patriarch, entered the house, took a bite out of one of the loaves, and almost broke his teeth. When he looked, he found a gold earring studded with diamonds inside the loaf of bread. He put it in his pocket without questioning where it came from, assuming it was his lucky day. He hated the taste of the loaf he'd found it in, though, so he threw the rest away. He took another one and cut it in half, and, what do you know, he found another earring like the first. The maid was summoned and beaten, so she confessed and told her lady's secret. As for Zbaida bint Rassaa, she was locked in her room, and her two sons were taken away from her. She wasn't allowed to eat or drink, and that was how she became paralyzed, out of weakness and humiliation. Others said that when she was locked in her room, she tried to slit her throat with the shards of a broken mirror out of despair, but she didn't die and was left paralyzed. Some people also said that her father-in-law, Othman Ennaifer, beat her legs with a stick, the way people hit animals. The beating was so severe that the nerves in her feet became paralyzed. As for the lover, Franco, they said he melted like a grain of salt. They thought that he must have gone back to his hometown in Sicily when he heard the news, and he was never heard from again.

Do you believe this story, Sultan of Tunis? I didn't. It was too similar to the fairy tales grandmothers tell about the ring the poor fisherman finds inside a fish and how he becomes a rich trader, thanks be to God. Still, it's a mass of intertwined secrets. With the help of what I could piece together from family members' stories, I was eventually able to untangle them. In addition to what I heard from Si Mhammed the day he accused Zbaida to clear his own name, I also happened to overhear a conversation between Si Othman and Lella Jnayna that guided me to the source of the tangle.

I was passing by the sitting room window during the *qailulah* when I heard Si Othman talking. His voice was sad, which was unusual. God forbid I eavesdrop on anyone, Sidi Mehrez, but one of my feet went numb at just that moment, so I froze in place against my will, waiting for the numbness to wear off. Si Othman was talking to Lella Jnayna; I don't remember everything he said, but I remember most of it. He said, "Whenever I remember that ill-fated day, I still feel short of breath. I start gasping and heaving, and people sitting around me ask if I'm all right, but I don't answer. I know you know what's wrong with me, Jnayna, and you know that I know. You know I'm ruminating on that same story, and you understand my regret without me saying anything. I regret it, Jnayna. Today I'm saying it out loud. I regret it beyond what words can describe. I often wish that it never happened. But God decreed his will in heaven, and I can't object to what God plans or how he carries it out."

Unfortunately, I didn't hear Lella Jnayna's answer. Luiza suddenly emerged from the storage room and stood staring at me suspiciously, so I kept walking as if nothing had happened. Was that conversation about Zbaida and the accident that paralyzed her? I will never know, but I think it must have been. Si Mhammed refuses to talk when I bring it up. If he says anything about Zbaida, it's always something mysterious that casts doubt on her reputation, but he never explains anything about what happened. As for that maid, Luiza, she's a sealed box of secrets that can't be opened with sweet words or bribes. She closes up like a stubborn clam whenever I ask her anything concerning her lady or her lady's teenage sons, Mostafa and Mohammed Habib.

I love Mostafa, Sidi Mehrez. I look at his handsome face whenever I get a chance, when people around me aren't looking. I secretly pray that one day I will have a son who looks like him. He's fourteen years old. He obeys his mother and is polite and sweet, unlike his brother, who's one or two years older than him. That boy, whose name is Mohammed Habib, inexplicably hates me. Actually, I think he hates the entire family, except maybe his uncle Mhammed. He scowls at everyone for no reason, and he rarely answers their greetings. He's rude, especially to his mother, but he's also disagreeable with his father and grandparents. He always has a sour expression.

Yesterday, he knocked on my bedroom door after lunch. Si Mhammed was asleep, so I spoke to him from the window, asking what he wanted. He answered me grouchily. "I want my uncle. Open the door, my uncle's wife; you shouldn't get used to talking to men from your window."

"Your uncle's sleeping, and it's *my* room and *my* door; I'm free to do as I want."

"Yeah, we know you do what you want—we can tell from the half-washed clothes on the line. Catch you later."

He left me boiling like a pot. I wished I could scratch his face with my nails, I was so angry. A boy of fifteen (at most!) was trying to tell me how to behave properly. I beg you, Sidi Mehrez, use the power of your shrine to curse him. May God *not* bless him. But I didn't come here to curse anyone . . . I came here to ask for your help, to figure out how to deal with my faggot husband.

He really is a faggot, I swear to God, Sidi Mehrez. It's a new word I learned from Zbaida, the day she explained to me my dear husband's status among normal men. Si Mhammed got very angry when I mentioned the word in front of him and gave me a horrendous beating. That's when I began to seriously plan to run away and come to you.

Forgive me, Sidi Mehrez, I forgot to mention something. I forgot to tell you how I found out that he prefers men over women. Please forgive me. I'm confused and not sure what to say, and I'm doing everything all wrong. Also, I spent most of my life at home; I can barely read and write. I don't know how to speak eloquently like Zbaida, the educated one who knows how to read in Arabic and French.

When I visited Zbaida the day Luiza recommended I talk to her, she refused to speak. When I repeated what her maid told me, she pursed her lips in surprise, as if she didn't understand it any more than I did. She was sitting on a wooden rocking chair next to the window in her room, her legs covered with a pink linen blanket, richly embroidered and carefully ironed, and she had a big book in her lap; as we talked, she snuck occasional glances at its pages. Before this, I'd never seen her in light clothing, so I seized the opportunity to examine what I could of her body. I searched for any trace of an old wound that might provide evidence for one of the stories about the accident that paralyzed her. She had a long neck. No sign on her body. No scratch, let alone a deep wound. The neckline of her pink shirt revealed milky cleavage between two firm breasts, whose shape didn't seem to have been changed by pregnancy or breastfeeding. She noticed that I was staring at her, so I moved my eyes away and pretended to change the subject. On the opposite wall was a huge oil painting, somewhat clumsily done. It depicted the bey of Tunisia wearing his luxurious royal attire and receiving a large sword on a feather pillow from a distinguished gentleman, who seemed to be foreign. I asked her, pointing to the painting, "Is that Sidi Lamine Bey?"

She laughed and said in the tone of a teacher working with a somewhat dull student, "That's Sadok Bey, Mohammed Sadok Bey. Have you heard his name before, Fawzia? He's the bey who gave in to France and signed the ill-fated treaty that made us colonized. That's the French colonialism, Fawzia, that honorable patriots are now fighting to end."

I got bored after that, when she started going on about the resistance movement and its patriotic leaders. A long, heavy lecture that I don't remember a single thing from. She was probably trying to bore me, to get me to leave her alone so she could finish her book. But I kept calm and fixed a sweet expression on my face, nodding from time to time, pretending to understand. After that dull digression, she got back to the painting; she pointed to it and mentioned a name I can't remember for the foreign man facing the bey, claiming that it was the emperor of France. She declared imperiously that the painting depicted a real meeting between Sadok Bey and that emperor in Algiers ninety years ago.

I said, untruthfully, trying to move the conversation into territory adjacent to the questions I came for, "The foreign man in the painting looks a lot like your oldest son Mohammed Habib."

She raised her head in surprise and didn't comment. I took advantage of her silence to reroute the conversation. I asked her how old she was when she had Mohammed Habib. From her answer, I estimated that she was in her early thirties. Six years older than me at most.

There was a heavy silence that I broke by saying, with a voice I purposefully made a little bit sad, "I wonder if I'll have a child at your age, Lella Zbaida."

"You've only been married two months, Fawzia. Inshallah you'll get pregnant soon and will have both boys and girls."

She made that comment with her eyes trained on her book, trying to avoid looking at me. I decided to take a chance. "Where will the baby come from, Lella Zbaida?"

". . ."

"Aren't they born from the place where their father spilled his seed?"

". . ."

"Have you ever heard of a virgin who returned from the toilet holding a newborn?"

I saw her shudder. She made as if to stand up from her seat, then remembered her disability and sank back down. She closed her eyes and tilted her head back with a sigh. Then she opened up, and what she said made me cry a lot. She explained to me that my husband, Si Mhammed, was not the beast I imagined him to be. She said that he was an unfortunate man who nature made differently than most men. She said we don't choose our inclinations any more than our defining characteristics, that we're born with them. She also said a lot about upbringing, experience, society, and ethics that I didn't understand. Listening to her, I heard for the first time in my life that some males have sex with each other. My mouth was hanging open; I looked like an idiot in math class. She said that Si Mhammed had been sleeping with men since his early youth. He'd been avoiding marriage and wouldn't have married at all if it hadn't been for his mother, Jnayna. She said that his mother was the root of the problem; she suspected that her son might be abnormal but still insisted on him getting married. She probably thought that if he got married, his condition would improve and his inclinations would change. Luiza's words sprang to mind: *The flawed one's defect can't be hidden . . . It all ends in marriage or revelation . . .* I slapped and scratched my face in grief, listening to Zbaida. *How unfortunate you are, Fawzia! You wanted to marry a man, and they married you to something that is not a man and not "not a man."*

"What is this called, Lella Zbaida?"

She cast her eyes down and didn't answer. I asked again. She pronounced a difficult word in French that I didn't understand and then another, just two letters long, but I didn't recognize it. She searched in her memory for the Arabic equivalent of the two words. She mentioned the word in classical Arabic, insisting that it was associated with some people mentioned in a surah in the Quran. I forgot the classical word, Sidi Mehrez, and only the last word she gave me stayed in my mind.

IV

"Are you a faggot, Si Mhammed?"

He gaped at me in disbelief. "What did you say, Fawzia?"

I said it again with the confidence of an ignorant person. I didn't know it was an insult; I thought it was the name of an illness, like asking if he was schizophrenic or consumptive. I didn't realize I had hit on a sore spot until I saw him lose his mind in rage. He immediately attacked, showering me with blows and kicks and calling me profane names that I wouldn't have thought him capable of. He "enrolled me in the ranks of women" that night, as they say. He emptied his manhood for the first time as he should and *where* he should, but with indescribably violating force. I didn't hear his snoring that night when he turned away from me. Instead, he breathed in uncontrollable short gasps for an hour before quieting down. I was soon taken by sleep—or maybe unconsciousness—but I thought I heard muffled sobs in the dark.

Our relationship went from bad to worse after that night. But at least it gave me a long break that allowed my body to partially heal, because Si Mhammed had resolved to stop sleeping with me. The apathetic expression that never left his face disappeared and was replaced by a frowning mask with knitted brows. He started staying out late a lot, and when he came back home, some time before dawn, he went to bed tottering from drunkenness, mumbling and smelling of alcohol.

One night he came back home early and cheerful-looking, which was unlike him. It was the start of fall, and cool breezes had started to diminish the unbearable heat. He was drunk, as usual, but he was at least aware of what he was doing and saying. He sat cross-legged on the bed and invited me to sit next to him. I was a little afraid of him, but I complied. I faced him, putting my palms on my thighs and tucking my dress tightly under my knees out of modesty, as if I were sitting with a *mahram*, like a brother or father. But the *mahram* was sitting facing me, naked except for two stinky socks. He looked down, playing with his mustache and thinking, as if trying to figure out how to approach the topic he had in mind. Then, abruptly, in a tone somewhere between hopeful and begging, he said, "I want you to give me a child before the divorce."

The word startled me. Divorce? After less than three months of marriage? What would people say about me? Who would believe me if I told the truth? And would I even dare to do that?

"Did you hear me, Fawzia?"

" . . . "

"My marriage to you was a mistake. I could never love you—I

don't feel with you what a man should feel for his wife. You don't move me, and you mean nothing to my body. I've been trying for a while now to convince myself that those feelings will come the longer we live together, but nothing has come but disgust and boredom. I love another woman."

It seemed to me that he was emphasizing "another woman," intentionally stressing its syllables. Tears sprang to my eyes, but I didn't say anything.

"Well, what do you think?"

"About divorce?"

"The divorce is a settled matter. I am asking you about the child."

You have some nerve, Mhammed Ennaifer, I thought, turning the matter over in my mind. The vile man wanted me to be a divorcée with a baby in my womb or on my lap so I couldn't cast doubt on his manhood. He considered the child a means of proving his innocence to his family and society. I wiped away my tears and straightened up. "And why do you want a child from me? You could have one with this other woman," I said, stressing the word *woman*, as he had. He had clearly prepared himself for this question and answered without hesitation," The other woman has openly admitted to me that she's infertile, and I don't want to be deprived of having children."

I became so angry that I turned into a bully. Did he think I was an idiot who could be so easily fooled? I don't know what came over me, but I said to him, "And what's the name of this other woman, the infertile one? Mohammed the grocer, Salah the coppersmith, or Ali the coffee shop boy?"

He glowered at me. His nose twitched, and his chin trembled, and I saw the yellow color of death seeping into his face. His head drooped between his shoulders, and he seemed to me like someone who had suddenly grown feeble from anger, as if he couldn't talk or move. But a black hatred glowed in his eyes, and I realized that the only way to escape dying by his hand that night would be to call for help.

I jumped out of bed and sprang towards the door, opening it and putting one foot out, placing myself half-in and half-out of the room. The surprise paralyzed him, and he didn't move. Then I said, intentionally raising my voice a bit, "And if you lay so much as a finger on me, I'll expose your big secret to the whole neighborhood."

He shook with anger. He was still sitting there like a ball of rage, cross-legged in his stinky socks. He grabbed the blanket to cover his privates and hissed, "Lower your voice, bitch! People are sleeping."

I became hysterical and lost the ability to control my body. I felt as if my limbs were leaving their sockets, each heading in a different direction. My right arm shot forward and snapped back, raining heavy blows on my face and chest that I could hear but not feel. Meanwhile, my left arm flew up and fell on my head, over and over, like an iron hammer. My legs were trembling and stomped the ground under me as if I were a chained animal that wanted to run away. I think he quickly realized that the matter was going to get ugly if he couldn't calm me down. The wall separating us from Zbaida's room wouldn't be able to block the approaching scandal for long. He shot towards me like an arrow and held my hands behind my back as if he were hugging me, whispering in my ear, "Calm down, Fawzia." His arms encircled my chest as he pulled me back into the room. He closed the door with his foot and sat down on the carpet next to the couch, pulling me down to the floor. I broke down crying in humiliation, trying to push him away, but he didn't let me go until I stopped crying in his arms. He caressed my head, combing my tousled hair with his fingertips and running his hand tenderly across my cheek to wipe away my tears. When he was sure that I was calm, he stood up and went to the low dresser to get the silver vial of rose water. He sprinkled it on his hands and started dabbing it on my face and the upper part of my chest. The scent of rose water covered the smell of his socks, and his sudden sweetness covered the sensation of boiling over in my chest. When I looked at him, I saw a terrorized man, small and broken despite his massive body. His eyes were red, as if he were secretly crying with me. We sat there exactly as we had been sitting earlier, but on the floor this time, like the poor in your entrance hall, Sidi Mehrez.

V

"Don't believe what Zbaida and her maid say about me, Fawzia."

He started with those words. His voice was shaky, and there were tears in his eyes. The confessions started to pour forth. He said that Luiza hated him because he'd rejected her a few years ago when she propositioned him, a week after her divorce. She'd come to his rooftop shed late at night as he was eating suhur, claiming that she was chasing a cat that had run up to the roof after stealing a big mahi mahi left over from dinner. She offered to tidy up the shed, since she was already holding the broom she'd used to chase the alleged cat. He had doubts about her intentions but decided to test her by giving her the benefit of the doubt. He welcomed her help and watched her quietly as he finished his rice pudding (flavored with a touch of cinnamon, the way he liked it). She turned her back to him and started sweeping. There was an obvious flirtation in her movements as she swept the broom left and right, as if she were dancing to the rhythm of a hidden music. She swayed her hips with every stroke of the broom and moved her buttocks indecently. She collected an imaginary pile of dust and pretended to sweep it into an old olive-oil-spotted newspaper she found on the table, bending over in a blatantly sexual position in the process. But Si Mhammed didn't react and didn't say a word. That's what he told me. Then Luiza looked back to face him, bringing her fingertips softly to his face and putting on a coquettish tone, "You have a grain of rice—two, actually—on your lip, Si Mhammed."

She started slowly passing her fingers over his mustache and lips as she stared at him, hard. There was no room for doubt then. He caught her hand and squeezed it violently. He didn't let it go until she screamed in pain and the look of seduction in her eyes became one of supplication and fear. He took the newspaper she had used to collect the dust, carefully opened it, and then shook it over her head before throwing the paper in her face, whose brown skin tone had turned blue. He pushed her away with his foot disdainfully, so she ran towards the door as he insulted and cursed her.

He didn't tell anyone in the family about the secret, fearing that she would be fired, but she treated his nobility with meanness. Years after the incident, she fabricated an imaginary story inspired by her sick illusions. She claimed that she found him in the shed one Ramadan night fornicating with one of his male friends. No one believed her but her lady Zbaida.

"Believe me, Fawzia, Zbaida doesn't like me, and she's probably the one who incited her maid to fabricate those lies."

It was obvious I didn't believe him. I must have raised my eyebrows and pursed my lips without realizing it, like someone who's disagreeing with what they're hearing. He sighed and clapped his hands in despair, "Don't force me to uncover family secrets, woman. No matter what, she's my brother's wife."

I smiled derisively, nodding my head. He understood that his false decency wouldn't convince me and that he needed to provide more explanation if he wanted me to believe him. So he aimed his bow at his brother's wife and released a hail of poisoned arrows.

VI

Where is all this cold coming from, Sidi Mehrez? What am I supposed to do about the frost creeping through the cracks in this worn-out straw mat and mercilessly biting my bare feet?

The darkness in the shrine is starting to scare me, and the wind howling through the cracks in the door is filling me with so much terror that I don't know whether I'm trembling from cold or from fear. There's a din coming from the *zawiya* courtyard: tin vessels rolling, the curtains over the doors flapping—or maybe clothes fluttering on the line—and a forlorn creaking sound I can't place, all giving the night a terrifying rhythm. As if a newborn storm has suddenly begun to rage from every side, banging and destroying everything its demonic fingers can reach.

Are you angry at me, Sultan of Tunis? Are the wind and the cold my punishment? Did I desecrate your clean, honorable shrine with the story of my impure husband, and now I merit your wrath instead of your satisfaction? Or are you angry because Zbaida's being gossiped about and her honor is being violated here in your house as she sits at home, oblivious and disabled?

Zbaida doesn't deserve for you to get angry on her behalf, Sultan of Tunis; she doesn't believe in the holy saints. She makes fun of them, God forbid, and mocks the people who visit them. Once, when she heard Lella Jnayna talking about the miracles of Saint Saida Manoubia, she laughed and said, "Another of her amazing miracles is that she managed to make the people of Tunis believe that all her alone time with Abu al-Hasan al-Shadhili in his cave in the Jellaz hillside was purely for knowledge. The same goes for her alone time with Bousaid al-Beji."

She said that and burst into laughter, then went back to thumbing through her book. Lella Jnayna nearly lost her mind hearing Zbaida make fun of Saint Lella Manoubia and talk about our masters, the saints of Tunis, with such disrespect. She regretted talking about the subject in front of that "Westernized" woman whose religion was spoiled by the Catholic schools. She told her so angrily, then started asking for forgiveness and mercy from Lella Manoubia, Sidi Abu Al-Hasan, and Sidi Bousaid, so they wouldn't harm this ignorant woman who didn't know what she was saying.

But they did harm her, Sidi Mehrez. During the six months I spent at the Ennaifer house, I saw her have two epileptic episodes. Her body would shudder violently like a terrified chick, and even when the episode calmed down, she would continue shaking and shivering. When the seizure finally ended, she lay as still as a corpse, tears flooding her eyes, nothing left of her but her faint breath.

In my opinion, they most likely harmed her in bed, too. Or perhaps her husband also got his share of the curse. I often pressed my ear to the wall separating our rooms, both night and day, but I never heard anything: not a laugh, not a shout, not a muffled cry of pleasure. There was a funereal silence in her room whenever Si Mohsen entered it. Sometimes I could hear voices without words, the sounds of a short argument followed by long sighs and sharp exhalations like sobs.

This wind is getting stronger; it's about to take the door off your shrine, Sultan. As though you're still mad at me? God forbid, it wasn't my intention to spy on the secrets of locked rooms. I swear by your honorable shrine, I was just checking to see how thick the wall was, so I could tell, based on what I heard, what my neighbors could hear from our side. But what I could hear from Mohsen and Zbaida's room wasn't enough to satisfy me.

Only once was Si Mohsen's voice loud enough that I could hear his words clearly. Zbaida was whispering, so I didn't hear anything from her, but he answered her angrily with his voice raised, saying, "You didn't leave me with any other options!"

". . ."

"You should've seen this coming. I'm not an angel, and I'm not a devil."

". . ."

"I'm fine, thank God. But you should consult one of the good books and get some help."

". . ."

I heard him laughing. "Is she really still asking this? Tahar Haddad's book, of course."

I would hear this name repeated in Zbaida's room more than once, Sidi Mehrez, always by Sidi Mohsen. He only mentioned it when he was shouting and angry. But I was never able to understand the context he mentioned it in. Once, I tried to lure Luiza into a conversation about it, hoping to get some idea about the story. I knew there was no point in asking a direct question, so I decided to trick her. I invited her to my room and pointed to the bell-shaped iron bars on the window that rust had started to erode, and said, pretending to be innocent, "I beg Si Mhammed every day to fix these bars before they come off completely and the problem gets harder to fix."

Then I added, clapping my hands to express my aggravation, "Si Mhammed won't mingle with contractors and doesn't know the good from the bad. I should ask Si Mohsen for help so we can hire someone we can trust."

"It's an easy fix, Lella Fawzia; it just needs a bit of welding here and there. Any blacksmith's apprentice could do it."

"I heard Si Mohsen talking about a good blacksmith he knows; I think his name was Tahar . . . ?"

She looked confused, her eyebrows furrowed, as if she were trying very hard to remember. I wanted to help her, so I repeated the name, "Tahar the *haddad*, the blacksmith."

Her eyes suddenly glowed darkly. She stared at me for a long time, blinking nervously, her lips pursed in obvious anger. It seemed as though she were going to raise her hand and slap me, but she asked God for forgiveness and sought his protection from Satan, then turned and left without saying anything.

VII

The night Si Mhammed told me about his disagreement with Zbaida and her maid, to prove that what they'd said about him was false, he spared no effort in staining their reputations. But in all of it, he didn't mention a blacksmith named Tahar or an Italian trader named Franco. Although curiosity was prodding me to ask about them, I feigned indifference because of the fit of fury that had overwhelmed me and the role of the silent, angry woman I was playing. It prevented me from showing interest in the person talking to me or asking him questions about anything that was unclear. I just kept listening to him, sometimes looking down and sometimes at the ceiling. I showed no reaction, as if I were made of rock, as questions burned in my chest, so many questions that still remain unanswered.

He didn't talk about Luiza for long. In addition to the story of that Ramadan night on which she'd tried to seduce him, he told me about a solitary adventure she'd had with a carver on Rue de l'Eglise. The man had his way with her on top of the worktable in his shop, in the middle of the dust and marble shavings. After that he started pointing and laughing at her whenever she passed his shop, telling the story in obscene detail to the riffraff he hung out with.

Si Mhammed says that he begged his father, Si Othman, to kick her out when he heard the story from some of his old friends at Zaytuna Mosque, which isn't far from the carver's shop. But her lady Zbaida got very angry and foamed like the sea with rage; she claimed that he was slandering her maid. So Hajj Othman, who had grown old by then, listened to her; he'd softened with age, making it easy for Zbaida to trick him and bring him over to her side.

The truth is that Zbaida is a master in trickery, cunning, and slyness. Or that's what Si Mhammed said. His proof was that she'd "gotten off scot-free." If the Queen of Sheba had done what she did, the Prophet Solomon would've personally cut off her head. He added, smacking his legs with his fist, "Zbaida did something despicable and somehow avoided punishment. And when she got sick, people treated her with nothing but sympathy instead of the contempt she deserved, and that just encouraged her to keep sinning."

Instead of thanking him for his intelligence in uncovering the secret, his brother argued with him, content to be the cuckolded husband. And his father blamed him for the consequences of the incident.

That night, Si Mhammed went on and on about all these generalities that didn't quench my curiosity or satisfy me. I kept fidgeting inside, hoping to find out more, but my tongue—my vanity—wouldn't cooperate. I told myself I had to be demure and patient and ask later what I couldn't address then. But I was wrong to think that way. Since that night, Si Mhammed has refused to talk about anything related to Zbaida's story. Even stranger is that he's started lecturing me whenever I try to dig into it, telling me to stop gossiping about people.

8
The Tale of Si Othman Ennaifer
(*Rue Tourbet El Bey, Winter 1951*)

I

Life slips away between our fingers, and each breath brings us closer and closer to our deaths. Even if we get everything we want from this world and live our lives the way we want in every respect, we still won't be happy, and our tears of regret will never dry. Don't you see how long this grudge between your two sons has lasted, Jnayna? Don't you look back at the years gone by and ask what we did during these years and how we spent them? Why won't you deal with the problem? What's preventing you from doing something good and mediating their conflict? Why has the disagreement between the two continued all these many years? Isn't it time for this estrangement to end, and for this schism to be replaced with forgiveness and kindness?

Yesterday, Tijani Ben Abdallah, your son Mhammed's father-in-law, spoke to me at the cemetery, as we stood around the grave of our neighbor Amjad Shawashi, waiting for his corpse to be buried and to offer his children our condolences. He pointed at your son Mohsen as the crowd noted him walking alone between the graves towards the dead man's family: "Isn't it strange, Si Othman, that we never see your sons Mohsen and Mhammed out together?"

I tried to change the subject: "Shouldn't I feel it strange, Si Tijani, to be standing next to Amjad's grave? Just yesterday we were chatting in his shop in Souk Chaouachine."

He recited, "There is no power nor strength except by God," and asked God to protect him from Satan. He went silent for a moment, casting his eyes down as if pondering our friend's passing. But then he continued, asking, "But my daughter Fawzia told her mother something odd. She said that during the four months she's spent as a bride at your house, she's never once seen her husband Mhammed talking to his brother, Mohsen. They do live in the same house, Si Othman, or am I wrong?"

The grave digger had already started burying the corpse, so I seized the opportunity to quote from the Quran. "Yes, Si Tijani. We were created from dust and to the dust we will return. 'Every being on earth is bound to perish. Only your Lord Himself, full of Majesty and Honor, will remain forever.'"

Si Tijani immediately wiped his face and beard in a pretense of devotion before answering me with a sly smile, "Praise be to God, Si Othman. As God, may His majesty be glorified, said, "The believers are but brothers, so make settlement between your brothers."

The malicious man paid no heed to me after that, knowing full well that he'd put paid to the argument with that final, decisive blow. A solemn silence descended on us like a mountain, until the crowds started to move, forming lines heading towards the departed's family. I hurried ahead with the other mourners and left Tijani behind. He was elegantly dressed, as usual—overdressed, really—so he was still back between the graves, stumbling on the hem of his *chokha* and *qaftan*.

If you want the truth, Jnayna, then take it from me: Your new daughter-in-law Fawzia knows everything. I'm sure she told her family the story of that fateful night in detail. Do you expect any better from that cursed maid Luiza than exposing people's secrets and staining their reputations? She's the only one left in the ring now that Khaddouj is gone, so she doesn't miss a chance to attack us. If it hadn't been for Zbaida and my pity for her, I would've ousted that rotten woman from my house, even before hearing the awful story Mhammed told us about her.

Imagine, Jnayna, it was only a month or so after your son's marriage that I heard the bride and the maid whispering to each other next to the cistern. Fawzia was listening intently to Luiza, who spoke for a long time, looking right and left, watching for anyone spying on them. When they saw me and realized that I was unhappy about their suspicious meeting, their expressions changed. They'd been relaxed and whispering, but then they went quiet, embarrassed.

I managed to catch a few words from their whispered conversation, though, as if deciphering a code. I asked you about it that day, Jnayna, but you didn't help me out; you just changed the subject altogether. You should be honest with me today and speak, before I take your sons by their necks and bang their heads against the wall. What is it that Mohsen knows and is keeping secret, buried deep inside, out of concern and a desire to be a good son? And what was in that viper Luiza's head when she told Mhammed's wife, "Sidi Mohsen is the only one from the Ennaifer family who believed me, and here you are paying the price, Lella Fawzia."

What price is your daughter-in-law paying, Jnayna? Why does she seem to hate her husband and us and her life here so much? I see that you stopped being nice to her a while ago and have stopped speaking kindly to her. You probably never liked her, even though you chose her as a wife for Mhammed. I heard you saying to Beya that Fawzia's time living with us has exposed her hidden flaws and that now you realize that she's rude, mean, impatient, and unpleasant. Based on what you said, she's nothing compared to your older daughter-in-law, Zbaida, who's gentle, kind, well-spoken, and gracious.

May God forgive you, Mhammed. You ruined my relationship with Zbaida that night. You brought Satan into our house, and in a few seconds, you brought down an edifice that we thought would never collapse. What good did we do by exposing what was exposed? What did we gain by making the Rassaa family our enemy? If Mhammed had never touched the bundle of bread in the maid's hand that day, Jnayna, if he'd restrained himself, if I had stopped to think and each of us had gauged the consequences, would we have had that fight? God damn the anger that blinded our judgement, spoiled our affection, and caused all these problems.

Whenever I remember that ill-fated day, I still feel short of breath. I start gasping and heaving, and people sitting around me ask if I'm all right, but I don't answer. I know you know what's wrong with me, Jnayna, and you know that I know. You know I'm ruminating on that same story, and you understand my regret without me saying anything. I regret it, Jnayna. Today I'm saying it out loud. I regret it beyond what words can describe. I often wish that it never happened, but we have no time for regret.

II

I was confused and ashamed the night I apologized to Ali Rassaa, the night he regained consciousness. I visited to congratulate him and invite him to attend Mhammed's marriage ceremony. Yet I, Judge Othman Ennaifer, who shake the walls of the sharia court when I walk in its halls, entered the house of my in-laws feeling hesitant, with one foot forward and one back. If you hadn't insisted, I wouldn't have found the courage to face the man after all that happened that awful night. May God forgive you, Mhammed. You threw an ember of unrest onto a peaceful threshing floor and kept fanning it until the fire engulfed almost everything. But that night, the man was just happy to have come back to life after death stared him in the eyes, so he was inclined to reconcile without a quarrel. But he did allow himself to prick me with sharp needles from time to time, an innocent smile fixed on his face.

As he talked to me about his childhood at the royal palace in the Bardo district, I discovered that he was two years younger than me, despite his white beard and wrinkled forehead, which made him seem at least ten years older. In his youth, he lived the lifestyle of the beys in a rich family. But then the wheel of fate turned in the opposite direction when their patriarch passed away and they became the target of relatives' injustice. When his father, Rafiq Rassaa, was appointed as an artillery commander in the royal guard at Bardo Barracks, the family left their house on Tourbet El Bey and rented the upper floor of a small palace. It was owned by an Italian family and surrounded by a sprawling orchard that was originally owned by one of the royal family members from the 17th-century Muradid dynasty. As a child, he looked out from that height onto the social mosaic of Tunis. This shaped his early consciousness of Tunisian society in all its contradictions and his precise understanding of the human soul with its complexities and illusions. This is what he told me, with an expansive look on his face: "Seeing is believing, Si Othman."

He repeated this sentence several times while telling me about events he witnessed when he was ten or so. These events left their traces on him as a young boy and shaped the personality that people came to know later. They made him open-minded, "which is something the fundamentalists condemn." He stressed the syllables of the word and winked, pretending to laugh.

I accepted the first prick of the needle, Jnayna, with the forbearance and smile of someone who couldn't recognize an indirect accusation. I listened to him telling me about Madame Laura, the wife of the Italian living on the first floor of the palace, and about her fidelity, despite her open doors and exposed cleavage. And about Khala Daddo, the wife of the orchard caretaker, and her moral corruption, despite being closely guarded and well covered.

Two events remained in his mind. He told me about them enthusiastically, clearly urging me to take a lesson from them. The first involved Khala Daddo, the wife of the gardener Baba Flawi, and her story with a young Italian veterinarian who used to visit the palace from time to time to check on the cows in the barn and update their vaccines. The veterinarian was in his thirties; he was a big guy, handsome and strong. He was deeply shy, and his cheeks would get red whenever Madame Laura, the Italian owner's wife, came to talk to him about the state of the barn. The second was a story that happened between that young man and Madame Laura herself. He searched the old notebooks in his memory and told me, "My grandmother from my mother's side, God bless her soul, used to visit us at our Bardo residence from time to time. She would often visit us towards the end of the summer or in early fall. The carriage would cross the orchard surrounding the palace until it conveyed her to the stairs leading to the entrance. As soon as she poked her head out of the carriage, she would see Madame Laura, in her vibrantly colored short dresses with their low necklines. She would be drinking tea or coffee (or maybe some juice) on the high patio overlooking the orchard, lying on a rattan chaise longue under a jasmine trellis, surrounded by expensive mats and pillows. She would lie down on her back with her knees bent, her legs perpendicular to her slender body, and the dress would slip down, showing her thighs. The young Italian woman with the captivating laugh never missed the chance to wave, welcoming my grandmother with a smile on her face each time she visited. Yet my grandmother, who we called 'Mother Zeinab,' would answer the greetings with merely a nod. She transformed the thirty-three steps of the winding staircase up to her daughter's home into a string of prayer beads for her careful repetition. As she negotiated her ample body up the stairs, you could hear nothing but her tongue reciting, 'Good heavens! Good heavens! Good heavens!' or 'God forgive us, God forgive us, God forgive us!' And sometimes the prayers turned into curses aimed at the Italian disbeliever who exposed her buttocks in public."

Si Ali laughed, asking God to have mercy on his grandmother and all the departed Muslims, and then resumed. "My grandmother wouldn't even wait for her sweat to dry before she started her lecture, which my mother knew by heart: 'I'm afraid for you, Farida! How could you let your husband see this Italian woman morning and night? You have no problem with her lying like that, showing off her thighs? If I were you, I wouldn't stay one more day in this house. You're foolish. Men are stray dogs who salivate over cheap meat. Tomorrow this corrupt woman might bring you a baby in her arms and say to you, 'Zis is ze son of Si Rafiq Rassaa.'

"My brothers and sisters and I would laugh out loud at my grandmother's imitation of Italians trying to speak Tunisian Arabic. My mother was phlegmatic and taciturn, but her face would darken for some time, and signs of annoyance and concern would come over her calm features, though she tried to hide them under a puzzled smile.

"Then my father would come home after his work in the barracks, tall and attractive, and my grandmother would see him in his magnificent military uniform: black trousers with a red stripe on each leg, a jacket with golden buttons and decorated with silver medals, and the shiny bey coat of arms embellishing the front of his chechia, its long tail hanging down to the middle of his broad back. He would greet her with a smile, his teeth white like snow, rubbing his pointy mustache. As soon as he entered the room, my grandmother would start to slap her thighs with her hands in agitation, whispering to my poor mother, 'I am afraid that Italian woman is going to steal this young man away from you.'

"I'm not sure if my grandmother enjoyed torturing my mother with those thoughts, which clearly bothered her and wrapped her happy days with my father in a vague, unspeakable anxiety. But the impact of what she used to say about the immoral Italian unbeliever, who wanted to steal my father and harbored ill will towards my mother, shaped our early consciousness, my siblings and I, imparting to it a hidden fear of foreigners that was mixed with a kind of hatred that we couldn't explain.

"But our experience coexisting with that Italian family soon caused us to feel torn. The simplicity of Madame Laura in her daily life, her genuineness with her neighbors, and her kindness to both young and old, all of which we'd personally witnessed, seemed to be at odds with the negative stereotypes. We'd heard that Europeans were so unclean that when they went to the toilet, they wiped themselves with whatever they found nearby, instead of cleaning themselves with water like civilized people. Yet that young Italian woman with the captivating perfume used to fill our pockets with candy and fine chocolates—chocolate whose magical flavor I can still taste, and I am now an old man of seventy-five."

Si Ali lowered his voice, craning his neck to cast a glance at the window overlooking the courtyard and make sure that none of his family members could hear him, and then he said to me, smiling, "I had a crush on her, Si Othman. Her perfume used to waft towards me when she bent over to plant two warm kisses on my cheeks, and I would feel something in my chest, though I couldn't name it. Heat would rise to my head when she caressed my short hair with her soft hand and put some sweets into my pocket, saying, '*Bellissimo ragazzo*.'

"She used to send me home with some homemade traditional cheese, as well, but my mother, disgusted by its strong smell, would immediately throw it away. She would say 'Bismillah,' frustrated, and add, 'God provides and God disposes . . . This is no good, no good at all. Is this all that's left to us, getting bewitched by Italians?'

"Madame Laura also used to bake delicious-smelling European pastries and share them with us from time to time. We had to devour them in secret on our way home, and any leftovers ended up as feed in the chicken coop.

"Because I loved her so much, I used to spy on her; I would watch her from an observation post on the roof of the house as she walked among the trees, smelling one flower, caressing the petals of another. Or sometimes she would fill her woven basket, covered with red cloth, with ripe fruits that she picked, whatever was in season: figs from the old fig tree, apples, peaches, almonds—everything the orchard offered. I noticed with some jealousy how interested Baba Flawi had become in her and how he would run behind her with a bouquet of violets or jasmine necklaces. She never refused his presents but, instead, accepted them with a big smile, raising them to her nose as a sign of affection and bowing her head in gratitude. Even more disturbing, though, were her conversations in Italian with the Italian veterinarian as they left the barn and headed to the courtyard to drink fresh orange juice under the jasmine trellis on warm spring evenings. Then I felt like she was a stranger, and the childish naivety I had attributed to her due to her broken Arabic faded away. They would be often joined in these evening chats by Filippo, her tall, skinny husband who wore a black hat. They would talk and laugh loudly, but the young veterinarian would stay reserved and quiet.

"One evening, we heard a loud mooing in the barn and knew one of the cows was in labor. But the mooing started to get more and more intense until it became like a hideous scream. Baba Flawi couldn't help the cow, who was kneeling on her front legs and shaking, having lost a lot of blood. He ran to call for the veterinarian, Alberto, at his house near the estate. I, along with my brother, Mahmoud, who was a year and half younger than me, was standing behind a post in the barn, watching the scene with a pounding heart. Madame Laura arrived quickly, wearing rubber boots, tight brown trousers, and a pistachio-colored woolen shirt. I still remember that scene in detail, as if it hasn't been six decades since it happened. She started talking emotionally to the veterinarian while holding the cow's head, rubbing her forehead, encouraging her in Italian, and addressing her by a name I don't remember. As for the Italian veterinarian, he took off his jacket and threw it onto the hay piles, then put on two rubber gloves. He rebuked Baba Flawi when he tried to help him with some tricks he knew, and the gardener left, angry and mumbling. My brother and I held our breath, fearing that Madame Laura would see us there and kick us out, as well; she wouldn't have let children witness scenes of labor or slaughter.

"A few minutes later, Alberto was able to save the calf, thanks to his experience. The cow calmed down, stood back up, and started licking her calf, cleaning the remains of the placenta off it. As for Madame Laura, she screamed in joy like a child and started jumping like a butterfly next to Alberto, who took off his gloves and smock to wash his hands and arms from a wooden basin, splashing water on his neck, armpits, and chest despite the cold, looking at her with admiration and smiling. It was a beautiful scene that was spoiled by an unexpected act. When Madame Laura handed him a clean towel to dry off his body, he suddenly grabbed her hand and pulled her towards his naked chest, trying to kiss her by force.

"When I looked at Mahmoud, I found him glued to the post, pale and staring blankly. I myself was afraid and pulled between two conflicting voices in my head: one reproached me for watching and ordered me to run away, while the other urged me not to deprive myself of the pleasure of a forbidden spectacle. Before I'd made my decision, Alberto had pushed Madame Laura to the ground with his strong body and pinned her down, burying his face in her breasts and belly. We didn't understand that she was resisting him until we saw him put his hand over her mouth to muffle her screams, and we didn't believe she'd gotten the better of him until we saw him retreat, blood streaming from his forehead. The brave young woman had hit him with a shovel that she grabbed from the top of the hay pile where she'd fallen during the struggle. In less than two minutes, it was all over, and a new path, questioning some basic axioms, had opened in my mind. Wasn't this Madame Laura, the immoral disbeliever, the man hunter who exposed her buttocks to men, as Mother Zeinab said? Why, then, was she so desperate to protect her honor and the honor of her hat-wearing husband? Weren't the revealing clothes and the improper sitting position unmistakable signs of moral decay? How could this charming woman combine displays of her beauty and body on one hand, with chastity and fidelity on the other?"

III

Si Ali was looking at me meaningfully as he asked these questions, Jnayna, as if waiting for an answer. I understood what he wanted but stayed silent, waiting for the rest of the story. He stopped for a moment to fish a silver box out of his *jebba* pocket and offered me an imported cigarette, but I politely declined. Then he called a servant boy and ordered him to prepare the pipe for his guest and to fill it with the special leaves. I understood that he meant cannabis. I smiled and didn't comment. He continued, "The incident of Madame Laura with the veterinarian, Si Othman, was the first part of a two-part lesson. The second part would come only a month or so later. After around a week or ten days, the veterinarian showed up again, the wound on his forehead starting to heal. We knew that Madame Laura hadn't told her husband, probably to protect his longstanding friendship with his fellow Italian. She started avoiding him, however. He began entering and leaving without attracting anyone's attention, especially in the late winter and early spring, when the Italian owner frequently sent Baba Flawi to the markets in Tunis to buy new shoots and seeds to plant for the next season.

"Baba Flawi was in his forties, a big man with a big head, as if he were an ogre from a fairytale. I heard my father saying that he had been a wealthy farmer from the region of Msaken; he had orchards of olive and almond trees that brought in enough money to comfortably take care of him and his siblings. Then life turned its back on him. After the revolution of Ali Ben Ghedhahem, General Zarrouq raided the Sahel region and, on the order of Sadok Bey, took away residents' livelihoods, money—even their wives' jewelry. Baba Flawi wasn't the only person affected: the same was done to hundreds of others in Msaken, Kalaa Sghira, Monastir, and all the coastal villages that had defied the army. All because they had supported the uprisings in the villages of Ouled Majer, Ouled Ayar, El Frashish, and Drid against tax increases. Baba Flawi couldn't bear to become a day laborer working for his neighbors, like his siblings did, so he migrated to Tunis and worked in a number of jobs before settling at the palace.

"But he was prideful and his pride made him malevolent and suspicious. Whenever he left the palace, wearing the gray clothes he favored both summer and winter, he would lock the gate of his house—a modest dwelling at the edge of the orchard—with a thick chain, imprisoning his wife and daughters. We used to find this behavior strange because my father, despite his own zealous protection of his family honor, never locked my mother and sisters in. He would allow them to go for walks within the walls of the palace grounds, so long as they covered their faces and didn't go out into the street.

"The funny thing is, Khala Daddo and her daughters were able to escape the house and go out into the orchard through a small window in the bathroom. It was meant to let in daylight and fresh air, and it wasn't covered by an iron grate like the rest of the windows. And because it was high and relatively narrow, it never occurred to the hapless Baba Flawi that they could use it to get out whenever they wanted. So we would see them coming out of it, one after another. The mother first: she was a medium-sized woman, and the harsh conditions of life hadn't yet managed to steal the softness from her body. Then her daughters followed, ordered by age: the youngest one, then the middle one, and finally the oldest, who was six years old, last. While we boys busied ourselves chasing the girls and spying on their innocent games among the trees and bushes, Khala Daddo would disappear for about an hour. Then she would suddenly reappear, calling her daughters. They would immediately run to her and reverse the path of their escape, the daughters first and the mother last, climbing up on an empty barrel that they had placed under the window."

As Si Ali told the story, Jnayna, he laughed fit to burst, as if he were reliving those long-ago moments. Whenever I remember that he lived only a few short days after that visit, I become surer that the human soul, as it approaches death, starts longing to relive past events. It's as if they're compensating for the imminent loss of what will never happen by returning to what has passed. Deep down memory lane, Si Ali exhaled the smoke from his cigarette, his eyes wandering along with the smoke as he continued. "In those days, I was still angry at Alberto, the Italian veterinarian. I didn't think that the shovel blow—which had left an ugly wound on his forehead—was punishment enough for what he'd done to Madame Laura in the barn. I was thirsty for justice, and it just so happened that that period coincided with my summer break. I started watching the veterinarian's comings and goings from a distance, searching for a way to take revenge that would heal my fury. I thought about teaming up with Mahmoud to take him by surprise and push him into the open cistern. Maybe he was one of those people who didn't know how to swim, so he would drown and die. But I was afraid of the consequences if he survived and complained to our father. I also thought about going to the barn before him and opening the door leading to the bullpen. When he entered, I would stir up the bulls by screaming and banging hard on the barrels to get them to leave their stalls and kick him while he was busy checking the cows. I had to revise this plan, too, however, after I tried screaming and banging on the barrels before he arrived but the bulls didn't move. I kept spying on him, though, waiting for an opportunity or an idea. And that's how, one morning, I saw him knock on the locked door of Khala Daddo and her daughters after Baba Flawi had left for the tram station.

"The way he knocked on the door caught my attention. He knocked twice with the palm of his hand, following that with a single rap and then repeating the same rhythm twice. What was even stranger was that he left right after knocking, without waiting for an answer. He walked slowly towards the outer gate of the palace wall, occasionally turning to look behind him. A minute later, I saw Khala Daddo's head emerge from the usual exit, followed by her slender body, then the bodies of her daughters.

"My brother busied himself watching the girls play in the orchard, as usual. But for the first time, I kept my eyes on Khala Daddo. I saw her cover herself with a thick black *safseri* that covered her from head to toe. She pulled the lace edge so far over her beautiful Amazighi face that you couldn't see her at all, not even her eyes.

"She set off in a hurry, looking through the tiny holes in the lace of the *safseri* to find her way along the same path that Alberto had taken. As she left through the outer gate, she quickly disappeared from my sight. Our father forbade us from climbing the outer wall of the estate for any reason, but I was dying of curiosity and so disobeyed his orders, scraping the inner part of my arm as I struggled to see over it. The wall was high, but there was a hole in the stone that I put my foot in, lifting my body as much as possible with my arm muscles. That's when I saw Alberto walking on the path heading away from the barracks, followed at a distance by a ghost wearing black, walking with a swinging gait. From time to time, Alberto glanced back at the ghost and smiled."

IV

When the servant arrived carrying the pipe, Si Ali stopped talking. You know, Jnayna, that I'm not a big fan of cannabis, but I suppose it doesn't hurt to have a little fun sometimes. I straightened in my seat and slipped the stem of the long pipe between my lips. The scent was mesmerizing, so I closed my eyes and listened to Si Ali resume his story. "I waited for Khala Daddo until she came back, around an hour later. Her face was still covered by the *safseri*, so I couldn't gauge her mood. She called her daughters, as usual, to go inside through the small window before Baba Flawi came home. The honorable house with its iron chain fell silent again, as if nothing had happened.

"I told Mahmoud what I'd seen, since he was my partner in the plan to get revenge on the Italian. I found that, like me, he was inclined to think the best of Khala Daddo: maybe she went to the veterinarian's house to do some cleaning, to earn a little money to help her cope with life's hardships. A modest Muslim woman, obedient to her husband and accepting of her seclusion, committed to wearing Islamic clothes—even beyond what was required—could only be a synonym for honor and virtue. How innocent and naive children are. I stopped thinking about her and went back to thinking about the veterinarian and how I could get revenge on him for what he'd done to Madame Laura. The summer break was about to end, and my enemy's visits had started to become so infrequent that I was about to throw in the towel. But then one of the cows' udders became inflamed, and blood started flowing from it along with the milk. The veterinarian was called in the morning, offering me my chance on a silver platter. He examined the cow and determined that she had a very infectious disease and must be culled from the herd. Baba Flawi took her away, following the Italian owner's orders as he left for work, to get rid of her. Baba Flawi left to call for Aammi Khalifa the butcher, and we heard him order his wife to prepare the necessary bowls to hold the slaughtered cow's offal. Everyone was busy with the work of slaughtering, skinning, and cutting, and no one realized that the veterinarian had vanished like a grain of salt in water, as had Khala Daddo. I was the only one who knew where they were, and the only one who knew what they were doing. It was a shock for the boy I was then, and it changed his views on chastity and virtue forever.

"Alberto had warned everybody, especially Baba Flawi,

that they should stay away from the barn until he had ascertained the scope of the infection among the rest of the herd. He claimed with his broken Arabic that the disease could easily infect humans and claimed that its consequences were dire and could cause paralysis or blindness. Khala Daddo, who came with the tubs to hold the offal, listened to what he said and recited some mumbled words of protection. Within a few minutes, the butcher arrived, and everybody gathered around the sick cow, except for Madame Laura, who would hide whenever she saw the shadow of Alberto at the estate. As for me, I wasn't paying attention to either the cow or the knives, but had focused my attention on the veterinarian, secretly praying that God would up and infect him with the disease he'd made us afraid of. But he didn't seem worried about infection or danger at all as he snuck out of the crowd and went back to the barn. Shortly afterwards, I saw Khala Daddo join him, pulling the heavy wooden door closed behind her."

I will not repeat to you, Jnayna, Si Ali's description of what he saw through the cracks in the barn door, or what precisely the veterinarian and the inattentive gardener's wife were doing. It was a shock for the boy, who discovered a new, wild way for men and women to interact and, at the same time, the gulf between outer appearances and hidden realities. He elaborated, after finishing the story, on the moral he took from all of this. He said, lighting a second cigarette, "I knew at that early age that connecting chastity with external appearances and modest clothing was a fallacy that only an ignorant and naive person could believe. I understood that keeping women locked in the house and constricting their movement wouldn't prevent them, if they so desired, from doing what even free women won't do. There were two opposite examples before me, each of them harvesting an outcome that seemed at odds with their actions. Baba Flawi, so cautious and suspicious, vicious and jealous—his wife, that modest and respectful woman, cheated on him despite all the locks and barriers he erected. And as for the

Italian owner who didn't prevent his wife from mingling with men, his honor was protected and his reputation preserved, despite the ample opportunities she had to sin."

V

You see why Ali Rassaa told me about these events, don't you, Jnayna? The man was implicitly justifying to me his misguided philosophy of raising his daughters like a decadent European. And as for the term "cuckoldry," which I indirectly attributed to him when we argued that ill-fated night, he was dressing it up as a special sensitivity that came from experience and careful reflection on the best way to deal with women.

I felt that he was justifying the mistakes he made as an adult with his experiences as a child, though during that visit he maintained his role as a sensible scholar, experienced visionary, and wise man giving lessons. But regret has a smell that exposes the regretful, Jnayna, no matter how proud they are or how hard they try to hide it, and the odor of regret on Ali Rassaa was unmistakable. He must've reproached himself a thousand times for allowing that unbeliever Tahar Haddad into his house, enabling him to poison his sons and daughters' minds with his fairy tale ideas about liberating Muslim women and encouraging them to follow the European model. Can you imagine: "emancipating" them from the hijab, making them equal partners with men in inheritance, and so on, all nonsense God doesn't approve of.

I knew the man superficially, Jnayna. I followed the campaign that was launched against him by two newspapers, *Al Zahra* and *Al Nadim*, as soon as his book was published. Then I saw him later at Hajj Banna's perfume shop arranging the bottles, organizing the big jars they mix perfumes in, and dusting the shelves. It never occurred to me, when I went to the shop to buy you that basil perfume you like, that the quiet employee with the forlorn face and despondent movements was the heretical writer Tahar Haddad, who, with his deviance and moral turpitude, had provoked scholars, the media, and most of the Tunisian people. I found that out by chance from my friend Sheikh Ben Mrad. I was passing by the souk one day, on my way to the late Amjad Shawashi's shop, accompanied by Sheikh Ben Mrad. At that time, in the early '30s, he was a first-year teacher at Zaytuna University and was still associating with us, before he became stubborn and arrogant and changed his friends, when he became the Sheikh of Islam during the time of Moncef Bey. That day, the sheikh nodded his head towards Banna's shop and said with clear pleasure in some misfortune, "Do you see those miscreants, Othman?"

I looked left and right, but I had no idea who he meant. When I asked for clarification, he mentioned his name, asking for God's protection, and said angrily, "The apostate who was a student in my class at Zaytuna University and then, after that, started attacking and taunting us, accusing us of being backward fundamentalists, and telling us to stop following God's lawful sharia."

"And what's our friend doing at Banna's shop?"

"Banna felt sorry for him when he was fired from his job by ministerial decree, so he hired him to work there for a pittance."

He hadn't even finished his sentence when he veered towards the shop, pulling me with him. He greeted Hajj Banna, who jumped up to greet us. Then he addressed Haddad, who pretended to be busy organizing a display at the back of the shop, "Come here, boy. Bring some cologne for Si Othman; it's on me."

I looked at the man. He was young and brown-skinned, the age of our son Mohsen or a year or two older. He looked up at us, recognized the sheikh, and understood his intention. His face tightened, and he didn't answer. He gently closed the display case, then went towards where Hajj Banna had sat back down. He leaned over and whispered something in his ear before quickly leaving the shop.

"I sent my apprentice on a mission, Sheikh Mrad, but I will serve you. What kind of cologne does Si Othman prefer?"

Sheikh Ben Mrad got angry. He fixed his turban, caressed his beard, and addressed the shop owner harshly, walking towards the door: "We won't buy anything, Hajj. It seems to me that your apprentice will bring you bad luck. How can God bless your business when you support his enemies? Good night."

I eventually forgot about that incident, Jnayna, and I never went back to Banna's shop, to avoid any awkwardness. It didn't occur to me that I would hear Haddad's name again until the incident at our house. I asked people about him after that fateful night, but I couldn't find anyone with anything good to say about him. I was told that his family and friends had abandoned him when they found out about his heresy and disrespect of religious laws, so he died alone, a persona non grata. People said he was originally from the south; his family migrated to Tunis from El Hamma in Gabes, but he was born here in a poor house on Rue Kaaiki. His father was a trader who owned a chicken shop in the Marché Centrale, along with his brother.

Isn't it one of life's great injustices that a chicken seller's son could find his way to the great mosque of Zaytuna, to study with the sons of nobles and dignitaries? What's even stranger is that he didn't end up heretically reading the Quran over dead people in cemeteries. Even though his teachers called him stupid and said that he didn't memorize much from the Islamic texts, commentaries, and annotations, he managed to get his degree—the *Tatwi*, Jnayna, after he failed twice! He spent nine years at Zaytuna Mosque instead of seven.

Although the *Tatwi* would've enabled him to work as a notary public like our son Mhammed, it seems that Haddad knew his own worth and realized that he couldn't compete in that business. So he chose not to open his own office, preferring instead to work as a bookkeeper at Mohammed al-Khmiri's shop in Souk El Attarine. Then Ali Rassaa helped him, or so people say, to become a secretary at a charitable association. Five years before his death, God wanted to give him a preview of his torture in the afterlife, so he got fired from all his jobs, and people started throwing stones at him in the street. If he hadn't sought protection from some of his tribe who'd migrated to the Sidi Mansour quartier, the people of Tunis would have killed him. They say he sent several letters to the protectorate authorities complaining, but they didn't answer him, so he was forced to work as a shop employee to feed himself.

I don't know how Ali Rassaa met him towards the end of his time at Zaytuna. He hired him to teach his daughters when their schedule at the French school permitted. Is there any rational person who would do this? It wasn't enough that he sent his veiled treasures to a school that disdained our traditions and religion! No, he doubled down on his mistake with an even worse one: he brought a strange man into his house to be alone with his daughters, on the pretext of teaching them Arabic language and literature. How misguided and stupid! Can't anyone with a little bit of brains understand that "avoiding harm is better than reaping benefits?" And what's the benefit anyway of teaching chickens to crow like roosters? What's the benefit of teaching girls the principles of reading and writing, except equipping them with what they need to write letters to strange men? Would Zbaida have received a letter from anyone at all if she'd remained hidden in her house like our daughters, protected from prying eyes, with no need to acquire skills that would harm her rather than benefit her? Are Zbaida and her educated sisters better off? Do they have a higher status or a more perfect mind? Are they happier than you, Jnayna, or than your daughters, Beya, Nozha, and Mannana?

There's nothing in this life more harmful to women than trying to imitate men. A woman loses half of her femininity any time she holds a pen instead of scissors and a needle, or puts a book in her lap instead of an embroidery hoop and ball of wool. Then, bit by bit, her voice gets louder and her head fills up with useless knowledge; her treatment of her husband changes, and she starts to disagree with and bully him. It's rare that one of these educated women stays with her husband for long. She always overestimates herself and oversteps, so after a few months, she ends up either a divorcée or ignored in her husband's house, neglected, no one paying any attention to her. Then the husband gets tired of her and exchanges her for another wife, one full of femininity who doesn't read or write.

As God is my witness, I advised Mohsen to avoid the Rassaa girl, but he didn't listen to my advice. He was stubborn as usual, just stuck his fingers in his ears, so to speak, and said, "She's the only one for me." I said to him, "She was raised by nuns. If they didn't teach her how to moo, they taught her how to cluck."

My words only made him more stubborn. I told him what Mhammed had said about her when he found out his brother was planning to ask for her hand. I was agitated, hoping he would come to his senses: "Your brother says she was at the Taraqqi Club last year during that debate organized by the Society of Cultural Prosperity. Mhammed himself saw her applauding for that crazy woman Habiba Mismari or Minshari or whatever her name was, defending unveiling and attacking those who were defending the hijab, accusing them of being backward fundamentalists."

Your son answered me without shame, "God bless Mhammed and his valuable intelligence report. Now I know I made the right choice."

Your oldest son is clumsy, Jnayna, and obviously he inherited a lot of stupidity from his maternal uncles. The cursed boy forced me to accept it as a *fait accompli.* I was afraid that if I insisted on refusing him, he would go back to Germany on the first ship, to marry some European woman who would raise my grandchildren in licentiousness and debauchery. I accepted it against my will, and I didn't even know then that the bride was spending time alone with an apostate who was teaching her Arabic and who would become, a few months after her marriage, the biggest enemy of the nation.

VI

Ali Rassaa didn't talk, during our reconciliation meeting, about his past with Tahar Haddad. I think he was as surprised as everyone else when he published that book, which infuriated both the elite and the masses. I'm sure he was even more alarmed when he discovered, too late, that he'd entrusted his daughters to a renegade and an enemy of the religion. He'd even paid him money to spread his poison in their young minds. Worst of all, the man wounded him not only in life but also in death. Wasn't his corpse already cold by the time Haddad's letter reached his daughter?

When he called for Zbaida that fateful night, bellowing like a camel and ordering her to leave our house, she clung to Mohsen's arm and refused to follow his orders. I saw his face go as pale as a cholera patient's and watched with bitter pleasure as he saw with his own eyes the fruit of her corrupt upbringing. What more could we expect from a girl who went to school, read books written by unbelievers, and got a taste of freedom? Nothing but disobedience and disrespect. Then I told him something that broke what was left of his pride, "Don't worry, Si Ali. Tonight, Mohsen will swear the oath of divorce, and she'll come back to your house humbled and obedient."

He refused during the confrontation between us to condemn his daughter for anything. He kept asking me to show him the letter that had unleashed all this chaos so that he could decide whether his daughter had made a mistake. But the letter had disappeared, Jnayna. I remember that I threw it at Zbaida after I jabbed at her with my cane, but no one who witnessed the incident saw it after that. I told him my recollection of what I'd read, but he claimed that I was settling accounts with his daughter based on my misunderstanding of the written words, not the content itself. "On top of that, the person who receives a letter isn't responsible for the intentions of the sender. What right do you have to condemn Zbaida for the mistake of the person who wrote the message and the ignorance of those who read it?"

He was a master of arguments, Jnayna, sharp-tongued and shameless. I accused him of moral decay, negligence, and a failure to zealously guard over his women, while he accused me of fanaticism, ignorance, and living in the Stone Age. If it hadn't been for my son Mhammed, who supported me from time to time with some harsh words that confused the sheikh and silenced him, I would've hit him in anger with my cane like I did his daughter. As for your son Mohsen, he was standing like a statue, neither moving nor speaking. He stared daggers at his brother, reaching up every so often with a handkerchief to wipe away the blood still dripping from his nose after their fight. Mahdi, Zbaida's twin brother, who'd accompanied his father that night, also remained silent. But Mhammed paid no attention to them. That night, he was worked up in a way I'd never seen before. He probably didn't want to support me and condemn Zbaida as much as he wanted to humiliate Mohsen and rub his nose in the dirt. He was the one who told Ali Rassaa the thing that made him lose his mind, drove him over the edge, and finally put an end to the long argument. The sheikh was thundering and clattering, thinking he'd won the day when he embarrassed us by asking to see the message and then accused us of not having proof. But then Mhammed dealt him the fatal blow. He looked him straight in the eye and said, "We thought you would call your daughter in to question her. We thought you would teach her a lesson, have her apologize to her husband, and beg for his forgiveness. That's what a well-bred person does. Yet here we are; we hear what you're saying and see what you're doing, and we're shocked. We see you defending and justifying. You're prettying up a rotten dish; you're sprinkling putrid meat with spices. It's clear which spoiled goods are for sale at the Rassaa house: sanctioning fornication and gilding character flaws with immorality! The poet was right when he said: 'If the head of the house is playing the drums, you can't blame the family for dancing.'"

The old man was speechless. He staggered, as if Mhammed's words were a physical blow to the face. His body quaked and his eyelids flickered. He started mumbling, as if he'd lost all his eloquence in one fell swoop. He looked from his son Mahdi to Mhammed to Mohsen, as if to confirm that his son-in-law and his son, who was as silent as a tomb, had really witnessed what had been said without uttering a single word to defend him. Before he roared for Zbaida, whose disobedience would destroy the little pride he had left, he spat on the ground in Mhammed's direction and said, "Goddamn you, you ill-bred bastard!"

VII

After Ali Rassaa and his wife and son left, disappointed and angry, Mohsen went to Zbaida. She was huddled in her place in the corner of the entrance hall like an orphan kitten on a stormy day. Who would have believed that, a few minutes later, she would become a predator? Without saying a word, Mohsen grabbed her arm roughly and pulled her towards their room upstairs. You, Jnayna, had gone there before them to check on Mostafa in his crib after he started crying again. You didn't see the poor woman submissively following him with her head bowed. For my part, I leaned on Mhammed's arm and started slowly walking towards the sitting room, feeling severe pain in my leg.

Suddenly Mhammed decided to add more fuel to the fire. It had started raining again, but he raised his voice above the sound of water in the gutters and spoke, pretending to direct his words to me, "That wretched woman! What luck: on the same day her secret's exposed, her beloved dies, her father disowns her, and her husband's about to divorce her. A triple loss,

God willing, and all Mohsen has to do to divorce her is say the word three times, too."

You didn't witness Zbaida's reaction that day, Jnayna. You certainly heard her howling, but you didn't see her lunge towards Mhammed like a rabid wolf. With a single movement, she freed her arm from Mohsen's grip and attacked Mhammed. She suddenly transformed from a sweet kitten soaked by the rain into a raging predator driven by instinct. When Mhammed shook my arm from his, leaning back with his body to avoid her as she leapt towards him, I lost my balance and fell. I felt, then, something like a dagger tearing the ligaments of my ankle and cutting deep into the flesh. No one came to help me because all eyes were focused on Zbaida, who had dug her nails into Mhammed's neck, as if she were trying to kill him. Her diamond ring cut him below his chin, and he screamed in pain as he tried to push her away, to no avail. I stayed in my place, lying on the ground like a piece of furniture, watching helplessly as the situation spun out of control. That awful night was to lead us to another long chapter of horror, just when we thought that the dawn was near.

9
The Tale of Si Mahdi Rassaa
(*Hammad Lif, Winter 1943*)

I

The streets of Tunis are full of German soldiers now, Zbaida. They're roaming the roads with their harsh military gait, their heavy black boots hitting the ground in rhythm. Their armored vehicles are spread around the city, in every square, and at the city gates, blocking all the strategic entrances.

There are tanks stationed like metal monsters near Bab Jedid, Bab El Khadra, and Bab Souika. Unsmiling officers, wearing imposing military uniforms adorned with that distinctive Nazi symbol, appear from the tops of the tanks from time to time. On Place Bardo, next to La Kasbah Barracks and in the European quartier behind Bab El Bhar, there are heavily armed military vehicles with anti-aircraft artillery on top. The trenches that were dug in the fields of Sidi Jebali and in the Collège Sadiki garden and other places, both within the wall and outside it, are filled with residents of the city. Men, women, children, and old people all run towards them in groups whenever they hear the sirens, day and night, to hide from the hell of the Allies' bombs falling from the sky.

You're safe here, Zbaida. I'm sure you can hear the rumbling of cannons and the roar of planes from where you're sitting, but thank God, you're safe from their bombs. For the first time in his life, your father in-law, Othman Ennaifer, made a wise decision. Hammam Lif, where he moved you to escape the turmoil of war, is relatively safe. Allied aircraft coming from Algeria usually avoid it; the bey's palace is there, and for diplomatic reasons, it's unlikely that Moncef Bey's residence will become a battlefield.

Your father, Hajj Ali, also planned to move to the summer house in Hammam Lif when the battles started, but your mother refused, saying that she was surrendering to God's will. She was lying on the green couch in the sitting room, peeling some roasted chestnuts and listening to "Frag Ghazali" on the radio (its volume turned up to cover occasional explosions), when the Hajj tried to talk to her about how serious things were. She sat up and looked at him. She slowly swallowed the chestnuts in her mouth and then answered him contemptuously, "No one will die before their time, Si Ali; when your time is up, your time is up. I won't leave this house, even if they knock it down on top of my head."

She's still of this opinion, unwavering. Nothing can shake her, not your father's daily news about casualties, or your brother Bakkar's pleas that the constant terror will give him hepatitis. Whenever she hears explosions or sees the missiles lighting up the night to expose targets, she just touches the closest wall and recites the Verses of Refuge, *Al-Mu'awwidhatayn,* topping them off with the prayer she usually recites when there's lightning or thunder. Then she heads for the kitchen and goes about her business as if she can't see the smoke in the sky or hear the earth-shattering explosions. Hajj Ali was forced to find inspiration in his wife's bravery, composure, and deep faith—and give up the idea of departure.

As for your younger brother, Bakkar, he spends all day listening to the radio, moving from one channel to another, listening to the news. He began spending less and less time outside and more time at home, and now he no longer leaves the house at all. The Lycée Carnot closed its doors, just like the Collège Sadiki, the Lycée Alaoui, and all the other schools in Tunis. But, in spite of that, you can still see a small number of students leaving home in the morning, heading to shops where tutoring sessions are offered. What's even crazier: if some of them are daring and get close to the German armored vehicles, the soldiers smile at them and throw them candy and chocolate, and sometimes canned cheese and tuna. Do you see what they're doing, Zbaida? That wicked Hitler is deceiving the Tunisian people. It seems that he gave orders to his high-ranking officers to butter them up. With every newscast, the Italian station, Radio Bari, tells us that the German Reich has no interest in our country and that the entire region of North Africa means nothing to Germany. As for that lunatic Hitler, he still claims in his speeches and statements that his only concern is to cleanse the area of Allied domination. But no reasonable person believes that. It's impossible for anyone who knows the Nazi ideology, their plans to dominate the world and impose on it the superiority of the Aryan race, to believe them. Despite this, nearly everyone today, except for the Jews, trusts Hitler. They think that the Germans are a godsend and have descended on Tunisia to save them from French colonialism. As if they don't know that falling into the hands of Hitler the Nazi or Mussolini the Fascist would be a thousand times worse than submission to the feeble Vichy Government.

Also, let's assume that we believe "Aammi" Hitler and welcome his good intentions. Do you think an Axis victory is guaranteed, Zbaida? What if the Allies win and France comes back to set up gallows in Place Bab Saadoun? Or brings people before the firing squad at La Kasbah Barracks in retaliation for their alleged conspiracy against France and their alliance with the enemy? Some say, "Don't all signs point to the military supremacy of the Axis forces? Didn't Belgium and the Netherlands fall? Didn't the French sign the truce of 1940, submissive as pups?" But the English have the answer! Don't be fooled by the surrender of the French and their neighbors so long as Great Britain hasn't had the final word. It was not for nothing that the old empire was called the mistress of the sea. I swear to God, her fleet could resist the Germans for an entire century. Didn't she defeat Napoleon the Great after fifteen years of resistance? Also, the news from Russia about the Soviets' resistance in the Battle of Stalingrad shows that Germany is on the verge of a disaster.

Talk to your husband, Zbaida. I'm tired of talking to him. His stubbornness is no longer acceptable. He refuses to understand that he's under suspicion because he lived in Germany for a while and because he speaks German. To be honest with you, I'm worried about him. I'm afraid some informants might accuse him of collaborating with the Germans. The accusation alone is punishable by death, and France is now prosecuting people based on suspicion.

Two days ago, your stubborn husband came to my clinic on Boulevard Bab Mnara. He was complaining of chest pains. Don't worry, Madame Ennaifer. His heart is healthy and strong; he just had a bad cold. During the check-up, I tried to convince him that the future of the war hasn't been decided yet, and that he has to be careful of showing his support for the Germans, but he insisted the Nazi army is invincible. He kept laughing at me sarcastically, saying, "What do you understand about military plans and strategic maneuvers, boy? What looks to you like a German retreat is all part of their hit-and-run tactics. A maneuver to make the opponent overconfident so that they get careless and make it easier for the Germans to pounce again. It's nothing but tactics, boy."

That stupid position of your husband's is shared by some of our comrades in the party. Dr. Habib Thameur told us about the contents of the letter Bourguiba sent from his prison in Fort St. Nicolas last summer, but they weren't enthusiastic about his opinion and didn't even see any wisdom in it. Do you know what Bourguiba wrote? I didn't see the letter they smuggled to Dr. Thameur in the civil prison, but I was told that it literally said, "Germany won't win the war; it's impossible for it to win. It will be crushed by the two colossi, the Russians and the Anglo-Saxons."

In that leaked letter, Bourguiba was most likely giving orders to our leaders and fighters, telling them to communicate with the French leaders close to Charles de Gaulle, and to support France—not the Germans and Italians. I'm not sure whether time will prove him correct, and I'm not at all sure about the French. Isn't it possible that, if the Allies win, they'll just divvy up the cake among themselves? Then Tunisia might get rid of the French Protectorate only to find itself a British or American colony. I think, Zbaida, the best thing we can say right now is what your wise mother says every day, as she quietly stirs her pot to the rhythm of bombs and rockets. She runs her fingers through her hair under her scarf and says, "God, give the unbelievers power over the ungodly, strike the tyrants with tyrants, and get us safely away from all of them."

II

I know you feel you've been mistreated, too, Zbaida. It's been eight years since that night, eight years you haven't been allowed to visit your father's house and have been deprived of seeing your family. But your mother and father can't be blamed, either. Who could accept being insulted in the presence of his daughter and not seeing her get angry and support him? Instead, she disobeyed his order and didn't leave with him, even after he ordered her to do so . . . ? You broke their hearts that night, especially because they came to defend and protect you. You insulted them and made your in-laws gloat over their failure. But as God is my witness, I swear that, despite their anger, they were in terrible pain over what happened to you. If it hadn't been for Luiza, who brought them news of you day after day, describing your gradual recovery and how you were overcoming the pain, they could never have resisted visiting you in the hospital, and they wouldn't have been able to stand not seeing you for this long. Also, for God's sake, do you really think that I've been visiting you for all these years behind their backs? No, they know everything. They know I didn't stop writing to you during my time in France, and that I never stopped visiting you at your house on Tourbet El Bey over college breaks and afterwards, once I was home for good. Do you really think the books that Hajj Ali Rassaa buys from the Librairie Annabi at Bab Souika and sends with Luiza for your son Mohammed Habib—books by Manfalouti, Mikhail Naimy, and Gibran, and the novels of Voltaire, Montesquieu, and Stendhal, and French poetry collections—do you really think they're for your eight-year-old son? Did you think that the imported Turkish delight from Anatolia, the halva, the baklava trays, *bjawia*, trays of sugared almonds and ambergris cookies, the glass *fechka* of distilled rose water, the sweet geranium oil, *atarchya,* and all the other treats I brought you before the war—do you think any of them left the house without the permission of the Sultana Bashira Djellouli? Don't be ridiculous. Also, do you know why I left my clinic in these dark circumstances and rode the train to the suburbs for you, despite the danger? Your mother raised her voice this morning so that Hajj Ali, who was busy reading, would hear her. She put her right hand on my head, as she does every morning to protect me before I leave the house. She made her prayer a little longer than usual this time and started elongating the syllables in a singsong voice, her fingers combing my hair, with no concern for the hairstyle I spent half the morning working on:

> *Mahdi, may God stand you tall and make your enemies fall. May he make your troubles go and raise you above your foes like the crescent moon, high atop the mountains in the blessed sky. Pride and wealth in tow, may your deeds echo and the Prophet's blessings grow. May your words soar and blessings pour at heaven's unlocked door. May you shine like the moon and every path open before you. May God shield you and His blessings fill you.*

Then she held my chin and started haranguing me in such a threatening tone that anyone listening would imagine that the radio had suddenly switched stations. "Mahdi, I won't be happy with you if you don't go to Hammam Lif to see Zbaida—today, not tomorrow. If you don't check in on your sister and her two sons, the milk I fed you from my breast will become *haram*, what you eat from my pot will be bitter, and I'll be angry at you, whether I'm present or absent, awake or sleeping, alive or dead."

Then she took her hand off my chin and started rapping me on the chest with both fists, encouraging me to stand up as she continued. "My poor daughter. She must be worried sick because of the news of victims in Tunis. Tell her that we're all okay and not to let Mostafa or Mohammed Habib open the door or stand at the windows. Who knows? Stray bullets, God forbid, don't discriminate between young and old."

I see that you're laughing, Zbaida, but your mother has the right to be worried. Three days ago, I told her a painful story that has gnawed away at her, making her see visions during the day and giving her nightmares at night. When I was in the clinic around 11 A.M., as usual, providing free urgent care, the sirens suddenly started howling and all hell broke loose. The explosions were very loud and gave the impression that the destruction was only a stone's throw away. Even though I usually avoid the trenches and their crowds—instead trusting in God and my mother's prayers—I ran with the patients to seek refuge in the Bab Jedid trench. I found that it had become a canyon of mud after the heavy rain the previous night. A skinny little girl of seven or eight slipped from her mother's grasp as she gently lowered her down into the trench, and she fell into my arms. We lost sight of her mother because of the pushing and crowding, so she stayed in my arms waiting for the distress to ease up and the raid to stop.

She was wearing an old woolen *qashabia* for warmth, the hood of which was stiff with dust and dirt, and on her feet were thick socks encrusted with mud and a pair of rugged rubber shoes. Despite her poverty and dirtiness, her small face radiated a captivating, angelic beauty. She grabbed my hand when the bombing started, and I felt the coldness of her trembling fingers. I patted her small head gently to comfort her, and I talked to her from time to time, taking advantage of the short interludes of quiet between explosions.

I found out that her name was Habiba and that she had lost her father a few days before. He had been struck in an air raid targeting a freight train, while he was working with some other employees at the Tunis railway station to repair the track. I found out that her four younger brothers were all killed, buried under rubble, after their roof collapsed during the raid that destroyed most of the Sidi Bashir quartier. No one survived but her and her mother; when the disaster occurred, they had gone to see her wounded father in the Hôpital Aziza Othmana, where they found out that he'd died of his injuries. She said that now she spent most of the day wandering aimlessly in the street with her mother and that they sheltered at night in the entrance hall of Al Haliq Mosque. They slept on a piece of thick cardboard donated to them by some kind people, and they covered themselves with half of a woolen blanket her mother had managed to save from the debris of their home, where the other half was still lodged under the steel and stones. As she answered my questions, she narrated her family tragedy without a tear, as if, with a child's innocence, she was telling a story that didn't mean anything to her, or recalling a bedtime fairy tale her grandmother had told her. I was astonished and speechless, first because of the scope of the tragedy and second because of her neutral tone, and she didn't give me a chance to offer any words of sympathy or consolation.

As soon as the bombing stopped and the all-clear siren went off, I helped the little girl get out of the trench and followed her with my eyes as she rejoined her mother, holding her hand and disappearing into the crowd of people and vehicles. But the image of her waving to me from across the street haunted me for the rest of the day. Since she told me where they sheltered at night, I immediately started planning an evening visit to Souk

El Silah, where Al Haliq Mosque is located, to give her and her mother, the stricken widow, something of what God had predestined for them.

I looked at my watch. It was midday, and I still had a long day at the clinic. I was not excited about going back to work. I realized that I was filthy, my white coat a dirty rag stained with mud. So I changed direction and walked towards Al Pasha Cafe on Boulevard Bab Mnara. I used to go there a lot before the war, anytime I had gaps between patients at the clinic. I would take my notebook and pens and sit in a calm corner, far away from the noise of backgammon and cards players, and write my weekly articles in French for *La Dépêche Tunisienne* and *Le Petit Matin*. Both newspapers have stopped coming out recently because of the interruption in publishing and distribution, but I've stuck to my routine, driven by habit to sit at the cafe and scribble down some worthless thoughts on the front and back of my empty cigarette pack. I always give the pack, with whatever's written on it, to the waiter, Mouldi. I assumed for a long time that he asked for it because he loved to read and it was a sign of appreciation for the pen of the doctor journalist, but then I found out that he was using them to hold whatever he had stolen each day from the small share of coffee and sugar, which is heavily rationed.

Next to the Ministère de la Guerre building, my thoughts scattered when I heard the sound of bullets. Three or four consecutive bullets, then a frightening silence followed by a heartbreaking howl that seemed to come from the throat of a wounded animal. People ran in front of me, emerging from alleys on all sides, and I saw them turn after about a hundred meters onto a small street that led to Bab El Allouj. I heard some of them shouting, "The Germans shot a little girl."

I felt my stomach clench. A horrified voice rang out in my head: "It's her! It's her. Habiba. The girl from the trench." But how could that be possible when God was merciful and compassionate? How could I believe that the Most Merciful would heap all the calamities of war on the head of that poor woman, taking first her husband, then her four boys, and finally her remaining daughter? This is what I thought as I ran, following the curious crowds.

I saw a group of people standing in a circle on the street corner. I started pushing them aside, yelling as loudly as I could, "I'm doctor, let me through, I'm a doctor!" I wanted them to open a path for me into the circle so I could save the wounded person. Then I saw her. The same *qashabia,* now stained with blood, in the arms of the poor woman. The head with the angelic face had lost its back half, and part of her brain was spilling out, blood streaming from the cracks in her skull. "Stray bullets," people said. It was as if a donkey had taken a bite out of a pumpkin. This little girl was uprooted from her place by the bullet so hard that she spun in the air two or three times, then fell forward on her stomach, lifeless, her eyelids trembling. As for the German armored vehicle from which the bullets were shot, it sped up and didn't stop to find out what had happened.

When I told the story to your mother, she broke down in tears, as if she'd just heard the news of a relative's death. She insisted, once she calmed down, on finding the girl's mother in her nighttime shelter at Al Haliq Mosque. She said, "Let's give her a place here in our house, Mahdi, until she finds something, and if she wants, we'll hire her to join our maids so she won't have to live off of anyone." But the woman never went back to the mosque after the day of the incident. This is what I was told when I asked. No one knows what happened to her. Ever since then, your mother has been suffering from something like hallucinations. She sends the maid to your sisters' houses every day and instructs her to tell Nafissa, Mna, and Qmar to keep their children inside and away from the windows overlooking the streets.

Nafissa's young boys dropped out of school early and started working at their father's shops in Souk El Bey, so the grandmother and her advice no longer have any authority over them.

Even if the crisis of war forced Nafissa's husband to close some shops, opportunism and greed pushed the honorable family to transform a few of them. They became secret warehouses for exorbitantly expensive black-market goods like clothes and food staples, which have become rare these days. Not only has local production stopped, but imports are delayed because of the interruption of maritime shipping. As soon as Wednesday morning arrives, your father, who is no longer satisfied with the small rations allowed by the authorities, accompanies his black servant with his woven basket on his back, and they go to the warehouses of our brother-in-law Monji Shammamat in Souk El Bey so that Hajj Ali can buy essential goods for Sultana Bashira, at twice the original price. With these, she's able to maintain her strategic stock: soap, flour, oil, sugar, tea, and coffee.

As for Mna and Qmar, I learned that they're traveling with their children this week to a farm called Barsh Farm in the Beja countryside. The farm's owner is the president of the Destour Party chapter there. It seems that he's a good friend of Mna's husband, who worked for some time in Beja as a deputy judge attaché at the Justice Council. As God is my witness, I tried to talk your sisters out of going: typhus fever is spreading in that region, and it's killing people mercilessly. My biggest fear is that, in fleeing the bombing with their children, they'll be like someone fleeing a drop of water, only to find themselves under the spigot.

III

There's no point hiding your feelings, Zbaida; I know you better than anyone. I know you've been suffering for a long time. Your sisters' injustice towards you has caused you a lot of pain. They believed the rumor, so they started avoiding you and cut off all ties. I think they were afraid that the echoes of what happened might reach their husbands, and then they might find themselves marked by the spreading stain. I can hear you telling yourself that they cut you off and forgot they even had a younger sister called Zbaida, and I know you're right, but I still give them the benefit of the doubt. Don't forget that Si Tahar Haddad, may God bless his soul, was their teacher during that period, too, or maybe before that, as far back as Nafissa. They all agreed, implicitly, without even discussing it, that they had to hide that part of their personal history. First when Tahar published his book on women, amid all those rumors about the corruption of his opinion and his faith, and then later when he was accused of having a relationship with a married student.

I've avoided talking to you about this for all these years, Zbaida. Doubt ate me up in the beginning, and I thought the worst of you. I was afraid that if I asked, you would make a confession that would break me and leave me too ashamed to hold my head high among men. So I told myself, "Hold on to your doubt, Mahdi. Doubt's more merciful than a certainty that would shake you to your core and erase Zbaida from your life."

But uncertainty kept growing in my chest like a tumor, and it spoiled my happiness when we heard you had overcome the crisis and recuperated. During the short breaks I spent in Tunis, I tried over and over to learn the details from Hajj Ali. But it was like someone hitting their head against a wall that's both deaf and dumb. If I kept insisting, and I presented him with my assumptions and conclusions, he would look at me askance and say grumpily, trying to end the conversation, "You were there with us, Mahdi; you saw it with your own eyes. Your sister made her choice, and she has harvested the fruit of that choice. Like people say, what goes around comes around."

As for Hajja Bashira, she was no less determined than he was to avoid discussing the matter. Whenever I brought it up, she would get irritable and sigh, before saying exasperatedly, "Turn the page, Mahdi. 'May God never expose our private affairs to anyone.'"

For years after the incident, I kept seeing your odious

brother-in-law Mhammed at the Khali Ali Café under the ramparts of Bab Souika, but we never talked. He would sit close to the cafe counter with a group of his annoying friends, some other dinosaurs from the Destour Party executive committee and some reactionary sympathizers. They would watch me with scornful expressions, whispering suspiciously as I climbed the stairs to the upper section with my friend Ahmed Deraai. After I came back from Paris with my medical degree five years ago and my name became well-known in the Tunisian Francophone press, I picked up the habit of sitting there with my comrades of the pen, like Abdelaziz El Aroui, Hedi Labidi, Zine el-Abidine Snoussi, and a group of others working in media, politics, and literature. During those conversations, many of the group members told me about Si Tahar and the misfortune that caused his tragic death in the prime of his youth. None of his loyal companions knew that he died of heartbreak except his best friend, Ahmed Deraai, but Si Ahmed remained true to him and protected his secret. He never said a word on the subject during all the time I was with him, working with news editors-in-chief who were his acquaintances and friends.

You probably don't know, Zbaida, that I owe my fame in the world of journalism to Si Ahmed. My narcissism has led me to hide that fact from even the closest of the people close to me, to make them think that I'm the genius of my era and that I climbed the ladder to glory on my own merit. The truth is that if it weren't for Ahmed Deraai, today I would be an unknown doctor whose opinion no one cared about. Ever since my father talked to him in passing about his teenage son's passion for reading and writing and praised my fluent writing in French, the man took it upon himself to encourage me to enter the world of media, and to make it easy for me to meet the masters of it.

I remember the first time we met over a cup of tea, at his invitation, at the Broke Bank Café, the place where the Sheikh of

Writers, Larbi Kabadi, hung out. I was then in my baccalauréat year, and I had heard of this cultural café that was frequented by the poets and writers of Tunis. I would sneak a look at its customers whenever I found myself in Bab Mnara, but I never dared to go inside. There, with two cups of black tea with mint in front of him and a hookah in his hand, Si Ahmed told me about the circumstances in which he met my father through Si Tahar in early 1924. He said that his loyal friend, who'd been his classmate for many years at the university of the Great Mosque, took him one day to see my father at the grand vizier's office and ask him to intervene for him and his acquaintances, after the problem his naughty pen had gotten him into. The revolutionary-minded Zaytuna students had dared to criticize the bey of Tunisia in a telegram they addressed to him. They had criticized his weak position on the naturalization issue, and he was about to be jailed under the accusation of insulting the bey. I listened to him, astonished at his audacity and enjoying the smoothness with which he narrated precise details from many years ago. On that day, Si Ahmed seized the opportunity to give me a quick test. He took a white piece of paper out of his coat pocket and cut it into two halves. He put half in front of me and the other half in front of him and gave me a pencil. "We're going to play a game."

That's what he said, winking and laughing. He asked me to write two paragraphs of similar lengths in French, one justifying naturalization and defending those who were naturalized, and the other criticizing it and showing its dangers to identity and religion. Before I could completely grasp the instructions, he had already started writing two paragraphs on the same subject on the other half of the paper, declaring that whoever wrote the most convincing piece would not have to pay for their tea. His eyes sparkled later as he read what I'd written. He got his matchbox out of his pocket and lit the edge of his paper on fire until it became wisps of black ash in the wind. As for my paper, he carefully folded it and put it in his pocket, then said, laughing, "You're excused from ever paying for tea, from today until the country gets its independence."

After that meeting, Si Ahmed took me under his wing. He started passing by the school from time to time as the evening sessions wrapped up and taking me with him to the various newspaper offices. He would introduce me to the papers' owners, saying, "Mahdi Rassaa is like my younger brother. Remember his name! His pen reflects a disciplined mind and a sweetness of expression, and I owe his father, Hajj Ali, a debt I will never be able to repay."

Si Ahmed continued to write to me during my time in Paris as a university student. He would urge me with every letter to be more involved with the Society of Muslim Students of North Africa and to write political and social articles in their journal. Later on, he helped me get published in Tunisian papers. Then, at last, I became the writer you know, my name already listed among those of well-known journalists while I was still a student in France.

On the horrendous night of the incident at the Ennaifer house during my break in December 1935, I knocked on Si Ahmed's door in El Halfaouine, searching for a truth that could put out the fire inside me. You were still at the hospital, Zbaida, hanging between the Earth and heaven.

IV

I found Si Ahmed Deraai drowning in a bottomless well of sadness. He broke down crying when he saw me. He seemed like another person, difficult to recognize: his eyes were swollen, and his shoulders were sagging, as if he was carrying all the mountains on earth on one of them and all the waves of the sea on the other. His handsome face was hidden under a short prickly beard, topped with a mop of tangled hair that hadn't seen a comb for days. When I went to shake his hand

and express my condolences on Si Tahar's passing, he threw his arms around me and started sobbing on my shoulder like a small child. Then he leaned his arm on me and ushered me into a small, musty room that was cloudy with smoke. The ashtray on the table was filled with cigarette butts, some of them barely smoked, and scattered among stacks of paper and newspapers were cups of different shapes and sizes with dried-up coffee grounds inside them. Judging by the white and green fungus sprouting from cracks in the grounds, some had been sitting there for quite some time.

I felt embarrassed watching him try, with unsteady hands, to hide some orange peels, olive pits, and fresh breadcrumbs on the table under the newspapers. Then he pushed away the shirts and woolen jackets that had piled up on a chair to the right of the door before offering me a seat.

Deep down, I was angry at them all: him, Zbaida, and Si Tahar, who had died before we could settle matters. How did they manage to hide what was between you from me? How did they dare to sit with me, look me in the eyes, and laugh in my face, all the while keeping this secret? And where could Si Ahmed have gotten the cheek, as I told him that you were between life and death, to pretend that he didn't know you and didn't know anything?

I saw the shock on his face when I told him, avoiding going into detail, "You didn't see me at Si Tahar's funeral because Zbaida, my twin sister, was admitted to the hospital in critical condition the same day."

But he turned away quickly, pretending to be busy looking at some papers on the table, and then said, without looking at me, "You have a twin sister? I wish her a speedy recovery. How's she doing now?"

"I came to ask you about her."

He looked at me, pretending to be surprised. He was holding a book whose cover had been ripped off; he was about to hand it to me, then changed his mind. He met my alert, harsh gaze and took a step back. He probably read in my face that I was silently accusing him. He cast his eyes down for a short moment, as if trying to figure out the best way to answer my accusation, without an absolute denial or a complete confession. "Are you sure you want to dig up this ancient history, Mahdi?"

I answered him with determination, crossing my arms, "If either of you had been clear and honest, what happened wouldn't have happened."

He heaved a sigh, setting the book down gently on the table. I glanced at it, but its torn cover prevented me from reading its title. He sat behind the table and started rubbing his head with both hands in a mechanical, repeated movement that was almost convulsive. I kept watching him, silent, until he made up his mind and said, "Don't think badly of my friend. Tahar is dead now, and God will judge him based on what he did, good or bad. You and I are here, and what our tongues say today will determine how God judges us later. Man is destined for change."

I interrupted him in a tone that came out unintentionally sharp, "I prayed the Friday prayer before knocking on your door, and I have no desire to listen to a sermon in your home. No more beating around the bush; just tell me: What was going on between my sister and your friend? A simple question, my friend, that demands a simple answer."

Something like anger sparked in his eyes. He probably didn't like me talking to him so sharply, especially since he's about fifteen years older than me. He started slowly rubbing his eyes, as if trying to stall for time until he calmed down. Then he looked at me, his features radiating sincerity, and said, "As God is my witness, there was nothing untoward between Tahar and your sister. Nothing. No one knows about the story but your father, may God give him a long life, and me. There was no need to talk to you about it because everything ended a long time before we became friends. The matter was closed for good the day of the ceremony at the Casino du Belvédère in October 1930."

He fell silent for a short moment, riffling through the papers on the table before reaching again for the book with the ripped cover. He held it up and said, "Do you see this small book? It's the masterpiece of our time. I pray that God will let you live long enough to see the day when the people of this country leave their resentments behind and give this book what it deserves. And give its writer his due when they realize that he was the leader of enlightened thought. It was only because he was so ahead of his time that ignorant people threw him into the fire."

He exhaled angrily, thumping the table with the book, before continuing furiously, "We wanted the honor ceremony at the Belvédère to be a celebration of this book, and we invited family members, intellectuals, and friends. We thought it would be the beginning of Tahar's glory and a herald for people who believed, like him, that reforming this nation means reforming its social structure. But the book was a curse on Tahar that he was never able to overcome, and the ceremony became a watershed moment in his life; the time before it came out was paradise compared to the burning hell that followed."

He continued telling me about the dark days that followed the celebration at the Belvédère, about Tahar's shock, watching in agony the campaign that was launched against him by Hassan Al Jaziri, the editor-in-chief of *Al Nadim* newspaper, and Mhammed Ben Hussein, the editor-in-chief of *Al Zahra.* He read with astonishment the satirical poems about his atheism that Jalal Eddine Naqqash, Mahmoud Bourguiba, Salah Souissi, and others wrote in Classical Arabic, stirring up Ahmed Bey against him. Si Ahmed told me about how his friends abandoned him, distancing themselves for protection from the overwhelming anger of the masses. He also related the position of Zaytuna scholars, who wrote to the prime minister, Khelil Bouhageb, asking him to confiscate the book and make its distribution illegal, claiming it contained violations of sharia and other statements that the Muslim community could not keep silent about.

I knew most of those stories from my conversations with old friends of Si Tahar at Taht Essour Café. But I couldn't bring myself to interrupt Si Ahmed, to go back to the subject that I came to discuss. I was abashed by the tears falling on the book as he bitterly recounted the events he lived through with Si Tahar during those difficult months. While you, Zbaida, were getting married to your groom Mohsen, Tahar's body was being married to the arrows of general resentment.

V

I don't know if you met with Si Tahar after your marriage, Zbaida, and I don't want to know. I also don't know whether he told you himself about what happened to him after his book came out, or whether you're hearing this for the first time from me. But I can see from the tears you're trying to hide that the wound is still fresh, as if it happened yesterday. My opinion might surprise you, and you might not like it, but I'm convinced that our father made the right decision when he refused your marriage to Tahar Haddad that night at the Casino du Belvédère. Yes, Zbaida. Your teacher asked your father for your hand, in case you didn't know, and he did it in line with the Holy Quran and the sunnah. But according to Ahmed Deraai, Hajj Ali Rassaa, that distinguished gentleman, mocked him. He was rude to him, becoming the first to fire an arrow into his body. A body that, in the words of a great poet—that you, the lover of Baudelaire, probably don't know—would come to be so pierced with arrows that the arrowheads starting shattering against each other.

Stop crying, Zbaida, and listen to me. Please stop looking at me like that; words get mixed up in my chest when you stare at me so accusingly. Just imagine if you'd married Tahar Haddad and then he became unable to provide for you and himself when he was stripped of his civil rights. Isn't it possible that he would hate you and resent you, that the social differences between you would get wider and wider with the rise of the wave of disrespect that drowned him in its turbulence? You would've regretted it when you stood by, helpless, and watched the man you loved turn into the shadow of his former self. How could he stay the same person when, overnight, he became the enemy of the nation, the target of children throwing stones and men following him with insults and slander?

"Tahar lived through a long nightmare that only ended when he was buried."

That's what Ahmed Deraai told me that day, with a lump in his throat. I listened to him and thanked God that Hajj Ali, by marrying you against your will to Mohsen Ennaifer, saved you from living with the man through his long nightmare. I don't know what excuse your father used to reject him the day he asked for your hand. I've never been able to get a single word out of him on the subject. I don't for a moment think that he'd read his book and was punishing him for his ideas. I think it's more likely that his refusal was for classist and chauvinist reasons, rooted in the *beldi* complex of those under the illusion, like that madman Hitler, that they're a race above other races and that their noble bloodlines shouldn't mix with those of other Tunisians. But maybe it was a blessing in disguise, Sister. The Sheikh of Islam declared that "Haddad's new Arab woman" was dead on arrival. Would you have taken on her identity and made her address your home? Do you think the people who gave him the social death penalty and questioned his work as a notary public couldn't get a fatwa to charge him with heresy, too, making it *haram* for him to be with his wife and forcing him to divorce her?

Oh, yes, Zbaida. The calls to charge Haddad with heresy were rising, and the general public was convinced he was either an atheist or an apostate. It was possible that he would be tried, based on spurious accusations, as happened before him to Abdelaziz Thâalbi. It was also possible that he would be executed as an apostate and hung if the authorities obeyed his attackers and forwarded their testimonies against him to the court. The poor man wrote his death certificate with his own hands when he wrote his book about women. Would you have been willing to marry a dead man who wandered in the souks like a tortured spirit, getting accosted by children told to chase him, and insulted by homeless people, beggars, and drunks?

A month after the launch ceremony, after widespread anger and repeated harassment forced Si Tahar out of his usual spots at the Place de la Kasbah Café and Assabbagh Café on El Morkadh, he was sitting with Si Ahmed at the Tuta Café in El Halfaouine, feeling defeated and angry. He'd heard sad news that day that made him even more upset. The Zaytuna faculty council had fired his friend Mhammed Salah Mhidi from his teaching position in Tunis and banned him from teaching at its branches elsewhere, all because of his encouraging remarks at the launch ceremony. Si Ahmed told me about what happened that evening. "I tried to make Tahar feel better, but to be honest, I was even more furious than he was. The hypocrisy of these turbaned sheikhs with their prayer beads who can't say anything without sprinkling in verses from the Quran—yet at the same time have monopolized all the religious properties and wealth for generations! It's too much. I was infuriated; I felt like I'd lost a relative by murder and had to avenge him. I mentioned them by name, one by one, and cursed them all. All the while, Tahar was staring into the void, silent except for the occasional soft sigh or groan. Suddenly we noticed a group of children coming from a Quranic school nearby in single file, reciting something that rhymed in unison, though we couldn't make out the words. We took a closer look and realized that they were advancing as one towards where we were sitting on the café terrace, raising their voices so they could be heard by the patrons. It only took a moment for me to realize that they were reciting, in a theatrical choral performance, a few poetic verses satirizing Tahar and inciting the populace against him. I had read the poem a few days ago in *Al Zahra*; it was attributed to one of the Zaytuna sheikhs who didn't reveal his name. The words shot like poisoned arrows from the innocent little throats:

"Beware new-fangled thoughts and fear the trick;
If you mingle with Haddad, you'll get the stick.
He's a boy who Satan fooled and stole his mind
So he became an enemy of religion divine!

"I prepared myself, wanting to scatter them, and searched through the crowds gathered opposite the café for the damn teacher who'd sent them to us. But Tahar held my arm, pulling me back down into my seat. So I sat there, forced to listen to the insults, one after another:

"He interprets the Quran with ignorance,
Claiming he's here to defend what's right,
But he breaks sharia ordinance
If it's against his corrupt delights."

Si Ahmed said that the Quranic school students didn't let up until they pointed to Haddad in a collective theatrical act, finishing their performance with a final verse that he recited to me but I forgot; I think it started with cursing him after accusing him of deviance and apostasy.

This incident only the pettiest of the harassment Haddad endured. He was attacked once, when he was entering the Khaldounia Society, by a group of students trying to force him to leave. When he asked them why, they claimed they were defending the place from desecration because access was forbidden to an enemy of the nation and its identity, who parroted those who resented Islam and Muslims. Tahar stood up to them, and because he was a sturdy fellow before he got sick, he managed to take care of the business that took him there. But then they waited for him outside and threw a bag of garbage on him, scraps collected from the butchers and greengrocers, and walked behind him reciting a new poem in Tunisian Arabic by Hajj Othman Gharbi that had been published a few days before in his satirical newspaper, *Ezzahou*:

> *"Help us, God, to stick to our religion; don't expose us to the scandal of that mook.*
> *Guide us, God, to the right path; help us close our eyes to Haddad's book."*

After that incident, Tahar retreated inside himself and started to avoid public places. He rarely went outside and wouldn't even go for a walk unless accompanied by some of the friends, at least the ones who hadn't deserted him after the tide of public opinion turned against him. But that only made the people who hated him fiercer. Deraai told me about the details of a fight on Place de la Kasbah; Haddad would have been badly injured if not for divine protection. He was sitting with his friend Hedi Labidi and a group of supporters when they heard a barrage of shouts from some thugs who had gathered in the street in front of the café, accompanied by several louts who were attracted by curiosity and joined in with the screamers:

"Atheists . . . France's dogs . . . "

"God damn you . . . You're not men . . . "

"Enemies of God! Beheading you's not enough . . . "

"Inshallah you'll spend eternity in hell . . . "

"Heads of the snake . . . Rats' tails . . . "

Si Tahar wasn't successful in calming his friends, who rose up as one to answer the curses with even more insulting ones. A fight broke out with fists entangling, heads cracking against each other, and kicks and punches following one after another from every direction. Chairs were scattered and tables flipped over with everything on them. Then some French soldiers stationed at La Kasbah Barracks interfered, hitting the assailants with the butts of their rifles, and the fight dissolved, leaving some injuries and bruises on both sides. Haddad himself wasn't physically injured during that fight, but his pride suffered a grave blow, and he lost confidence in himself and people. After that, he avoided going to cafés, fearing not for himself but out of pity for his friends, who had taken it into their own hands to support him in his crisis and protect him from harm.

Deraai said he tried very hard to make Tahar change his mind about secluding himself and staying home. He would try to tempt him to go for walks in the orchards and suburbs, far away from the riff-raff, as he used to do during the happy times with two of his poet friends, Aboul-Qacem Echebbi and Mustapha Khraief. He refused to give up and continued trying to tempt him into a trip, giving him options of which friends he'd like to go with them, until finally he agreed to go to the suburb of La Marsa on the road to Sidi Bou Said. They left after lunch, not knowing what destiny had in store for them.

Deraai told me, "It was a beautiful clear day, despite the light winter sea breeze. There were some giant white clouds in the sky that looked like mountains of soft cotton. That day, Si Tahar seemed happy; there were signs that he was celebrating life, as opposed to the mood he'd been in ever since he was hit by disaster. He walked, surrounded by his friends and breathing in the fresh air, as if he were fortifying himself for the coming days of loneliness and isolation. The path was empty at that time of the day, except for flocks of goldfinches hopping from branch to branch on the eucalyptus trees that spread as far as the eye could see. The scene of the hill overlooking the sea stirred the emotions and brought up sad memories. Our friend Tahar started singing with his sweet voice some classical Arabic music of *muwashshah* and *ma'luf,* and some songs by Sayed Darwish that he'd memorized. His companions responded with joy, singing along in a harmonic chorus. The group was still walking up and down the hills until they saw at a distance a large group of people walking together. It was a demonstration by the supporters of the Destour Party coming back from the house of Chedly Khairallah, the editor of *La Voix du Tunisien* newspaper, and it was coming towards us. It was a big crowd, chanting slogans in unison in support of the newspaper and its editorial board, which the colonial authorities had threatened to shut down. As soon as the demonstrators recognized Haddad, something like an earthquake exploded among them. Their harmony was disturbed, their shouting died down, and they started muttering to each other and preparing themselves. There was no option but to confront them, as there was no exit to the right or left that the small group could use to avoid the collision. Moreover, the men's pride wouldn't allow them to run away. As the distance between the two groups closed, the demonstrators became more agitated. Suddenly their slow march turned into a run, as if evil were rushing towards us. They raised menacing fists in the air. We were sure that we were going to get hauled along the ground in that valley, or we would get dragged until we cried like leaking buckets or we would get beaten to death. But we continued on our way, walking together very close to each other, like vulnerable herds in times of imminent danger. When there were only a few meters separating the two groups, the calls to punish the enemy of Islam started: they accused Tahar of spreading lies about the prophet and the Mothers of the Believers. There was only the distance of two fingers separating us from tragedy. But God is generous, Mahdi. Our relief came like a miracle from the source of the distress itself. Suddenly the mass of demonstrators parted as some men pushed and elbowed their way to the front of the group, then yelled out like thunder, 'Haddad is under our protection until he gets back safely.'

"These men were from his tribe in El Hamma and his neighbors in the Sidi Mansour neighborhood. They were about six people out of sixty or so, and they surrounded Haddad like a shield, protected him from the aggressors, and pushed people aside until they involuntarily parted for him. We cleaved through the angry crowd with him and didn't come to any harm except for the occasional flying insult or spit blown back to its sender by the wind.

"Among the people who saved us that day from the violence of the demonstrators was a baker from Sidi Mansour called Karrita. He was a muscular man, as big and tall as if he were one of the trees on the roadside. He stretched out his arms and positioned himself in front of Haddad, who looked as if he were walking behind a tank or a wall. When some wicked hands rose into the air, grabbing the man and pulling at his clothes, he twisted towards them, hitting, kicking, and swearing. Karrita was the most zealous constituent of the Destour Party and the biggest supporter of its members; he would generously spend some of his small income on the meetings and donate his money to the party budget. The day after this incident, he opened his shop around dawn to display his various loaves of wheat, bran, and barley, but by midmorning, nothing but a stray dog had passed the threshold of his shop. His bakery was in an alley branching off a main street. He went out to see what was going on, and to his surprise, he found a group of participants from the previous day's demonstration stopping passersby at the corner and whispering something suspicious to them. When he followed one of them to ask about the matter, he answered him, annoyed, 'May God guide you to the right path, Karrita. Are you selling God's bounty to people and then renouncing Him? Are you feeding us *haram* food without our knowing? If you believe in Haddad so much, let him support you.'

"When the baker heard that, he picked up a metal bar he used to push the trays into the oven and headed towards the men hanging out at the corner, bursting with anger like a volcano. As soon as they saw him coming towards them, they ran away, and he couldn't catch any of them. He went back to the bakery and sent his employee with hot bread to the usual customers, but all but a few of them sent it back to him. He didn't earn much that day. When he learned that the instigators were mainly party members, he complained to the party's executive committee. But Klibi and the other high-ranking members just brushed him off. They told him that people wouldn't tolerate someone who supported unbelievers. The boycott of his shop continued for about a month, so he decided to send his employees to sell the bread on carts far away from the quartier."

When Deraai finished, Zbaida, I asked him about the baker, but he said he didn't know whether he was the one who sent his boy with that letter the day Haddad died. But he thinks he probably was, because that baker was the closest person to Tahar during the last few days of his life. He visited him during the time he spent at the Hôpital Militaire and provided for him.

VI

What was in that letter, Zbaida? I asked Deraai about it, but he didn't know anything. What your father-in-law, Si Othman, said about it the night of the incident was vague and fragmented; even its writer was unknown. Your father-in-law praised God and asked him for forgiveness, then said, "The apostate wrote to her asking her to meet him."

He went silent for a moment, then said, "God knows which pit she'd find him in now. And Satan knows how many times they met, while we were blissfully unaware, thinking she was an angel when she's really . . . God forgive me."

Can you imagine, Zbaida, how I felt listening to him say all this about my smart, well-mannered sister? Can you imagine your father's grief when the only proof he could use to reject that accusation was the letter the Ennaifer family had lost? Where did you hide the letter, Zbaida? Why would Tahar write to you when you belonged to another man?

I asked Deraai that question, but he denied my implication, almost scolding me for my suspicion. He spoke with confidence.

"The last contact he had with her was the day he told her he would ask for her hand at the book celebration. After that night at the Casino du Belvédère, he buried the secret of her in his heart. Or rather, he buried his heart itself under the dust of time. I never heard that he wrote to her or that she wrote to him. I don't think he would hide a secret from me, especially since I was there through all the seasons of his pain."

Si Ahmed Deraai cast his eyes down for a short moment, then, hesitant, continued, "The truth is that he only saw her once, by chance, a few months after her marriage. He came across her near Le Passage, as she was leaving the Théâtre Ali Ben Kamla. Their eyes met, and their hearts trembled, but no happiness or sadness appeared on their faces. Your sister was holding her husband's arm as he leaned towards her, talking and laughing, and he seemed happy. As for Tahar, he had just left a failed meeting with the lawyer César Benattar in the European quartier. He had suggested Tahar sue *Al Nadim* newspaper for defamation and publishing fake news but then mysteriously changed his mind about defending him. As soon as Tahar saw her and she saw him, he looked away, and she did the same. He continued on his way as if he had not seen her, but he was shaking. But just as he was about to pass her, something unexpected happened. He heard a man's voice calling him. 'Si Tahar? Isn't it?'

"He looked in the direction of the voice with his heart pounding and found, to his surprise, that your brother-in-law Mohsen Ennaifer was talking to him. He was still trying to swallow the lump in his throat and making a herculean effort to control himself so his agitation wouldn't expose him, when he saw your brother-in-law extending his hand. He said, 'I wanted to ask you about your friend Mohamed Ali El Hammi. We were good friends for a while, but then I lost track of him. In the early '20s, we were classmates at a university in Germany. We used to sit in the same auditorium, eat lunch at the same cafeteria, and live in the same dorm. I remember that he contacted me one summer seven years ago, inviting me to join the Economic Cooperation Society that he'd founded. I went to their first meeting at the Khaldounia School. I heard your name there and saw you give a speech before Mohamed Ali El Hammi, so I knew you were one of the founding members. When I listened to what you said, though, I found your socialist project utopian and too difficult for Tunisia and its fragile economy to adopt. I wasn't enthusiastic enough to get involved, and I told El Hammi he should drop it. A few months later, I found out that he was arrested for being involved with the union movement, so he dissolved the cooperative companies and founded the General Confederation of Tunisian Workers, all of which proved I was right. Then I heard that he'd been exiled, and he started writing to me every so often from Egypt. In his last letters, he told me that the pasha he worked for fired him because of his politics, and that he was going to travel to Hijaz. But then I never heard from him again . . . '

"Tahar glanced furtively at Zbaida and saw that she was trembling, her face as red as burning embers. Her husband had gotten carried away; he self-corrected and introduced himself, but he didn't seem to notice anything amiss. Tahar answered him in a voice that came out low and hoarse, 'I'm sorry to have to tell you that Mohamed Ali passed away.'

"'Good God!'

"'He died two and half years ago in Jeddah, where he was working as a taxi driver. It was a car accident.'

"'I'm so sorry for your loss, Si Tahar. I know he was more to you than just a comrade in activism from the same region—he was a close friend.'

"Then Mohsen Ennaifer turned to his wife. 'Isn't it frustrating, Zbaida, that an economic thinker and union leader could meet such a sad end? May God bless his soul! If only we could say that it was just the French Protectorate engaging in tyranny and rejection of noble work—that would be some comfort, at least. But this is Si Tahar Haddad, a social and religious reformer who's become the target of the sheikhs at Zaytuna.

They've accused him of apostasy and set their rabid dogs on him: barking in the columns of tawdry papers that aren't even fit to wrap fritters in."

VII

Deraai said, Zbaida, that Haddad cried that day and was in severe pain. When Mohsen wished him a good day and good luck, he bade farewell to you with his eyes as your husband wrapped his arm around you and ushered you towards the tram station. He couldn't bear to go back home. When Deraai checked on him early that night, he found him lying on a reed mat on the roof of his apartment. He was calm, listening to a phonograph of Sayed Darwish singing, "I fell in love, and I am finished." He was silent, as if filled with tears and about to break down. He wanted to cry but couldn't, and when he tried, the tears wouldn't come. Then he sang along, his voice hoarse, breaking, "My darling and I are in love . . . there's nothing like it, even in my dreams . . . I love her even when we fight . . . being away from each other is a crime . . . if I'm content with her leaving me . . . I should say *farewell* to this world."

Then he jumped up and stood on the edge of the roof, looking down into the void. He started repeating the last sentence over and over, as if he'd lost his mind, "farewell to the world . . . farewell to the world," and Deraai thought he would throw himself off the roof. He pulled him back from the edge, pretending to give him a hug, wanting to immobilize him and calm him down again. The poor man burst into bitter, hopeless tears, then entered what seemed like a fit of rage. "Leave me alone, Ahmed! What's left for me now? I'm as useless as the knee of an amputated leg."

He started shaking, but Deraai held onto him until he calmed down and relaxed. When he let go, Haddad picked up the phonograph and threw it down onto the rooftop, smashing it, then started shattering the records over his knee, breaking them into halves, thirds, and fourths, then began throwing them and sending them flying through the air. They glided a ways before falling on the heads of people walking in the street, like meteors from the dark sky. He looked around but couldn't find anything else except the small clay stove with a teapot on it that smelled like burned tea. He kicked it, and the teapot fell over, but nothing spilled from it, not even a drop. He stood there for a moment panting, as if trying to decide what to do next, and Deraai just looked at him, not knowing what to do or say. Then Haddad ran to the stairs and went down to his apartment. He was gone for some time, then reappeared with books and papers in his hands. He started tearing them up and throwing them into the small clay stove, shouting at his friend as if resuming a previous conversation, "And this is *Tunisian Workers and the Emergence of the Trade Union Movement.*" Then he stopped talking for some time, watching his first book be consumed by the flames. When the ashes started to scatter, he threw in more papers, saying in a bombastic tone, sarcasm mingling with vengefulness:

"These are my newspaper articles in *Al Omma*, *Al Sawab*, *Al Zaman*, *Lisan Al Shaab,* and *Ifriqiya*."

"And these are my poems about you, Zbaida, Mohsen Ennaifer's wife."

"This is the notary degree from the clerics at Zaytuna."

And so he continued, throwing page after page of theological commentaries and analyses into the flames. He stirred the embers with a stick, sweat dripping into the fire. Then, on the verge of collapse, he threw in the last book and said, "And here's the leader of the gang. The great pharaoh. The banisher of pleasures and the repellant of friends. The roadblock to livelihood and the destroyer of horizons. Your 'woman in religion.' Your 'woman in society.' The book I wanted to be a lamp in the night of darkness and backwardness, but that instead became a song played to the deaf or a mosaic shown to the blind. Into the fire you go, all of you who are blind and deaf. Into the blaze you fed me to as tinder."

VIII

Do you think you would've found the strength to live with a man so broken-hearted that he had almost lost his mind from the injustice inflicted on him? You can't compare Mohsen, with his beautiful mind and his poise, to an angry writer who became the victim of his readers. So how could you expose yourself to danger because of a love story you lived when you were just a teenager? Should I believe Deraai, who says Haddad never tried to contact you after your marriage, even though you lived in his mind and heart until the last moments of his life? Or should I believe your father-in-law and brother-in-law, who swore to God that there were letters and meetings between you and him? Or do I believe your husband, who has concealed his secrets inside a shell thicker than a walnut's, especially when he never mentioned to me that he knew Tahar or had met or spoken with him?

Why are you denying that you hid the letter, Zbaida? Why are you keeping it from us when, if you're telling the truth, it's proof of your innocence? Soon your two boys will grow up, and their vile uncle will tell them about their virtuous mother's scandal, and they'll ask you about the letter and its contents. You poor woman, what have you done to prepare for that day? How can you live with your husband when the fire of doubt is flaring up inside him, only getting stronger with time? Put him at ease, Zbaida. You've almost reached the limits of human patience. Tell us the whole truth. Put him at ease . . . And me.

10
The Tale of Si Mohsen Ennaifer
(*Jellaz Cemetery, Winter 1978*)

I

Peace be with you, Bahiya. I haven't spoken your name for twenty years. I haven't come back to you since I buried you with my own hands. I never told anyone about you, and I won't, not until resurrection day. Forgive me, Bahiya. I wronged you in death just as I wronged you in life. Twenty springs grew up around your remains, and no one looked after your tomb. I didn't write on your tombstone that you were the wife of Mohsen Ennaifer, like you asked me to. I pretended as usual that I didn't understand. And I didn't fulfill your wish by giving you someone to stand next to your tomb, after a long life hopefully: a child of your own to pray for you and put out some water and ryegrass seeds for the birds. I did what I had to for you to think that you were either infertile or your husband was sterile.

I hid you from sight, Bahiya, and I deprived you of your most basic rights. I used to see you point to your empty belly and sketch a round shape with your hands, wrinkle your forehead and purse your lips, then put your forefinger next to your temple, imploring, as you did whenever you begged me, in vain, to spend the night at your old apartment in El Hafsia. I was laughing, Bahiya. I laughed a lot when you made those same unclear sounds with your damaged throat; they were the same, in your concise dictionary, whether you were happy, sad, satisfied, or angry. And how rarely you got angry at me, darling. I would leave you alone for a week or two weeks, but when I came back, you welcomed me after my absence with a beaming face, flooded with longing. You couldn't hear the key scraping in the lock, Bahiya, but praise be to God, who made it up to you by giving you a sensitivity surpassed only by your amazing intuition. When I arrived, I would find you behind the door waiting for it to open, and I would hear you running towards it before I even turned the key. You would put your hand on your heart whenever I expressed my surprise, and laugh that laugh whose magic you'd never heard yourself.

I decided to marry you the day I heard you laughing in the lobby of the tax office. You knew that you were beautiful, Bahiya. When you entered the lobby hall with the tray of *kaak warka* hanging from strings around your neck, men with full bellies hurried to beat the hungry to you, clamoring for attention. They devoured your generous breasts with their insolent eyes. If any of them dared to examine the goods exhibited on the tray, you would smack their hands with the edge of your soft palm and release your captivating laugh.

I still remember when you first entered my office, the doorman hot on your heels. You invaded the office with a smile like clear running water. There was a dimple in your chin and two more in your cheeks that made anyone looking at you long to press their lips against them. You stood silent, staring at me with a look that was almost reproachful, and the *kaak warka* tray rested against your waist, as if it was your lavish chest that was exhibited. Your dress was honey-colored with daffodils, daisies, and lavender flowers strewn across it, as if spring had entered my office. I felt perplexed, as if I were the one invading your private space, not you invading my office. I cleared my throat and said, stuttering, "Welcome, Mademoiselle. Do you need something?"

Your smile widened, but you didn't speak. Your dimples deepened until they seemed to call out, like a tunnel to overwhelming pleasure. I was still perplexed and you still silent when the doorman scurried in and grabbed your forearm in his big hand. Trying to drag you outside, he said, "Forgive me, Boss; I don't know how she got past me. She's just a girl selling *kaak warka*; she can't hear or speak. The daughter of the Jewish man, Pascal, the sweet shop owner at the end of the alley."

You were bravely defending yourself, even though he was twice your size, and there were two words on your tongue that you kept repeating with a kind of gentle anger: "Yezzi. Yezzi. Atu. Atu."

I would later come to know that these two words "yezzi" and "atu" meant "let me go" and "give me," "come," "yes," "no," "thank you," "I love you," "Happy New Year," "I'm cold," and "I want a child from you" . . . And countless other things. How beautiful your clarity was, Bahiya. How beautiful your language, free of the ruse of rhetoric and the warble of oratory. You left me the option of free interpretation because you only meant what I understood. You couldn't lie, so long as you only said what I wanted to understand of the pure truth.

That day, I asked "Aammi" Hamza to let you go. I took two *kaak warka* from you and gave you double their cost, and you put your hand over your heart and said "Atu." You said it in a tone that melted me. Then you spun around in a way that made your dress swirl in the air like the robe of a Mevlevi dervish dancing, and my heart danced with it.

When I got home that evening, I gave one of the two *kaak warka* to Zbaida, but she didn't want it. I gave the other to the two boys, Mostafa and Mohamed Habib, and they shared it. As soon as night fell, I sat on the couch with a pillow behind my back and started flipping through a French magazine. Zbaida was on the bed reading one of her fat books, and there was your honey-colored dress fluttering in my mind so unexpectedly that the words in front of me shifted into zigzagging and curving lines, as if tracing your tender body on the page. Suddenly I found your *kaak warka* in my hand; I had unconsciously picked it up from the nightstand and bitten into it, staring off into space. Zbaida stared at me in surprise and said, "Are you back to eating sweets?"

I pursed my lips in annoyance and nodded. I said a lot of things that were between me and myself. I'd been talking to myself for a while. Whenever Zbaida asked me something, I would answer her with a nod or a gesture, and my inner tongue would start weaving a long speech that no one could hear but my insides. "You're surprised I'm eating sweets, Zbaida? Of course I am. Why wouldn't you be surprised when you know that you didn't leave anything to make me happy but bitter oleander? You made me lose my ability to enjoy all the tastes; sweet, bitter, salty, and sour are all the same now. My days with you have become as tasteless as food mixed with laundry water or cooked on the wood of the Zaqqum tree in hell."

And as if Zbaida were listening to my conversation with my insides, she pursed her own lips in resentment and then went back to her book, saying, "It's up to you. But don't forget all the dangers of diabetes that my brother Mahdi listed for you."

"Who made me sick with diabetes, Zbaida? Who's the evil witch who transformed me in one wicked night from a strong young man who could break rocks with his bare hands into an old man with no ambitions or determination, bored and sick?"

Yes, Bahiya. I hid my hypertension and diabetes from you, just like I hid their causes. I didn't want to talk to you about the horror of the night that pulled me into such tribulation that by the next morning, I'd become a broken man, aged before his time. I didn't want to embarrass you when I saw that you had spent all day preparing different juices and pastries for me. So I would happily take them from you and eat from your hand, ignoring the warnings of the doctor, who had forbidden me to eat sugar.

Do you hear me, Bahiya? I know that your soul is here above the tombs. It's warm, active, and playful despite this bitter cold. I feel its whoosh when it flutters around me. I can almost feel the tender palm of your radiant soul caressing my back, which is weighed down and aching from these heavy years. Why did you leave me so early, Bahiya? Who allowed you to die before me while you were still so young? Who did you leave me for, me, this old man whose hair has gone gray and whose back has become bent? Who will bake a cake for this old man's seventy-seventh birthday, Bahiya? Who will take his withered body into her generous embrace and tell him dreamily, "Yezzi atu"?

II

The morning of the day after we first met, Bahiya, I pricked up my ears waiting to hear your laugh in the hall. There was a lot of noise, and the racket of the Tax Office clients, whether coming or going, was drowning out the sounds of people passing on the main street. My heart would skip a beat every time someone knocked on my office door, as if I had a date with you. Then I got tired of waiting for so long, and I busied myself with work and focused my mind on it. A little bit before noon, the door opened without permission, and you entered like a butterfly, all light and cheerfulness. Your hair, which the day before had been braided and looped into the shape of an oblong *kaak warka*, had been freed of its shackles and flowed over your shining face, like night covering up the day. You wore a light pink lipstick that made the gap between your front teeth more beautiful. A sly look shone in your big eyes that said, with full self-confidence, "You were waiting for me; don't even try to deny it." You found me standing up to welcome you, and I had never stood for anyone but Henri Kleman, general director of the Tax Office, when he showed up for sudden inspections every month or so. I looked, and there was your tray filled with *kaak warka*, like your bodice, overflowing with its fruits. I spotted an attractive beauty mark lying next to your left pomegranate. You were mute, but your body was talkative, Bahiya. I was a deserted body in need of someone to speak to, like a lonely hermit who lost his sight in a forgotten cave on the icy peaks of Tibet.

Thirteen years, Bahiya, and my body still couldn't forgive Zbaida. Thirteen years of burying its desire under a plank of ice. It takes care of itself when it reaches the verge of explosion.

It plays with the pleasure, beats it, provokes it, and satisfies it, but it can't bear to address the body of the wife who was sentenced to abandonment without divorce. After she left the hospital and was getting better, she started trying to seduce me in bed, all innocence. I told her, reciting an ancient pre-Islamic formula of divorce: "You are now like my mother to me."

She thought I was joking. She gave a pampered laugh and said coquettishly, "That's against sharia, and the penance is fasting for two months. Poor Mohsen. You'll lose so much weight."

"So now you know the stipulations of sharia law, too? Who taught the Catholic schoolgirl Islamic jurisprudence?"

Her face blanched for a moment when she understood what I was hinting at. But she righted herself quickly and went back to being playful, baring her slender arms in a show of seducing me. Then she added in a whisper, so as not to wake Mostafa, who was sleeping in his crib, "I know things that you could never guess. And don't be fooled by the damage to my legs; 'My face still has what pleases the sight, and my body that which delights,' as the saying goes."

But I had already shaken her off, Bahiya, like a sleeper who's been stung by a scorpion shakes out their sheets. I turned my back to her every night, and I rebuffed her if she started her games to excite me. When it became hard to resist her, lying just a few inches from me with the scent of jasmine perfume emanating from beneath her negligées like burning desire and filling my nose, I left her bed and made the couch my bed. I would hear her sobbing in the middle of the night, but I would bite my lip, press my legs tightly together, and lean into the pain until my energy faded away and I fell into a fitful sleep. And I wonder: was I punishing her or punishing myself?

I've spent thirteen years as if I were a widower, Bahiya. My wife has been sleeping an arm's length away from me, and I've refused to touch her, as though to do so would be a sin, as if she were pork, carrion, or blood. I've realized that I'm stronger than I thought I was, and I've discovered that my stubbornness is a bottomless sea of darkness. The deprived body calls out to me, but it gets bridled by a proud soul, as though with a metal halter.

I came home one night during the first few months after the scandal, and she was waiting in the bedroom with a plan to break my stubbornness. In the four corners of the room, she had placed silver candlesticks holding red and purple perfumed candles, which produced a dim, romantic light. On the bed were elegant white sheets of embroidered cloth, as well as a long bolster and two big pillows decorated with satin ribbons knotted into the shape of a butterfly. The curtains were tightly drawn, and there was a brand-new silk rug on the floor. Oum Kalthoum's record was playing, with calm music and a heavenly voice: "I swear by you, you're the wish, the plea . . . You're the aim, the prize, the key . . . And in you, my deserter, a fervor I find . . . That leaves every lover bewildered, entwined . . . "

I stole a glance at Zbaida, and there she was, wearing a crimson silk nightgown I hadn't seen before. She'd changed her hairstyle, and the room was pervaded with the scent of a perfume I didn't recognize, one that seemed to contain the sweet taste of the forbidden.

She was sitting by the window reading, but as soon as she saw me come in, she threw the book aside. It flew through the air, its pages flapping and causing the candlelight to flicker, before it ended its trip at the base of the armoire. Her eyes followed its trajectory happily, and then she looked at me, smiled, and opened her arms like someone inviting an embrace. In the dancing light of the candles, I noticed that she had dyed her hands with henna and had delicate designs on her left wrist, drawn with black *harkous*. When did she do all of this? I didn't know. I pretended to be cold, ignoring her happiness to see me, and said drily, "Hi."

"No 'hi' and no talking . . . not until you tell me what the *harkous* hidden under the lace is saying to you."

She said it laughingly, pushed a light blanket off of her knees, and pulled back her dress, revealing the *harkous* design on her right inner thigh, ascending in fine, elegant lines until it was hidden from view by a flutter of red lace. My throat felt dry. I was on guard and anxious. I examined myself, but the only problem I found was my weak resolve. Zbaida was on the verge of victory. She had taken off the mask of modesty and was staring at me with a mixture of audacity and obscenity. I think that if she'd been able to stand up, she would have thrown herself at me. I stood hesitating, not knowing whether to advance or retreat, and in my chest two men were fighting. The one who had fallen was about to surprise the man standing over him with a thrust of his sword and kill him. As for Zbaida, she started touching her neck as though stroking it, as if she were dipping her fingertips into a pool of polished pearls. All the while, she sang along with the record, "When, my handsome man, will I see your satisfaction, see your anger fade away?" and started beckoning me with her henna-colored finger.

I advanced towards her, frowning like someone who'd been defeated. She asked me to move her from the rocking chair to the bed, and I did, as I had every night since I brought her back from the hospital paralyzed. When I laid her gently on the bed against her pillows and was about to straighten up, she threw her arms around me, pulling me to her neck tightly. That was the first time she'd ever done that; she'd never initiated anything so boldly, contenting herself with sending modest signals to see if I would respond. I couldn't free myself from her, and it felt wrong to push her, given her frail condition. So I yielded to her arms, as rigid as a tree trunk encircled by a serpent. But Zbaida didn't give up. She held onto my shirt, pulling it up to free it from my belt. Then she slipped her hand under the cloth and started caressing my back, scratching it with her fingers gently up and down, and my skin erupted in goosebumps of pleasure, the tree trunk scraping off its bark, about to come back to life. I was fighting myself, pretending to be unaffected, when she whispered softly in my ear, "Aren't you tired of this yet, Mohsen? How long will we stay in this torture?"

". . . "

"What can I do to make you believe me?"

"Confess."

The word came out of my mouth sharp and decisive, like the final verdict in a courtroom. I said it with the force of all the anger boiling inside me. Immediately, her arms around my back slackened, and she sighed deeply. She quickly pulled her hand from under my shirt and pushed me gently, so I sat up straight.

I saw tears pooling in her eyes and spilling quietly onto her silk nightgown, leaving dark spots on it. Suddenly, she shrank from me like an oyster that had opened its shell in the sun and, instead of warmth, received a squeeze of lemon. I waited for her to answer me, or at least to try evading the question in a way that wouldn't spoil her plan to break through my stubbornness that night. But she stared into space for a moment before busying herself with changing the record and adjusting the needle of the gramophone, which was next to the bed. After a few seconds Cheikh El Afrit started singing: "I am tired and bored . . . of this bitter life with you . . . " I left the room feeling that my head was filled with a thousand afreet, and I slammed the door behind me.

III

After that night, Zbaida never again tried to seduce me in any conspicuous way. Her pride prevented her from trying again, fearing to expose herself to another failure. As for me, I considered her reaction a tacit admission that my suspicions were legitimate, and I interpreted her silence as a sign that couldn't justify the unjustifiable. Over time, we both got used to our new life. In front of others, we were a married couple with no hatred or resentment between us, and, when the door closed on us, we became more like siblings, nothing between us but affection and tolerance, and occasionally some fighting. One outcome of this unnatural situation is that our behavior at times became hostile. She often made up problems and would start crying and screaming. Sometimes she said that she missed her eldest son Mohamed Habib, who was "detained" at her father's house, and accused me of negligence and lack of fatherly feelings because I didn't try, out of respect for my in-laws, to take him back by force. Other times, she complained about Khaddouj's controlling behavior with her maid Luiza, and asked me to put my foot down to deter the aggressor and teach her a lesson. Then she would get angry and throw a fit if she saw me remain neutral, uninterested in the maids' fights. She even hinted once that I was having an affair with Khaddouj, God bless her soul, a sinful relationship to make up for the marital bed I'd deserted. In the aftermath of a fight between Luiza and Khaddouj, in which faces were scratched and hair was pulled, and in which I didn't interfere between them in any way, she said, "Why are you defending Khaddouj? Are you afraid she might get mad at you if you stand by Luiza and leave you lonely?"

"Who's going to leave me lonely?"

"Khaddouj. The piece of charcoal that you've replaced this beautiful white alabaster with. Some men are like that; they love the smell of garbage."

I laughed a lot that day on the inside, but I hid it. Zbaida was accusing me of an affair with Khaddouj, who'd raised me like a son? Women are insane when they're consumed by jealousy! Let her think whatever she wants, I told myself; I'll let doubt nibble away at her heart, as it has eaten at mine all these years, without ever being satiated. Nothing breaks a woman's heart like the suspicion that her husband has another bed. She remains in a state between belief and denial. She can't completely believe it, tack up his obituary in her heart, and prepare to forget him. But neither can she completely deny it and treat him as if nothing's happened. I looked at Zbaida blankly that day and then smiled coldly to torture her more. She screamed at me, her patience running out, "Nothing? Don't you have anything to say?"

"I learned from the best, Professor Zbaida. How many times have I asked you questions, and you kept silent? Now it's your turn to ask and receive no answer."

Two or three weeks later, I heard her mention the word divorce for the first time. Three years had passed since that fateful night, and her legs weren't getting any better, despite the exercise and the physical therapy sessions she did every two days with a French doctor who visited her at home. The conversation got heated between us over some small matter that I don't remember, and she said suddenly, "Divorce me, Mohsen. Why are you retaining me against my will when you don't even want me?"

I was surprised by the question, and I didn't answer immediately. Since the day she held my arm and disobeyed her father, I'd thought that divorce was her greatest fear, but now here she was, asking for it herself.

"You know the way to the court. Go and sue me for divorce if you wish. Aren't you knowledgeable about personal code matters?"

"Are you really telling me to go to court? Are you mocking me, Mohsen, because you see me nailed to this chair, unable to do anything for myself, whether good or evil?"

"What do you want, Zbaida? Divorce? Never."

"Are you just being stubborn? Or are you enjoying seeing me helpless in your house?"

"As usual, you don't understand a thing. We would've divorced a long time ago if you hadn't been in that chair."

"Is it pity, then? I hereby relieve you of it. I don't want you to feel sorry for me."

"Do you really think you're worth pity, Zbaida? God, no. I don't think you deserve any compassion from me. I'm just doing my duty. It's unmanly for a man to divorce the mother of his children when fate affects her health."

IV

I was lying, Bahiya. My opinion about divorce wasn't about me being chivalrous or noble, as I made her believe. It was more complicated than that. When I saw her bloodstained that fateful night, I almost lost my mind. My mother told me a few days later, when I'd come back to my senses and started talking to people, that I had run out into the street with her in my arms, wailing like a woman who had lost her child. I don't remember how we got to the hospital, or how the nurses took her from me and lay her down on the gurney to take her to the operating room. All I remember is that I kept praying to God to save her until I fell asleep. Later, they told me that I passed out; that was my first diabetic shock, Bahiya. When the nurses woke me up, I found myself lying down on the ground, as if I were one of the beggars in the entrance hall of Sidi Mehrez's shrine. One of them, speaking broken Arabic and with signs of regret on her face, asked me, "Are you the husband?"

I leapt to my feet as though I'd been stung, and I didn't become aware of myself until I had grabbed onto the nurse, shaking her violently and asking, "Is she okay? Is she alive?"

She reassured me that she was still alive but informed me that she had entered a coma that might last for a long time. I asked to see her, insisted, but the nurse gently suggested that I go back home because visitors wouldn't be allowed until further notice.

I didn't leave the hospital for four days. My body started to smell, my clothes became dirty, and my joints became so stiff that I couldn't stand up without feeling dizzy. I spent the days imploring the doctors for good news and the nights praying for God's mercy. I checked the inside pocket of my jacket from time to time for the letter that had arrived in a bundle of bread and opened the gates of hell on us. Khaddouj had secretly slipped it to me the night of the incident after retrieving it from Mohamed Habib, who was playing with it. I read it over and over during those four days, but I couldn't make up my mind about it:

> *I'll be gone soon. I left the distilled fruits of my thinking and my heart with Karrita the baker in the Sidi Mansour quartier. They're for you. Send Luiza to pick up the book and the poetry manuscript. Tahar.*

I looked at the small piece of paper on both sides, hoping to see something new on it. I put it in the sun on a stone bench in the hospital courtyard for hours, thinking that perhaps writing in invisible ink would appear. If one of the workers or visitors had paid attention to me, they would surely have thought that I was a spy on a mission or an intelligence officer conducting an investigation. Or maybe a crazy person who thought he was one or the other.

I walked through the hospital hallways, talking to myself. My mind said that there was nothing suspicious in the letter, a writer offering his books and poems to a passionate reader through a middleman. What was the problem? Why had Hajj Othman made such a fuss, raised his cane, and caused all these problems? But as soon as I made peace with this opinion, some old images would pop into in my mind and take me back to my bewildered square one. I remembered a meeting between Tahar Haddad and Zbaida near the Théâtre Ben Kamla when she was in the early stages of her pregnancy with Mohamed Habib. It was a holiday, and she'd told me that she wanted to see *The Miser,* by Molière, which was being produced by the Arabic Acting group. Since we married, Bahiya, I'd gotten her used to frequenting the theaters and following the works of George Abyad, Fadhila Khetmi, and Ibrahim Akkoudi shown at the Rossini Theatre, despite the opposition and anger of my father, God bless his soul.

As soon as we came out of the theater, we saw Tahar Haddad. I had already heard rumors of the controversy surrounding his book about women, whose audacity didn't please the fanatics in our country, who had then conspired against him. I greeted him on the pretext of asking about a mutual friend, claiming to be worried because I hadn't heard from him. In fact, I'd already learned about his passing in a foreign country. The truth was that I wanted to comfort him during his crisis and show him the support of the enlightened people. I introduced him to Zbaida in glowing terms, and I thought then that it was the first time they'd met. I noticed that day that the man was oddly unsettled. His face was flushed, and it seemed to me that he was sneaking glances at my wife; as usual when we went out, she hadn't covered her face, so I didn't think badly of him. As for Zbaida, who before the meeting was very active and joyful—she applauded the actors onstage and would have, if not for her modesty, whistled and shouted—she was silent the rest of the walk home. She didn't say a word, as if suffering from a sudden grief. When I remembered that meeting while wandering the halls of the hospital, I became very suspicious. I took the letter out of my pocket for the thousandth time and read it again. That's when I realized that he'd said "send Luiza." I didn't know then that he'd been a teacher at the Rassaa house, and it was as if a bucket of cold water had been poured on my head on a very cold day. How could Tahar know the name of Zbaida's maid if there had been no intimate communication between them?

My feelings were still swinging between satisfaction and anger, between doubt and certainty when I heard, at the end of the fourth day at the hospital, the final say. I was standing in the hall when the lightning bolt fell in the form of good news. I heard the nurse's voice speaking in broken Arabic, calling urgently, "Monsieur Tahar! Monsieur Tahar!"

There was so much joy and enthusiasm in her voice that I turned to look for this lucky Tahar who was going to get good news. The hall was crowded with men, young and old. One of them ran to her, but she pressed past him with her big body and walked on as if she didn't see him. I realized that she was coming towards me. When our eyes met, she said, smiling, "Monsieur Tahar, the patient's awake."

I looked behind me, but I didn't see anyone. Who was this crazy nurse talking to? I said with a forced smile, "You're mistaken, Madame. I'm not the person you're looking for."

Her brows knit in surprise, and she shook her head, then said, "Aren't you the husband of the patient Zbaida Ennaifer? She's been asking for you ever since she opened her eyes."

My heart was beating violently, and my mind was on the brink of exploding. Should I be happy that she'd woken up from her four-day coma, or preoccupied wondering why the nurse thought my name was Tahar? I said to her cautiously, "Yes, sorry. I'm Mohsen Ennaifer; my family members call me Tahar. Did she mention my name?"

"Oh, Monsieur Tahar. Your name is the only thing on her lips. She must love you so much: someone waking up from a coma always reveals their hidden secrets. She's not fully conscious yet. Now go back home, shave your beard, take a shower, get some rest, and you can visit her tomorrow during visiting hours. *Au revoir.*"

V

The next day, I didn't dare go back to the hospital, Bahiya. I sent Khaddouj and sat waiting for her at the café across from the visitors' entrance, secretly hoping that she would come out and tell me that Zbaida hadn't woken up and that the nurse who'd spoken to me the day before was an old woman fabricating stories. But Khaddouj was gone for an hour that seemed like an eternity, then came back with bad news. Wiping her tears with the edge of her *safseri*, she said, "Lella Zbaida has regained consciousness, but—"

I interrupted her eagerly, "When did she regain consciousness?"

"Yesterday, Sidi Mohsen. But she's still in the intensive care unit. She asked me about you, but—"

I said sarcastically, "She asked you about me? That's nice of her. What did she say exactly?"

"She said why didn't Mohsen come with you, Khaddouj? But—"

"She said 'Mohsen,' just like that? Are you sure you heard the name right?"

I burst into hysterical laughter, and Khaddouj stared at me with an open mouth. No doubt she was saying to herself, "Sidi Mohsen has lost his mind over fear for his wife." She waited with her gaze averted for the laughing fit to end, then told me what she'd been trying to say each time I interrupted her.

She said, crying, that one of the nurses had told her that the patient had lost the ability to move her legs and that the chances of her walking again were very slim.

I went back to her the next day outside of visiting hours, shortly after sunset. I gave the guard twenty francs to let me in from the doctors' entrance. I gave a male nurse another twenty francs, so he took off his smock and put it on me. I stood behind the glass of the intensive care unit, looking at her from a short distance away. Her eyes were closed, and her chest was rising and falling softly. She seemed thinner than usual in the white sheet that surrounded her small body. That was the day, Bahiya, that I started talking to myself. "So you didn't die, Zbaida, and I can't mourn you and then forget you. You didn't come out of the accident safe and sound, either, so I can't congratulate you and then torture you the way a lion does its rival, to avenge my damaged dignity. You've come back to us half alive and half dead. A half-death isn't enough to forget you, and a half-life won't allow for punishment." Then I saw her moving one of her arms and blinking, and I quickly slipped away.

"How can I face you, Zbaida? How can I look into your

traitorous eyes? Do I send you the divorce papers while you're lying in bed, disabled? How can I decide your fate, and the fate of two boys who are still babies, based on an untrustworthy source? Even if the nurse told me the truth—and I don't think she would lie—would any rational person judge someone who's feverish and hallucinating? Also, could I ever leave you, Zbaida? Where would I get the strength to leave you, when my soul is still attached to you, unable to imagine life without you?"

Bahiya, the days that followed were cruel, like whips of fire on the back of a dying old man. It was difficult for me to tell anyone in my family about my doubts; after all, I had stood by Zbaida's side on the night of the accident, acted hostilely towards my father, and assaulted my brother because they'd treated her roughly and cast doubts on her behavior. I asked my family to keep the details of that fateful night a secret. None of our relatives knew about the incident, and no one visited Zbaida in the hospital. What made it easier for Mama Jnayna to hide the matter from the neighbors is that, at the time of the accident, Zbaida was still lying in with Mostafa, and my mother explained away her seclusion as postpartum indisposition. As for Mostafa, who was a few weeks old, my mother gave him to my sister Beya and asked her to breastfeed him with her son for a month until Zbaida got better, and then we gave him back to her.

The first time I met with her after the accident was hell. The hospital director gave permission, after her brother Mahdi (who has an enviable network) got involved, to move her from the women's room, where she'd been for three days after coming out of the coma, to a small room in a corner of the men's section that was usually reserved for the medical staff or their relatives. Once she was moved to the private room, I could no longer pretend I was too uncomfortable to visit her in a room filled with women, so the moment of confrontation had arrived.

I entered the room that evening with a surly expression on my face. Five days had already passed since she regained consciousness, and I'd been imagining scenario after scenario for the meeting, all depending on her reaction. I divided my thoughts into many situations, hoping to find the perfect approach to get the truth without exposing myself to the humiliation of the question. I decided that to save face, I couldn't tell her what the old nurse had said about her repeating the name Tahar during her hallucinations; I would make do with asking about the letter and nothing else. I was ready for anything that day, except for what actually happened.

She was lying on her side, facing the wall, when she heard my steps. She whispered weakly, without turning, "Luiza?"

I pretended to sneeze lightly to hide my shaking voice and said, clearing my throat, "It's me, Zbaida."

I heard her call my name with emotion as she struggled to turn over and face me. I approached the bed and supported her, and she burst into tears. It wasn't crying in the usual sense, Bahiya. It's not possible to describe it in words, not even using the venerable dictionary Arabs have created for the degrees of crying, from sobbing to wailing and lament. She made a sound that seemed to emanate from deep within her, echoing as though it came from all her pores as well as her throat. A sound with no tears or mucus, as if it were an ancient language body the body used to mourn itself. I was terrified, and my limbs trembled as Zbaida clung to my neck with both hands, screaming her strange scream in my face as if vomiting all of her sadness, anger, pain, and despair onto my head. I felt like someone who found himself suddenly in front of the open gates of hell, on the edge of a cliff, and chained, with the fire blazing in his face. Where did Zbaida get this sudden power from? What kind of solidity did this tiny body have at the very moment it seemed most broken? Isn't it strange that expressing weakness can be such a demonstration of strength?

I took her into my arms, shielding myself from her with her body. I hid her face between my neck and shoulder, trying to mute the grief that was escaping from her. It was the last thing I expected myself to do in my first encounter with her. She neither resisted, nor revolted in my hands. By the time a young nurse hurried over to us, asking what had happened, the wave had already receded, as suddenly as it had come, and the roaring sea had become a tranquil lake with swans floating peacefully on its surface. When I felt that she was becoming restless in my arms, I let her go, and I sat on the edge of the bed watching the nurse go through her assessment protocol. I took advantage of her answering the nurse's questions to gaze at her. Her eyes were dry, with no trace of a single tear, and they were surrounded by dark bluish circles. Her eyelids were drooping and wilted, and the left corner of her bottom lip was still horribly swollen from the blow she'd received on the night of the accident. Her face was pale and her cheeks hollow, as if she'd lost half her weight in these few days. She was beautiful, Bahiya. Beautiful despite the blueness, the swelling, the wilting, and the paleness. The thick hair on her forehead was calling my hand to push it gently out of her face, and the bruise under her chin was calling my lips to kiss it as a sign of sympathy. My eyes filled with tears I didn't feel, and I almost smiled at her—but caught myself at the last minute.

When the nurse left, we fell silent. I looked down, and she did the same. I sighed, and she sighed. The white blanket had slipped a bit, exposing part of her legs next to me. They were stiff and motionless, like two logs. When I gently extended my hand to straighten the blanket, it was as if I had poked her eye with a stick. Her sudden cry scared me, so I pulled my hand back, apologizing, and said, confused, "Do your legs hurt that much?"

She answered through heart-rending sobs. "It hurts me not to feel your hand on them."

After a short moment of silence, she added, "Tell me the truth, Mohsen. Am I paralyzed?"

Good lord! I came to ask her for the truth, and now she was asking me questions, and I was answering. I said, without hesitation, "You're not paralyzed, no, nothing like that. You're fine, and you'll be able to run home in a couple of days if you want to. Just have some patience, Zbaida."

"Your eyes are telling me the opposite. You're all lying to me. Mahdi isn't telling me the truth, and Luiza won't stop crying. God help me! I'm lost! I'm lost . . . "

She repeated the expression over and over in agony, hitting her face with her hands until her swollen, bruised lip split and blood spilled from it. When I tried to stop her from harming herself, she started slapping me and pounding her fists against my chest, still wailing, and didn't calm down until two nurses ran into the room. One of them held her down as the other tied a strap around her arm before injecting her with a sedative. I don't know what happened after that. All I remember is the cold sweat that took me by surprise, soaking my shirt, and the violent dizziness, and then the world went dark. That was my second diabetic shock, Bahiya.

VI

Bahiya, Bahiya. There is no solace left after your passing, nothing but Mohamed El Ezaby's song, which I'm listening to on the car's cassette deck now as I bring my granddaughter Hind, Mostafa's daughter, home from preschool.

Bahiya Bahiya.
Your eyes are so beautiful
And all the story is about the eyes of Bahiya.

My dear little Hind sings along in her childish voice, and I laugh so hard I almost pass out. The four-year-old has a sweet lisp that makes some of her letters lean towards "L." So it sounds like she's saying "woe, the eyes of woe" when she sings "Baliya, the eyes of Baliya."

I wonder whether my granddaughter with the beautiful face

and golden braids feels, with the amazing intuition of children, that her grandfather's life suffered from a *baliya* that no one knows about? A *baliya* thanks to which he discovered that God loves him. Don't they say that if God loves someone, he'll send him a test? God put me to the test with Bahiya, after I had already buried my heart and given it to the worms of ennui to feed on. But it was resurrected in your hands, the heart of a young man ready to greet life's pleasures.

When you invaded my office that second day, I read so many words in your eyes. From the tray hanging around your neck, you took a bundle that you'd hidden from your customers behind the rows of *kaak warka*. You untied it with your slender fingers and presented it to me with a shy smile. In the bundle were three almond cookies, still warm. How rude I was to ask you about the price, gesturing to the cookies as I did so. There was a flash of anger in your eyes, and you shook your head like someone who'd been disappointed. I was still embarrassed and looking for a way to apologize when you left the bundle in my hand, turned around, and walked quickly towards my office door, which you had left open, a boon for the eyes of curious employees and workers.

You didn't come to our offices for several days after that, long enough for your loyal customers among my colleagues to miss you dearly. They'd gotten used to waiting to drink their black coffee until your delicious *kaak warka* arrived. As for me, I was preoccupied with misfortune. During that period, my father-in-law Si Ali Rassaa got sick and eventually died. He lost consciousness suddenly while sitting at the dinner table, and he was unconscious for a long time until the doctors finally gave up on him and allowed his relatives to take him home to die in his own bed. Luiza brought us the news, and it became imperative to end our dispute with them before fate decided the matter. I asked the director-general for an urgent leave from work. I accompanied my mother to the Rassaa house for reconciliation, and we took Zbaida in her wheelchair; she insisted on seeing her dying father and asking for his blessing before he passed. It was as if Si Ali Rassaa had been waiting for his daughter to regain consciousness. As soon as she arrived and he heard her voice, he rubbed his eyes and sat up, as if he'd only been sleeping. We were celebrating his recovery and happy that he'd accepted our invitation to my brother Mhammed's marriage, when we were stricken by the news of his collapse in the mosque courtyard, at the feet of the invitees, his heartbeat gone, like a leaf falling from a tree.

I took two extra days off to prepare for the funeral and attend the condolence rituals. And you, Bahiya, once your anger towards me subsided, you started coming back to the Tax Office, and you became alarmed by my absence. The doorman told me, laughing, that you'd been at my office door ever since you tried to open it and couldn't. When the wait became too long, you roamed past the other offices, gazing at faces like someone searching for something lost. He made a conclusion based on his own small mind and warned me, the morning I returned to work, "Those Jews are a greedy people, Boss. They have no friends but money. So long as the deaf-mute girl has tasted the sweetness of your outstretched hand, she'll be glued to your door, just like the Jews are glued to the land of Palestine. Didn't you hear about the Zionist Ben Gurion declaring a few months ago that he was founding the state of Israel on the land of Palestine? Those Jews are like an epidemic. God forbid! If they go to a place, they destroy its people."

He was quiet for a short moment, pursing his lips in resentment, as though his nationalistic feelings had made him forget why he'd come to talk to me. Then he found his train of thought again and continued, quickly, "If you allow me, I'll make sure that she never sets foot in the building again."

I dismissed him with a frown, telling him to leave you alone and stop giving unsolicited advice to his superiors. I didn't find myself interested in talking to him at all that day. I thought he most likely wouldn't understand, but he would probably try to debate me anyway, with all his ignorance and fanaticism, and he would probably defeat me—I'm quick to surrender when dealing with fools.

I hung my jacket and fez on the metal coatrack next to the door. The room had gotten stuffy during my absence, so I decided to leave the door open to let in some fresh air. As soon as I sat down at my desk and started going through the files that had piled up, I heard that captivating laugh jingling in the lobby. That day, Bahiya, I decided to wash away the filth of my depressed soul with your laugh. Thirteen years of sadness weighing heavily on my heart: Zbaida's tears, sighs, and moans; my mother Jnayna's screaming at my brother Mhammed to shut down the rumors and complete half of his religion; and the looks of black hatred that I exchange with him when we sat at the dinner table or met on a narrow path. As I returned from a funeral, I was eager for joy. And you were the epitome of joy on alabaster legs. Your laugh lit a lamp inside my heart, and in its light, I saw an empty land I couldn't imagine still existed. I saw it surrounded by a jungle of cacti, tribulus, neurada, colocynth, and other prickly plants. Here was your laugh, opening a gap in the impenetrable fence and roaming in that empty land, plowing it softly and finding there, beneath the cracked earth, the dormant seeds of a thousand orchards.

As soon as I heard your laugh, I left my office and stood up by the door, looking out into the lobby, searching for you in the crowd of clients. I saw you on your knees playing with a little boy accompanied by an adult my age. You offered him a *kaak warka* coated with sugar and took the money from the adult. As soon as you stood up, you raised your eyes towards my door and saw me rooted to the spot, gesturing to you to come upstairs. You flew to me and landed on my heart like a dove landing on the nest that holds her chicks, reassured, tender, and cautious. When I greeted you with a handshake and you put your hand in my palm, I felt as if I were holding ostrich feathers. I closed the door behind you, and you looked annoyed. You took two steps back, and in your eyes was the fear of someone who has experienced, after a long time working in the street, the vileness of men and their lack of appreciation. I don't know how I asked you, trying to articulate the sounds so you could read the words on my lips, "Are you engaged?"

You went silent for a moment, a touch of surprise on your face. I thought you didn't understand the question, so I started acting out the movement of putting a ring on my left ring finger, as you watched, your expression frozen as though you were enjoying my confusion. When I was about to give up hope of getting an answer, I saw you smile shyly and shake your head. Without thinking or prior planning, I found myself grabbing your left hand and spreading your fingers with my fingertips. Before you overcame your astonishment and I came back to my senses, I picked up a big *kaak warka* from the tray hanging next to your chest and hung it on the tip of your ring finger.

I didn't see either happiness or anger in your features. You pulled your palm away gently; then you pulled off the *kaak warka* and put it carefully back in its place on the tray. Your face remained ambiguous, like a closed book whose title has flaked off. As for me, my face turned red and gave away all its secrets. I pretended, to hide my awkwardness, to choose some *kaak warka* from the tray. As usual, I paid extra, but this time, you insisted on giving me back the change. You bade me farewell with a gentle nod and headed towards the door, walking with confidence and modesty. What did you think that day, Bahiya? Did you think I was making fun of you or trying to convince you to sleep with me? Or did you deem it excessive for an almost fifty-year-old man to want to marry a girl that hadn't yet reached twenty?

I was eaten up with regret. What kind of devil drove me to propose what I proposed while my wife was still mourning her father, whose body wasn't even cold? Was it jealousy of my brother Mhammed, who was soon to be married, while I had been like a widower for years? Or was it the madness of the midlife crisis that attacks men in their fifties and makes them act like teenagers again, after their virility has faded, their muscles have wasted away, and their gray hair has spread to their sideburns? I started pacing my office like a wounded lion, rebuking myself and weaving sad ends to my story with you, "What if the girl tells the employees here, that vile doorman, the workers, the clients? What if she tells them what happened between us? You miserable man, what kind of scandal have you cooked up with your own two hands?"

Then I remembered that God had protected you from slander and gossip when he chose for you to abstain from speaking, and I calmed down a little.

I went back home that evening with a tendril of love like ivy growing around my ribs. Its pressure got more and more intense as the night progressed, and my pain became unbearable. I felt my heart beating like the heart of a dying person. Zbaida was in bed, dozing; every so often, her grief for her father would wake her up, and she would begin sobbing again. I sat on the couch staring at the ground between my feet and gasping for air, as if I were ascending to heaven. At dawn, I suffered from a severe headache at the back of my head, and I couldn't stifle my moans. My head was about to explode. There was a huge mill churning inside it, rumbling and clanking. Zbaida noticed and asked me, terrified, in the darkness. "What's going on, Mohsen?"

"Nothing. Nothing. Go to sleep."

But she didn't go to sleep. She kept calling to me and repeating the question until I told her about the headache splitting my skull and how I was on the verge of vomiting because of the pain. She implored me to come next to her. She persisted in her pleading, and I was too weak to oppose anything. She turned on the light, sat up, and asked me to put my head on her knee, and I did. She massaged it with her fingertips for a long time in slow, small circles from the front to the back. Then she repeated her movements in the opposite direction. I felt much better. The knocking in my head stopped, and the sound of the mill slowly started to fade. I opened my eyes, looking at Zbaida with an expression of gratitude. When she stopped, I groaned and asked her to continue. She started rubbing my eyebrows with her thumbs, back and forth, and then put her palm on my temple, caressing it gently. When the light of dawn started to sneak in through the window, she turned off the lamp. The darkness enveloped us again. Within moments, I'd fallen asleep with my head on Zbaida's knee, and she nodded off with her palm on my cheek.

I saw you in my dream, Bahiya. It was a horrendous nightmare. I saw myself walking in a neighborhood I was unfamiliar with, terrified, as though I were being chased. I was walking deep into narrow alleys with old, dilapidated buildings. Every alley led to another alley, longer than the last, as if I were in a maze. From time to time, women wearing revealing clothes would look out at me from the balconies of the row houses. Some of them called me by name and beckoned to me with obscene gestures. Others poured buckets of brackish water into my path, and it splashed onto my face and clothes. I walked faster as licentious laughter rose behind me. Then the buildings disappeared, and I found myself in a place that looked like an endless forest, trees extending as far as the eye could see. My throat was dry, and I was sweating. The prickly plants in my path scratched my arms and caught on my clothes. From time to time, I was surprised by a lurking snake that would hiss at me, flicking its forked tongue, and I would run. I heard the barking of a dog slowly gaining on me. Suddenly a whole pack of stray dogs were running after me, a terrifying froth at their mouths. I stopped, searching among the dense bushes for a stone to throw so they would leave me alone, and my eyes fell on a large, dried-out *kaak warka* in the dirt. There was no stone, or even pebble, in sight. I picked up the *kaak warka* and threw it at the dogs, but it flew in the air, spinning, until I could no longer see it. Then it reappeared, coming back to me like

Pharaoh's staff. Suddenly, the dogs barked and stopped running, and I was chased by the *kaak warka*, which scared the hell out of me. I ran; it ran behind me. I sped up; it sped up. When I was too tired to run anymore, I fell to my knees, and it floated over my head, neither passing me nor falling behind. When they saw me kneeling, the dogs ran towards me again, barking louder, and the snakes slithered towards me from all sides, their hissing drowning out the barking. The *kaak warka* approached my head, almost knocking off my fez. I screamed, calling out for my mother like a small child. Suddenly, a woman in a white dress appeared out of nowhere, carried by a white cloud so close to the ground that it almost touched it. I looked up and saw you, Bahiya, with a tray of *kaak warka* hanging against your chest as usual. You gave me your hand, and I stood up and rode with you on the cloud, which lifted us above the forest, above its dogs and snakes, as if it were a flying carpet.

I woke up after that to Zbaida's hand stroking my cheeks. She said that she woke up because of my screaming and calling for my mother, and she knew it was a nightmare. She asked me to tell her about it, and I pretended I didn't remember. She asked about the headache, which was still bothering me slightly, but I claimed that her magic hand had cured me. When I sat up, wanting to stand, she put her hand on my forehead as if checking for a fever and then passed her palm over my face quickly as if to wipe away the nightmare sweat. When her fingertips reached my chin, her hand slowed. She put her forefinger between my closed lips and gently slipped it between my front teeth and touched my tongue. At that moment, the only thing I remember was me kissing her lips desperately. I was dizzy from the nightmare and the headache and didn't know what I was doing. I saw her face flush and her breath quicken, and within a few seconds, years' worth of ice melted in the magma of exploding desire.

When everything was over and the body had quenched its thirst, I found myself drowning in a sea of sadness. The patience of thirteen years was wasted for the joy of one hour, and the cascade of fleeting pleasure didn't put out the volcano of my doubt and anger. Worse than all of that were the images I saw in the moment, and I wasn't sure whether I should be happy or sad about them. I remembered your face as I kissed Zbaida, and I imagined your slender body under my hand as I touched the body that had gained more fat from inactivity. You were there in my bed, with all your vigor, beauty, and youth. It occurred to me that Tahar was there in Zbaida's bed, too, even if he'd been dead for a long time. A horrendous feeling of humiliation came over me. Is there anything worse than feeling like a tool used to satisfy a sexual urge?

I know now, Bahiya, that I was exaggerating my thoughts and doubts. It occurs to me from time to time, now in my old age, to ask for forgiveness from Zbaida for the silent torture she suffered. I believe that God will call me to account because of her when I join you and face him.

That would be the last time, Bahiya, that this happened between me and my wife. I never went back to her bed after I married you and you satisfied my physical desires. My heart didn't soften even when she sometimes cried and wailed, asking me why. And when I tried, two months after your passing, in a moment of weakness, to rekindle what had been between us, she pushed me away with disgust, as if I were a despicable beggar at the door of a tyrannical prince. That day, what she said dug a black hole in my heart, only God knows how deep. In one movement, she pointed with her fingertip to her mouth and then to the ground at her feet and said, "If the phlegm comes out, Mohsen, we don't take it back."

VII

After what happened between me and Zbaida that dawn, I became sure that I needed to safeguard my chastity from her. I didn't want anyone but you, Bahiya. I interpreted the nightmare of running through the alleys and woods in a way that fit what I thought was right, which helped me move forward with my nascent plans.

I saw the running in terror as evidence that I was afraid of committing sins. As for the snakes lurking around me, they were the Jewish and Italian ladies of the night I'd begun to consider visiting when I stumbled across them while spying on my brother Mhammed, God bless his soul, to get to the bottom of the secret Luiza revealed to us one Ramadan night. As for the dogs chasing me, they were the barking desire in my body due to years of deprivation. I used to think that the *kaak warka* in the dream was a sign of imminent danger, but it was only your love, which wouldn't forsake me even if I neglected it, and would accompany me wherever I went, protecting me from the sun. Your arrival on a cloud to save me from the snakes, dogs, and aimless wandering was proof that you were my angel, who would save me from going astray. It was a vision, then, and not a nightmare, and someone who could interpret it correctly—like me—was worthy of talking to your father immediately.

So that day, I asked about the shop of Pascal the Jew on the street parallel to the Tax Office, before going to work at 8 A.M. There were two men standing and chatting in front. They were holding orange blossom biscotti and dipping them in juice, which I could tell from its color was lemonade mixed with *rosetta* almond drink. I stood on the opposite sidewalk next to a skinny, dusty boy sitting on a short wooden chair, a wooden step stool and some shoe shining tools in front of him. I gave him my foot and focused my eyes on the small shop. There was a big man with a big belly standing behind the counter. He was wearing a white smock and a black hat, and I heard the customers calling him Pascal. I assumed from his appearance that he was in his sixties or a little less. He had laughing eyes and a loud voice and seemed to me to be a humorous man; he welcomed his customers and answered the greetings of people on the street by lifting his arms up high in the air, as if he were an actor onstage saluting the audience. His movement was graceful, despite his heavy weight.

"Can you give me your other foot, please, Sidi?"

I withdrew my right foot from the top of the tilted wooden box and put the left one there instead, and the shoeshine boy continued his work. I kept staring at the shop owner, trying to learn about his personality before I sprang on him what I had in mind. The two customers left, and I saw him putting a tray on the counter whose aroma reached me at the same time as it reached the boy, who sighed. Pascal pulled a knife with a square edge and wide blade from his apron belt and started cutting the contents of the tray vertically and horizontally, six slices each way. I felt the boy tap on my calf to let me know he'd finished his work. I gave him his fee and crossed the street, heading towards the shop. Pascal greeted me before I had even reached him. He raised his arms and shook his head left and right, saying, "Good day, Sidi. This is your first time here—welcome!"

I greeted him back with some flattering expressions and asked him about the tray in front of him. He said proudly, "Tunisian sorghum bread sprinkled with sesame, delicious and aromatic. You won't find anything like it in the souk." I asked for three pieces and a glass of lemonade. Pascal laughed, surprised by my appetite. I gestured for the shoeshine boy to come over. He ran, worried that I'd found something wrong with his work. When he saw that I was giving him the lemonade and two pieces of the millet bread, his eyes sparkled happily, and he mumbled his thanks: "May God bless your parents and feed you from the fruits of paradise."

Then he added, while drinking the lemonade, "And may God open your path and meet your needs."

I was in need of his last prayer. But God didn't answer. Pascal shut the door in my face and refused to give me what I needed. If I hadn't tricked him, I would never have gotten you, Bahiya. I told him, as I was standing at the threshold of his shop with the piece of millet bread in my hand, almost crushing it unconsciously, "You have a girl that sells *kaak warka* at the Tax Office, and *mashallah*! She is polite, sweet, and smart."

He laughed happily and said, rubbing his stomach proudly, "Which one of my daughters?"

"I realized then that I didn't know your name, Bahiya. Everyone at the Tax Office called you "Bakkousha," the deaf girl, and I couldn't reference you to your father by your disability, so I kept mumbling, as if trying to remember a name I forgot.

"Wided or Bahiya?"

I didn't know how to answer him. I found both names suitable for you. But Bahiya sounded better and more poetic. I was still unsure what to say, until I heard him saying, pointing behind me, "This one?"

My heart leapt, and I expected to see you there. Instead, I saw a comely face with a slight resemblance to you, but a bit older. Wided greeted me and entered the shop quickly, and I lost sight of her behind a curtain leading to the back. Pascal could tell from my reaction that I meant his other daughter, so he said, seeming emotional, "It's Bahiya, then. The beauty of girls. Smart and kind. If God had given her a tongue, she would have dethroned Elizabeth the wife of George the Sixth, king of Britain, and would sit in her place."

I said to myself, a lump in my throat, "Then let her dethrone Zbaida, wife of Mohsen Ennaifer—no need to fight the English!"

Our conversation was interrupted by the arrival of some new customers. I stood nearby, waiting for a chance to broach the subject I'd come there to discuss. But it was time to go to work, and the queue in front of the shop was getting longer and more crowded. So I convinced myself to postpone the matter until evening.

I spent the rest of the day distracted. When I remembered some brief scenes of my morning with Zbaida, I found myself sighing, depressed. My God, how much my wife had changed over the years in which I hadn't touched her. Her buttocks had gotten large and saggy. They used to look as if they were sculpted from ivory. Her calves were wasted and shriveled, their muscles loose from years of inactivity. Her belly had started to resemble fritter dough that, when the cook flips it over with his hands, his fingers sink in. There was nothing left of her but her beautiful face, as glorious as daybreak, and the tiny tear that trickled from her eyes whenever she reached orgasm. I used to kiss it, laughing, in happier days, proud of my virility.

I didn't kiss her tear that morning, Bahiya. Rather, a new feeling came into my heart, like the stroke of a dagger. Something worse than the resentment of the victim against their oppressor, and worse than the pain of someone betrayed by their beloved. When she let out her final moan and I saw the tear slip from beneath her right eyelid, slide down her temple, and disappear into her hair behind her ear, something crazy occurred to me. I held her by the shoulders, still pressed against her, and shook her violently, screaming at her, "Who are you crying for, Zbaida? Wait until I die, then wail."

She looked at me goggle-eyed, mouth half open in surprise. Then she turned her face away from me, to the left, without saying a word. I became more irritated. I held her temples between my fingers and turned her face towards me violently, screaming at her until my saliva misted her face, "Confess, Zbaida! You were wishing you could've lived these moments with your lost beloved. When I touch you, do you remember him? Are you crying about losing him?"

I ruminated on that suspicion all morning as I paced around in circles in my office like a bull turning a waterwheel, waiting for the evening to arrive so I could go back to Pascal's shop. In the meantime, I remembered, in pain, old memories from my honeymoon with Zbaida that made my suspicions all the more probable.

VIII

When I closed the door of our room on Zbaida the night of our wedding, she trembled like she was cold. She was wearing a thick dress embroidered with sequins and yellow beads and another dress hidden beneath it, made of thick velvet to protect her from the November cold in Tunis. We got married on a quiet night. The wind had stopped, and the downpour of rain had come to an end, after falling for days. My mother had begged my father to postpone the wedding until the summer, but her pleas resulted in nothing but fights, one after the other, that ended in her total surrender. Zbaida's father informed us at the end of October, after a long wait, that he was agreeing to the engagement. He gave us only one month to prepare the wedding and welcome the bride into her new home. My father agreed for my sake, when he saw how eager I was to meet the conditions so that everything would go well. Mama Jnayna didn't have any option but to comply, so she pretended to be pleased. But as she worked on preparing her dress, she asked for God's mercy and showed her objection to the proceedings with her pursed lips. Whenever I entered the house, then, I would find her busy preparing something for the wedding party, but she would immediately start complaining, saying with an anger that she didn't bother to hide, "Glory be to God! Would it be the end of the world if you got married in summer like every other young person? What kind of wedding will this be in the rain? What happens if we set up the stage for the band and the chairs for the guests and then the autumn rain surprises us? How can I wear the ensemble I prepared all those years ago for this blessed day if it's freezing cold?"

I would just kiss her head to placate her. She would relax and laugh when she saw me rushing around impatiently. She would pray for me and trill joyfully, "May God make you happy, my son. I hope that Rassaa's daughter is a good girl and will make you happy."

I still remember the night of my first wedding, Bahiya, as if it hasn't been forty-eight years. The night of Friday, November 24th, 1930, one day before my twenty-ninth birthday. Everything went as well as I could have wished. The singer, Leïla Sfez, arrived ahead of schedule. With her beautiful voice, she fired up the stage, which was set for the occasion in the middle of the courtyard. The girls danced to her music underneath a large green tarp that Khaddouj had prepared in the afternoon. She had secured it with thick rope to each of the four corners above the courtyard, protecting the dancers from the cold nighttime dew. Meanwhile, Raoul Journo—who was not yet the shining star of Tunis's music scene—was in the center of the men's gathering in part of the roofed portion of the courtyard. He thrilled the attendees with his strong, melodious voice performing the Andalucian *taqtouqat* and the Eastern *adwar*. Everyone was eating and drinking and having a good time, singing and dancing. I was the only one impatient for the singers to conclude, as if I were sitting on a red-hot ember. Impatient for the party to end, the guests to leave, and to be left alone with my bride.

When they had finally gone, I found her shivering. I sat her down on the edge of the bed; she was wearing her gold beaded dress. I snatched my burnous off its hanger and spread it over her shoulders. Then I took off my fez and knelt in front of her. I extended my hand to her, but she didn't give me hers. She seemed so shy that if her shyness covered over Mt. Boukornine, it would calm it down. So I grabbed her hands to hold them in mine, and found them like two discs of Siberian ice. I began to rub them and blow warm air on them as she sat there, as rigid as though she'd been turned to stone by Medusa. I spoke to her, as I kissed her hands between every sentence or two, about my passion for her. I told her how I had followed her on her way to high school for days, but she never saw me. About the shape of her black leather school bag with its two golden buckles, about the number of buttons on her gray school smock with its two front pockets, about her blue shoes with their modest heels and her brown athletic shoes with rubber soles, about the cheerful way she greeted the groom as she got into the carriage that took her from home to high school and the elegant way she jumped down from it as they arrived. I released her hands after mine had transferred some of their warmth. Then I said to her, laughing, as I raised her chin for a moment to get her to look me in the eyes, "Ever since I first saw you, Zbaida, I prayed to God that he would bring you close to me, if our closeness would bring good. And if our closeness would bring evil, that he would banish the evil . . . and then bring you close to me."

I scored something approaching a smile at this. That encouraged me to go on. I sat down on the side of the bed next to her and pulled her to me, resting her head on my shoulder and putting my arm around her. Then I placed my other hand over her eyes to get her to close them, careful not to smudge the kohl. I spoke to her in a soft voice, as if I were soothing a baby to sleep. Then I said, humbly, as if praying, "Your image never leaves me, day or night. I imagine you standing there in front of the armoire wearing a nightgown. And you lying down in it here on the bed. I imagine your belly becoming big and round. Then I imagine us having one child crawling on the carpet and another in his crib, kicking the wood with his little bare legs and giggling."

I heard her sigh, so I continued in a dreaming voice, "I love you, Zbaida. My love for you destroys my sleep and doesn't let me rest. I sleep, and you are my bed; I wake, and you are my blanket. You go with me wherever I go. When I'm performing my prayers, I see you. I see you at my office, between my notebooks and the boxes of files and registers and papers. I see you in the café, dancing among the cubes of sugar in a clear glass of green tea."

Zbaida finally spoke, and I heard her voice for the first time. She gently removed my hand from her eyes first, then straightened up, leaning away from me. So I drew my arm back from around her shoulders and helped her take off the burnous. She turned towards me and looked at me with mischievous eyes, shining with a light hidden by the glint of the golden beads she was wearing. Then she said, in a tone of wonder mixed with teasing, "A poet, too! And here they told me you were an economist! Do they teach you poetry in the schools for economics, too?"

I sensed some derision in what she said, but I softened the edges and assumed good intentions. I looked up at the ceiling, like a pupil whose teacher has surprised him with a question he doesn't know the answer to. Then I answered her, wide-eyed and laughing affectedly to show amazement and approval, "Is it possible to trade in poetry, as well? Honestly, it's a great economic idea, Zbaida. It could solve the international banking crisis. A client could, for example, request a loan of fifty thousand francs, and the bank could then give him five poems by Abderrahmen Kefi and let him deal with it on his own."

I said that and guffawed, remembering the poems Kefi wrote taunting life and people with its obscene language. She didn't get it, so she pursed her lips, annoyed. Then she laughed an artificial, sarcastic laugh that was closer to a snort. She said, after she clapped her hands together as if lamenting or disapproving, "Are Kefi poems worth that much? Or maybe you don't know any other poets, so you thought he would be a good example?"

I laughed then, thinking she was joking. It didn't occur to me at the time that she was testing me. She was secretly comparing between the present and the absent, between the culture of the economist next to her and the culture of the writer and poet. She was setting a trap with every question, and I fell into them with the naivety of the inattentive. I said, laughing, "What can I do? It's God's punishment. I don't understand anything outside of calculus, statistics, and equations."

Then I took off my jacket and undid my tie. I got closer to her and winked, saying suggestively, "But I am very cultured, nonetheless; you'd be surprised by how much I know. I promise to teach you everything . . . "

Then I added, laughing as I opened the armoire and went through the silk and feathered garments folded neatly inside. "We can start by choosing the clothes for the first lesson."

But I didn't give my first lesson that night, Bahiya. In fact, nothing happened between me and Zbaida for two weeks. I was like a domesticated monkey, and she was like a shy gazelle. Whenever my lips approached her face, she would move her head away as if fleeing great harm. She would stand up, looking around her as if searching for an exit to save her from a looming problem. And because I was inexperienced and in love, I couldn't decipher her code. I thought she was rejecting me because she was shy and was teasing me. But she turned away from me out of hate and arrogance. I didn't want to force anything on her, and I didn't deprive her of anything in return. When I found out that she loved theater and singing, I accompanied her to theaters and took her to private concerts that were organized regularly in the houses of my French friends. With me, she lead a glorious life that you didn't get even a tenth of, Bahiya. So, with time, she started coming out of her shell and softening up. I started to get to know her personality, and I realized that she was funny and joyful, eloquent and interesting when she spoke. Whenever she delved into a topic, you couldn't feel bored, and if she was brief, you wished that she would keep talking. What's more, she was smart and witty, and all this made me even more ardently in love with her. By the time she'd given birth to our two sons, I thought that I knew all her secrets, that I knew her like I knew the lines of my palm, and had memorized her like Muslims memorize surahs from the Quran. Then the storm, after five years of blessing, took me by surprise. When I looked around me, I found Zbaida like a deep, dark well, and Mhammed my brother, the son of my mother and father, may God bless his soul, crueler to me than a poisoned arrow in my side. I started examining myself, and

I realized that I was weaker than a nest of larks trampled by elephants, and more delicate than a clod of dirt picked up by a boy and thrown into the well.

IX

When I went back to Pascal that night, I found him getting ready to close the shop. He had already shut and latched the door and locked it using two heavy keys. As soon as he noticed me standing behind him, he said, apologizing, "Good evening, Sidi. We're closed now, but you'll find what you need in the morning, if God gives us life until then."

"I'm here to ask for something you can take care of before morning, if you wish."

He raised his eyebrows, taken aback and suspicious. But he didn't reject my request to sit at the Ben Jeddou Café near his shop. I ordered us two coffees. Then I introduced myself and mentioned to him that I was married and the father of two sons, and that my wife was paralyzed. I told him that I wanted to take a second wife, on the condition that this marriage would remain secret so as not to insult the pride of my disabled wife. He frowned and started smacking his cup on the table nervously, until the foam spilled over. He put it down, annoyed, and rubbed the fingers of his right hand on his left palm to get rid of the sting from the hot coffee. Then he looked at me and said, "Do you mean, Si Ennaifer, that you want me to marry you to my daughter Wided?"

He didn't give me a chance to answer before he continued angrily, "Without a party or making it public, as if she were an orphan?"

Smiling, I kept my eyes fixed on him and mumbled, "Not Wided. Bahiya."

His eyes gleamed in astonishment, and he stared at me with what looked like anger; then he stood up and leaned towards me with his hands on the table. His lips trembled, and he was about to say something but didn't. He seemed to be searching for the right words. Then he said, with a voice he deliberately raised, just a little, "Listen to me, Sidi. If you're here to joke with me, then your joke isn't funny; it's heavier than lead. And if you're here in all seriousness, then you should know that I don't have girls suitable for marriage."

He called the waiter over, rummaging in his pockets for change to pay for the coffee before leaving. I held his arm and gently pulled him back, trying to get him to sit down again, and said, "Pray to the Prophet, Si Pascal."

The formula slipped off my tongue before I thought about it, but he looked askance at me, becoming visibly more irritated. He most likely interpreted my words as a mockery of his Jewish faith. He put his francs on the table and walked towards the door. There was no option for me other than to go after him and try to placate him, but he refused to come back with me. Finally he stopped on the sidewalk, at the end of his patience, and spoke to me gruffly: "Okay, go ahead. I'm listening."

I explained the matter to him quickly, emphasizing my best intentions and my plans to do the right thing if I was accepted. I said, sighing, to conclude my speech, "I'll buy her a place in El Hafsia, close to your shop, so you can visit her everyday if you like. Her mother and sister can stay with her whenever they want during the times I spend at the other house. I'll pay you the dowry you want, buy the bride the appropriate jewelry, and register the apartment in her name. I don't ask for anything but secrecy."

He seemed hesitant, and I thought he was about to relent. But he shook his head after a moment of silence and said, "Bahiya, no. I'll marry you to her older sister if you wish."

"Si Pascal. Please. If all I wanted was to marry another woman, I would've done it a long time ago. I wouldn't put myself in this ridiculous situation. But I saw Bahiya and fell in love with her, and only God knows how much I love her. I'm happy with her the way she is. Do the right thing and don't reject me."

He fidgeted, then pushed me back inside the café. I found that the waiter had already cleaned our table and taken away our cups. Pascal ordered two more and started speaking, his voice shaky, "Listen . . . "

Then he was silent for a short moment, as if trying to find my name in his memory. I helped him, so he resumed, saying, "Yes, yes, Mohsen. I was about to say 'Listen, my son,' but the word stuck in my throat, then disappeared. I don't think I'm sufficiently older than you to consider you my son."

As he said this, he glanced at the hair that was receding from my forehead, and the gray hair at my temples. I swallowed the barb with grace, raising my hand to my chin in embarrassment, trying to hide the flabby skin that had started to gather below it. He took a big sip of coffee and continued, "Bahiya is the apple of my eye. As you know, she has a disability. She had a fever when she was three years old and lost her hearing, but we didn't notice anything at first. Then it didn't take long before she forgot her words because of her deafness. She became mute, and we thought she'd become stupid, or something had happened to her brain. But she was getting cleverer and more skillful despite her muteness. And her deafness made her sharp."

Then his tone changed, and he raised his finger in my face in warning, "If you think she's below you because of her disability or her religion, then I have nothing to talk to you about. But if you're serious, and appreciative of who she is, then you should know that my daughter is independent, and it's up to her to decide. I won't force her to do something she doesn't want to do. Be patient, then, until I consult her and see what she thinks. The girl is the age of your children, and she may not be willing to share her husband with another woman."

We agreed that I would visit your family at home on Saturday evening to ask for your hand, the way these things are traditionally done. If you accepted me, we would hold our secret marriage contract ceremony a week later, and I would move you to your new apartment before the end of the month.

From the house of my father-in-law Ali Rassaa, who had died three days before, I went to Sylvan's shop at Souk El Berka. I bought you a bracelet that, after that day, wouldn't leave your wrist until it was taken off by the woman who washed your body and wrapped you in your green shroud, embroidered in golden thread with "There is no God but God." I also bought you a gold cuff and a diamond-studded gold brooch in the shape of a bird spreading its wings. I still have it hidden in the box of my important papers, and I'll give it to my granddaughter Hind for her next birthday, if God lets me live until then. That day, I put the velvet boxes in my jacket pocket and went down to Souk Trok. I chose an expensive pink silk cloth that you would use to make that beautiful dress out of, the dress that made me lose my mind whenever I saw you in it. I walked towards the address that your father had given me, with light, confident steps, as if borne aloft on a cloud of joy. I was certain that you were waiting for me anxiously and longingly. The eyes don't lie, Bahiya, and your eyes had spoken the sweetest words to me over the previous days. I climbed the long staircase leading to your apartment on the third floor of an old building on Rue Qaa El Mezoued. I was able to find the street thanks to the vocational school on the left of the turnoff, just as your father had described. When I arrived at your door, I was gasping for air and very sweaty from climbing the stairs. I stood for a moment until I caught my breath so you wouldn't think that I was a weak old man. After a minute or two, I knocked gently on the door and straightened my fez and tie. I stood there for a long time, and no one opened the door, making me worry. Was it just an illusion when I imagined that she wanted me like I wanted her? Was Pascal mocking me, luring me here only to leave me disappointed on their doorstep? But a four- or five-year-old boy poked his head out of the neighbors' door across the hall and examined me with curious, mischievous eyes. I asked him, pointing at the closed door, "Is this Pascal Wazzan's apartment, young man?"

He shook his head and didn't say anything. I was tongue-tied. I repeated the name again fearing that he had misheard me, but he continued to shake his head with the confidence of someone who knew what he was talking about. Was I on the wrong floor? Was this the wrong building? I said in a pleading tone, "Do you know the man I'm asking about?"

He nodded. I asked him if he knew where he lived. He burst into laughter before disappearing behind the door, which he left ajar. I was still standing there, not sure what to do, when I saw Pascal reopening the door, your naughty brother smiling mischievously behind him. Your father affected a laugh and invited me to sit in the guest room, saying, "You're lucky the neighbors didn't open the door for you, or you'd be in trouble by now."

He explained to me that an old Jewish man lived in the opposite apartment with his seven daughters. He had been planning to immigrate to Israel because his business stagnated during the war, and then some thugs attacked him at the souk in the aftermath of Ben Gurion's declaration about founding of the State of Israel in the Jewish holy land. So now he wants to marry his daughters off here in Tunisia, no matter what, so he can afford to travel.

It didn't occur to me then, Bahiya, that your father was telling me what would become his own plan only two years later. After he married you to me and married your sister to a jeweler from your faith who would later emigrate with her to Canada, Pascal sold the sweets shop and the apartment in which I asked for your hand; then he came over with your mother, one evening, to bid farewell to you. Through his tears, he asked me to take care of you, and after a few months, he sent us a telegram to say that he'd settled with your mother and brother in Acre in Western Galilee with a group of Sephardic Jews.

X

From that day on, I became your whole world. But I was a world with two forces fighting over it. As soon as one of them found some peace, the other would ruin it. You never felt that I was yours, despite the legitimate marriage contract, and despite all the gifts I gave you to make up for my constant absence. I remember that you weren't very happy with the apartment I bought for you in El Hafsia, where I visited you every Tuesday and Friday evening. And I actually remember you frowning disapprovingly when you saw the stacks of money I gave your father as a dowry. Your father had stipulated during my first visit to your home that I give him five thousand francs, no more, no less, in return for keeping the matter of his daughter's marriage to Mohsen Ennaifer secret. It was a very large amount, so I gave him half in cash and wrote him a promissory note for the second half. He didn't leave for Israel until I'd paid him the rest of the amount. Had your father asked for more that night, I would've agreed without hesitation. You were beautiful in your modest white skirt and your sleeveless pink shirt with its high collar. You came in to us carrying the tray of *rosetta* and walking slowly, as if you were walking barefoot on my heart; watching you felt like a delicious massage. You raised your eyes to me when I reached out to take the glass from the tray, but my arm trembled, and the drink sloshed onto my fingers. Your naughty brother snorted with laughter. When your father asked you if you were happy to be the second wife of a Muslim man, your cheeks got rosy, and you didn't blink. Your mother and sister trilled joyfully, and I raised my hands by myself to recite the Fatiha, as your father mumbled something that I think was from the Torah.

We were joined in matrimony at your parents' home in the presence of two witnesses who were invited by your father. I furnished the new apartment in less than a month and moved you there two or three days before the forty-day memorial gathering for Si Ali Rassaa. I stipulated that you stop working at your father's shop and never come to the Tax Office. I also requested that you stop going out as much as possible and stay at home instead. I had become cautious and suspicious: he who has burned his tongue on soup will blow on salad. I was afraid you would object because you were used to freedom and had become familiar with the streets, but you agreed without hesitation. During the first few weeks, I kept sneaking out of work to see you outside of the days that we'd agreed on. I would put my jacket on the back of my desk chair and my fez atop a stack of papers, and I would order a coffee to make the employees think that I was in the building. Then I would casually walk out as if I were going to take care of some business nearby, and as soon as I'd turned onto a side street with no Tax Office windows overlooking it, I would run without looking back.

I became young again with you, Bahiya. My mood improved. My tension faded away. I started paying more attention to my looks and clothes until Zbaida began to have doubts. She started fabricating problems, both with and without reason, and then she would get angry at me before resorting to her broken record of tears. I would comfort her sometimes and find excuses for her most of the time. A few months after I married you, Mhammed's young wife moved into the room next to ours. Now the walls became talkative, reminding her that she was living through a romantic drought with a negligent husband. But as for me, during those first days with you, I was like a traveler on sunbeams or someone riding a shooting star. I would glide like a feather through the highest heavens. Then something suddenly occurred to me and brought me back to earth, confused and perplexed. What if you got pregnant, Bahiya? How could I have a child that people would call the son of a Jewish woman? Should I hide his existence from people the way I hid yours? What if I died and left the child with a mute mother? Who would give him his rights, and who would explain to Mostafa and Mohamed Habib that they had a half-brother? I decided to reveal the secret of my marriage to Khaddouj and entrust you to her if something happened to me. But I quickly ruled out the idea. Who would listen to a black maid saying that she knew a secret nobody else knew? I had to reveal the secret to someone who had moral authority over my wife and children. Someone who would make them fear God if they denied my child's legitimacy and refused to give him his rights. I decided to inform Lella Bashira, Zbaida's mother, that I was secretly married and that I held her responsible before God, if she outlived me, for recognizing my children from my second wife. I hid your name and origins from her, and I claimed that we hadn't yet been joined in matrimony out of respect for her late husband, who had passed away so recently. She rebuked me harshly, but she accepted the situation, and she asked me to keep it secret. As I left her house, I felt that a heavy weight had been removed from my shoulders.

But Lella Bashira didn't live more than a few weeks after that stormy meeting. She was sick, and her health deteriorated. We didn't know about her illness. She spent her final days in bed; she stopped eating and talking, and then she stopped moving. They would touch her, but she didn't feel it, and when they talked to her, she didn't answer, even with a blink. Shortly after that, she died peacefully, and the secret and the promise died with her. I couldn't find it in me to subject myself to another attack if I revealed your secret to my mother or one of my sisters. I decided to entrust my case to God. I started praying that he would bless me by making you infertile, so you wouldn't bear a child whose future I would have to worry about.

Six months after our marriage, Khaddouj died. And because one tragedy is not enough, signs of pregnancy began to appear on you. Your cravings were the strangest thing I'd ever seen. You started eating uncooked rice with water, crunching olive mill pomace, and sucking on bars of soap. You hated sweets and their smells. Your mood became difficult, and you were always on the verge of crying. But you were happy with the pregnancy. You would point to your belly, laughing, and then dance your arms right and left, like you were rocking a baby. May God forgive me, Bahiya. I gave you two pills like the ones I gave to Khaddouj when I caught her preparing to hang herself to hide her scandal. They were two pills that would stop the embryo from growing and lead to a miscarriage, as my French friend Guillaume Chazal, the gynecologist at the Hôpital Civil Français (now the Hôpital Charles Nicolle) had told me. I had tested their efficacy with Khaddouj, so why shouldn't I try the same thing to hide my scandal? May God forgive me, Bahiya. I ground up the two pills and mixed them into the *lablabi* that you'd been craving. I added a lot of tuna, capers, and cumin to it so you wouldn't taste them in the dish. When you didn't like it after your first spoonful, I argued that it was the pregnancy aversions making the food taste bitter. I asked you to finish your plate, since I'd had to stand in a long line in front of a popular restaurant on La Place des Moutons to get it. That night, I told Zbaida that I was traveling to attend the funeral of an old friend. I avoided her eyes as I recited the script I'd spent my morning writing and rehearsing: "Sheikh Shedhli Allani died. He was a colleague of mine at the Tax Office before retiring less than a year ago. May God bless his soul."

I wiped away a tear, as per the stage directions. Then I changed my voice to sound sad and said, "The news broke my heart. I'll be leaving for Kairouan in a little while with one of my colleagues. We'll have to spend the night there with the family of my late colleague."

It was a weekend, and the next day was a day off. It was the first time I'd spent the night with you since we got married. I was afraid that you might start bleeding while you were alone at home and that you wouldn't be able to find someone to help you. But nothing happened, Bahiya. You woke up in the morning suffering from a light dizziness. You vomited like Zbaida used to when she was pregnant with Mostafa. Then you made my coffee and started eating your favorite morning meal, olives dipped in harissa and a glass of buttermilk. I watched your every move, and I was gripped by intense fear. What if the medicine I slipped you harmed the embryo without killing it? Would the child be disfigured or simple-minded, a constant reminder of my vile action?

I was pale all morning, watching you strut around in front of me with the duster in your hand. You were happy about the extended time I was spending with you; you moved as lightly as a butterfly and didn't seem to get tired. From time to time I would force a smile and ask, as if to spoil you, "And how is the mother of my child?"

You would raise your hand to your mouth and kiss it, both the palm and the back, as a sign of gratitude, a wide smile on your angelic face. I reclined on the living room couch staring into space, worried like someone waiting for something to happen, not sure whether to be happy or concerned. As soon as the noontime call to prayer sounded, I heard you moaning in the kitchen. I ran to you and found you bent over, your arms on your belly, pressing down on it because of the severe pain. Your face looked bloodless, as if it had been coated in turmeric or dyed with pomegranate peels. I was stricken by a feeling I don't know how to describe to you. A fear mixed with hope, or a regret mixed with hope. I was afraid you would suffer some unforeseen complications, but I also felt the relief of someone who's about to escape a crisis. I inspected you visually but didn't see any sign that the bleeding had started. I supported you as you dragged yourself to the bedroom and helped you lie down on the bed. We were in the early days of January, and the apartment I had bought in haste had windows facing west, so it became an oven in the summer and a refrigerator in winter. I touched your hands and legs, but they were as cold as marble on a freezing night. I folded back the cover that you had carefully smoothed in the morning and tucked it tightly around you as you continued your sad moaning. Then I went to the stove to make you lemon verbena tea, hoping it would help reduce the pain. I remembered, as I watched the surface of the water begin to wrinkle in the pot, what Khaddouj had told me about her ordeal that year: "I tried everything, Sidi Mohsen. Hot mint tea, sitting on a copper bathing container, lifting heavy things, jumping from high up, sneezing and coughing strenuously. But nothing worked to abort the fetus."

My eyes wandered over the containers arranged on a wooden shelf over the kitchen counter. There it was, the container of dried mint calling me to help get rid of the source of your pain. I scooped out a big handful and put it into the boiling water, which made a green foam. I contemplated it for a moment before your sudden screams brought me running back to you. I found you uncovered, looking with bewilderment at a large spot of blood that was gradually spreading on the white bedsheet. We were no longer in need of mint. But there was grief and shock in your tearful eyes. As soon as you saw me come in, you pulled the cover back over you, worried, as if you were ashamed for me to see you in that state. I could read on your face a feeling of shame, the shame of someone who couldn't protect what they were supposed to have kept safe. I hugged you and tried to comfort you, but nothing worked. I left you that day hating myself and disgusted with what I had done.

For several days, I fed you horse meat and lamb spleen so you would quickly recover what you'd lost with the bleeding. I asked your mother, who hadn't left the country yet then, to accompany you to Dr. Chazal at the Hôpital Charles Nicolle. I told her, giving her a sealed envelope, along with the doctor's fees in another envelope, "Give this letter to Dr. Chazal in person so he takes good care of Bahiya. I want to make sure that the miscarriage didn't cause any damage to her womb. The doctor will do what's necessary to assure future pregnancies."

I was lying. May God forgive me, Bahiya. I had already agreed with the physician that he would act as he saw fit so you wouldn't get pregnant again, and I bought his silence and complicity with money. I gave him three quarters of it in my first meeting with him, and I sent him the last quarter with your oblivious mother. The doctor explained to your mother, with some difficulty, that his exam had confirmed that the uterine wall collapsed during the miscarriage, and that you needed to spend two or three nights in the hospital for a surgical intervention. Based on her personal experience, your mother disapproved of the doctor's strange diagnosis, just as, when she took the two envelopes from me, she told me I was wasting money on trivial things that happened to all women and never caused lasting harm. But she grudgingly obeyed the doctor's decision.

I don't know what Dr. Chazal did to you during the time you spent in the women's ward, but you came back after three days leaning on your mother's arm, your face frighteningly yellow. You kept away from me in bed for a month or more because of the pain during intercourse. I felt terrible guilt as months, then years, passed, and again and again you pointed to your belly in confusion and asked me with your eyes why it wasn't round. And then, finally, you became convinced that you had to be infertile; the first pregnancy had only been a fluke.

XI

Had the child you lost been born, Bahiya, then grown up and lived, you would've left him motherless at the age of nine. Would Zbaida have cared for him after she became, over the years, an old turtle withdrawn into her shell, with reading glasses on her nose and a magazine or book in her hand?

When I lost you, still in the bloom of youth, strong and beautiful like a fresh pomegranate, Zbaida had already passed forty by four years. But disability and sadness had added to her real age so that she looked more like an old woman in her sixties. Every day, she would sleep until midmorning and then call Luiza when she woke up. Her maid would wipe down her face and limbs with a cotton glove with soap foam on it, then help her comb her hair and put her clothes on. Then she would squat in front of her and wait patiently. Zbaida would put her arms on Luiza's shoulders, then wrap them around her neck. Luiza would hold her firmly and straighten up, with a red face and bulging veins, and carry her on her back despite her heavy weight. She would take her down the stairs, teasing and joking with her, until she sat her down in her favorite spot. In the summer, it was in the middle courtyard next to the cistern; in the winter, in Mama Jnayna's room next to the heater. After she had sat her down, leaned her against the pillows, and raised her feet onto a short chair to help avoid swelling, she would bring her breakfast and whatever books and pens she wanted. She would check on her throughout the day, bringing her whatever she needed until she started dozing. Then she gathered her papers and took her back to her room. If Zbaida wanted to sit in her rocking chair, she would sit her there, and if she wanted to lie down in her bed, she would lay her down. She would do all of that with a smile, never complaining.

That woman is strange, Bahiya. She's so loyal that it's as if she's not even human. She's served Zbaida for a long time. She has fed her and changed her clothes. She's clipped her toenails and massaged her feet. She's bathed her and told funny stories to make her laugh. She has carried her, supported her physically and morally, and taken care of her children, to whom she's been like an affectionate aunt and a sympathetic older sister. She has also born Mhammed's abuse far too often for Zbaida's sake, and he has always found her unbreakable.

I can't be certain, now, whether Luiza really hated my brother Mhammed, as everyone thought, or if she was hopelessly in love with him, a love that reached its extreme and became hate. But if we adhere to what my mother Jnayna, God bless her soul, used to say, then Luiza herself, and no one else, was the reason behind Mhammed's divorce. She made Fawzia bitter and angry, filling her head with real and fabricated stories, until one stormy evening, Fawzia snuck out of her room and disappeared. That night, Mhammed asked about her at her father's house, then at her maternal and paternal uncles' houses. Then he searched police stations and hospitals, but he couldn't find her. At dawn, she returned to the big house wet and stained with mud, as if she'd spent the night in a barn sleeping among cows. When Mhammed greeted her with a beating, almost losing his mind in rage, she cried and wailed and screamed loudly, claiming that she'd spent the night praying to God at Sidi Mehrez's shrine. No one believed her, and we didn't rescue her from her husband's hands until he was on the verge of killing her. Then she fled to her father's house. Mhammed followed her there and hurled the oath of divorce after her. I think he'd been waiting for her to make some small mistake so he could get rid of her without angering Mama Jnayna; thanks to her foolishness, she offered him instead a massive error that made it easy for him to divorce her.

Mama Jnayna didn't succeed in marrying him off to another wife, despite all her attempts. When I moved my family to Bardo after my mother's death in the summer of 1962, he stayed in the big house alone. Still, Luiza kept visiting him once every two weeks, to clean the house with whatever energy a woman in her mid-forties still had, and to cook different dishes for him that he would eat throughout the week. No one asked her to do it. What was even stranger is that Mhammed would kick her out when she knocked on the door, speaking harshly to her. But that didn't stop her. She started using tricks: she would wait for him until he left the house, and then she would enter in his absence, using my old key. When he came back early and found her wandering about her former kingdom as she used to in the old days, buckling down to scrub the courtyard or washing his clothes in the washtub, he would lose his mind, screaming and insulting her, but she paid no attention to him. It didn't take long for Mhammed to get used to her visits and give in to her stubbornness. He stopped being mean to her; instead, he started sitting next to her as she squatted in front of the washtub, handing her the clothes she'd forgotten to wash. He would do all of this silently, with a frown on his face, as if he were doing her a favor. When she got home, she would tell us about her day with him, laughing hard. If one of us expressed their astonishment at her insistence on serving him for free, or if Zbaida disapproved of her generosity towards someone who didn't appreciate her favor, she would strike her chest several times over and answer with determination. "Lella Jnayna asked me, on her deathbed, to keep an eye on him. She didn't ask her daughters, the daughters of Othman Ennaifer; she asked me, Luiza bint Sassi Weld el-Aarem. Do you want me to betray her trust?"

Then Luiza would sigh and repeat the same story for the thousandth time. "Lella Jnayna pointed to me as her chest rose and fell and the foam of the soul leaving her body gathered in the corner of her lips. She motioned for me to bring my head closer, and when I did, she held my braid with her trembling fingers and whispered in my ear, her voice rattling, "Take care of your brother Mhammed, please. He has no children, no money, no shoulder to lean on. Don't abandon him. Please."

Luiza continued to check in on Mhammed and take care of him from time to time for about eight years, until—in his last days—he'd gotten used to her. His disposition softened, and he stopped being so prickly and started joking with her, or so she told Zbaida. Sometimes she saw a look of gratitude in his eyes. Then fate struck. She knocked on the door one winter morning, a week after her last visit, but he didn't open the door for her. She opened it with the key and went inside, calling him, but she didn't receive an answer. She thought he might have woken up early to take care of some business. She entered the kitchen first and found it neat, except for some moldy dishes piled up in the sink. When she was done cleaning them, she headed to Mhammed's room to collect his dirty clothes. The door was ajar, and as soon as she passed the threshold, she was struck by a putrid odor, the kind you might smell passing a dead cat in the street. She didn't need to look closely at Mhammed, who was lying in his pajamas on his bed, to recognize that he was a corpse that had already started decomposing. Luiza said that he was wearing one slipper, as if he had sat up in bed, getting ready to get up, but death was faster, and he fell backward instead, his mouth open and his eyes bulging. The neighbors called the police when they heard her screaming, as she ran through the quartier asking for help. The detective didn't find anything suspicious in his death, especially after the pathologist diagnosed a tear in the blood vessels near the aorta. Mhammed died alone at the age of sixty-nine. He wasn't buried until six days after his death. In his funeral procession, people followed behind an empty coffin because the burial had been delayed so long that body smelled. I didn't realize that I would grieve his loss the way I did. Something from him stayed in me, despite the forced reconciliation my father demanded from us on his deathbed.

XII

When my father felt that he was dying, he called for Mhammed. Two weeks prior, he had suffered a stroke in his sleep. By the time he woke up, his right half was paralyzed, the corner of his mouth was crooked, and he'd lost the ability to speak. He wasn't alive enough for us to wish him a recovery or dead enough for us to forget about him. Then God's pardon spared him a few days later: his tongue began to loosen up slowly, and he started pronouncing some faltering words that were difficult to understand, as if he were pulling them from the bottom of a well or uprooting them from a quarry in a rocky mountain. Mama Jnayna told me that he had asked for Mhammed over his last few days and then told him, his breath short, "Go to Zbaida's room and kiss her head, then bow to your older brother and kiss his shoulders and apologize to him."

Mhammed fidgeted and didn't answer. My father stared at him with a look between anger and hope. He gestured to him with his head, beckoning him closer. Mhammed bent over, kissing his head and rubbing his forehead. But he pushed him gently away with his healthy arm. Then he closed his eyes and mouth and didn't speak again until his soul left his body and he and his family had been relieved of their burden. Mhammed realized that Hajj Othman was warning him that he wouldn't forgive him if he didn't heed his request. Mama Jnayna kept lecturing him about the consequences of disobeying his parents, and finally he agreed to initiate the reconciliation.

He spoke to me the next day as I was getting ready for work. He didn't show real remorse when he apologized; instead, he explained to me coldly that he was obeying the last wish of his dying father. But he was very embarrassed when he knocked on Zbaida's door. I watched him from a distance, waiting for him to come out so we could go see our sick father together and bring him the good news. He disappeared into Zbaida's room for a second, then came out again, his face the dull blue of a person suppressing his anger. I don't know what he told her or how she responded. When he got closer, I asked him, and he answered, "There's no hope for your wife. May God forgive her."

I asked her in the evening, as she was undoing her braid before the mirror. She sighed and said, "Your brother's a goddamn spineless bastard."

That day, Mhammed and I entered the room where Hajj Othman was shrouded under the heavy blankets. His eyes were fixed on the ceiling, rapt, as if a window had opened up there and no one could see it but him. He was looking through it as if at his seat in heaven. We talked to him, but he didn't blink. We hugged each other next to his bed and kissed each other's cheeks noisily while Mama Jnayna trilled next to his ear, hoping that he would pay attention to us. But he was absent, or a kind of absent. Or perhaps he understood, with the clarity of someone about to die, that we were acting in a kind of play to please him, and he hated to participate.

It was a cold hug, yes, and insincere kisses, and a hesitant, shaking ululation, but it did help over time in melting the ice. We stood next to each other in the cemetery two days later, receiving condolences, and we walked back home together, helping each other carry the heavy burden of mourning.

Oh, Bahiya! I buried so many loved ones in that cemetery, before you and after. My first was Mohammed Shedhli, the twin of Mohammed Habib, who came into this world a few minutes before his brother. Then he left before making it even forty days. Then Khaddouj, our loyal maid. My close friend and confidante. She wilted, dried up, and was consumed by a malignant tumor while I was busy, paying no attention to death because of the joy of new life. I would remember her for a short period, then forget her for a long one every time I tasted the honey of newly wedded bliss from two generous palms still decorated with henna.

After Khaddouj, time took from me my father and mother, my older sister, and my only brother.

Consecutive ordeals would break the back of the strongest man. But as God is my witness, Bahiya, no ordeal, aside from your loss, was harder on me than the one I faced that night. The fateful night of December 7th, 1935.

XIII

I'm telling you the story of what happened more than forty years ago. Events hidden in my heart that nobody knows about, save the family members who were there to bear witness. Family secrets, locked in their owners' chests, forced into a dark corner and covered with a thousand veils. And why wouldn't they hide these shameful events that, if exposed to the curious public, would be a blot on their noble bloodline for generations to come?

Forgive me, Bahiya. I wasn't able to trust you with my secret, even after I found out that you were deaf and mute. Zbaida's betrayal taught me to doubt everything, to be wary of everything. But now you've been in your grave these twenty years, and nothing remains of you but a bag of bones under a cold tombstone. So now, allow me to reveal the hidden secret, my story of tragedies and sorrows.

Our house was a haven of affection and peace. The quiet was only broken by my two boys, Mohammed Habib and Mostafa, crying when they got hungry, or by Khaddouj and Luiza fighting over a bucket or broom. Then the tables suddenly turned, and everything fell apart. Fate was cruel to us, turning affection into hatred, and joy into silence and sorrow. Our peaceful haven became hell—we became distant from each other and from the happy days we had known.

Out of nowhere, the house of Judge Othman Ennaifer witnessed events that wouldn't happen in even the lowliest houses. The wife made a fool of her husband, and her own brother-in-law revealed the secret. He wasn't forced to reveal it, either out of pity for his brother or concern for his honor. Rather, he revealed it in an act of revenge and spite, like someone who'd just caught their longtime enemy red-handed.

How did Zbaida betray me? Why and where and when? I won't know until I die. Did she really cheat on me, as I pictured in my head, or was it nothing more than an illusion, the figment of a paranoid imagination? Is it possible that the whole story was just a heartbeat, a fleeting vessel of fate? I will never know. And there's no use finding out. There's none so foolish as the man who convinces himself that emotional betrayal is somehow less vile than physical.

I still had faith in her and the love that united us the night I attacked Mhammed, wanting to kill him. He had stabbed me in the back, and I attacked him, an iron bar in my hand. I swear, I was about to bury it in his eye, and I would have if the appearance of Zbaida hadn't drawn me away from him. She came out from her room, calling for me. And because my worry for her was greater than my rage at him, I let the bar fall from my hand and ran to her. So he escaped a certain death, and I escaped from the gallows, or the prospect of a life of regret behind bars.

My faith in her and in our love was strengthened that night when I saw her attack Mhammed, scratching his face with her nails and gouging a deep wound under his chin with her ring. This all happened after Si Ali Rassaa left, angry at her for disobeying him and refusing to leave the Ennaifer house. He left with his wife and son, and we all scattered. I took Zbaida by the arm, wanting to talk to her alone in our room so she could explain the letter and the bundle of bread. She followed me, quiet and obedient, while my father walked, leaning on Mhammed and dragging his bad leg. The night would have ended there, with no harm done, had it not been for Mhammed throwing more fuel on the fire. After only two steps with our father, he addressed Zbaida in the most provocative language, threatening her with summary divorce. She went crazy; she pulled her arm from mine with a violent strength I wouldn't have believed possible, then jumped on him screaming like a fighter in the ring. I can't say what was going through her head at that moment, only that she seemed like a person carrying an unbearable weight, and Mhammed's words were the last straw. She pushed him with both hands; when he fell, taken by surprise, she dug her nails into his face and clothes. My father lost his balance, teetering for a moment before falling on his face, his turban coming undone. Mhammed cried out in pain, the blood from his chin running down his neck and dripping onto his chest. He refrained from attacking her back, only pushed Zbaida as hard as he could and then ran towards his room upstairs. She ran after him, a sight that was difficult to believe. Should I have gone after her, instead of helping my father get to his room like I did? Yes, that was my fatal mistake. But how could anyone have known what would happen in the darkness of the stairwell? And how could anyone leave a lame old man lying on the cold marble in the rain, to run after a twenty-something young woman chasing a cowardly man?

Mhammed and Zbaida disappeared into the maw of the covered stairs, but I could still hear their footsteps as I pulled my father into the shelter of the roofed walkway. I kept my eye on the open balcony of the upper floor, expecting them to appear at any moment. I wasn't worried. Mama Jnayna had gone up to our room to check on Mostafa; she came flying out when she heard the screaming, looking down at us with a frightened expression. I reassured her from where I stood in the middle of the courtyard, saying, "Don't worry. The Hajj tripped, but we helped him back up. Check on Zbaida—she's heading towards you, hunting your son, and she's almost caught him."

A bit of black humor seemed to fit the mood. It seemed such a ridiculous scene, like a partridge trying to hunt a bear; I never for a moment thought the chase would end as it did, or that it would have such grave consequences. Why didn't the partridge spread her wings at the critical moment and fly over what fate had planned for her? How did she end up, in the blink of an eye, in a pile at the foot of the stairs, shivering and trembling like a slaughtered chick? No one really knows what happened. Mhammed told us, running towards her like the rest of us, "She tripped on her *fouta* on the top step and rolled down."

Zbaida, when she woke up a few days later, had a different story: "Mhammed pushed me with his elbow when I grabbed his shirt from the back. I lost my balance and fell."

Neither of them changed their story after being confronted by the other's. Mhammed swore to God that he hadn't touched her. She swore that he was responsible for her fall, even if unintentionally. We were never able to figure out which of them was lying. All we knew was what we had heard that night: a horrific scream, several thuds, and then an ominous silence. I arrived to find her lying, lifeless, at the foot of the stairs, the pool of blood under her head spreading alarmingly. It was a nightmarish scene worthy of the goriest foreign horror movies. To this day, when I remember the blood that trailed behind us as I carried her out to the street, I can't believe she survived. The head wound turned out to be less serious than I'd thought, less serious, in fact, than her other injuries. Because, in addition to a concussion, the doctor diagnosed fractures in the pelvis and spine that had affected the spinal cord.

We both came out of the accident paralyzed, she in her legs and I in my manhood and motivation. I became accustomed to having a new companion trailing after me, rarely far away. It was a malicious and deformed companion, making life, despite all its wonders, seem narrow, making its taste bitter in my mouth, enamoring me of lethargy. This companion's name was ennui. I would begin something, only to lose interest after half an hour and move on to something else. But after starting the new thing, I would feel guilty and go back to the first. And as soon as I was about to start it, I would again lose interest. I would start and stop new things all day, without accomplishing anything and without having any desire to accomplish anything. I had no interest in my work, I fumbled my prayers, and I began to be suspicious of my closest friends. If one of them told me something, I would think he was lying; if one of them gave me advice, I would imagine he was conspiring against me.

Months passed in this way. I didn't talk to anyone in the house, and they didn't talk to me. They thought that Zbaida's disability had broken me, not realizing that the brokenness was caused by my sudden loss of value and meaning. Then I remembered something that, amidst the distress, I had forgotten. But I didn't go after it, too afraid and ashamed. I remembered Sidi Mansour's baker, who had delivered the ill-fated letter. How could I have forgotten him all this time? How could I have stopped searching for him when he possessed half (if not all) of the truth? Was it the fear of certainty, surprising me with its caustic cruelty? Or was it the deeply rooted cowardice of a lover avoiding the naked truth, so as not to sully his image of his beloved? I contemplated the matter; perhaps there was some mercy in the persistence of doubt, one that could only be appreciated by someone who'd been burdened with painful knowledge. I hesitated for a while, then made the decision to open the wound and probe the pus inside.

I stopped by the baker's shop about four months after the accident, in the spring of 1936. It wasn't hard to find; everyone in the quartier knew the story of Karrita. When the residents boycotted his bakery—on account of the controversy around Haddad's book—he'd been forced to hawk his bread in the middle of the road. But, as the sheikh who directed me observed, time heals all foolishness: the matter was quickly forgotten, and the bakery got back to business as if nothing had happened. Tahar Haddad alone paid the price and left this world in the prime of youth. Yet I shared with him the debt, remaining in the world hollow and useless, like an oud with no strings.

I thought, at first, of sending Khaddouj to the bakery, pretending that she was coming on Zbaida's behalf. She would take what had been left in the baker's care—the book and poetry manuscript mentioned in the letter—and save me from a humiliating confrontation. Before long, however, I cursed myself for my cowardice and weakness. Luiza might have already been to see the baker and told him the whole story. She could have taken everything and warned him not to trust any messenger from the Ennaifer family, the two agreeing to deny knowing anything. I was the only one who could dig the truth out of him—gently if he cooperated, violently if he did not. That's what I told myself as I stood facing him, ready to bake him in his own oven if he so much as thought about lying to me.

XIV

Do you hear the tumult outside the cemetery, Bahiya? The atmosphere is still tense, even though it's been a week now since that black Thursday. Many leaders of the Tunisian General Labour Union have been arrested, and there were several dead and injured among the demonstrators after Bourguiba's regime opened fire on them the day of the general strike. Mostafa himself would have fallen among the martyrs, if not for God's mercy. The boy inherited all my stubbornness, Bahiya, and then added some of his own. I warned him how fierce an aging lion is when he starts to recognize his impotence, but Mostafa and his wife went out anyway. They marched in the peaceful protest that started from Place Mohamed Ali, and the military met them with fire and iron. It was unbelievable: Tunisians who yesterday confronted the colonizers' tanks as a single body are now fighting each other like enemies and turning a deaf ear to calls of reason and unity. These days, Tunisia is devouring its children like a mythical beast, and those children, never satisfied, are eating each other. As for Bourguiba, he's an old lion who will attack one and all to hide his weakness from the people. Mostafa said that the person running in front of him fell after receiving a bullet in the head. The last thing he said before he was shot by the treacherous sniper: "Long live the union! To the legacy of Farhat Hached!" As for the protester who was running next to his wife, he got shot in the knee and was trampled underfoot.

Forgive me, Bahiya. I haven't been able to drive my car by myself for a while now because the diabetes has damaged my eyes. Mostafa drove me here today, thinking I wanted to visit the family graves. I left him waiting for me in his car in front of the cemetery with my granddaughter Hind, who we picked up from school at 3 P.M.. Look at her! Here she is, coming towards me from the gate, calling for me. No doubt Mostafa sent her to rush me, since the tension in the capital's streets is still high. Dozens of cars have been set on fire over the last few days. Look at that surprised expression on her face. She's probably saying to herself, "My grandfather Mohsen has lost his mind! He's started standing by the graves of strangers." Look at that happy face and those intelligent eyes, Bahiya. Don't you think she looks like Zbaida, as I described her to you?

The Arabic teacher at the Lycée Rue du Pacha says she has an amazing talent and will be a great author, the likes of Mahmoud Messadi. She's only fourteen years old, but her pen breathes magical texts. A few days ago, I overheard a conversation between her and Zbaida. Hind was reading a paragraph from an essay she wrote as homework, and when she finished reading, her grandmother applauded in delight and said, kissing her cheek, "How on earth did Mostafa the math teacher and his wife the science teacher produce this amazing young author?"

Hind answered with her quick wit and sweet tongue, laughing joyfully, "Aren't I the granddaughter of Princess Zbaida, who always has a book in her hand?"

At this moment a devil spoke in Zbaida's voice. I heard her sigh a long sigh and say confidently, "Indeed, you are my granddaughter, Hind. You're the granddaughter of Zbaida and the granddaughter of Tahar Haddad."

11
The Tale of the Beginning

I

By the light of a flashlight I bought on my way here, in the souks of Tunis's Old Medina, I begin cautiously descending the narrow, twisting staircase leading to the cellar of my great-grandfather Othman Ennaifer's house. The distance between one stone step and the next is large and inconsistent, forcing the person going down, if they're young and strong, to jump with both feet; if they're in their late adulthood, like me, they have to walk like a crab, descending sideways with one shoulder in front, like someone going through a narrow entrance.

I move one foot after the other with difficulty, keeping my back against the short, unplastered wall where the stairs start. I strain my elbow behind me to rest on the wall and keep me from slipping, dirtying my coat sleeve with some sticky, smelly black fungus. The low ceiling seems, when you look at it, like an upside-down green field because of the dampness. There are small spiders—and other, larger ones—hanging from it. I tear their webs out of my way with the handle of the flashlight so they won't get on my face or in my hair. From time to time, I hear some suspicious, faint sounds behind the dusty, cracked earthenware jars and scattered jugs below the stairs. But there's no reason to fear scorpions or snakes in the Ennaifer family cellar, or that's what Khala Luiza, may God bless her soul, told me a few years ago when she encouraged me to go look for the box of secrets. Poisonous reptiles, as opposed to rats and sewer beetles, don't like the smell of rot, so they don't nest in city cellars. The only thing I have to worry about is my memory's stockpile of stories about jinn, demons, and ghouls with human heads and goat hooves. I need to get rid of those and use the strict mind of the international law professor at the Université de Carthage; I need to find that fine line between the tangible, visible world on one hand—and the world of the unseen, which this deep darkness and the house's long vacancy are inviting into my thoughts.

About a year and a half ago, Salim Ennaifer, the son of my uncle Mohammed Habib, contacted me to let me know that he'd made an agreement with a real estate agent to sell the big house on Tourbet El Bey to a man from the El Kef region. The man was a trader of leather clothes and traditional furniture and was planning on converting the house into a workshop and storage space. I begged him to grant me the right of first refusal, then asked him to give me a month to consult my husband and get the money together. The truth is that I had been wanting for a while to buy my siblings' and cousins' shares in the house of our ancestors. My grandfather Mohsen had inherited it from his father Othman, God bless their souls, after my grandfather bought his sisters' shares. I still have very clear images in my memory of visits to the house as a child. In them, a little girl whose father calls her "Handouda" struts around in her new Eid clothes, wearing a headscarf the size of the courtyard at the Lycée Rue du Pacha. Then she enters the rooms of her father's uncle, the lame old man, to greet him shyly and kiss him on the cheek, repeating with a stuttering tongue, "I wish you health and long life, Sidi Aammi Mhammed." Making the scene even warmer in my mind, the lame old man gives me a hug, laughing, and puts a silver coin in my hand as a gift for Eid. But aside from the warmth of these memories, I became interested in the big house thanks to the stories Khala Luiza told me before she died, about the dangerous secrets the walls were hiding, how its many rooms and its wide courtyard had been the stage of tragic theater. Over time, the desire to own the house grew within me. I became obsessed with the idea of walking through it and unearthing the secrets in its corners, especially since Khala Luiza had told me, among other things, about a metal box she had hidden in the basement herself; she asked me to bring it out from darkness into the light.

But several factors forced me to take my time and delay discussing the matter with my partners in the inheritance: the severe economic crisis that lingered in the country after the January 14th revolution, the fear of the future with the political deadlock, and the increase of danger from terrorism. So the house remained empty for years, subject to the ravages of time that started eating away its wood, gnawing at its walls, and digging into its ceiling. The lack of maintenance and the negligence on the part of the heirs made the situation worse. When they finally decided to put it up for sale and found a buyer, I rushed and approached them with the same price that the stranger had offered, asking them to consider me first since I was a co-owner of the property. My cousin Salim was surprised at what he called "a failed investment in a pile of stones," and my husband, who hails from a village in the Sahel, was not excited about what he considered "a pathological need to hold on to the symbols of classist and regional belonging." But I was stubborn and borrowed some money from the bank, which I added to the sum I received for an old apartment in El Hafsia behind Hotel Ayachi. My grandfather Mohsen had left the apartment to me before he died and had insisted—for a reason I would come to learn later on—that I not reveal its secret, as long as he lived, to my grandmother Zbaida. So I was able to gather the price of the big house if I deducted my legitimate share as decided by Islam and bought out the shares of the other heirs.

I never considered using the house, though, after I had become its sole owner, because the necessary maintenance work was more than I could afford on my monthly salary, after living expenses. So the ancestral home remained like a thick, ancient shell, closed on its secrets until further notice. Also, my fear of intruding into an abandoned cellar and wandering through closed rooms in which my relatives had died, one after another, tempted me over time to cast doubt on Khala Luiza's stories. We had often listened to her, my daughters and I, generation upon generation, telling us magical stories whose characters, events, and plots were amazingly diverse, making them both better and harder to believe than the stories in *A Thousand and One Nights*. She did all that with so wild an imagination that if Jules Verne had had even a bit of it, he would've dived with us a lot farther than *Twenty Thousand Leagues Under the Sea*, and if Pierre Boulle had just half, he would've discovered behind the *Planet of the Apes* a full galaxy of planets of elephants, frogs, and even lice and ticks. Couldn't Khala Luiza have woven, with the loom of her imagination, a finely made fabric of lies? A marvelous fabric, as wide and long as an old person with dementia, riddled with boredom and illness, might have time for?

As the days passed, my mind became more inclined to accept this possibility. I forgot about the cellar and the treasure trove of secrets buried there, and focused my efforts on my academic research, my lectures and readings, and the daily life of one of Bourguiba's New Women, with its hectic running between work, the street, and home. And just when I'd become convinced that I shouldn't go near Tourbet El Bey until I had the money, an architect, and a team of contractors, an amazing encounter happened between me and the dedication on a poetry collection manuscript, its edges nibbled by rats.

II

I see, in the light of the flashlight, two red spots hanging in the air. I hold my breath, thinking about a thousand possibilities, but before my heart drops into my stomach, the image of a cute little rat standing atop a woven basket locks into place. It has long whiskers and a pink nose that twitches in curiosity. When I focus the flashlight on it, it flies like an arrow in the direction of an old pile of furniture and disappears under it.

These creatures have never scared me, even when I was a child. The only thing more amazing to me than their squeaking (which sounds to me like birdsong) is their strong social organization of families, with solidarity among members. When I was little, if it hadn't been for my fear of the adults' reaction, I would've kept the mice that fell into our traps as pets, out of compassion. One of the first things that made me aware, at an early age, of adults' cruelty and capacity for doing awful and unjust things is what Khala Luiza used to do, under orders from my grandmother Zbaida, to the mice that greed led into the metal trap. She used to fill a big bucket with water from the garden faucet, then put the trap with its mice into it, immersing them in water from every side. The mice would thrash against the bars and then twitch before they finally went still and flipped over onto their sides or backs, drowned. I remember that, twice, I happened upon my mother repeating the same crime with kittens that were less than two days old, born to a cat that lived among us and trusted us, and gave birth frequently. When I complained to my father, describing with pain how bubbles came out of the blind kittens' noses as they struggled in the water, he shrugged his shoulders and said, "Hind, it's God's destiny for them."

I don't remember how old I was when I managed to forget the ugliness of these scenes that had filled my nightmares. But I remember that they were the first thing that taught me the relativity of good and evil and the arbitrary nature of *halal* and *haram*. More than anything, they taught me to be cautious of human beings and not to put too much faith in their deceptive kindness or inclination to beneficence. I strongly believe that the compassion I feel for the weak now, whether people or animals, is partly due to what remained in my memory of those disgusting scenes.

In the darkness, towards the back wall of the cellar, I see the dresser with broken legs and five huge drawers that Khala Luiza described for me. She said I would find the box in the middle drawer, wrapped in blue cloth. Khala Luiza didn't lie about the dresser, then, but God knows what I'll find when I manage to open it. A lizard might jump out at me, or I might find a nest of mice. It could be too difficult to open the drawers if the wood is rotten or termite-eaten. If the wood has expanded from the humidity, the drawers may be so stuck that they may as well be nailed shut. And how do I get there in the first place with all these obstacles in front of the dresser, like a desert that can only be traversed by a creature with wings?

Just two days ago, I would never have thought about invading an abandoned cellar based on the advice of a ninety-year-old woman who suffered from dementia in her old age. What's wrong with me? Who cares about closed boxes that have been locked for a quarter of a century, or more? What would I even find in old papers whose exact written content Khala Luiza was ignorant of, and whose source she refused to reveal? Would these papers, and their ink, have survived the test of merciless time? Following that train of thought, I decided that the matter wasn't worth the trouble, but finding that yellowed manuscript yesterday was a shock.

A week ago, I contacted the director of the Bibliothèque Nationale in its new location on the Boulevard du 9 Avril 1938 and informed her of my intention to donate some valuable manuscripts and books that my father had inherited from his father, and his father had inherited from his grandfather. Those books had been decorating a large, glass-front bookcase in my father's home in Bardo. My father, God bless his soul, had always boasted about it in the presence of visitors, even though he never took a single book out of it and never let us do so, either. When my father passed away and my siblings and I decided to rent out the house, no one wanted to keep the books, and I didn't have enough space for them in my apartment. So the books remained hidden in boxes that cluttered up the storage room on the roof, and they were threatened from time to time by rainwater leaking from the window cracks or sneaking in under the door. Then one day, I saw the painter we'd hired to whitewash the roof carrying the boxes on a cart attached to his motorcycle. When I asked him about it, he told me that my husband, God bless him, had given them to him to sell in the weekly souk or to the shop owners who trade in old books at Souk Edabaghine, for a small amount of money. I decided that day to save my ancestors' books from an unknown fate. I took them back from the painter, giving him thirty dinars instead, estimating that he would make about that much if he sold my priceless family heritage on the street. When I told this funny and sad anecdote to some of my political science colleagues in the professors' cafeteria, some of them advised me to donate books to a university or regional library—or even to the national library, the Bibliothèque Nationale, if there were rare and valuable books in the collection. I immediately started emptying the boxes and going through the books, sorting out those that were qualified for a new life with someone who would appreciate their value and others that had been too damaged by time and humidity, which I put in a small pile to get rid of.

Among the treasures I found was an ornate manuscript copy of *The Revival of the Religious Sciences* by Al-Ghazali, two volumes written in Thuluth font from *Al-Futuhat al-Makkiyya* by Ibn Arabi, and a treatise by Ibn Azoum Al-Qayrwani, as well as another one by Ismail Tamimi disputing the claims of the Wahabis. There were also old volumes about the Arabic language whose authors I don't remember and many books from the Middle East in grammar and Islamic jurisprudence, Islamic philosophy, theology, and Quranic exegesis. In the pile that I assumed were not worth donating to the Bibliothèque Nationale, I put the books that were badly damaged—and there was one bound volume with no title that caught my attention. It had been nibbled around the edges by some rodents, and, as if that weren't enough, most of its pages had been damaged by the damp, which left black spots on its pages. The thing that caught my attention on the manuscript was a sentence written in French on its cover in a neat handwriting that seemed familiar. Translated, it said, "Received from the baker Karrita in the Sidi Mansour quartier on 4/16/1936."

My chest tightened, and I couldn't breathe; the manuscript in my hand felt like burning embers. Was this my grandfather Mohsen's handwriting? Who else wrote the letter K like that, like a butterfly about to take flight? I recalled at that moment Khala Luiza's story about the bread bundle that a baker from Sidi Mansour, whose name she didn't mention, sent to my grandmother Zbaida. Was the book in my hand the proof that Khala Luiza was telling the truth?

I opened the manuscript to the first page, my fingertips trembling eagerly. There I read, in bold black handwriting in the middle of the page, "The Poetry Book of Tahar Haddad." I breathed deeply, trying to calm down so I would be better able to deal with more surprises. On the top left of the first page were some lines written in a thin, blue script in the shape of poetry verses; some of the letters had faded away under black spots, and others had fallen prey to the rats' teeth. But there was a clear, elegant signature under the lines that had survived the test of time. I looked at it closely and found the name "Tahar" in an ornamented Arabic script, and under it an almost obliterated date; the only thing I could make out was "Sebtamber," written in this weird way. I understood that I was dealing with the dedication of a poetry book written, signed, and dated by the author himself. The dedication was addressed to a woman whose name was mostly hidden under a small black spot, nothing but the final letter still visible: an "a," tied up into a neat bundle. I rubbed the spot with my thumb, hoping to see the name of my grandmother Zbaida, but the paper crumbled and eroded under my fingertips until the spot became a hole. I tried to add in the missing letters based on the context, the rhyme, and the meter, and I was better able to make it out:

To the honorable ______a:

I am tired of this life and these woes
I go to bed sad, my heart is broke
My eyes are sleepless, and their river flows
Acting out what the hand of time forcibly spoke
My ribs tremble when I remember on what
I forever wasted my beautiful patience
There are masters who disappear and leave their loves
Moaning as though stabbed with a lance
You left me alone, my forbearance exposed
Where can I find solace? I've lost the patience that was filling me
I am enduring illness that admiration caused
I find only suffering, and my passion for you is killing me.

Tahar

__ Sebtamber ____

Everything was clear now. That's what I told myself as I flipped through the yellowed papers of the manuscript, some with writing on both sides. Most of the poems were political and social, and a few were love poems. I read their titles and the first stanzas of each, and then I remembered that I had read most of them many years ago in Tahar Haddad's poetry collection, which had been published about twenty years ago and that some intellectuals had discussed on the National Radio.

That day, Khala Luiza, who was almost eighty years old, was sitting in the kitchen with her ear to the radio, in front of the piles of garlic that she was peeling for our yearly provisions. My mother and I were helping her half-heartedly and chatting. As soon as she heard someone on the radio show mention the name Tahar Haddad, she started smacking her mouth with her hand, gesturing to us to stop talking so she wouldn't miss any of the conversation. I remember that I laughed a lot at her when she shook off the garlic peels from her hand, then put her right hand inside her shirt and got out a silk bundle tied tightly with a thread from a ribbon. She opened it carefully and gave me a dinar, saying very seriously, "Hind, go buy me a copy of Sidi Tahar's book today, the one they're talking about on the radio. Today, Hind and not tomorrow. And give me back the change."

My mother smiled and didn't comment. I took the dinar and kissed her head and said, pretending to be serious, "Really? May God forgive me, Khala. An entire dinar for a book? What if the bookstore doesn't have change for a dinar? Can't you find one or two hundred francs, just in case?"

Luiza laughed with her toothless mouth, looking at me in disdain from under her old glasses. Then she said, taking back the dinar, "All right, give it back, you little idiot. It's my mistake for giving you my money. Are you making fun of me, you daughter of a dog (no offense to your father)? In my day, people used to buy a piece of jewelry with a dinar, and nowadays you think it's not enough to buy some papers?"

"But what makes you want to buy these papers, my dear Luiza? Why are you spending your precious money and wasting your capital on paper? Did you learn how to read behind my back?"

Here her voice shook as she said, "The book's not for me, brat. It's for your grandmother Zbaida."

Silence reigned after that. She went back to peeling her garlic, her eyes distant and dreaming, as though she were looking into worlds that no one else could reach. I teared up, my good mood taking a turn for the worse. It had been thirteen years since my grandmother Zbaida was laid in her grave, but Khala Luiza erased all those years with one sentence, as if it hadn't been long at all. I don't know whether she forgot from time to time that her lifelong companion had died, or if she just refused to believe it. But for whatever reason, Khala Luiza never ceased to unintentionally force me, as long as she lived, to remember a sad day in my life, a dark day from when I was a second-year undergraduate student at the Faculty of Law.

III

It was the beginning of February 1984. It was a very cold and rainy Friday, the gutters of the sky overflowing, as if crying along with me. I ate my breakfast quickly and took a taxi to Bardo, where my grandmother and Luiza lived by themselves after the death of my grandfather six years before. It was supposed to be a celebration of Akram's release from the Bouchoucha detention center. I had bought a chocolate cake the night before from the Italian bakery, Pâtisserie Garza, on Rue d'Athènes and had hidden it at my grandmother's in Bardo so that my mother and father wouldn't see it and start interrogating me. What my parents and siblings don't know—what had never occurred to anyone—was that my grandmother was my close friend and confidante. I would tell her about my loves and trust her with all the ins and outs of my heart, and she would listen to me with an open mind, as if she were a girl in her twenties, and would react and understand. I had been telling her about Akram ever since my heart first beat for him in the college auditorium, and I cried in her arms the day he was arrested with some of our classmates during the Bread Riots.

Akram wasn't a union member, or an official member of any political party or organization. Like me, he was an extreme leftist who wasn't pleased with anything, thanks to the genes he inherited from his father, who'd been a leader in the Communist Party in his youth. The day things got really bad between the demonstrators protesting the bread prices and the security forces, with their weapons and hand grenades, we were walking peacefully, holding hands on the wide sidewalk, talking about the old leader, who'd left the country for his entourage to plunder, and predicting the fall of the regime. We were optimistic about this revolution of the people, who were finally rising up to defend their livelihood. When we got tired of talking about politics, we started singing Léo Ferré's song about time that passes without leaving anything beautiful for us, and we promised each other, laughing, to prove it wrong.

Suddenly, we found ourselves in the heart of the commotion. There were people running and the police chasing them, stones flying from one direction and tear gas bombs from the other. We ran with everyone else towards the side streets, but the police came after us with their truncheons and guns. We could hear their heavy boots behind us and their obscene curses filling our ears. At the bend of Rue de Paris, I felt a blow on my shoulder that knocked me to the ground. Before I could grasp what had happened, I felt a thick hand catching my hair and dragging me by it with unmatched violence. I don't understand what kind of demon controls those masked cops, transforming them into machines that hit, kick, and curse indiscriminately. Do they take hallucinogenics before going out to suppress unarmed demonstrators? If not, how do you explain the desperate effort of that giant cop, dragging a weak twenty-one-year-old girl across the pavement—one who hadn't raised her hand once to throw a stone or opened her mouth in a single chant? Would he have let me go himself, after mopping Rue de Paris with me, if Akram hadn't attacked him with his bare hands? I don't know. The important thing is that Akram hit him to rescue me from the police, and he got hit and kicked in return; he cursed and was cursed; then he yelled at me to run as more cops surrounded him, pushed him to the ground, and beat him severely, dragging him over to a blue armored vehicle, where they handcuffed him and threw him inside. He spent a month and two days in detention, during which time his father made a scene and threatened to file a complaint with international organizations. Then Bourguiba pardoned all the prisoners arrested during the demonstrations who hadn't been found guilty of a crime, so he was released. The impotent old leader was happy with the outcome of the situation, and the stupid people just buried their dead, treated their wounded, and then went out into the street shouting "Long Live Bourguiba" as soon as he went on TV and uttered his famous sentence, bringing the good news about repealing the increase in dough prices: "We are going back to where we were before the increase."

When I told my grandmother Zbaida what had happened during the demonstration on Avenue Habib Bourguiba, she praised Akram at length. She wiped away my tears with her fingers, then sighed and said, "You should be happy about what happened, you crazy girl. Real love is a stance on the ground, not words that can blow away in the wind. By standing up for you, Si Akram proved that he loves you. When you get older and look back on this, you'll realize that love has a tax that everyone pays, sooner or later. Look at it this way: your Akram has already paid that tax, and now it's your turn."

Then, after a short silence, she rubbed her paralyzed legs and added, her features sedate and tranquil, "Be careful not to give up love once you've found it, Hind. Sink in your teeth and fight the entire world for it. Do you understand?"

Then she added, her face once again radiant, "In a few days, when Akram gets out of jail, God willing, bring him here so I can meet him."

When I gave her the good news that Akram would be released the next day, she was the one who suggested I throw a party. She gave me two five-dinar bills and said, "Buy a nice cake today. Tell the baker to write on it, 'Where there is life, there is hope, Our Hero.' Then contact your classmates at the university and fix a time to surprise him with a small party in the quad or cafeteria. This misfortune needs to end with a beautiful memory."

When I opened the box and showed her the cake that evening, she frowned disapprovingly and said, laughing, "That cake is small, Hind. Did you inherit your mother's stinginess?"

It never occurred to me that those words would be the last I would ever hear from her. I gave the cake to Khala Luiza to keep in the refrigerator, and I let her know that I would be coming by the house in the morning to take it before going to the university. The next day, I told my parents I was going on a class trip and then raced the sunrise to my grandmother's door. I opened it, as usual, with my copy of the key. The living room light was on, shining into the hallway, so I raised my voice in a cheerful greeting, but I didn't hear anything back but absolute silence. I told myself that my grandmother was most likely praying and that Luiza was busy with her chores in the kitchen; she was accustomed to getting everything done early. I peeked my head into the living room, but it was empty. I wasn't worried as I walked down the hallway towards my grandmother's room, raising my voice to call for her and for Khala Luiza. But as soon as I turned in the direction of the kitchen, I was struck by the terrifying scene. Khala Luiza was crumpled on the ground in her pajamas, and next to her feet was my grandmother Zbaida, lying on her face in her white bathrobe. I was stricken by a temporary paralysis, glued to my place as firmly as if nailed to the ground with pegs. I'm not sure how long I stayed like that, but soon my tongue came loose, and an anguished cry issued from my chest as all the pieces of the painful scenario assembled themselves together in my mind. My grandmother Zbaida must have started her day with her weekly bath, as she did every Friday morning, and Khala Luiza must have helped her bathe, then carried her on her back when she finished, as she does every day. They were unaware of the deadly gas leaking silently from the water heater, breathing it in until they fell to the ground unconscious. I ran to the windows and doors and opened them to the strong winter wind. Then I went to the living room where the phone was and called the fire department and ambulance, then dialed our home number, shaking in fear. Ten minutes later, my grandmother's house in Bardo was filled with people. My father was the first to arrive, followed by my uncle Mohamed Habib, accompanied by Salim, his eldest son. They helped each other carry my grandmother to her bed and then covered her with a heavy blanket, putting Luiza next to her. Salim was speechless, his face yellowish and desolate; as for my father and my uncle, they started crying like children, so I didn't dare ask the question that was eating me up: Was my grandmother dead? Was she alive? What about Khala Luiza? My confusion didn't last long; it was quickly dispelled when the ambulance arrived. After a short exam, the cover was pulled over my grandmother's face. The two doctors moved to check Khala Luiza, putting an oxygen mask on her nose and injecting her with several drugs. Because the rescue team arrived when it did, Khala Luiza survived after spending only a night at the hospital. The paramedics were able to save her because she hadn't stayed for long in the bathroom where the fatal gas leak had occurred. As for my grandmother, her time had come, and she bequeathed us the remaining unlived years of her life. She passed away on a Friday, without saying goodbye.

Akram didn't come to my grandmother's funeral. All my university friends came, except Akram. He made do with a brusque phone call at the end of the third day. He claimed that he was sick because of the conditions at the prison, but a mutual friend of ours who visited me every day during the three-day mourning period—and would later become his wife—told me that he hadn't missed his lessons at the university. To this day, I don't know the reason behind his sudden coldness towards me. Was it difficult for him that I'd seen him in a moment of weakness that day on Avenue Bourguiba, screaming in pain and begging the cops to stop, so he ended our relationship to save face? Or is it that he held me responsible, if indirectly, for what he went through, both the prison and the beating, so the love in his heart gave way to black resentment? I don't know. The important thing is that I never forgave him for abandoning me in my time of need and considered his indifference to my grandmother's death a betrayal of her spirit, especially since she had loved him and had high hopes for him without even having seen him. My memories of him are linked in my mind to that death, so just the thought of him upsets me. He's a famous politician now, one expression of all the toxic mold that grew in our country after the revolution. I met him a few months ago at a conference organized by the Women's Union about combating violence against women. He was presiding over one of the panels. He spoke that day about police violence against women in the detention centers and during protests, and he called on civil society to pressure parliament to craft a national plan to protect Tunisian women from verbal and physical violence. He reminded us of the role of modern societies and organizations in supporting the social path towards full equality between men and women. He was glancing at me as he spoke, proud of himself. When I asked for the mic to speak during the discussion that followed, he introduced me to the audience, smiling and saying with gravitas, "Let me introduce you all to Professor Hind Ennaifer. She's one of the best graduates of the Université de Tunis in international law. In addition to that, she's a dear colleague from my college days and an independent activist. She herself was the subject of police violence during the student protests in the '80s, so who better to speak on the subject?"

I intentionally neglected to compliment him as he had complimented me, and I saw his face darken in anger. He looked away when I started to outline the gains Tunisian women had been able to achieve thanks to the Code of Personal Status, whose inspiration the leader Habib Bourguiba had gotten from the pioneer of social reform, Tahar Haddad. I emphasized that Ben Ali, the ousted president, had supported these gains and hadn't gone back on them; this caused some angry murmurs from the new falsely revolutionary women, even though some of them had been trilling just the day before in the governing party's cooperative committee when the dictator Ben Ali's title, "The Change Maker," was mentioned. I went further with my provocation. I reminded the audience that the enemy of real equality between men and women was not those who wore Afghani clothes, shaved their mustaches, or grew their beards. The fact was that most of the modernists who celebrated National Women's Day with their wives and lectured at conferences and on media platforms about women's rights and equal opportunities, when they went back home, they took off their suits and ties and showed their true colors: the skin of masculinity filled with superiority complexes and the delusions of potency in its most naive sexual meaning.

I glanced at Akram. He seemed busy drawing long perpendicular lines on the papers in front of him, as if he were bored by what I was saying and his thoughts had wandered. There was an old vendetta between us, and it was time I settled the score. I addressed him in person in front of the audience. His mustache trembled as he listened to me describe his daily life as if I could see it. I said, smiling as if joking, "Ladies and gentlemen, take for instance a modern leftist like Si Akram, who's here with us this afternoon. He will leave the conference hall shortly and go to his usual haunts in some hotels, to sit with his activist comrades. Meanwhile, his wife, who I know very well because she was a classmate of ours at the Faculty of Political Sciences, will have left her law office at Rue de Paris and retrieved her car from the Palmarium parking garage. She'll stop by the supermarket on Avenue de La Liberté and pick up the children from their schools in Omrane; then she will drive them home to El Menzah. She will prepare a snack and a warm drink for them and help them do their homework, and then she will go to the kitchen to prepare their dinner as they recite the texts they memorized for school. When Si Akram comes back from his evening out with friends, the children will already be in their pajamas and ready to be tucked into bed. What do you think he will do then? He'll either sit down to watch TV until his wife is done preparing tomorrow's breakfast and the snacks for the children to take to school, or he'll go into his office to check social media as his wife finishes ironing the shirt he'll wear at his next political meeting, where he will lecture on equality between men and women."

IV

I'm trying, with great difficulty, to get around the obstacles that separate me from the dresser with its five drawers. That huge dresser whose middle drawer I'm supposed to open now, to find the box I came for. I wonder what kind of secrets are buried in it. Is it worth all this trouble? What if I open the drawer and find it empty, containing nothing but my disappointment? With my flashlight, I scan the mountain of old things that separate me from my goal. Most of them are old tools that are extinct in the souqs now; the new generation doesn't even know their names or what they're used for. I pause at a rectangular piece of wood with parallel ridges on it, and I can't suppress a smile. How can I forget the wooden washboard that Khala Luiza wanted to put inside the washing machine with the clothes to guarantee that the laundry would come out as clean as in the old days? I remember that my grandfather Mohsen's family was one of the first families to add a semi-automatic washing machine to its household appliances. But Khala Luiza refused to use it, preferring to hand-wash clothes. When my grandmother Zbaida forced her to give away the washtub, to lighten her load, she started expressing her annoyance at what she disapprovingly called "the kitty paw washer." Then, with her considerable faculties, she came up with a devilish trick that remained a subject of jokes among us for many years. It occurred to her that she needed to supply the machine with an extra tool that the German engineers who designed it hadn't thought of. So she started trying to slide the washing board into the machine along with the clothes so that the scrubbing would meet the authentic, "old-timey" standards. If it hadn't been for my grandmother Zbaida, who heard the banging and knocking and rectified the situation, the story would've been longer and more fun.

I step on something I can't make out, though I hear a muffled snap. I aim the flashlight at my feet and see a leather briefcase whose original color is difficult to guess. A large, swollen briefcase that undoubtedly contained something solid that broke when I accidentally stepped on it. My curiosity flares up, so I try to open its metal locks, hoping to take a look at its contents. But the rust and dust make my efforts useless. I'll take it with me and treat its locks with some olive oil at home. This is what I tell myself, gripping its handle cautiously, keeping its dust away from my clothes.

Now there are only three feet between me and the middle drawer of the dresser. I lift my leg high to step over an open birdcage so enveloped in spider webs that it looks like a solid box. It's a small cage, only missing a Tunisian flag tied to its wires to make you think a demonstrator must have held it up during the Avenue Habib Bourguiba protests during the January 14th revolution. It's still in good shape, strong and made to last. I think it's worthy of another life in my own garden. I pick it up by its metal ring with my index finger and thumb. The person who hid it here was doubtless preparing it for another life, too, as soon as the opportunity arose. For some reason it's difficult for people to get rid of birdcages. They keep them after they no longer need them, as if they have an ancient feud with freedom. I smile at the idea while imagining where I'll put the cage on our veranda, just to the left of the swing. I'll buy a Tunisian goldfinch for it; just like the Tunisian people, they're good at singing behind bars.

Here I am finally facing the dresser, counting its drawers from above. One. Two. Three. This is the drawer. The cage is in my right hand, and the briefcase and flashlight are in my left. I wedge the flashlight between my knees and put the briefcase on a wooden barrel next to the dresser, setting the cage on top of it. I hold the heavy drawer with both hands. For the first time, beams of late-afternoon winter sunlight are sneaking through the clouds and through a small aperture high on the wall behind me. It seems that mother nature has decided to be my ally at this decisive moment. I pull the two handles at the edges of the drawer with all the force I have, but it doesn't move even an inch. I put the flashlight down and brace my foot under the drawer while I lean back with all my weight, holding the handles tightly. The dresser with its broken legs nearly falls on me. I stop, gasping for air. This is the one of the very few times that it occurs to me to ask God why, if the male is not like the female—at least in terms of muscle size—he had to create me female. Now what? Should I ask my husband to come to my rescue so that his arms can compensate for the failure of my brain to come up with a trick to open a stuck drawer? How do I explain the purpose of this adventure in an evil-smelling cellar? How could I expose family secrets to the eyes of an outsider, if we got the drawer open, found the box, and the facts that had long been hidden from curious people got exposed? There must be another solution. I tackle the drawer on top of it. If I can open it and pull it out, I'll be able to see the contents of the one underneath without having to move it. You still have some resourcefulness in your head, Hind; you got it from your grandmother Zbaida, who could find a solution for every problem. But that resourcefulness doesn't help. The second drawer doesn't move even an inch from its place, and nor do the first or fourth drawers. The bottom drawer is the only one that complies. I pull out a round metal tin, once a box of imported candy. I shake it to find out what's in it, and I hear the sound of rustling inside, like the sound of papers touching each other. I open it with some difficulty and see a pile of folded yellow papers. I retrieve the flashlight and start reading. I can tell right away that they're legal documents because of the legal preamble at the top of the page, the stamps and signatures at the bottom. Most of them are written in a script I can't decipher. They're undoubtedly old deeds for lands and real estate, most of which is no longer owned by the family. But wait a minute. This is a court order issued by the religious court in 1935. I look closer. It stipulates that Mohsen ben Othman ben Ennaifer must pay a 500-franc fine to someone called Rezgui ben

Fatima, a cleaner at the psychiatric hospital in Manouba. The stated reason is the use of physical violence . . . Unbelievable. My grandfather Mohsen physically assaulted someone? Who? A simple cleaner? What else? I open another document. My heart is about to burst out of my chest. This is a divorce paper. A document of the kind that used to be issued before the Code of Personal Status in Tunisia. I read the text with difficulty, and I feel dizzy. Is what I'm seeing real? It's impossible for me to believe this. I check the date of the document. February 15th, 1936. The divorce is clear from the text. Did he divorce her and then remarry her? Why does no one know about this? Could they have hidden this from Khala Luiza, who my grandmother trusted with her most intimate secrets? What other surprises is this cupboard of marvels hiding?

I put the lid back on the box, which I return to its place in the drawer, carefully folding the divorce document and placing it in my coat pocket. It needs examination in the sunlight to get to the bottom of it.

I turn back to the closed drawer, tasting the bitterness of my helplessness afresh. I hear the afternoon call to prayer from the nearby mosque. Soon the city will be plunged into darkness, and my time here alone in the cellar will become a clip from a Hitchcock movie. I hook my fingers back into the drawer handles with determination. Let it be a last try. I will either get what I want or give up and go back home with the briefcase and the cage. I pull and pull and pull. My eyes are closed, my facial muscles contracted, my neck veins bulging, and my throat is releasing a mixture of human and animal sounds. My grandmother Zbaida used to tease me when I was young and say that I inherited her patience and my grandfather Mohsen's stubbornness. A person who combines patience and stubbornness is unbeatable. When I was a three-year-old child, I somehow got my head stuck in the gap between the seat of a chair and its back. I don't remember anything about the incident but the fear I felt over being stuck like a mouse in a trap. But when

I got a little bit older and started to be more aware of things, I picked up the details from my father and mother. The incident had become a kind of family legend that people would retell whenever they wanted to remind someone of Hind's legendary stubbornness, which started early. My mother says that I carried the chair around for half a day, hanging like a collar around my neck, my back bent, my face red, and my forehead sweaty, trying to get out of it in every different way I could think of. Whenever someone from the family approached, wanting to help me extricate myself from the trap, I would scream at them and hold on to the chair with both hands, as if it were my toy, not my shackle. As soon as my rescuer stepped back and left me alone to my fate, I stopped screaming, my eyes would shine defiantly, and I would go back to moving my head around and trying different tricks with the chair. My mother recalls that I continued like that, struggling, for hours, but I didn't stop until I'd managed to get out all by myself, and then I applauded and cried out of happiness. I'll applaud out of happiness today, too, if this damn drawer opens and I leave this cellar with the box of secrets in my hands.

With the last "Allahu Akbar" of the call to prayer, I fall back on my butt, the drawer in my hand. I feel a sharp pain at the bottom of my back, but I don't care. I fumble with my left hand along the ground, searching for the flashlight, and with my right hand, I explore the inside of the drawer, checking its contents. No trace of the blue cloth in which Khala Luiza said the box is wrapped. My heart all but jumps inside the drawer and sneaks under the yellowed bedsheets that fill it. Nothing on top. Nothing beneath. Nothing in between. My throat develops something like a lump. I have no desire to check the other drawers, but I still do, without enthusiasm. This time, they open easily; I pull on them from the bottom, taking advantage of the space left by the open drawer. Small crocheted covers, sewing tools, and knick-knacks made of wood, pottery, and ivory, some of them broken. Letters still in their envelopes, addressed to my father's uncle Mhammed Ennaifer from a man called Larbi ben Issa. I put them in my pocket to read when I have a chance. In one of the drawers is a big notebook written in Arabic in the form of a diary, but I can't figure out whose. Under the notebook is a packet of old pictures. In one of them, I think I recognize my grandfather Mohsen in his youth, being embraced by a beautiful blonde woman. Behind the picture is something written in German that I don't understand and a signature with the name Katarina. In another picture, a plump woman is laughing. My grandfather Mohsen has his arm on her shoulder as she holds his left arm with her right, and they're smiling at the camera. On the back of the picture are a name and date: Bahiya 1950.

My cell phone rings in my pocket, and I jump as though I've been stung. My husband's voice is on the other side, with all the obscenity he thinks is normal and only foregoes if he's in front of other people, "Hind! Where the *bleep* are you? Your *bleeping* phone has been out of service for *bleeping* hours now. I was worried about you *bleepety bleep bleep*."

". . ."

"Hello? Hello?—hear me? Hello? Goddammit."

"Do you have old pictures in your cellar, too?"

"Pictures? Cellar? What the *bleep*? You're breaking up . . . Where are you, goddammit?"

The call drops before I can answer. I stand up sluggishly. I pick up the cage and the briefcase and climb the spiral staircase with slow steps. My back hurts, and my head, too. The beam of light gets bigger as the distance between me and the cellar door leading to the courtyard decreases. Here I am, finally, in the open air, filling my lungs with the scents of the old city. I look in the corners of the house for an old rag I can use to wipe the dust from the leather briefcase before leaving. I press on its locks again, to no avail.

It starts drizzling before I make it out of the alley. I walk faster towards my car, which I left at the La Kasbah parking lot.

It starts raining harder. I look at the cage swinging in my hand and find that it looks new again after being washed by the rain. As if it hasn't been decades. I suddenly feel that it's heavier than I thought. I set it down gently on the sidewalk, but the rainwater suddenly sweeps it far away. I see it tip over in the mud. I hug the briefcase with all my force, fearing that water will leak into it. I talk to myself. *There's still hope, Hind. The secret is here in the closed briefcase. And soon, very soon, the locks will be opened.*

Glossary

Aammi / Aamma (fem.): A title meaning "[paternal] uncle/aunt" and which may be applied to unrelated older people as a show of respect. These titles are particularly applied to denote respect for those who may not hold high social status, and so for whom the titles of "Sidi" or "Lella" might not be deemed appropriate.

adwar: An Arabic classical music form comprising a suite of complex vocal and instrumental compositions and characterized by intricate melodic modes and rhythmic patterns. *Adwar* are performed by a vocalist accompanied by a traditional ensemble.

akod: A slow-cooked stew made with tripe and seasoned with cumin, garlic, harissa, and tomato paste

aoussou: The two weeks in late July and early August that are the hottest of the year. Named after this period in the Amazighi (Berber) calendar.

Asr: Late afternoon, also the name of the prayer to be performed at that time.

atarchya: A floral water, like rose water but made with geranium petals.

Baba: Father, daddy; also used as a term of address for older men, particularly lower-status ones.

beldi: The aristocracy of old Tunis. Descended from the Turkish administrative caste of the Ottoman empire who intermarried with the daughters of influential Tunis merchants, they resided in the fine houses in the Tunis medina and enjoyed power and status throughout the 19th and early 20th centuries. In the years following independence, most of the remaining *beldi* moved to modern residences on the outskirts of the city; the Tunis medina became crowded with migrants from the countryside and fell into disrepair.

balgha: Traditional North African slippers, typically made from leather and characterized by their pointed toes and lack of a heel. They often feature intricate embroidery or decorative stitching.

ben / bint: "Son (of)" / "daughter (of)," common as part of Arab names.

bendir: A large hand drum with a snare, well known throughout North Africa for its use in Sufi ceremonies

bjawia: A bite-sized sweet made of pistachios and dried fruit held together in a gummy sugar syrup.

Boushkara: A bogeyman that supposedly kidnaps bad children. The story is used by adults to frighten children into good behavior.

Boutelis: In North African folklore, particularly within Tunisian culture, Boutelis is depicted as a malevolent jinn that visits individuals during their sleep. He is said to induce sleep paralysis by sitting on the chest of his victims or exerting an invisible pressure, rendering them incapable of movement or speech.

bouza: A traditional Tunisian dessert containing hazelnut powder, sorghum, sugar, and milk. It is consumed either as a pudding or sweet drink (according to consistency), especially during the month of Ramadan.

bsissa: A food made from grains (such as barley, wheat, or malt), roasted and finely ground with fenugreek, aniseed, cumin, and sometimes sugar. This dish is known throughout Tunisia and Libya and dates back to Roman times. The most common preparation involves mixing the *bsissa* powder with olive oil to form a paste, which is then topped with nuts and fruit (dates, figs, or pomegranate).

burnous: A long, woolen cloak with a pointed hood, distinctive to North Africa.

chechia: Pronounced sheh-SHEE-uh. A soft, round felt cap, dark red in color. Differs from a fez or tarboosh in that a fez is taller and rigid, while the chechia is flexible and fits snug to the head. It also represents a difference in social class: the chechia is traditionally worn by Tunisian men of all classes, including rural farmers, whereas the fez is associated with the Turkish-influenced upper classes and religious scholars (because a turban, the symbol of a religious scholar, can be wrapped around a fez).

chokha, qaftan,* and *farraja: These three items together form the traditional ensemble worn by Tunisian religious scholars, particularly those adhering to the Hanafi school of thought. The *chokha* is a tailored shirt, over which is worn the floor-length *qaftan*. The *farraja* is open at the front and as long as the *qaftan*, but looser and with wide, elbow-length sleeves. All are made of fine material and feature intricate embroidery.

Dar Joued: Pronounced *dar joe-WAD.* A religious women's prison in Tunisia, operational from the 16th century until its closure in 1957 following the legal reforms of Habib Bourguiba, particularly the enactment of the Personal Status Code in 1956. The institution housed women deemed insubordinate or rebellious.

darbuka: A goblet-shaped drum that is an essential part of traditional music throughout North Africa and the Middle East. It is played while resting under the arm or on the leg of the musician.

darwish / darwisha (fem.): In Tunisian Arabic, a *darwish* (pronounced der-WEESH) is a dirty vagabond or crazy person.

This term comes from the Arabic word for an ascetic Sufi wanderer, from which the English word dervish is also derived.

debla: Traditional Tunisian sweets made of flour and eggs, rolled into the shape of a rose, deep fried, then covered with powdered sugar or sugar syrup.

falaka: A method of torture (and, in prior eras, child discipline) that involves beating the soles of the feet.

fasoukh: An ancient incense mixture that is a mainstay of folk magic practices across a broad geographical area.

Fatiha: Known as "The Opening" in English, the Fatiha is the first chapter (sura) of the Quran, consisting of seven verses (*ayat*). It holds a central place in Islamic worship and practice and is recited in every unit of the Muslim prayer (salah).

fechka: Pronounced *FESH-ka.* A traditional Tunisian glass vessel characterized by its distinctive round belly and slender neck, designed specifically for the storage of rose water and various distilled essences. Its unique shape not only facilitates easy pouring but also serves to enhance the aromatic experience by concentrating the scent when opened.

fouta: A traditional women's garment, usually dark red in color, made up of a single long piece of fabric. The *fouta* wraps around the body, extending to mid-calf. The two ends meet at the shoulders and are secured with decorative pins. A short shirt (called a *blouza*) is worn beneath, sometimes leaving the sides of the waist bare. The outfit is secured with a sash around the waist, with the *fouta* bloused over the sash.

haddad: Pronounced hed-DAD. Blacksmith; as with the English "Smith," it is also a common last name in the Arab world.

Haddad, Tahar (1899–1935): A Tunisian reformist thinker, scholar, and activist who played a crucial role in advocating for the rights of women and reforms in Islamic society.

Haddad's seminal 1930 book, *Our Women in the Sharia and Society*, advocated for several radical reforms, including the education of women, equality between men and women, the abolition of polygamy, and the necessity of mutual consent in marriage. He argued these points from a progressive Islamic perspective, asserting that the conditions of women's rights and their treatment under traditional Islamic law needed re-evaluation and reform in the context of contemporary society. He was not a proponent of Westernization, but rather advocated for reform based on the principles of Islam itself and for the preservation of Tunisian language and culture. Although Haddad faced significant opposition and backlash from conservative elements within Tunisian society during his lifetime, his ideas would greatly influence Tunisia's first post-independence president, Habib Bourguiba. Bourguiba, recognizing the importance of Haddad's reformist vision for the advancement of Tunisian society, used these progressive ideals as a blueprint for the Code of Personal Status. The Code can be seen as a realization of Haddad's vision for a modern Tunisia where women enjoy equal rights and are active participants in public and social life. Note: The speeches from Haddad's celebration (both Haddad's and the previous speaker's) are taken directly from the historical record. The poem in the final chapter is from Haddad's collected works.

hammam: A public bath, which served as the main source of bathing for urban Tunisians of all social classes before the spread of indoor plumbing. Hammams are segregated by sex, with either different spaces or different times for males and females.

hamsa: A hand-shaped symbol, meant to protect against the evil eye.

haram: Forbidden by Islamic law. The opposite is "halal."

harkous: A substance traditionally made of oak galls and ferrous sulfate that is used to draw long-lasting designs on the body. It is used in a way similar to henna but is black in color and sits on top of the skin, rather than staining it like henna.

***Hijri* calendar**: The Islamic lunar calendar counted from the *Hijra*, the migration of the Prophet Muhammad from Mecca to Medina in 622 CE. Because lunar months are shorter than solar months, the *Hijri* calendar moves back 10–12 days every year, relative to the solar Gregorian calendar. Ramadan is the name of one of the months in the *Hijri* calendar.

El Hilalia, Jazia: The central mythological figure dominating the Hilali epic, an Arab folk saga which narrates in epic poetic form the 11th-century migration of the Banu Hilal tribe from the Najd plateaus to the fringes of Africa. Jazia held the highest social status within the tribal hierarchy as the sister of the Hilali alliance's leader and was known for her extraordinary beauty, bravery, leadership skills, and loyalty to her tribe.

ijtihad: The interpretation of ambiguous Islamic texts using intellect and reason. It is in contrast to *taqlid*, which is imitation and conformity to precedent. To be qualified to practice *ijtihad*, a scholar must possess expertise in the Arabic language, theology, revealed texts, and the principles of jurisprudence.

Isha: Dinnertime, also the name of the prayer to be performed at this time, which is the last of the five daily prayers in Islam.

jebba: A long-sleeved, ankle-length robe that is typically worn by men, especially during formal occasions and cultural ceremonies. Made from various fabrics, including wool, cotton, and silk, the *jebba* is often adorned with intricate embroidery or subtle decorations. It is generally worn with traditional trousers, *sirwal*, underneath.

kaak warka: "Paper cookie." Small donut-shaped pastry made of layers of paper-thin dough, filled with almond paste and flavored with rose water. Often served at weddings and special occasions.

kadroun: A garment similar to a *jebba* but made of heavy wool and worn during the winter. Unlike the *jebba* (which can be either plain or fancy), a *kadroun* is always simple and utilitarian.

kanoun: A clay stove or brazier that is utilized for both heating and cooking. The *kanoun* is characteristically designed to burn charcoal and can be used for making tea, coffee, or even for simple cooking tasks. Additionally, it functions as an incense burner, where incense is placed over the hot coals to perfume the air.

***Khal / Khala* (fem.)**: A title meaning "[maternal] uncle/aunt" that may also be applied to unrelated older people as a show of respect. These titles are particularly applied to denote respect for those who may not hold high social status, and so for whom the titles of "Sidi" or "Lella" might not be deemed appropriate.

khatin: A man who performs a circumcision. Traditionally, the *khatin* was a barber but in modern times is a nurse practitioner.

lablabi: A hearty Tunisian stew made primarily from chickpeas, garlic, cumin, and olive oil, often enriched with bread, harissa, capers, and sometimes topped with a poached egg.

Lella: A term of respect and endearment used to address or refer to women of esteemed status, similar to the use of "Sidi" for men. It translates to "lady" or "madam" in English and is often prefixed to the first names of women to signify respect, nobility, or social standing.

machmoum: Pronounced mesh-MOOM. A cluster of jasmine buds mounted on thin sticks and bound together tightly to form a small bouquet. The bouquet has a sweet and powerful aroma and is a salient symbol of Tunisian culture. Tunisian men sometimes tuck a *machmoum* behind one ear, especially on special occasions.

madfouna: A rich winter stew, dark green in color, made with beef trotters, Swiss chard, and white beans.

Maghrib: Sunset, also the name of the prayer to be performed at that time.

mahram: A person with whom marriage is permanently forbidden due to kinship. This includes close family members such as parents, siblings, children, and certain in-laws.

molokhiya: A stew made with the leaves of the plant of the same name (Nalta jute). The leaves have a distinctive flavor and viscous texture when cut, similar to okra. *Molokhiya* is an important part of the cuisine throughout the Arab world, but Tunisian *molokhiya* is distinctive in that the leaves are dried and ground to a fine powder, and the stew (usually with beef, onions, and spices) is cooked for four hours. This makes Tunisian *molokhiya* thicker in texture, but not viscous, compared to other versions. It is eaten with bread.

masfouf: A sweet couscous dish with fruit, olive oil or milk, and sometimes sugar.

mashallah: An Arabic phrase that translates to "what God has willed" or "as God has willed." It is used by Muslims and Arabs of various faiths to express appreciation, joy, praise, or thankfulness for an event or person that was just mentioned, while acknowledging that everything occurs by the will of God. The phrase is often uttered to ward off envy or the evil eye when admiring something or someone's beauty, achievements, or blessings. For example, when someone compliments a child's beauty, they might add *mashallah* to both show appreciation and invoke God's protection for the child.

mashrabiya: A type of projecting oriel window enclosed with carved wood latticework, common in historic buildings in North Africa. The *mashrabiya* serves several purposes: it allows for ventilation and cooling in the hot climate, filters sunlight to reduce glare and heat, and provides privacy for the inhabitants inside—particularly the women of the house, since one can see out without being seen. The latticework is often made up of intricate geometric or floral designs.

mhamsa: A variant of couscous featuring larger, pasta-like grains that form small balls. These grains are commonly incorporated into soups and a variety of dishes, offering a distinctive texture and an ability to absorb flavors well.

mkharek: A sweet consisting of fried dough coated in honey, hailing from the Béja region of Tunisia and eaten in particular during the month of Ramadan.

muhallil: A man who temporarily marries a divorced wife to make it lawful for her former husband to remarry. This practice is viewed negatively by many Islamic scholars and communities, as it is seen as exploiting religious laws and as demeaning to the dignity of all involved, particularly the woman. The practice died away in Tunisia with the adoption of the Personal Status Code, which secularized family law.

muwashshah and ***ma'luf***: Two forms of traditional music using classical poetry as lyrics, the latter going back to Andalusia.

nagara: A drum with a round clay base and a hide head.

Nouba: A Sufi ceremony of Andalusian origin, involving chanting and dancing.

osban: A traditional kind of sausage made of sheep stomach or intestines stuffed with a mixture of greens, herbs, rice, spices, and chopped organ meat. This dish is usually served alongside the main meal of rice or couscous, often on special occasions.

Personal Status Code of 1956: The centerpiece of President Habib Bourguiba's post-independence reform measures, this law banned or altered a number of customs relating to marriage and family sanctioned by sharia (Islamic law). It outlawed polygamy, set minimum ages for marriage, required women's consent to marriages arranged by their families, allowed either spouse to file for divorce in secular courts, and legitimized interfaith marriages. Although virulently criticized by conservative sectors of society in its time, it now enjoys wide approval and has become a cornerstone of Tunisian identity and sense of exceptionalism. It is widely recognized that Tahar Haddad's ideas, as expressed in his 1930 book, *Our Women in the Sharia and Society*, served as a blueprint for the Personal Status Code.

qailulah: A nap taken during the hottest part of the day, similar to the Spanish siesta.

qashabia: A heavy winter garment, similar to a burnous but with sleeves and a closure.

ruqyah: A recitation of suras from the Quran, intended as a cure for the evil eye, malevolent magic, and illness.

safseri: A traditional Tunisian women's garment, composed of a single long piece of white or cream-colored fabric and wrapped around to cover the body, including the hair. In the past, urban women would wear a *safseri* over their clothing when they were walking in public; today it is only worn by old women and is rarely seen.

shakshuka: A quick meal made of tomatoes, peppers, and sometimes other vegetables sautéed in a pan with tomato sauce, garlic, and harissa, and with poached eggs on top. Eaten with the hands, using bread to scoop it up.

Si / Sidi: In Tunisia, the title "Sidi" (sometimes abbreviated as "Si" before a name) is a term of respect that translates to "sir" or "my lord" in Arabic. It is traditionally used to address or refer to men of revered status, including saints, elders, and men of high social or scholarly esteem. It can also be used more generally to show respect in formal or polite conversation, akin to using "Mr." in English.

sirwal: A traditional type of trousers worn in Tunisia and other parts of the Arab and Islamic world. They are characterized by their distinctive silhouette: baggy around the pelvis and thighs but tapering to a tighter fit around the ankles. *Sirwal* are often worn under a *jebba* and can be part of both casual and formal attire.

Standard Arabic: The modern written language of the Arab world, which is closely related to the Classical Arabic of the Quran. Standard Arabic is not the native language of any group of speakers but is the language of education, broadcast news media, government, and writing in general throughout the Arab world. *Calamity*'s Arabic original was written in Standard Arabic.

tabouna: A round flatbread cooked on the interior walls of a traditional clay oven.

Tarawih: Special prayers performed only during Ramadan, which involve reading long portions of the Quran and performing many rak'as (prostrations).

Tatwi: The highest academic degree granted by Zaytuna Mosque in Tunisia in the early 20th century, awarded until 1933. Holders of the *Tatwi* degree were eligible for many religious and judicial positions and roles. For instance, those who earned this degree enjoyed a monopoly as legal witnesses (notary publics).

Tunisian Arabic: The vernacular varieties of Arabic spoken in Tunisia; in particular, the prestige spoken standard of the capital, Tunis. Tunisian Arabic shares many similarities with the vernaculars spoken in Libya and in Eastern Algeria but differs markedly from those of the Middle East and Egypt. Tunisian Arabic is not traditionally used in writing, though this has begun to change since the spread of internet access and the 2011 Jasmine Revolution.

taqtouqat: A genre of Arabic music featuring light, catchy songs with simpler melodies and rhythms than those of classical forms like *adwar*. They are typically performed by a lead vocalist with accompaniment from traditional instruments.

zawiya: A religious and educational institution, rooted in Sufi Islam. These establishments are often associated with a particular saint or Sufi leader and serve as places of worship and spiritual learning. *Zawiyas* act as custodians of the saint's legacy, housing their tombs or relics and becoming centers for their veneration. They play a significant role in the practice of folk religion, where the local community engages in practices that honor the saint's memory through rituals, celebrations, and pilgrimages.

zlabia: A popular sweet throughout the Arab world and South Asia (where it is known as *jalebi*), consisting of dough that is deep-fried in a thin spiral or pretzel shape, then coated in sugar syrup.

Zuhr: Noon, also the name of the prayer to be performed at that time.

About the Author

Amira Ghenim is a Tunisian writer and academic. She teaches Linguistics and Translation at Tunis University. Her novel *The Yellow Dossier* won the 2020 Sheikh Rashid Bin Hamad Prize. *A Calamity of Noble Houses* is her American debut.